The Bleed-Through Effect

by

AA Dasilva

Periphery Series

The Bleed-Through Effect

Cover Art by *Lisa Dawn MacDonald*

The Wild Rose Press, Inc.
PO Box 708
Adams Basin, NY 14410-0708
Visit us at www.thewildrosepress.com

Publishing History
First Edition, 2025
Trade Paperback ISBN 978-1-5092-6195-6
Digital ISBN 978-1-5092-6196-3

Periphery Series
Published in the United States of America

Dedication

To the readers, the dreamers, the believers...
This one's for you.

Prologue

Twenty Years Earlier

"Keep going," Mitch barked.

The boy inhaled, sweat gleaming on his forehead. His elbows locked and shook as he held himself in the rest position, exhausted from the forty push-ups he'd just done. "I can't." His voice trembled, barely a whisper.

Mitch squatted beside the boy, tilting his head so he could examine his face.

The boy kept his gaze on the asphalt beneath his hands. Then he lowered his body again—his chin almost touching the rough ground—and pushed back up.

"Good." Mitch nodded as the boy shakily resumed the push-ups. "Now tell me, what happened today, at school? Why did you attack that boy?"

"He called Mom crazy." He huffed, his push-ups coming quicker. Easier.

"And what did you say?" Mitch stood abruptly. He clasped his hands behind his back and paced in front of the boy.

"She's sick. That's why—"

"No!" Mitch snapped. "She *is* crazy. She's in a mental institution. You're old enough to know now."

The boy stopped, elbows locked, arms quivering. Sweat dripped from his forehead onto the pavement below, leaving dark circles where they landed. "She's sick," the boy repeated to himself.

A group of young soldiers walked past, staring at the boy and his father. "Damn, Lieutenant. He's just a kid," one of the soldiers grumbled.

Mitch ignored the commentary, staring at the boy with disdain. "Continue!"

The boy lowered his chin to the rocky asphalt and pushed up again and again and again.

"That's the thing you need to learn, Jared." Mitch stood tall and still as he spoke. "The universe—life—is an opportunistic thief. It will steal everything and everyone from you. Take and take and take. You can waste away fighting it like an animal, or—"

"You can steal it back," Jared finished.

"You're damn right, son. Like a quiet thief in the night, you steal that sonofabitch back. You can never have too much pride."

The boy continued his push-ups. Harder, faster, well past fifty now. His focus remained on the hard ground beneath him.

Mitch squatted beside him, watching the boy's unbroken focus as he continued his torrent of push-ups. "Next time someone tries to mess with your head—" He poked the boy's forehead. "—you calmly turn away in front of others, then burn his fucking house down when no one is looking."

The boy remained quiet, his arms burning and shaking, ready to give out. Sweat darkened his shirt, ran down his face, and streamed into his eyes. "Yes, sir."

"I won't go easy on you because you're my son. Respect is earned, Jared."

The boy's breathing was audible, and he wheezed and groaned, shakily making it to his one-hundredth push-up. With a loud moan, he collapsed onto the asphalt, his ribs absorbing the brunt of the impact. He winced, but quickly composed his face.

Mitch extended his hand and helped him up. "Next time, you'll do one-fifty."

"Yes, sir."

Chapter 1, Reality 1

Jared

I glared at my father. "If I wait any longer, it'll be too healed to do it."

He sat across from me, behind the plexiglass with the phone pressed to his ear. His grip on the phone turned his knuckles white, about to break the damn thing in half, or at least break a tooth, given the clench of his jaw.

Good.

Military police were strategically standing behind the booths every few feet, while the other inmates spoke with family or lawyers through the telephone-and-plexiglass system.

I had to be careful how much I said. The lines were tapped—video and audio recording every interaction was a given in a shithole like this. I shifted in my seat, then rolled up the sleeves on my orange jumpsuit. He scowled, and I allowed a careless smile to spread across my face.

He raised his eyebrows at me. "I'm sending a few more jumpers over to ensure everything is set up. The more information you have when you go over, the better. You're not going to remember anything. Not this time, at least. And it'll be easy to get…distracted."

Arrogant bastard. I wasn't afraid to have my heart stop. I was looking forward to jumping to my peripheral life and getting revenge while my body was kept in a coma here.

"The bleed-through should help me remember the gist of it. We've been sending files over for years. Have more faith, *General*."

"I don't operate by faith. I operate by facts, and fact is, we need another week. One fucking week, you hear me? That's an order!" He slammed his fist on the countertop.

I rolled my eyes and kept my gaze on the flickering fluorescent light overhead. I sighed. "Let me do it—" I glanced over each shoulder and leaned closer to the glass. "—now. Send a few jumpers to watch, see how it goes when I get there. Let them—" I cleared my throat. "—plug me back in. Then we can regroup in Maryland, at the hospital."

"You'll be guarded after that, put on suici—watch. You're going to need to get sent back and forth *at least* three more times before you start to build the ability to remember."

"I'll get the job done without being put on watch," I growled. "I always do. One of the guys started building memory retention after the second jump. Maybe I'll be exemplary, like I am with most things, and build them sooner." I held his cold glare.

Mitch narrowed his eyes at me. "You'd already be a trained jumper and we wouldn't need to track down people to jump for us if your *wife*—" He inhaled sharply, his jaw pulsing. "—and her *boyfriend* hadn't put a wrench in things."

My chest tightened. "They'll pay," I said calmly. "But we have plenty of back-up drives and equipment to get us started."

"It takes time and money!" He slammed his fist again, then took a steadying breath. "Both of which are going to be in short supply soon! And, with all eyes on our *business* at the moment, we have to be calculated, metho—"

I sighed. "Methodical. Yes. Send me. Get your—" I waved my hand dismissively. "—organization set up and all your fancy equipment and clients ready. In the meantime, send some jumpers to brief me. I'll take care of things."

His nostrils flared. "If you screw this up and end up there permanently, with no memories, that's on you."

"What's the worst that can happen?" I shrugged. "If I do, you'll be sending jumpers over to remind me to *torment* a certain jumper before each mission we send him on."

"You can't unplug her. She's—"

"You think I don't know who she is or what she does?" I slammed my hand on the glass, my patience finally wearing thin. "I was talking about *him*."

Mitch leaned back in his seat and smiled. He always loved when my control slipped.

A guard clomped over to me. "Time's up, Cardoza."

I held my hand up to him. "I still have sixty-five seconds."

I turned back to Mitch and ran a finger around the collar of my jumpsuit, which suddenly felt too tight. "I know what she does there. You've made me study this shit for four years. I'll remember what I need to."

"Well, then. Sweet dreams, Son." He slammed down the phone.

I kept the receiver crushed to my ear as he unfolded himself from the seat and sauntered out the door, and my grip on the phone tightened painfully when he disappeared behind an automated door. Freedom for him while I rotted in this hellhole. After allowing myself to be collateral to cover up Quantym, I deserved more. Better. Right now, the entirety of the U.S. thought me a mass shooter and had no idea about the program we'd been running for the better part of a decade.

"Cardoza!" The guard boomed.

I dragged my gaze from Mitch's now-empty seat to the man, with the phone still pressed to my ear.

They wanted crazy? I'd give them crazy. My father would buy the guards' loyalty later, anyway.

A feral smile stretched across my face.

The guard reached toward me. "I said, time's up, put the phone—"

I pulled on the phone, the metal wire snapping from the force, and in a quick movement, I was standing and beating the guard's face with it. Blood spattered across my jumpsuit as he grappled toward me with a roar, attempting to stop the torrent of blows I slammed on the side of his face. The receiver broke in half, and I swung it at him, the plastic lodging deep into his flesh. I was pulled backward by my jumpsuit, the collar momentarily cutting off my air.

In another instant, I was on the ground with the wind knocked out of me as several MPs tackled me and held my torso, head, and legs down. I'd landed on the barely-healed stab wound inflicted by my wife, and the warmth of my own blood soaked through my jumpsuit.

Perfect.

The guards took turns pretending they were subduing me, when really they were each getting a shot in, taking out their frustrations on another troubled violent prisoner.

I took a fist to the face, a kick to the ribs, and had my ankle stomped on. I turned my body slightly, and a heavy boot connected with my bleeding wound.

Fucking beautiful. Ab-so-lutely beautiful. Poetic, almost.

I grunted, absorbing the pain. Another boot connected with my face, and the metallic taste of blood flooded my mouth. I smiled as black dots swam in my vision. Blood leaked from my mouth and pooled onto the tile below.

"I'm coming, doll," I mumbled. My voice was unintelligible from my face smashed against the tile, and the grunts of the animals beating my subdued body. My vision swam as my eyes began to roll to the back of my head.

The darkness closed in, and I welcomed it like a bulletproof vest in a combat zone.

Chapter 2, Reality 1

Charlotte

My stab wound had finally healed enough to be submerged, and the long, hot shower was glorious. Stepping out, I shivered while swiftly drying off, anxious to get the hell out of Virginia. A week-long stay in the hospital for the deep puncture wound in my torso was long enough. And considering how fast the wound was healing, it was certainly overkill.

I pulled on a pair of soft cotton sweatpants, rolling down the waistband to avoid the injured area, then drew a cropped tee over my head. The bandage showed, but I wore it as a badge of honor. Proof that I'd been tested and tried but survived. Again. Against the odds.

I opened the bathroom door and looked at Sy, who leaned against the wall with my packed bags slung over his uninjured shoulder. The other side, under his collarbone, was bandaged from a gunshot wound—another parting gift from Jared.

I walked over to him and twined my arms around his waist, resting my head on his chest.

He rubbed my back, then trailed his hands down to rest on the exposed skin of my lower back. "Ready to get out of here?"

Taking a slow breath, I nodded and closed my eyes. "I can't wait to go home."

The door opened and he pulled back, resting a hand on my lower back.

"Alright, Ms. Cardoza, if you'll just sign here, and here"—the nurse motioned to the paper with a pen—"and down here, you'll be a free woman."

I took the pen and signed my discharge papers with a sigh.

Sy raised his eyebrows at me.

"Y'all have a safe flight home and get well soon." The nurse smiled and exited the room.

"Sad to be leaving?" He questioned my sigh.

"I don't like being called *Ms. Cardoza*." I shrugged.

"I have plans on changing that myself." Sy smiled and grabbed my hand.

"Oh?" I cocked an eyebrow and bit back a smile.

He gently wrapped his arms around my waist, and I looped my arms around his neck.

"Should I be worried *when* and not *if* I ask you?" he whispered in my ear, his breath awakening goosebumps on my neck.

"I'm just so unpredictable. I guess there's only one way to find out."

He kissed me and I parted my lips, letting him in instantly as my body relaxed into his.

I pouted when he released me and opened the door, not ready for our kiss to end. I licked my lips, savoring the pleasant taste of him that lingered, and followed him out of the hospital room.

I was glad Sy had already gotten to meet my parents. Their flight back to Florida had left last night, but they were already planning on making a visit to us up north once we settled back in.

Now, with Simon free from his contract, Jared

locked up, and his father, General Mitch Cardoza, under intense scrutiny by the government, we could move forward and leave all the death and corruption in the past.

Quantym—the organization led by Jared and Mitch—had been dismantled to a point that'd rendered it useless, and the database of jumpers were wiped on this side and on the Periphery. It'd take them years to rebuild it, and even then, they'd need to start off by giving all their attention to elite clients to fund it.

We headed toward the elevators, rode down a level, and exited through a winding hall that led to the main entrance.

An idling taxi waited outside to take us to the airport.

To take us home.

****

The plane landed with a jolt, the motion startling me from my ruminations. The captain announced our arrival in Rhode Island.

"Home." Sy squeezed my thigh.

I rubbed my sleepy eyes and caught Sy's gaze, returning his wide smile with my own.

After obtaining our luggage, we headed outside, where Sy's brothers, Jeff and Max, waited for us in an idling truck at the front of the airport. Sy pulled the back door open and put our bags in the bed of the truck before he joined me in the backseat.

"Glad to see you both home, and in one piece." Jeff smirked at us through the rearview mirror.

Max turned toward us and winked. "I had no doubts."

"I'm still gonna beat the shit out of both of you for letting her go to Virginia," Sy grumbled.

"Might want to let your chest heal first. Otherwise you'll have to take us on one at a time, and what fun would that be?" Jeff laughed.

"Let me?" I scoffed. "There was no stopping me."

Sy shook his head. "There never is. That's part of your allure, though. When it's not getting you killed."

Jeff and Max rolled their eyes and groaned.

"You've gone soft on us, man." Max shook his head.

Sy punched the back of his seat, and Max's body bounced from the blow, his head connecting with the headrest in the process.

"Ow." Max rubbed the back of his head and chuckled.

"Alright, brothers. Let's not antagonize or overexert the gunshot victim," I scolded.

"Oh, I'm going to overexert myself as soon as I have you alone," he muttered.

My face heated and I elbowed him.

Jeff and Max groaned again.

"Didn't need to hear that." Jeff shook his head.

"Then stop listening." Sy kicked Jeff's seat.

Jeff merged onto the highway, and we all erupted into laughter. He turned up the radio and took us home.

****

I'd listed my house for sale within two days of coming home, ready to put the past behind us.

Sy's brothers had already garnered a lot of interested buyers for the home they'd fixed up and listed next door, and with the need for housing for military families, my house and their flip sold within a few weeks of listing. Though, it turns out the flip wasn't necessary. The house was obnoxiously updated and beautiful, but the brothers were watching *me* months ago, trying to determine if I was involved with Jared's fake death and role at Quantym.

I understood their need to be close to me and learn the truth and was grateful for it, even. Without them, I'd likely have gone back to Virginia with Jared—against my will or under a false pretense—and fallen prey to whatever life he deemed necessary to move his and Mitch's organization at Quantym forward.

Sy and I were mostly physically healed, though I carried a heavy load of emotional baggage from the events that played out over the last few months. Simon seemed to settle back into routine with ease, being strong when I faltered.

The empty house echoed with the sound of my footsteps.

I walked over to the bay window, now devoid of curtains or blinds, and watched Simon pull out of the driveway, taking the last load of my things to his place.

Jeff used his truck and had already dropped off most of my furniture to a storage unit in Tiverton.

Now, standing here staring out my bay window, admiring the cherry blossoms and maples alight with leaves orange as embers and red as blood, I accepted the choices of my past. I wasn't going to deny that I'd loved Jared at one time or lie to myself that I'd been coerced or tricked into marrying him. No. He was a choice I'd made before I knew him, or myself, completely. It'd been a hard truth to swallow, but a truth nonetheless—I'd loved him, and he was toxic. Severing those ties took strength, and I had to choose to love myself *more* than his venomous "love" that would've eventually maimed or killed me. It was a harsh truth told only by experience and maturity, and just another decision, in a sea of a million others I'd made, that spun my life into the direction it needed to be to find myself where I was now.

Happy. Content. Loved.

The moment was bittersweet.

Turning from the window, I hugged my chest and walked lazily through the kitchen, then down the hall, peering into each room I ambled past. Memories flooded my vision, a stark contrast to what the empty house held today.

I ascended the stairs.

The two large empty rooms were illuminated only by the light spilling in from the dormered windows on either end.

A box on the window seat of one dormered window caught my attention, so I strolled over to the window and sat, bringing my knees to my chest.

The light-brown box was wrapped in a burlap bow. A tag hung from the burlap, and I turned it over to see my name in Simon's handwriting. I smiled, pulled the box onto my knees, and pulled on the burlap ribbon to release the bow. Gently placing the cover beside me on the window seat, I ran my fingers over the gift within.

The midnight-blue leather was speckled with pinpoint silver stars. Orion's belt—the most prominent constellation in the sky on my birthday—stretched across the front cover amongst a sea of other constellations and stars. I pulled the journal from the box, and the stiff new book crackled when I opened the front cover.

The first page was inscribed with a note:

We wandered through the dark
And stumbled upon the stars
Here's to the theories that became truth

And the stolen moments that brought us together
I died to find you. And I'd do it over and over again
to keep you.
-Sy

Smiling, I removed the fountain pen from the loop on the side of the journal, turned the page, and began writing the numbers that defined us. The numbers I'd committed to memory, the numbers that calmed me when I was anxious, and defined the new life that lay ahead of us.

Instead of the repetitive equations that continuously invaded my brain thanks to the savant syndrome I'd acquired from my head injury sustained in a car accident over four years ago, these numbers held the meaning to my heart, as opposed to calculating my physical place in time.

Simon's resting heart rate, the heartbeats that lulled me to sleep when I lay upon his chest at night, and my own resting heart rate. I drew my pristine memory of Simon's EKG rhythm the day I resuscitated him at Quantym. His heart rhythm connected with my flat line, a representation of when I'd died at Quantym after being stabbed by Jared, and ended in my rapid sinus rhythm when they'd shocked me and got me back. Two beating hearts, connected by death and love.

I leaned my back against the wall of the window seat and stared at what I'd drawn. Two pages, connected by the journal binding, were now completely filled with my sketches and numbers. To anyone else, it'd look like the musings of a crazy artist obsessed with numbers. To me, it defined our lives, our futures, our deaths.

I closed the journal and released a cleansing breath. My eyes slid shut.

A car door slammed, and I gazed out the window as Simon made his way toward the house.

The front door closed with a soft click.

I stayed seated in the window with a smile.

"Charlotte?" His deep voice echoed through the house.

His footfalls sounded throughout the downstairs layout as he searched for me, then on the stairwell, and I turned in the direction of the sound with a sly grin.

He emerged from the stairs, looking left and not noticing me on his right.

"Boo!"

He didn't startle as he sauntered over to where I sat.

"I *will* scare you one day." Disappointment laced my voice.

He smiled and slid his hands into his pockets. "Never."

I stood to meet him as he approached me. Looking up at him, then back down at my gift, I spoke quietly. "Thank you, Sy." I swallowed hard, recalling the night I'd burned my old journal.

He took the book from my hands and tossed it onto the window seat. Then he pulled me into his arms, and in an instant his lips were on mine, hungry and searching.

In his safe embrace, I kissed him recklessly like it was the first time. I ran my fingers through his hair, then pulled away and rested my palm on his cheek. "I love you, Simon."

"I love you, Charlotte. Always have, always will."

"What you wrote—"

He waved his hand through the air, then leaned down and gently bit my lower lip.

My body melted in his arms, the softness of my body

completely melding against the hardness of his.

He moved forward a few strides, until he had my back against the wall, his body crushing into mine as he kissed me senseless.

He grasped my shirt in his fist, and I pulled away with a gasp. "Not this one!" He had a penchant for literally tearing my clothes right off my body. I laughed and pulled my shirt up and off by the hem.

His fingers curled around the waistband of my pants, dragging them down until I stepped out of them, while keeping his lustful gaze on mine.

I pulled his T-shirt over his head and tossed it to the floor. His muscular tattooed chest pressed against my bare chest, and my skin tingled in response.

He grasped my hips and lifted me, and I wrapped my legs around his waist.

I shuddered when he hooked his thumbs under the flimsy lace of my panties, tearing through the delicate fabric until they fell away completely, the ribbon of pink fluttering to the ground beside us. He brought his hand between us, lighting my nerves on fire.

My gaze wandered to his waist as he unbuttoned his pants with his other hand, agonizingly slow.

"What do you want, Charlotte?"

I moved my hips and gasped when he pulled his hand away. "You," I nearly begged.

He hummed his approval of my response, then wrapped his hands around my waist and pushed into me.

"*Fuck*," he whispered. He buried his face into my neck, nipping kisses along my collarbone.

I rested my head back against the wall with my eyes closed. Time stood still as he relentlessly brought me to the edge of space and time. I clung to him, a dangerous mix of pleasure and need building within me with every touch of his rough hands, his sinfully deep voice, and his scorching, hard body against mine.

Our hot breaths mixed in between kisses, and my head fell forward against his large shoulder as he thrust into me again and again. Shooting stars swirled behind my closed lids as heat built and tightened inside of me, and a scream clawed its way from my throat as I shattered around him.

Sy captured my lips between his, groaning as he spilled deep inside of me.

My trembling body fell limp in his arms with my legs still wrapped around his waist.

"I will never get enough of you," he mumbled in between breaths.

Our chests heaved, both of us panting and breathless.

He reached up and grasped my face with both of his hands.

I opened my eyes and held his fiery blue gaze as my heart burned with the intensity of his love and reverence. "I never knew this"—I rested a hand on his chest—"existed. This feeling, this kind of love."

"You deserve more than I could ever give you, but I'm a selfish creature, and I'm keeping you for myself." He rested his forehead on mine and closed his eyes.

"Sy, you're the *only* one who can give me the one thing I want."

"And what would that be?"

"You."

He kissed my forehead tenderly. "You ready to go home?"

I nodded.

He lowered me to the ground, and I stood on shaky legs as he found my shirt and pulled it back over my head. I pulled on my pants and turned to put the journal back inside the box. After tying the ribbon, I grasped his hand.

"Let's go home."

****

When I woke up, the shower was running in the master bathroom, and steam wafted from the open doorway. I tossed the covers aside and stood by the floor-to-ceiling windows, then rubbed my hand across the window to wipe away the rogue fog from Simon's shower to watch the sun rise over the bay. Distant cars zipped over both lanes on the Mount Hope Bridge, and I was thankful I wasn't rushing back to work just yet.

My boss, Brian, extended my LOA without my asking when he and my co-workers learned I was *injured in the hospital shooting in Virginia.* The truth was much more complex than that, but for all intents and purposes, it was something that warranted time to recover from, both physically and mentally.

But the past didn't matter, just the future. And right now, my future was standing behind me in nothing but a towel with mischief in his eyes.

That evening, Sy emerged from the bedroom in a black button-down shirt and black pants. He cuffed his sleeve, exposing his muscular, tatted forearms.

"You look...alarmingly handsome." I sauntered up to him and trailed a finger over the tattoo on his chest that was visible with the top few shirt buttons undone.

"I clean up nice, don't I?" He leaned down for a kiss while buttoning up his shirt.

"But you—" He grabbed my waist. "—look

positively stunning." He spun me to face the mirror he stood in front of.

The dress I'd bought for the occasion was casual, but it was black, and pairing it with heels topped off the look.

I stared at our reflections in the mirror. "It kinda looks like we're going to a funeral."

He shook his head. "Black is timeless."

"I couldn't agree more." I grabbed my bag, and we headed out the door to meet my best friend for dinner to celebrate her husband's return from deployment. What I also knew, though no one else did, was tonight, Jess also planned on revealing to our close-knit group of friends the gender of their baby.

I smiled to myself, excited for all the reasons to celebrate. "I didn't know Thames served food."

Sy nodded. "They've got classic pub food, and it's decent."

"My favorite is a good pub burger. I haven't had one in a while."

He raised a brow. "Really? I've never seen you order one."

I nodded. "Well, I rarely indulge, but when I do, I go hard."

"Now this is something I want to see. Don't disappoint me by eating half," he teased.

I laughed. "I won't let you down. You'd be surprised how easily I can put away a burger and fries."

He glanced over at me, his gaze falling to my formfitting dress and back up.

"Can't picture it. I'm excited to see this." His gaze wandered downward again.

I crossed my legs and hugged my arms around

myself. "What?" I finally asked when his gaze wandered again.

"Just…nothing." He shook his head.

I gave him a pointed glance. "Now you have to tell me."

"I just like the idea." He suppressed a smile.

"Of me eating?"

He put his hand on my thigh, then dragged it upward and stopped on my flat stomach.

I froze.

"Of you letting go. Indulging yourself."

My shoulders loosened and I smiled, glad he wasn't going to say something about pregnancy. I'd still never told him, or anyone other than Mitch and Jared, that I'd lost an unexpected pregnancy when Jared and I had been in the car accident.

Sy parked, and we headed inside to meet our friends.

As soon as we breached the threshold, the back of my neck tingled, and I rubbed it. I tightened my grasp on Sy's hand.

He glanced down at me, concern etching into his features as his brows pulled together.

I shrugged. "Crowds, I guess."

"But this place is special," he countered.

"Where we met." I tipped my head in the direction of the booth where we sat that first time. "Right there."

He hummed, squeezing my hand a little tighter.

I looked up at him, and when I met his blue eyes, the unease at the back of my neck lessened.

Jess bolted out of her seat and ran toward me.

Her body slammed into mine, making me release Sy's hand and stumble back a step as she bear-hugged me.

"Charlotte!" she squealed.

"Careful, you've got precious cargo." I brought my hand down to the tiny bump between her hips.

"I do!" She released me and turned to the side, smoothing her shirt over the swelling.

"You wear him or her very well." I smiled. I tried to swallow, but my throat was suddenly dry. "I'm so thirsty." I brought my hand up to my throat, surprised to find myself parched.

"Oh, let's sit! How are you feeling?

"I'm good now. I don't want to talk about that. We're here to celebrate you…"

Steve walked up behind Jess and rested his hand on her shoulder.

"And you…" I smiled at Steve. "Welcome home. And congratulations."

He nodded and thanked me. He turned and shook Sy's hand, and the guys immediately began conversing about Steve's deployment.

Jess pulled me to the seat beside hers at the table. She poured me a glass of water from the pitcher in the center.

I took it gratefully, and gulped down half immediately.

"Wow, you were thirsty." She lowered her head and stared at me. "You okay?"

I smiled brightly. "Never better. Now, when are you going to tell us the gender?" I whispered.

"Patience! The cake isn't being served until after we eat."

"Oh my gosh, already a mother." I rolled my eyes.
She laughed.

My co-workers and friends began arriving. My boss

Brian, and his partner James, Angela and her boyfriend Rex, Nelson and his wife Shonda. One by one, each asked how I was feeling, and after I changed the topic, we settled in like old times.

We ate, talked, and laughed, and soon it was well past dinner, and the bar crowd started rolling in.

Before the place could get too packed, the waitress brought out the individual cakes for us.

Jess cleared her throat, and swiped her ginger bangs to the side. "Tonight, we're going to find out the baby's gender, but I wanted to say something first."

Our friends all quieted, and we focused on Jess.

The hairs on the back of my neck prickled, and I began tapping my finger on my thigh. I counted each finger-tap, hoping to lessen the unease that washed over me again.

"Charlotte, you've been an amazing friend. What some of you may not know, is when I was going through fertility treatments, Charlotte would walk to my house every night to give me my injections. I'm terrified of needles, but she made something so hard, surprisingly easy."

Our friends smiled.

I increased the pace of my finger-tapping. Thirty-one, thirty-two, thirty-three...

"Sy, you've made her incredibly happy, and I think I speak for all of us when I say—no one deserves happiness more than her."

Everyone at the table murmured their agreement, and Sy put his arm around me.

My neck tingled again, and I shifted in my seat. I glanced around the room, feeling like there were eyes—multiple sets of eyes—on me from afar. But just as I'd suspected, I saw no one looking. Nothing was amiss.

"So, tonight, I want you to be the first to know, Charlotte. You go first."

I glanced around the room again when the shiver hit. It was as if the room suddenly dropped a few degrees in seconds.

"Charlotte?" Sy leaned down and spoke into my ear.

"Huh?" I looked up to see everyone at the table watching me. "Oh! Me?"

Jess smiled and nodded. "You first."

I took my fork and speared a piece off the small cake in front of me.

I gasped, and a smile broke across my face. I brought the fork to Sy's lips, and he took a bite.

"Girl!" I exclaimed.

The table erupted in celebration, and for a few seconds I was able to ignore how incredibly wrong I felt as the freezing cold sensation made its way from my neck down my spine.

I'd felt this feeling before. Someone was watching me.

Chapter 3, Reality 2: On the Periphery

Jared

The headache hit hard and fast while I walked down the hall to the biggest conference room in the building, the sudden pain searing through the center of my forehead.

Charlotte walked beside me, her arms full of file folders, as she prattled about her upcoming presentation. "There's going to be how many?"

"How many what?" I snapped.

She stopped and turned to me with her brow pinched. "Are you okay? Oh, geez—you don't look good. Sit."

She pulled me into an empty conference room, and I collapsed into one of the chairs. Leaning forward, I pinched the bridge of my nose between my thumb and forefinger. "Forty-four." I finally answered when it came to me.

She was just returning to the room, a bottle of water and two pills in hand. "What?"

"You asked how many were going to be there. Forty-four." I took the water and pills from her hands, then looked up at her. "Charly," I grumbled.

"What is it?" She pulled a chair over and sat facing me.

She placed a hand on my leg, and I stared at it.

She rubbed small circles on my knee with gentle fingers. She was nervous.

"Don't fuck this up today." I squeezed my eyes shut, trying to will the pain away.

She pulled her hand back and bristled. "I told you—I'll do it, but I don't think it's right."

"I don't give a shit about right, Charly. This means a lot to a lot of people. Me, included."

"If you don't think I can handle it, why'd you insist I do it?" she snapped. She stood abruptly and pulled the pile of folders off the conference table to her chest.

I sprang to my feet and strode toward her so fast she backed herself into the wall. I glared down at her.

She lifted her chin. "What is your problem, Jared? One minute you're fine, the next, you're—"

I pressed into her, causing her arms to crush the folders against her chest, and I rested my hands on the wall behind her. "Get in there and sell this. I won't say it again."

"I planned to before, but now that you're being an ass, maybe I'm suddenly struck with a headache, too," she mocked.

"Try it. I dare you." I stared at her for a moment, then dropped my gaze to her mouth. Resisting the urge to kiss her, I rubbed a thumb across her full lips. "Take this off, I don't like it." I cleaned the red lipstick off with my thumb. The last thing I needed to piss me off was her drawing the wrong kind of attention to herself in a room full of men.

"Stop it." She tried squirming away, but the little space I'd left her with made it impossible. She inhaled a deep breath and scowled.

I dropped my gaze from her lips to her delicate neck.

I had the sudden urge to wrap my hand around her throat, and as quick as the thought came, it receded, surprising me. I'd never put my hands on her like that. And I wouldn't—not without a damn good reason.

Her mouth dropped open, and her green eyes clouded with…*hurt*? Good.

I couldn't justify my sudden anger toward her, but there had to be a good reason. She'd been bitching ever since I got her to sign on at Quantym, and a lot was riding on today's presentation. Doctors, scientists, government officials, and private investors may or may not choose to invest, depending on how well she sold her and Doctor Gustav's research today.

The fire in the server room over a month ago had set us back, but we were able to get most of what we needed off a hard drive in Charly's laboratory. All wasn't lost.

She couldn't recall where it'd come from, and while I wanted to say finding a back-up drive was odd, I knew it'd likely been planted from some jumpers sent over from the main reality. They did a shitty job of documenting where they'd put intel at times, and it drove me up a fucking wall. I had enough to deal with, and I didn't want to take on reprimanding jumpers from the other side, too. Mitch could deal with that.

We'd never let the investors find out about that small roadblock, anyway. Now, we just needed more jumpers and quick, since that list hadn't been recovered. Luckily, we still had a few that'd been holed up at the facility, and a couple that were active Marines, but we needed to find more. If Charly knew what the hell she and Gustav were doing, soon, we wouldn't need any. We'd be making our own.

She shook her head. "You need to get seen.

Something's not right. Jared, I'm serious. Maybe it's not a migraine this time."

My gaze shot back up to meet hers. "*You're* giving me a damn migraine, Charly. I'll meet you in there when the meds kick in. Give me ten." I backed away, giving her space to leave.

She held my glare for a brave minute.

"Go, now!" I barked.

She took another deep breath and stormed out of the room. Her small frame—practically swallowed by the oversized white lab coat—disappeared out the door.

I sighed and rested my forehead against the cold wall. Damn, the pain was excruciating. Maybe it was the throbbing in my head, but I suddenly felt like I was recalling all the day's events for the first time.

Overwhelmed by the sensation, I dropped back into the chair. Mitch would be in the conference already, and he was probably wondering where I was. But he'd ensure they started on time, with or without me.

At least someone knew what the hell they were doing. For all his flaws, my father was a damn good general. And, with him there, Charly would be afraid to screw up. They'd never gotten along, and for a moment I considered that fact. I never fully understood why Mitch hated Charly, though my father's failed relationship with my mother was probably all I needed to know. My mother had a mental breakdown and needed round-the-clock care, something he couldn't provide.

Being a man of black-and-white interpretations of the world, he'd always felt if she'd loved him enough, she'd have gotten better. She never did, so abandonment with a touch of jealousy, then. He hated Charly because she reminded him of who my mother had been before mental illness robbed her of her mind. Docile, beautiful, kind—with a level of intellect that veered on the edge of madness.

And today, she'd better use every damn one of those attributes to sell our program to the investors.

"Lieutenant?" One of my men knocked on the door and entered.

"What is it now?"

"Emergency briefing."

I waved my hand at him dismissively.

"The general sent me—" He cleared his throat. "—from the other side."

I raised my eyebrows. "Jumper?"

He shut the door behind him. "Yes, sir."

"And?"

"He wants you to know you're in an induced coma on the other side. You've jumped. The mission is to begin acquiring memories."

So that's what the damn headache was all about. Made sense. Something niggled at the back of my consciousness that told me my unexplained anger toward Charly was about to be clarified, too. "Meet me in my office after the presentation so you can fill me in on everything from the main reality."

"Yes, sir." He nodded and left.

****

The lights were already dimmed for the slideshow presentation, so I was able to slip into the room mostly undetected. My father narrowed his eyes at me, and I took the seat beside him.

He leaned toward me. "There better be a good reason for your late arrival," he whispered.

I ignored him and watched Charly at the front of the

29

room. She'd reapplied the red lipstick, and wore wire-rimmed glasses.

She shifted through a stack of folders nervously, looking up to smile at the crowd when she took longer than necessary. She cleared her throat. Twice. "Good morning. I'm Doctor Charlotte Cardoza. Today, with my colleague, Doctor Thomas Gustav—" She nodded in his direction. "—I'm, um, we're happy to present to you our findings and ongoing research for the Quantym program."

I stared at the ceiling for a moment. She was rambling.

Mitch noticed my annoyance, and his shoulders shook with one quiet, scornful laugh.

I met my father's gaze, shook my head, and suppressed a smile.

Mitch diverted his eyes back to Charly, then narrowed them at her.

At that same moment, she met his scrutinizing glare. Her cheeks flushed. "I'd like to start with a quick recap of what you probably already know and end with some exciting new findings in regard to navigating through the parallel."

The room stirred with anticipation.

She clicked on the slideshow. The screen lit up with a diagram designed like a sun—a large circle, with six ray-like projections spiking outward from the sphere.

"This diagram represents the main reality and peripheries as we know it."

She clicked a button on the remote, and the circle and each projection illuminated with a caption. "This, here"—she motioned to the circle in the center—"is the main reality, where we all start, and where most of our main consciousnesses are residing, even now." She stopped and clicked on a red laser pointer. She hovered the red dot over a projection captioned *Periphery: reality two*, and said, "And this is where we are right now."

"Impossible," a man called out. "If we're on the Periphery now, that mean's we've all died in the main reality already, doesn't it?"

"No, sir. We are the alternates. We're living, breathing, experiencing life, indeed, but many of us are still living in our main life in reality one. Unless you're a jumper, or hire one—" She paused as the crowd laughed at her clever pitch. "—there's really no way of knowing whether you still exist in the main reality or not. And, should you die and come here, you become one with your alternate, inheriting all the memories you've made here."

I glared at the man who had interrupted her. He wasn't a doctor, and his black suit and designer watch indicated he was likely a government official sent in from the CIA. I'd ask Mitch later.

"Now, these here"—she motioned to the projections labeled one through six, avoiding the seventh periphery—"are the peripheral lives we've been able to access. As *most* of you know—" She gave a small smile to the man who'd interrupted her. "—we've been sending jumpers here from the main reality for some time now, which is how we discovered we're in reality two. Today, I'm excited to tell you all that we've cracked the code on traveling through the peripheries. Now, Quantym can offer our clients more options than ever before."

I leaned forward. Holy shit. Not that I ever really doubted her, but I swelled with pride when the faces in the crowd lit up at her revelation. Investors would pay a pretty price to be involved in what Quantym could now offer. I leaned back into my seat, spinning the wedding band on my finger with my thumb, a habit I'd picked up after we'd gotten married six—almost seven—years ago. I crossed my arms and watched her gain more confidence as she got swept up in explaining the research.

"We mapped the peripheries via altering the jumping protocol. I'll spare you the scientific details, but in a nutshell, the unit of measure and trajectory of our energy lies in time."

She walked over to the whiteboard and began writing an equation that looked like hieroglyphics. The black marker squeaked as she furiously completed the equation that spanned the entire length of the board.

Gustav snapped on a light to illuminate her jargon.

So much for sparing us the details. I sighed, and Mitch snickered again.

She continued, "Hearts beat based on an electrical impulse. These very impulses are energy bursts that tie us to our lives. By altering how long a heart stops—or restarts, then stops again—prior to full clinical death, we're able to control which realities the jumpers access. And because energy always chooses the path of least resistance, we're able to map out where we want a jumper—or client—to go, by using this calculation and adjusting joules used during defibrillation and tracking picoseconds during asystole."

The douchebag who'd interrupted her before spoke again. "If that's the case, then the jumpers that are accessing these distant peripheries, what happens to them if they die suddenly? Will they go to the last reality they accessed?"

"Good question." She spun to look at her equation again, and put her hands on her hips. "We can alter the path of their heart's energy for only a small window of time. Once that window closes, if they die, they go where nature intended, to the next available life."

She spun around with a huge smile. Her smile faded when she was met with a room full of blank stares.

She used the laser pointer to point at the slideshow again. "The natural course of life starts here—" The red dot landed on the central circle. "—in reality one, also known as the main reality. Each death should move you in a clockwise motion from here"—she pointed to reality two, then three, all the way to seven—"in that pattern. Each life we enter into, we inherit the memories of that life immediately upon death. Unless you're a jumper, of course. Then, you keep some of your old *and* inherit your new. Bless them. I can barely recall what I had for breakfast this morning."

A few people chuckled. I might have, too.

"But for those who are searching for someone, seeking reassurance—" She drew in a deep breath. "—it can change everything. Allow me to explain." She took a sip of water, then glanced over at Dr. Gustav.

He nodded encouragingly.

"Case study number twenty-three was a client who'd lost her adult daughter. Now raising her three grandchildren and stricken by grief, she enrolled in the program to have us find her daughter and ensure she was happy on the other side. But her daughter was deceased in reality three, after a brave fight with cancer. So, we decided to send some jumpers further, to see where this client's daughter was living out the rest of her life. After altering the jumping protocol several times, we located her daughter, living her life in reality four, healthy and happily married, with her three children. We were able to report these details to the client, who was grateful to know her daughter's whereabouts in space and time, and comforted by this knowledge. It helped her work through her grief, and in turn, console her grandchildren as well. The positive effects of this knowledge are far-reaching, especially in this case."

The crowd murmured and stirred again.

"The next case study, number twenty-four, was a client who was recently diagnosed with a devastating neurodegenerative disease." She paused, shooting a quick glance at Gustav, then cleared her throat and continued. "He was given only months to live, and he wanted to be able to choose his next life, not leaving anything to chance. We sent a few jumpers over to reality three, where he was living a healthy, albeit modest life. He was a blue-collar worker, and struggled to keep up with the bills. The client, who was accustomed to his generous lifestyle here, didn't want to wake up in a life without the luxuries he was accustomed to, even though he wouldn't remember this luxurious life. So, we sent jumpers further. In reality four, he was disabled from a brain injury suffered at birth, and so the client chose to be sent to reality five, where he was a CEO of a large corporation, and without health ailments."

Several hands raised, ready to ask questions.

Dr. Gustav leaned forward toward the microphone at the podium. "Please hold all questions until the end of the presentation."

Some grumbled, but the hands slowly lowered.

"And, finally, the last case study we'd like to present today, will be presented by Doctor Tomas Gustav. For this one, I'll turn the floor over to him."

He bowed and thanked her as she stepped aside. "Good morning, ladies and gentlemen." Gustav's deep, accented voice filled the room.

"As you've all just learned from my colleague, we've cracked the code on navigating the periphery in a clockwise manner. I'm here to present to you my findings on what happened when we attempted to navigate the periphery in a counter-clockwise manner."

Douchebag interrupted Gustav. "To see if you still exist in the main reality?"

"Exactly. And I, personally, don't."

Collective gasps filled the room.

"I'm obviously not a jumper, because I don't remember my life in the main reality. But am I surprised I've died over there somehow? Given my old age, no." He shook his head. "But that wasn't the point in sending jumpers backward. The point was to see if it was possible."

"So, it was possible? That's how you know you died there, right?" A woman in the front of the room asked.

"It was possible, yes, to the detriment of the jumpers. The jumpers can return *here* unscathed, but sending them backward, breaks—melts—their mind in their main reality. Over there, they become invalid. The mind cannot handle the influx of memories in that fashion. So I've put a stop and a permanent ban on backward travel to the main reality. It's unethical, serves no purpose other than to confirm existence or death in that realm, and it's downright dangerous."

"What about the jumpers that you already experimented with?" the woman asked.

"They've been compensated generously for their

time, and given their altered mental status in the main reality, most have already died there and jumped here. Permanently."

Charly was pale as she stepped beside Gustav, then leaned toward the mic. "Allowing a client to choose their next life is also unethical, and I'd like to recommend a ban on designer deaths as well. Given we do not know what happens after you reach reality number seven—"

"Stop her. Now," Mitch growled.

I flew from my seat to the front of the room and grasped her elbow.

She resisted.

"Come with me, *now*," I demanded.

She mouthed *no* and continued, leaning toward the mic. "After one reaches reality seven, we cannot be sure that upon death they'll have anywhere—"

I stepped in front of her and leaned down toward the mic. "My apologies, my wife and I are late for another meeting." I turned away from the mic. "Gustav, finish up for us."

"Jared, no," she whispered, her green eyes pleading.

Gustav gave a tight smile and leaned into the mic. "I can take questions at this time." He shot a sympathetic look at my wife.

Almost every hand in the crowd raised, ready with a torrent of questions.

I pulled her toward the door and signaled to three of my troops. "Transport," I muttered.

In an instant, one soldier was in front of Charly, and two flanked her.

I was directly behind her, her back pressed to my front. We formed a diamond around her, her petite frame completely hidden to any passersby.

She struggled, but had no choice but to move forward as we walked in unison, corralling her out of the room, down the hall, and toward my car outside.

"What the hell, Jared?" She stopped, reeling backward against me.

I lifted her by the waist with ease and kept moving forward.

"Stop! Guys, what the hell?" She looked up at the men, who knew us well.

They all stared straight ahead, ignoring her. Just as they were trained to do.

"Shut up, Charly." I tightened my grip on her as she began to flail and kick.

"Let me go!" she shrieked. "Put me down! Stop, stop, *stop*!"

I sighed heavily, my headache reawakening as I put a hand tightly over her mouth. "I'll explain later. Just *shut the hell up* right now and get in the car."

It wasn't until I dumped her into the passenger seat that she finally wilted. Damn, she had stamina. And a set of lungs. My head throbbed.

I pulled myself into the driver's seat and locked the doors.

The troops made their way back inside the building without a word.

She turned to me, her breathing ragged and eyes brimming. *"What the hell is wrong with you?"*

I pulled out of our spot so fast the tires squealed, then headed toward the house. "You can't make recommendations for bans, and you know it!" I exploded. "Offering designer deaths is what we've been working toward, and you were going to recommend *against* it? Do you have any idea how much people will pay to choose their next life? *Do you?*" If my anger burned any hotter, fire would break through my ribcage. I'd never hurt her before, but now I wasn't sure I was incapable of doing so.

"You're offering a better life at what cost? If we don't know what happens after reality seven—"

"What happens to them after they *choose* is *their* problem, not ours!" I slammed my fist on the steering wheel.

She recoiled, then shook her head. "Then count me out. I'm not doing this."

"I don't need you to do this anymore now, anyway. You're out. Stay home and bake cookies or something. Gustav has the equation. He'll help us."

"Fine." She shrugged. "If you do this, I can't do this anymore, either." She gestured between us.

I threw my head back and laughed. It was the funniest thing she'd said all day.

"I'm serious, Jared."

"Stop acting like you split the atom, Charly. You helped us, and now we're going to help others."

"You call this *helping* others?"

"Allowing them to choose their next life? Absolutely. What happened to your faith?" I lacked faith, but she didn't. "If you believe in heaven after reality seven, aren't we just helping them reach it faster?" I mocked her.

"We're stealing time from them. Years, potentially. And from their families, too. The implications—"

"You worry too much." I reached for her hand, but she pulled it away.

"I'm not kidding. I can't compromise on this." She stared out the window.

"On what?" My irritation flared.

"My morals."

She was full of jokes today. I couldn't help it; I threw my head back and laughed again. When I stopped to take a breath, I stole a glance at her and saw a tear escape and roll down her cheek. She always cried when she was mad.

I shook my head. "Well, your morals were compromised the day you married a man like me." I chuckled again.

She didn't laugh.

I shrugged. She'd get over it. "You did good, Charly. Be proud. You're giving our clients a gift."

"It's not a gift. It's stealing from them, not telling them—"

"Enough!" I pulled into our driveway with a screeching halt.

She exited the car, slamming the door behind her.

I stormed into the house after her, slamming the front door behind me.

She was just finishing her ascent up the stairs, and I took the stairs two at a time after her. Just as I reached our room, the door slammed in my face.

"Open the door!" I pounded on the door so hard the frames in the hall rattled. Before I could kick the door in, it opened.

She turned and stormed to the closet, pulling both doors open.

Boy, she was being dramatic today. I grasped her elbow and spun her to face me, then looked down at her. The fire in my veins cooled when I took in her tear-soaked face.

She sniffed and swiped at her damp cheeks.

"Don't be mad, Charly," I coaxed, my voice gentling.

"I'm not mad"—her voice cracked—"I'm *devastated*. Who are you? Because the man I thought I married wouldn't—"

I stopped her by pushing against her and pressing my lips to hers.

She put both her hands on my chest and pushed me away.

I stepped forward and reached for her again.

She shook her head. "No. Say you won't allow it." She batted my hands away.

I suppressed the urge to grab her wrists and subdue her. She was bordering hysterical, and my patience was wearing thin. Too thin. I stepped closer to her, making her back away from the closet. "Allow what?" I asked softly, my gaze dropping to her lips now.

"Designer deaths."

"Okay. You win. I won't allow it."

Her shoulders sagged, her fight waning.

I didn't have to lie often, but this situation warranted it, so her trust in me was validated. Perfect.

"Seriously, Jared?"

I stepped farther into her, pushing her gently toward the bed. "I've told you time and time again. For you, anything." Well, mostly anything. Not like she wouldn't benefit from maintaining the lifestyle my position afforded us, anyway. Besides, that'd always been her way of coping—pretend she couldn't see what was right in front of her to feign her own innocence and defend her morals. It was a delicate dance I'd learned to navigate over the years.

She stumbled when the bed caught the back of her

thighs. She slumped onto the mattress, and I stood between her legs. She tried wiggling away, not ready to forgive me just yet. "Don't ever remove me from a room like that again, either," she snapped.

She tried to stand.

I climbed on top of her, my weight preventing her from squirming away now. "You're adorable when you cry." I dragged my lips across her jaw. The taste of her salty tears made my mouth water.

Goosebumps pebbled her neck at my touch, her body answering even when her mind wasn't ready to let it go. "You promise you won't allow it?" Her voice was desperate, pleading.

My favorite.

"I promise, Charly." I slid my hand under her shirt and over her stomach, caressing her soft warm skin.

****

"Wake up, Jared, dammit!" Mitch boomed. "You hear me? We don't have all day!"

I opened my eyes. A burning pain radiated from my left upper chest to my shoulder. Several doctors were clustered around the bed, a camera was recording, and Mitch was inches from my face.

I was in the hospital, resuscitated. A few scraps of memories from the other side lingered at the edge of my consciousness. I squeezed my eyes shut, the beeping monitor bringing the headache back from the other side.

"Do you remember anything?" Mitch demanded.

The headache. I remembered having a headache.

My throat burned like a sonofabitch, but I managed to release the last scrap of memory I'd dragged back with me. "You couldn't have waited twenty more minutes? I was about to get laid."

The room erupted in laughter.

Mitch clapped my shoulder. "Pardon the interruption," he scorned. "Hope you were doing more over there than that."

A few memories lingered beyond my reach. "I did. There's something big happening, but…"

Mitch leaned back in his seat and held up his hand. "Don't worry about it. I know. I've had a few jumpers brief me. She cracked the code. Designer deaths unlocked. We're going to make one hell of a profit." He chuckled.

The memories danced on the periphery of my mind. I couldn't confirm what he was saying was true, but I believed him. And if he was right, damn, that *was* important.

"Now we need to get my ass out of jail, so she can start working on that damn equation here." I muttered.

"Here poses a challenge. Your charm won't get her compliance here. She needs more…motivation than that."

Heat flooded my body as my blood pressure skyrocketed at his words, and I clenched my jaw. "Did the jumpers bring back the equation?"

Mitch sighed. "They've tried. Dumb bastards can't seem to retain it, says it's too long, too complex."

A flash of memory bolted through my mind—the whiteboard, filled end-to-end with the hieroglyphic-looking equation. Then the memory was gone, out of reach like a bolt of lightning.

"We don't have a mathematician that can look at part of it?"

Mitch scoffed. "We've had the *best* look at the bits and pieces brought back. They said it makes no sense at all. According to the jumpers, even Gustav can't work with it, or solve it over there. Only she can."

I inhaled sharply, irritation clawing at my insides. "Send me back," I bit out. "I'll make her so miserable *there*, she'll feel the bleed through so viciously *here*, and she'll beg me to stop. I'll make her a deal."

"Patience. With your fancy new equipment, we'll have you a trained jumper in no time."

I peered down at my chest. Stitched up inside of me was a brand-new ICD device—an implanted cardioverter defibrillator. Normally implanted in people who were at risk of sudden cardiac arrest, mine was implanted to *give me* cardiac arrest and resuscitation, enabling me to jump to the Periphery and back while in jail. Each jump, we hypothesized based on preliminary research, would strengthen the bridge in the mind. Eventually, it'd make me, or anyone exposed to the protocol repeatedly, capable of retaining memories. Capable of being a jumper.

Soon, we wouldn't need to seek people like Charly or Simon to jump to the other side. We wouldn't need anyone unwilling, or only signing on for money. We'd have trained, homegrown jumpers put on missions and paid for by the U.S. Government, to assist us in building Quantym bigger and better than ever before.

"So, how do we get her compliance here?" I spat. I didn't like having to ask questions I should already have the answers to. But in my still-compromised state, I gave myself some slack. My body was frigid, trembling uncontrollably as I acclimated to being zapped back from the brink of death. We were in a private hospital suite, surrounded by our personal hired medical staff who knew the protocols.

"We get her to come to you. If you can't sway her with your charm, control her with her fear." Mitch barked out a laugh. "You're getting extradited to the prison on base in Rhode Island, thanks to a few calls I made. With the bleed-through and her increased intuition, I have a feeling she'll go to see you. To ensure there's no way you're...impacting her life. She's already begun having nightmares, you know."

Brilliant. She would come see me, I was absolutely certain. And he was right. She'd feel the unease bleeding through from the other side. Once she learned I was jailed in the same state and no longer in Virginia, she'd want to see for herself that I was caged like an animal, incapable of accessing her. And oh, how very wrong she'd be. If there was one thing I prided myself on, it was my ability to manipulate, and with Charly, I was capable of unspeakable things. Another flash of memory bolted across my mind. This memory was from here, from the first night I met her. The night I decided she was the one, and how many actions I took to ensure she had no other options. Ending up with me wasn't just a choice, it was inevitable. I'd be sure to remind her of that.

If she doubted herself enough, eventually she'd let me take over. She always did.

I smiled and closed my eyes. "That brilliance robs her of common sense. She's so predictable, isn't she?"

"That she is." Mitch nodded.

Chapter 4: Reality 1

Charlotte

"Charlotte, Charlotte! I'm here, you're okay. You're okay." Sy wrapped his arm around my waist and helped me to my feet.

I'd had another nightmare. This time, my legs tangled in the covers, and I'd fallen out of bed. The last thing I remember was Jared standing over me, the gaping wound in his torso spilling blood onto the bed, soaking through the sheets. He held a gun at me, but then raised his arm until it was pointing at a sleeping Simon. As he went to pull the trigger, I bolted upright, ready to take the bullet. Only, it hadn't been Jared, or a bullet. It'd been a painful fall to the hardwood floor. It'd all been just another dream.

I put my hand to my forehead, feeling the tender spot where it'd connected with the floor. "That's gonna leave a mark, isn't it?" I slumped down onto the bed.

"Oh yeah, it is. Let me get some ice." Sy disappeared out of the room.

He returned with a bag of ice and applied it to the rapidly forming lump near my hairline. He tucked my hair behind my ear. "Tell me about it."

"The dream?" I shook my head. "Nothing to tell. I don't remember anything, just panic." I lied to protect him. He deserved better. I shouldn't be dreaming of my psychotic husband, the supposed-to-be-dead husband who'd attempted to kill both of us. But here we were, stuck in the past. Some things never changed, and I wasn't about to make him suffer along with me.

"PTSD is real, Charlotte. You have to confront your fears, do the work. It'll only haunt you if you run. Trust me."

I nodded. "My appointment is tomorrow, actually. I called last week."

Sy had dealt with his PTSD long ago, after the terrorist attack that killed his comrades and left him clinging to life. He understood.

His hand lingered at my jaw. "At the VA?"

I nodded again.

He slid closer. "Want me to go with you?"

"No, thank you. I'm meeting my co-workers for lunch afterward. I'm going to talk to Brian about returning to work."

His blue eyes clouded for a moment. "That's good, but are you sure you're ready?"

I sighed. "Idle hands are the devil's workshop. It'll probably be the best thing for me."

I studied his gorgeous face etched with worry, then dragged a finger over the tattoo on his neck, trailing it down to where it connected to the wing stretching across his chest. My dream was forgotten for the moment as I traced the outline of the phoenix inked onto him. I finally spoke. "Sy, I don't want you worrying about me. I'm fine."

He smiled and leaned closer. "I don't underestimate you. I just want to protect you." His lips brushed against my ear, awakening every nerve in my body.

"Well, that's lovely. But know what I'd rather have

you do?"

He raised a brow.

"Join me in the shower." I gave him a quick kiss, then rose from the bed and sauntered into the bathroom.

****

The next day, I arrived at my appointment early. I didn't want to go to therapy, but I also didn't want to run from my past. Whatever was haunting me, Sy was right, it'd only stop if I confronted it.

The therapist was nice enough. The first session was just basically a recap of my life, with a big focus on the accident that'd supposedly turned me into a widow. Then, I went with the story released by the media, that Jared's brother, Adam Cardoza, had a mental break and went on a killing spree, and I'd been one of his many victims while in Virginia. All of that was plenty of trauma to sort through. I took no chances of revealing Jared's fake death or Quantym, for fear she'd either deem me insane, or report me and I'd have Mitch or the CIA tailing me—possibly both.

I met with my co-workers for lunch afterward, and decided on returning to work at the end of the month. Lunch with Angela, Brian, Beth, and Nelson was more therapeutic than the session had been. They asked about the events in Virginia, but didn't press. They knew I'd gotten hurt, but how much I told them was solely up to me. I decided to give away only scraps of what'd happened, leaving the rest unsaid. Everyone seemed okay with that. No one would ever know Jared wasn't dead, or that I'd saved Simon from Quantym, which was what'd set the events in motion that'd put Jared—known to the public as Adam—Cardoza in jail.

A couple weeks later, at my fourth session with the

therapist, I was convinced it was a waste of time. I couldn't tell her the truth about anything. I had to filter almost every word out of my mouth.

She picked up on this and said, "Therapy only helps if we're honest with ourselves."

"I'm being honest. I just...don't know how to articulate every—"

"Honest? Let me ask you directly. Do you still love Jared?"

"No! How could—"

"Charlotte, that's not how this works. Don't get defensive. If you're dreaming of him, thinking of him all the time, even seeking therapy because of him, perhaps there's some unfinished business."

I stood brusquely. "The only unfinished business is my ability to come to terms with everything that's happened. And I thought your job was to help with that."

"Sit. I didn't want to upset you. Did you realize our sessions always revolve around him? You don't speak of your parents, your childhood, your friends, or even your boyfriend."

I blanched at her words, then sat at the edge of the plush wingback chair. "Because they're not the problem."

She leaned forward and put her wire-framed glasses onto her nose. She peered down at her notes.

Then it hit me. She didn't say *Adam*. She'd said *Jared*. A shudder shook through me.

"Why'd you ask me about loving Jared? My dreams aren't of him, they're of—" My lies were catching up with me, my stories coalescing and crumbling.

"He was your husband. You don't love him anymore because he died? Because you're angry he died?"

I drew in a breath. Therapy was making things worse when I couldn't tell the truth or keep my own story straight.

"I still love him," I whispered, then squared my shoulders. "I hate his brother. Hate him deeply."

She sank back into her chair and smiled. "Now we're getting somewhere."

After that particularly inflammatory session, I was in my car driving home when the ringing phone broke me from my intrusive thoughts. I slowed the car and hit the button on the steering wheel to answer the call via Bluetooth.

Angela's chipper voice rang through the speakers. "Hey, you! So…before you come back to work, I want to get you drunk."

"Aw, you all missed me in the trenches, did you?"

"Of course! Let's go for drinks tonight, and don't you dare say no."

"Ange, you know that's not—"

"Your thing, got it. But I'll bring Rex and you bring Sy, and maybe we can change the way you feel after a few stiff ones."

I thought about it for a moment. With Sy there, it didn't sound unbearable. Maybe I'd get drunk. When was the last time I'd let loose? Had I ever?

"Thames Place?" I asked.

"No, I know just the place. Small, not too crowded. We can play darts. They have axe throwing, too!"

"You don't value your safety, then," I teased.

"Nope. Not one iota. You'll go?" She squealed.

"I'm sure Sy will say yes. I'm on my way home now."

"Okay, I'm going to text you the address of the

place. You better not back out!"

"I might even wear heels."

"Hell, yeah! See you tonight!"

I ended the call and shook my head with a laugh. My friends were all the therapy I'd ever need. After today's session, I decided I wouldn't be going back to the therapist. But still, something lingered at the edges of my mind, pulled at an uncomfortable thread left hanging. Was the therapist under Mitch's direction? Is that why she'd asked about Jared the way she did? I'd be giving no more of myself to her or anyone else who wasn't in my inner circle. And as I pulled down Bayview Avenue and toward my and Sy's house, I felt confident—comfortable—with my decision.

I made my way to the front door, and my phone chimed with a text from Sy.

—I'll be back in a few, went to see Jeff and Max. Jay's getting deployed next month.—

I was glad he was spending time with his brothers. They'd need him to put in more hours at the construction business, given Jay's imminent deployment, something Sy hadn't been able to do while recovering. Life was beginning to resume its normal pulse of duties and responsibilities, and I welcomed the normalcy with open arms.

I texted him back:

—Tell them I said hi. Knowing Jay, he's glad to be getting shipped out. Angela and Rex want to get drinks with us tonight.—

—You're right about Jay. And for tonight, I'm down for it if you are.—

—OK. I'll get ready. See you soon.—

—I'll be sure to check the camera in the shower,

then. Xx—
—You wish.—

I dropped my bag and keys on the kitchen island and dashed upstairs to start getting ready.

****

I grunted and recoiled after the heavy axe left my hand. It landed in the white circle just outside the bullseye.

"Not bad." Sy nodded in approval, then handed me another.

"Who needs therapy—" I brought my arm back, grasping the wooden handle tightly. "—when you can throw these?" I emphasized the last word when I exerted myself on the throw. The axe landed with a satisfying clunk into the wooden target, next to the last one I'd thrown.

"I don't know, man. I wouldn't piss her off if I were you," Rex said to Sy.

Sy took a swig from his beer and shrugged. "She's cute when she's mad." He handed me the last axe.

Angela rolled her eyes. "Show 'em, Charl. Give it all you got!" She brought her straw to her lips and took a long pull.

I scowled at Sy and took the axe.

I winked at Angela, and brought my arm back again, releasing the axe with all my strength. The axe finally landed just on the edge of the red portion of the bullseye. I jumped so high, both my feet left the ground. "Yes!" I jumped again and whirled to face the guys with a gigantic smile. "Take that!"

Angela jumped from her seat and slammed her body into mine with a bear hug. She swung me wildly, then we held hands and jumped in unison, making a show of our excitement. Something about alcohol and axes—probably not the best idea when combined—fueled an adrenaline high for us.

"Fear that, bitches!" Angela yelled to Sy and Rex.

The guys shook their heads and laughed, while Rex retrieved the axes from the target.

Sy stepped into position, and it was his turn to burn some stress.

"So, no more therapy?" Angela inquired, handing me the remnants of my rum and coke.

I slurped loudly when my straw hit mostly ice. "Nah. I don't think it helps, besides—" I stopped speaking when the loud crack echoed through the place.

Sy's axe landed just outside the bull's eye, cracking the wooden target down the middle. With a clenched jaw, he reached for the second axe from Rex.

"You're not going anymore?" Sy asked with his back to me. He gripped the axe by his side with white knuckles, waiting for my answer.

"No. We'll talk later," I muttered. I didn't want to get into it. Not here, especially.

"You finished your drink *and* you hit the bullseye! I'm buying you a shot." Angela giggled.

I draped my arm around Angela's shoulders. "*You're* my therapist now! With friends, axes, our men, and self-medicating with alcohol, I'm *healing*. I can *feel* it!"

"It's a miracle!" She shook her body as if she was being exorcised. "Praise!"

We laughed, and she snorted—causing us to laugh until our faces were red and bellies ached. The alcohol had released me from my mental binds for the time being, and I was glad to accept the reprieve.

Another loud *thunk* caused me to look up in time to see Sy's axe connecting with the damaged wooden target again. He landed it right in the center, stealing my thunder.

"Well, damn," Angela muttered. "I still think you did great." She nudged my shoulder. "Be right back." She smiled and hopped over to the bar.

Sy grasped for the third and final axe. He was tense, no hint of a smile, his brow deeply furrowed. "Why didn't you tell me on the way here?"

"Not important. We'll talk later," I said to his back.

His shoulders lifted with each breath. He gripped the handle of the axe, spinning it in his hand as he stood staring at the target ahead.

"You okay, man? I think you need another beer. I'll be right back." Rex headed toward Angela at the bar.

"Sy." I stood and started toward him.

He turned halfway. "Wait. I'm not done. It's my turn," he bit out.

I froze.

His axe again hit the bull's eye with a deafening crack, splitting the target in two. The two severed halves of the board clunked to the ground with a loud clatter.

The crowd quieted and looked in our direction.

Sy didn't turn around. He was still breathing heavily, sweat beginning to lace his hairline.

"Damn, killing off that bad energy or what?" I tipped my head at the broken target.

"Killing." He barked out a laugh. "You know damn well who I was picturing when I threw these."

I flinched from the statement he hurled at me, and my heart thundered in my chest. "Me too," I whispered. "But therapy isn't helping with that."

He spun and pulled me into his arms. "I'm sorry," he murmured into my hair. "Damn, I'm so sorry."

"Don't worry about it. You're not as okay as you pretend to be, either, apparently."

"I thought I killed him. He was *supposed* to be dead. But you were dying, and I didn't have time to ensure—"

"Sy, stop."

"No, listen. Just hear me out. If I'd finished the job—I'm *trained* to finish the job—you wouldn't be haunted by him. I've killed hundreds who deserved it, yet the most important one, I failed. I fucking failed. I want every part of you to myself, and he's—"

"He's not anything, Sy! You've got to stop—"

"You beg him, Charlotte, in your sleep. I know what you're dreaming, and his name falling from your lips, begging, pleading with him, is killing me."

I pulled away and gritted my teeth. "You didn't fail me. I beg him to stop—to stop going after *you.*"

He raised a brow. "Me? If I didn't love you as much as I do, I'd go pay him a visit in prison and finish the job. I still might."

"Don't. Getting yourself imprisoned for life is exactly what he wants. Don't let him win."

I turned to see Angela and Rex coming back from the bar. A bar worker shut down our lane while he replaced the wooden target.

Angela returned, holding a tray with four shots. Rex held out a rum and coke for me, and a beer for Sy.

"Since we're all on a murdering streak, I figured we could all use a shot!" Angela passed out the glasses to each of us. "To throwing axes and kicking asses!"

"Oorah!" Rex bellowed.

"Oorah!" We cheered in unison after him, clinking

glasses and downing our shots.

Angela was next to throw some axes, and cheering for her felt good.

Sy stopped drinking after his last shot and beer, changing over to water instead. The alcohol didn't seem to have had any effect on him, though.

I, on the other hand, continued to be fed drinks from a much too enthusiastic Angela, who had mentioned earlier that her goal was to get me drunk.

I sat on Sy's lap and rested my hands on his chest. "You smell so good." I dropped my head to the crook of his neck and inhaled the heady scent of his cologne.

"You, love, appear to be utterly drunk." He smiled and wrapped his arms around me.

"Why'd you stop drinking with me?" I pouted. "I do believe it was you who said you liked to see me indulge."

"As long as I'm here to watch"—he pulled me closer—"and I don't drink in excess because I don't like losing control."

"I'd like to see you lose control," I taunted.

His eyes darkened. "No, no, you wouldn't."

I stood and pulled him up with me. I ran my hands through my hair and swayed my hips to the music.

He put his hands on my hips and leaned down to speak into my ear. "Don't, Charlotte," he warned.

"Or what?" I turned so my back was to him. I intentionally swayed up against him, losing myself in the music again. I was drunk. Most definitely drunk.

"Or you'll watch me lose control on every bastard who is eyeing you right now."

"Well, luckily you're the only one watching."

I heard him mumble something, but the loud music masked his words. I was immediately distracted when

Angela sashayed up to me, clearly as drunk as I was.

"Yeah, baby, that's what we came out for!" Angela pulled me toward her and started dancing with me. Our bodies swayed in time to the thrum of music. Minutes passed, or maybe it was an hour, I couldn't be sure. But when Angela turned and started dancing against Rex, I realized Sy was missing.

I left Angela and Rex—not that they'd have noticed with their tongues down each other's throats—to search for Sy. He wasn't at the bar, and I loitered outside of the restrooms for a bit. Going missing wasn't like him. He was usually hovering, watching, on alert. Especially when I was around.

Maybe getting drunk wasn't the best idea, after all. Maybe we had a bit too much trauma to work through for me to have gotten so utterly detached for a bit. Then I got angry. I was an adult who never let loose—he even admitted that. I had every right to get drunk where I was safe, enjoying myself, escaping reality for a time.

I darted into the ladies' room before I went to look for him again. While in a stall, I checked my phone. He'd sent a text over ten minutes ago.

—Just getting some air. Be back in a few.—

I freshened up and raced outside. I looked left—two girls ambled along the sidewalk toward another bar, then right, where two men stumbled along toward the bar I was at. Sy wasn't outside. I slumped against the cold brick wall and checked my phone again. I started to text him back when footfalls caused me to look up.

The two men, clearly drunk, closed in on where I stood.

One guy raised his hands over his head and gyrated his pelvis. "Saw you in there dancing. You gonna bring the show out here for us?"

His friend took a drag from a vape, and blew out a puff of smoke when he started laughing. The vapor surrounded his gyrating friend, enhancing the dramatic show.

The man pulled his friend away from me. "Leave her alone—her boyfriend wanted to kill you for looking, remember?"

I rolled my eyes and started texting again, not giving the men a second glance.

The sounds of their footsteps faded, as both men continued their trek down the sidewalk and away from where I stood, the moment forgotten. A car horn honked in the distance, over the steady bass emanating from the bar I was supposed to be inside of. Laughter from two girls down the street floated on the crisp night air, only to be broken by a sickening thud.

A scream seared through the noises of the night.

Sy was standing over one of the men, his fist connecting with the guy's face once, then again, and again.

I ran over to him. "Sy! Stop! What the hell?"

"I warned this asshole, and the second he thinks you're alone, he approaches you."

His fist connected with the man's bloody face again, and Sy abruptly released the man's shirt, allowing him to drop to the concrete with a thud.

The man's friend stood between Sy and his friend on the ground. "Chill, man! We were just messing around." He helped his friend to his feet.

Blood poured from the nose of the guy Sy'd beaten, who now swayed on his feet. He turned to me, his eyes wide. "You bitches run toward red flags like a bull. Nice guy you snagged." He sneered.

I grabbed at Sy's arm when his body locked up, ready to swing at the guy again.

"Stop!" I pulled him away from the men's retreating figures as they stumbled down the street and away from the unhinged lunatic, who just so happened to be my boyfriend. "Sy! What the hell?"

"I'm sorry, Charlotte. I shouldn't have come tonight, I—"

"Walk with me." I grasped his hand and started down the sidewalk, in the opposite direction from the two men. "So, it turns out you're not okay either, huh?"

"I'm fine. I just—have bad days."

"And today is one of them," I noted.

He nodded. "Yeah. It is. I thought therapy was helping you. I *want* it to help you."

"I think *you* need therapy. I didn't know you were suffering like this. You hide it well."

"I want to be strong for you. But sometimes, I get so angry—" He inhaled sharply. "Mostly at myself, for not finishing the job. But I also get mad at anyone who may do you harm. I'm furious that I can't protect you from the fallout—the nightmares—that plague your sleep."

"It's a trauma response. I'll let go at some point. It takes time, though."

"I don't know that I'll ever let go, knowing that Jared and Mitch aren't *dead*."

"Well, I don't know if this makes it worse, but I'm glad you didn't kill him. And before you say anything, let me finish. I'm glad you didn't kill him because what if he was dead and I had these nightmares anyway? Knowing you, you'd think I harbored some kind of anger toward you for finishing the job. You'll never let yourself win, don't you see?"

He shrugged. "Maybe it's because I feel like I don't deserve you."

I stopped walking and faced him. "Don't say that, Sy. Please, don't ever say that. You're the man I love. I need you to understand that, okay?"

He brushed his thumb along my cheek and leaned down to kiss me.

I pressed tightly to his body, holding his face in my hands as I kissed him—I wanted him to feel how badly I wanted him, needed him.

A tinkling bell caught my attention. I pulled away from him for a second to look at the shops and bars lining the street. Then I turned back to him and traced my finger along the tattoos that trailed up his arm.

"What?" He raised his eyebrows.

The bell that'd chimed was for a tattoo shop across the street. I glanced across the street and back to Sy again, then nodded in the direction of the shop. "That."

His gaze went to the tattoo parlor and back to me. "I don't believe it."

"I want one. And I know exactly what I want."

He shook his head and smiled. "Text Angela and Rex. We're probably gonna be a while."

Chapter 5, Reality 2: On the Periphery

Jared

It was only my third time jumping, but I looked forward to the shocking jolt to my chest, as sick as that sounded. I itched to get this mission underway, to escape jail while my body was kept in limbo in the cell, monitored by my father and the other doctors we'd hired privately in the main reality. There wasn't a guard in that damn jail that my father couldn't buy. Another perk of the money and power Quantym offered us.

The Periphery was my playground, and I was already starting to build the bridge in my mind needed to bring memories back and forth. I always loved being in control, and being able to live in two lives, control and manipulate the narrative both *here and there* was more intoxicating than a drug.

I felt the heat in my chest before the stabbing pain seared through my heart. As darkness descended, a rush of excitement came over me, and I welcomed death with open arms.

My father was a lot of things. Powerful, committed, narcissistic, violent—but he was also the smartest man I'd ever met. I respected him. And he had the patience of a saint. He'd waited until I'd begun to build memories to have me briefed completely on the events happening in the main reality. Now, when I jumped to reality two, he had me briefed immediately by jumpers on my arrival. Soon, I'd barely need to be briefed at all. I'd retain *and* acquire memories upon arrival. *Soon.*

The intense headache was becoming familiar, too. Another reminder I'd jumped. I opened my eyes, rubbed my temples, and realized I was seated at my desk inside Quantym.

Two soldiers sat across from me, waiting to brief me.

Memories of the morning here in reality two tumbled into my consciousness—a quick flicker of Charly still sleeping in bed as I got ready this morning stirred something indescribable deep within me. I quickly sifted through the other memories of what I'd been doing over here, and damn it if she didn't pop up in almost every one.

I was told of the events in the main reality—about my fake death, and the Marine, Simon, grabbing the opportunity to steal my wife before I could return for her.

His influence had nearly dismantled Quantym in the main reality, and his influence got Charly to turn on me—stab me—in the main reality.

I saw red—I wasn't just going to murder him, I was going to ensure he was wiped from existence in every life that existed. Hell, I wished there was a way to ensure he'd never existed at all.

Once Charly cracked the code in the main reality and we didn't need outside jumpers anymore, he was going to pay. Dearly. Though my wife had only betrayed me in the main reality, she might've well have done it here, too. Loyalty should bleed through, and the fact that it didn't told me her insubordination ran deep. After she watched what I had planned for Simon, I was certain she'd not step out of line again.

But like my father, I needed patience.

Mitch was smart enough to know that giving this intel to me before I could begin building memories would be like throwing a Molotov cocktail into reality two, with high emotions and little control. Instead, he waited until now, when I was gaining control, to drop the bombshell on me.

And it was all the motivation I needed to help build Quantym back even stronger than before.

After my men finished bringing me up to speed on the details from the main reality, I leaned back into my chair and crossed my ankles on my desk. I was in jail in the main reality. Granted, my father had bought most of the guards so we had control on the inside, but still. I studied my desert-colored combat boots and considered the information I'd been told. Jail was going to be a temporary stay while he rebuilt on that side, and my mission was to influence Charly—*here and there*—to crack the code on the other side. Once she could get us to navigate through all seven peripheral lives in the main reality and here, our profits would increase, our clientele would increase, and we'd be heroes in the eyes of our investors. Power and money—we were about to own the elite one percent both here and there.

"Where is she now?" I looked over at Morgan, one of the men who sat across from my desk briefing me.

"May I?" He motioned to the computer at my desk.

I nodded and waved my hand at the PC.

"The general had us download this before your arrival today. Said it's more accurate than the one you've been using. Can pinpoint location down to a meter," he spoke while clacking away at the keyboard. "This icon, here"—he nodded at the infinity logo—"log in, and she's—"

I leaned closer to the screen when I saw the blinking red dot on the screen. "Right there." She was still home. I suppressed a smile when another memory of her popped into my mind—her showering this morning just before I left the house.

"The tracker is in her cell. You can access the app from your PC or phone."

I nodded. "Good."

My other troop, Jackson, cleared his throat. "I know you told her she wasn't needed anymore, but Gustav still can't seem to crack her equation, so the general has asked—"

I narrowed my eyes at the men. "I'll get her back to work. In the meantime, I want the two of you to keep tabs on the Marine, Simon Donovan. I want him tracked at all times, understood?"

"The Silencer?" Morgan stared at me, dumbfounded.

I gritted my teeth until my jaw ached. "Yes, *the Silencer*. Put him on my app, too. I want to see where he is at all times."

"Yes, sir," they said in unison.

I waved my hand. "Dismissed."

I stared at the computer screen in front of me.

Charly was leaving home, and the house was mere minutes from the hospital.

I planned to head into a few meetings, then I'd get her to show me the protocol to navigate all seven peripheries, before letting her leave her position at Quantym. If Gustav couldn't do it, I'd have to learn it myself. It wasn't out of the realm of my capabilities.

I was about to close out the app when a green blinking dot appeared. Son of a bitch, they were fast. Simon was on my radar, across base at PT. I'd be keeping an eye on both of them, staying a step ahead this time. I'd learned from my past mistakes, and as much as I hated to admit it, Mitch was right. Emotions only muddied the mission. I'd not be making that mistake this time.

I strolled into my father's office and sat in the chair facing his desk.

He didn't look up when he acknowledged me. "Questions for me?" He continued reading the paperwork before him.

"They brought me up to speed." I crossed an ankle over my knee.

"So, did she agree to come back?"

I sighed. "She doesn't have a choice. I'll have her show us the protocol, then she can be relieved of duties."

He raised his eyebrows and looked up to meet my gaze. "Then why are you here?"

I looked up at the ceiling and pulled a deep breath into my lungs. "I wanted to stop in on a few of the meetings. Make my presence known. I've got tabs on Charly and Simon, and they're not going anywhere."

Mitch closed the folder on his desk and folded his hands on top. "Time is of the essence. I've got the meetings covered."

I leaned forward. "I'll be going to the meetings. I want to see Gustav, ensure no one is going to tell Charly we're offering designer deaths."

He shook his head. "Still trying to stay out of the doghouse? Get your emotions out of this. They've no place here."

"Emotions? No. I'm taking the path of least resistance. She'll comply, and I have my ways of ensuring that."

"Speak of the devil herself," Mitch muttered.

A throat cleared and we both looked up to see Charly at the door.

"Um, don't mean to interrupt, but I'm dropping off some things to Gustav. Morgan said I'd find you here."

"So, you're going to stay home and bake now?" Mitch sneered.

Her back straightened. "Actually, no. I've been in touch with a few former colleagues, and they've offered me a per diem position doing in-office evaluations."

I rose from my seat and walked over to her. "Don't accept anything yet. We need to talk about this."

"Oh?" She shot a quick glance at Mitch, then looked up at me.

"These colleagues, are they part of the team you operated on Simon Donovan with?" I sealed my anger under the fakest smile I could manage.

She nodded and swallowed, twisting her hands in front of her.

I stepped closer, speaking in a placating tone. "Speaking of Donovan, aren't you supposed to meet with him one last time? Get him to sign on at Quantym?"

She shook her head. "I'm out. I'll have Diogo cancel all my meetings, reassign them to—"

"No." My anger simmered just under the surface, ready to break through and scald her.

Mitch stood. "Guess you don't miss him too much." He cocked his head and smiled.

Her mouth fell open and her eyes widened. "What the hell is that supposed to mean?" She stepped forward, ready to go head-to-head with him.

He towered over her and let out a grumbly laugh. "Unbelievable. See, Jared? Emotion. It's just a construct of weakness. Nothing more."

She put her hands on her hips and leaned in. "I *operated* on Simon—er, Mr. Donovan, years ago. And I was trying to get him to sign on to Quantym per *your* request. Are you implying I had anything other than a professional relationship with him, General?"

Mitch put his hands up in submission. "I just think you'll be able to convince him more effectively than me. But I'll do it. You're no longer needed."

She whipped her head to look at me. "Can you believe him? What the hell is this shit?"

I shook my head. "We have a lot we're reassigning because of your…abrupt departure."

"Maybe if you'd handled the presentation differently the other day, it wouldn't be like this! And now your father is accusing me of unethical behavior? On the heels of everything—"

"Stop! Now! This conversation is over. Gustav is taking over for you, and before you're relieved of duties, finish what you started!" I snapped.

"What I started?"

"Yes. Get Donovan to sign, and I want to watch you use the new protocol." I clenched and unclenched my fists, waiting for her refusal. There was only so far she could push me this time. My father would love to see my control slip, especially on her.

She tilted her head. "Designer deaths?"

I rolled my eyes. "No. I told you I wasn't going to allow designer deaths. We have a jumper assigned to go to Periphery four. We've contracted him for a very important client."

She shook her head. "No."

Careful. Breathe. Don't take her by force. Not now. Not yet.

I inhaled sharply and plastered on an empathetic smile, allowing my eyes to soften. "It's not what you think. He's looking for a child. These parents, they're devastated. The mother nearly committed suicide. We haven't found him in reality three. This is important."

She puffed out her cheeks while blowing out a breath, then crossed her arms. "I want to see the file."

I gave her a withering look. "You don't believe me?" *Breathe.* My gaze went to her delicate throat and back to her aurora-colored eyes. *Just breathe.*

Mitch interjected. "I'll have the file this afternoon. Be in the ORA wing, room 298 at 1500. And after the jump, you'll be relieved of duties." He shot me a knowing look.

I loosened my fists.

She held his gaze before backing away. She looked up at me, hurt clouding her eyes. "And Mr. Donovan?"

I shrugged, then bit out, "Finish what you started."

And if he touches you, I'll kill him with my bare hands. The words sat at the tip of my tongue, barely contained in my venomous mouth. I released a breath when she turned and stomped away. I didn't let my control slip, didn't let myself *feel*. She was a means to an end, nothing more.

Chapter 6, Reality 2: On the Periphery

Charlotte

I could feel Jared's eyes boring into my back as I strode away, swallowing back the burn that threatened to close my throat completely. When I locked eyes with him, I knew he'd be in a mood. It was happening more and more lately, that hardened, stone-cold look he'd get, usually accompanied by a migraine.

I blinked rapidly, keeping my head down as the white tiles disappeared beneath my feet. I couldn't do this anymore. *Maybe he has a brain tumor.* I started reconciling his behaviors with the symptoms of a brain lesion, but other than his callousness, he didn't fit the diagnosis. So what, then? His father? Had our morals never aligned, and perhaps I was only seeing him clearly now? No. *Something had changed.* I could feel it, *see* it in the smile he'd suppress as if he knew a dark secret when his eyes went cold like today. I'd been a good wife. Done more than he'd asked. Always more. A muddy memory caused my skin to crawl—cameras, there were cameras everywhere.

The day the server room caught fire, I kissed Simon Donovan. It had to have been the smoke inhalation. The whole incident seemed far away, out-of-body now. And, I'd avoided him ever since, which wasn't easy. He'd been my only friend for years, and as faithful to my husband as I'd been—I couldn't lie to myself and say I didn't look forward to seeing Simon, the one person who *saw* me. Heard me. Knew me. While my husband was busy ensuring my compliance, Simon was listening to me. Seeing the hollow shell I was becoming as more of my freedoms and autonomy were stripped away by…

I pushed the thought away.

Things changed the day of the fire, proof the universe could be both cruel and kind in its synchronicities sometimes. Simon could walk because I'd operated on him after his injury, and years later, he walked me out of that burning building. Simon saved my life, and I never spoke to him again, because there was something else, something more—but my shame and guilt refused to allow me to dwell on it for too long.

"Charlotte, dear!" Doctor Tomas Gustav jumped from his seat at the lab bench to greet me.

"Tomas." I took his outstretched hand in both of mine, giving him a warm handshake.

"So glad you're back." He turned away and began digging through a stack of folders. "The general and Lieutenant Cardoza have been asking me to work on your equation, but it's beyond me. Here, sit. Let's go over it again." His salt-and-pepper hair was in disarray when he turned back to me with a file folder in his hand. His eyes lit as he motioned for me to sit beside him.

I leaned against the lab bench and put a hand on the doctor's shoulder. "I'm sorry, Tomas. I'm not here to work. I've resigned my position. I-I don't agree with the ethics of what it can be used for." I was surprised I said it out loud to him.

"Ah, Charlotte. That is the sign of a *true* scientist. You have to listen to your gut. If it's telling you to stop, then stop." He closed the folder and pushed it away.

I looked up at the white board in the lab that still had my writing all over it, from the days before I'd completed the equation, and I wondered when they'd erase it, erase all traces of me that lingered in this contemptible facility.

"You're not mad?" My stomach fluttered with nerves. I was letting down a whole team, not just Mitch and Jared.

"Mad?" He scoffed. "I saw what he did that day, and I wanted to stop him. Removing you like that—"

"Don't worry about it." I waved my hand dismissively. "It needed to happen, to give me the push I needed to break away. I never wanted to leave my old job in the first place."

He nodded.

I smiled. "It's been wonderful working with you and the rest of the team."

"So, back to neurosurgery?" He stood and smiled, looking over his wire-rimmed glasses.

I shrugged. "Probably. I just want to make a clean break here. Figure some stuff out." My words hung in the air, holding more personal weight than I'd intended.

Gustav leaned closer. "No matter what, you'll be okay. You hear me, Charlotte? Don't doubt yourself, or your instincts. Instincts are more accurate than science."

I patted his shoulder. "Thanks, Tomas. Here, these are for you." I plopped a briefcase full of files onto the lab bench. I opened the front zipper and removed a glass container. "And this is so you remember me fondly." I grinned.

Gustav opened a corner of the container and beamed. "My favorite, Kvæfjordkake! Thank you,

Charlotte."

I hesitated and puffed out a breath.

He put the container down on the bench and leaned closer.

"I know this is poor timing, and I'd never want to get you in trouble, but—"

Gustav held my gaze, waiting for me to finish.

Internally, I debated whether I should just use my badge to access the record, but decided against it. I wanted to see how it played out, whether Jared would truly lie and risk everything, and how far he'd take it if I found out the truth without him knowing.

I spoke in a rush. "There's a jump happening, and Jared wants to watch me use the protocol. He said it's to track someone for a client, but I overheard—"

Gustav turned to his computer and badged in. He began clacking away at the keyboard. "What room?"

"ORA wing, room 298. Today at 1500."

"The client is...very well known." His gaze darted across the screen and his eyes widened. "Assessing alternate lives for her imminent departure due to...oh. *Oh*."

"What, what is it?" I nearly toppled him off the stool to see the screen myself.

He harrumphed. "Celebrities can buy anything now."

"You have *got* to be kidding me."

A beautiful young celebrity had been caught in a cheating scandal, and her career was being canceled. She was a humiliated, fallen-from-grace star who planned on finding a better alternate life, and *killing* herself to go there.

"Are we going to offer physician-assisted suicide to

healthy celebrities? Is that on the menu of services now, too?" I slammed my fist on the lab bench. My heart was cracking, breaking, tearing straight down the middle. Jared lied. Again. He knew how much this meant. I made it clear what was on the line if he proceeded with designer deaths. Our marriage. *Us.*

I looked away from Gustav and blinked rapidly through blurry eyes.

"This is the first of this kind that I've seen. But I'm sure there'll be more." Gustav shook his head. "I have a family, Charlotte. I'm so close to retirement, my pension. I can't just—"

"I'm not judging you, Tomas." I slumped into a chair beside him and rested my elbows on the lab bench. "Who's the jumper for this mission?"

After more clacking at the keyboard, Gustav cleared his throat.

I put my head down on my folded arms.

"An injured veteran Marine. He's done a few missions for us before."

"Name?" My voice was muffled, I kept my head in my arms and stared at the black bench top.

"Seth MacDowell."

I hadn't met this particular jumper yet. Most of our jumpers were service members, as those were the most-likely people to have survived a near-death experience. Quantym would target the injured vets with offers impossible to refuse, offers that could ensure financial security for life.

"Speaking of injured Marines. Have you gotten Simon Donovan to sign on?" Gustav asked.

I lifted my head from the bench. "No. He's not interested."

Gustav laughed. "I'm sure the general will increase his price, then. There's only so much you can refuse before you're considered *galen*." He swirled his finger near his temple.

"He's not crazy. He's smart." I stood and hung my lab coat on the back of my chair. "Not everyone wants to sell their soul."

Gustav stiffened.

"Not you! No, not you sweet Tomas. I meant the jumpers."

He nodded, but his shoulders remained tight.

I gathered my belongings, leaving the lab coat behind.

"Take care now, Charlotte."

"You too." I smiled at him and glanced around the lab before heading out the door of the Quantym lab for the last time.

Chapter 7, Reality 1

Charlotte

"You're lying. You're lying again!" I screamed. Tears escaped and rolled down my cheeks, the wetness bringing my consciousness back as the dream receded.

I moaned and rolled into the pillow to escape the sunlight pouring into the room.

Simon trailed his fingers along my spine, awakening goosebumps that prickled over my skin.

"Who's lying?" he asked softly, though he likely knew the answer.

I groaned and avoided his question. "My head—I'm never, ever drinking again."

"Another dream," he murmured, continuing to draw lazy circles along my bare back. It wasn't a question. It was a statement of fact. "I'll get you something for the hangover."

His soft touch disappeared, and the mattress released when he stood and left the room, returning a few minutes later with water and two painkillers.

"Thank you, Sy. I—" I gasped when I looked down at my hand. "It's perfect!" I sat up on my knees and reached for his hand, pulling him closer to study the fresh ink.

He put the water and pills on the nightstand. "Even alcohol doesn't mute your abilities." He sat back on the bed.

My mind took me back to the evening before, where we sat together in the tattoo parlor getting complementing tattoos. On the small triangle of skin between his left thumb and pointer finger was a small EKG rhythm—my tachycardic sinus rhythm from the day I was resuscitated after being stabbed by Jared, wrapped within an infinity symbol. My tattoo was similar, but was between my right thumb and forefinger, an infinity symbol struck through with a heart rhythm in V-fib, the fatal rhythm that I'd resuscitated Sy from that same day at Quantym, then trailing into the bradycardic rhythm that brought him back to life *here*. To me.

I tapped my temple. "Being a savant has its perks. Immaculate memory." I kicked my feet and squealed when I interlaced our fingers and the tattoos touched where our hands met.

"Pretty sure you freaked out the artist when you started calculating tattoo needle punctures per minute…"

"Then per second, and how many in total—" I laughed. "He definitely thinks I'm nuts."

"I like to call it brilliant."

I lowered myself back onto the bed, rolling onto my side as Sy settled in beside me.

He resumed tracing swirls along my back.

I squirmed and giggled when he hit a particularly ticklish spot.

"You should be mad at me. I wouldn't blame you if you were," he said.

"Mad? No." I shook my head.

"I'm sorry about last night." He closed his eyes for a few heartbeats.

"I understand the anger, and the fear, too."

"Anger, yes, but fear? I don't—"

I drew in a breath. "Fear of loss."

He nodded.

I met his gaze. "Apology accepted. Next time you want to lose control, I'll wear an old shirt, and let you get your frustrations out by ripping it off me like the big, hulking green superhero."

He laughed. "I like that idea."

"Sy, my dreams. Do you think it's—" I stopped abruptly, realizing I was about to sour the moment. I didn't want to talk about Jared, but the dreams were increasing in frequency, in vividness. I recalled something my friend Becca said months ago—that events happening on the Periphery could bleed through, affect our dreams, our mental state *here*, if things were bad enough *there*. Was it possible? No, Jared was alive, locked up, not a jumper himself, and without his hired jumpers available. There was no way…

"Talk to me, Charlotte."

"Has Joel heard anything else about the case, or trial date? Is Jared staying in jail or…" I trailed off.

Simon's hand stilled, and he rested his palm on my back. "It's going to trial, last I heard."

"So, we'll be called as witnesses?"

"Probably. But these cases can take years before…"

"Do you think Mitch can get him out? I mean, he was able to fake his death and assign him his brother's identity, so…"

Sy shifted, and I sat to face him. He rubbed a hand over his face. "My brothers and I have been keeping a close eye on the general and Jared. Mitch is in Virginia, still doing damage control. His hands are tied. He's under intense scrutiny and without the money and power of Quantym. Trust me, any move he makes, Uncle is watching. And, as for Jared, he's locked up in the maximum-security brig in Virginia."

"What if we told them everything? Can't DNA prove he's Jared, and—"

"Them." He let out a gruff laugh. "Who? Someone higher-up in the military that the general hasn't bought— if there is anyone? Do you really want to open that can? Think about how many people were involved in covering this up. The ID's, the records, the burial. This spans military branches, civilian branches, states. I don't want all eyes on *us*."

I nodded. "You're right." A random thought struck, and I wondered about my friend Becca again. "How is Becca Diogo?" She was my lifeline when I was alone with Mitch and Jared in Virginia.

"Haven't heard from her since we left. I'm sure she'd love to hear from you. Call her."

I grabbed the two pills from the nightstand and washed them down with a swig of water, then pulled my cell into my lap. "Maybe I'll send her a text. Do you think she'd come up to see us?"

"Maybe. But she's probably reassigned duties, maybe even deployed." He shrugged. "Only one way to find out."

I sent her a text:

—*Hi, Becca. Thinking of you. Would love to talk when you have time.*—

Immediately, my phone began chiming with a face call.

"I'll go make coffee." Sy headed downstairs.

I hit the answer button and grinned when Becca's smiling face greeted me.

"Charly! How ya healing?"

"All better. How about you?" I pushed a stray lock of hair from my face.

She leaned closer to the cam and squinted. "I'm good! Is that…? Aw, yeah, it is! Let's see the ink!"

I laughed and lifted my hand so it was back in view of the camera. "Sy got another one, too."

"Nice." She lifted her arm, examining her tribal tattoo. "I'm due for more soon."

"So, you're still in Virginia?"

She nodded. "I'm getting transferred to Fort Dix in a month."

"No more Quantym?"

She shook her head. "Like it never existed at all."

I shifted and crossed my legs underneath me. "Yeah, about that. You mentioned something about the bleed-through effect, and I know this is going to sound weird, but—"

She leaned in and lowered her voice. "He's still locked up, if that's what you're going to ask. And his father hasn't left base. He's been tied up with lots of meetings with attorneys."

"So, there's no way anything *intentional* could be impacting me now?"

She sighed. "Who knows what's going on over there. I mean, you and Sy jumped, and if you did anything that might've changed things over there…"

My stomach twisted. "Oh. Right."

"But I don't think Jared or Mitch have the capability of jumping or sending jumpers now."

"Okay. Just wanted to ask."

"Nightmares?"

"How'd you know?"

She smiled. "Charly, you've been through hell and back. I'm sure you're grappling with everything. I'm honestly in awe of you."

"Thanks Becca. I don't have a choice, you know? I'm just taking things day by day. But sometimes, I just feel like…never mind."

"Hey, you can't start and not finish. I walk with you in the dark and the light, remember? What do you feel like?"

I rose from the bed and shut the bedroom door before whispering, "Like he's somehow watching me. Waiting, planning something. These aren't normal dreams, or nightmares. They're vivid, sometimes even bleeding into my daydreams, my quiet waking moments."

She frowned. "Okay, now you've got my attention. What does Sy think?"

"That I need therapy. I went, but it didn't help. I can't even talk to anyone about this except for you, Sy, and his brothers. Sometimes I feel like the whole thing was a dream."

She leaned back in her seat and rubbed the back of her neck. "Okay, listen. I wasn't going to tell you, but I'm sure Sy will find out at some point. Promise not to freak out, though."

I inhaled sharply. "What is it?" I brought the cell closer to my face to watch Becca as she nervously shifted in her seat.

"With the program shut down, and a lot of soldiers being transferred, they don't have as many staff, and—"

"Becca…" I pressed as she rambled.

"They're transferring Jared to the prison on base in Newport, Rhode Island. Now, before you freak—"

"They're WHAT?"

"Listen, hang on, it's not what you think. With things being reorganized here, it's nothing too suspicious. I know it feels like it, but believe me, it's not. Even the general is staying here."

"No, no. Something's up." I shook my head.

She leaned in. "Look, I dug around when I heard, but I got nothing. If I find out anything shady, you'll be the first I let know."

"Okay, okay, yeah, thanks." I tapped my finger on my thigh, counting the taps, trying to regulate my breathing and heart rate.

"Charly, you're going to be okay. And if you need me, I'm here. Even if you just need to talk about everything that happened."

"Thanks again, Becca. I gotta go."

"Don't be a stranger. Take care, now."

I smiled before the call disconnected and the screen went black.

Well, shit.

****

We idled at the red light, and I stared out the window, watching a few flame-colored leaves twirl to the ground, landing on the ground twenty-three and twenty-four seconds after they'd popped off the branch. Sy and I were headed to Jeff's for dinner, a gathering for the family before Jay's upcoming deployment. Sy had just told me about Jared's upcoming transfer—Joel briefed him this morning.

I hadn't told him what Becca confessed to me a few days ago. I wanted to see if he'd tell me when he learned about it, too. And now that he did, I felt like crap for keeping it from him. I felt like I never made the right choice when it came to anything involving Jared. I was irretrievably messed up. Maybe I'd never be okay, and I'd self-sabotage everything good that came my way.

I finally spoke and broke the silence that'd settled over us after his announcement. "Do you know when?"

"A week, maybe two." Sy stared straight ahead.

Did he know that I already knew? Was I acting suspicious?

I nodded. "And you guys don't find it…suspect?"

"We've dug and dug, but we got nothing. Not an ounce of evidence that this was his—or Mitch's—doing."

I nodded again.

"I debated whether or not to tell you," he confessed.

At least that made me feel a little better. Though I'd kept it from him, he considered keeping it a secret, too.

I reached for his hand. "I'm glad you told me."

He interlaced our fingers. "I know you like living on the water, and Florida has a lot of waterfront properties we could look at. Plus, your parents would be ecstatic."

I shook my head. "I'm not letting you leave your job, your brothers, or your home, because of *him*."

"I'm not offering for him, I'm offering for you."

I squeezed his hand. "I'm fine," I lied. "He's locked in a cage, and I have you to distract me." I rested my head on his shoulder.

He kissed my hair. "You'll always have me to distract you. But there's something else to consider."

"Hmm?" I hummed, closing my eyes and breathing in the heady scent uniquely Sy.

"Work. You're going to be on the same base. Do you think that might be—"

"Triggering? No. I worked there for years after I

thought he was dead, I lived in the house we were married in while I grieved," I scoffed. "He's not going to be going out for recess."

"Okay. Let's take it day by day, if anything changes, come to me. We'll talk. Don't feel like you need to hide anything from me."

I cringed internally. Crap, he most definitely knew Becca told me.

"I will. I'm working on being more open, but old habits and all. You can call me out on it, you know," I offered.

"I trust you, but you try to take everything on yourself. I want to be there for you."

I shrugged. "Yeah, like I said, old habits and all. I don't want to burden anyone."

He looked at me with raised eyebrows.

I sank back into my seat.

"You'll never, ever be a burden, Charlotte. Even when we're old and gray and barely able to recall how to tie our shoes. I'll be grateful every single day we get to be together."

"Well, you're a little older than me, so I'll be obliged to tie your shoes for you," I teased. I stared out the window again, glimpsing the sights of fall in Newport passing by, as a bit of melancholy settled over me. "The night we went out with Angela and Rex, you said something about feeling like you didn't deserve me. Truth is, I rarely feel I deserve *you*. Thanks for always being the calm to my storm."

He smiled. "Always, love. Storms are beautiful and powerful."

"When they're not destroying everything." The words tumbled from my mouth before I could stop them.

"Sorry. I'm just in a mood, I guess. Who's going to be at Jeff's tonight?" I changed the subject.

"Just the family."

As we pulled into Jeff's driveway, I looked over at Sy and gave a wide smile, sliding my proverbial mask into place. I was okay, I was going to show everyone— no matter how shattered or scared I felt inside. *I was okay.*

****

I woke from a sound sleep when a large hand grasped my arm tightly. Pulling against the painful grip, I cried out as my grogginess faded and awareness descended. Panic swelled, constricting my chest and causing my heart to pound. I fought against the unrelenting hold, the blankets and sheets tangling at my feet as I flailed my arms and kicked my legs.

"Charlotte, no! Charlotte!" Sy's deep voice was filled with dread.

I stopped my kicking to see him thrashing beside me, holding onto my arm with all his strength. "Sy! Wake up!" I wailed.

"I will kill you!" he growled.

His words sent a cold shiver down my spine as I fought against him.

Prying each of his fingers from around my arm, I wrestled myself away from him, then stood and counted and paced, shouting his name over and over. Rushing to his side of the bed, I grabbed his shoulders, screaming, begging him to wake up. Sweat drenched his shirt, just as I felt beads of sweat bloom across my hairline.

He bolted upright, his face shrouded in shadows and darkness. His pupils were blown wide and filled with lethality. He grasped both of my biceps, our faces inches apart.

"Please, no, Sy!" I wailed, anticipating he was about to bring us to a place of no return.

He gasped, his rounded eyes filling with awareness as the dream bled away. "Oh, no, no, no! Charlotte, did I hurt you?" He huffed and panted.

I pulled away. "No."

He dropped his face into his hands. "I'm so sorry. Oh my God, I'm so sorry."

I inched closer and rested a hand on his shoulder. "It's okay."

"No, it's not."

"It's him," I said matter-of-factly. "The bleed-through effect."

"No! No, I have PTSD too." His shoulders slumped.

"Stop denying it," I bit out.

"I'm not denying anything! I had a nightmare."

"And *I'm* having nightmares because they're doing something. I know it!"

He looked up at me, his blue eyes drowning in sorrow. He gently pulled me onto the bed and held me, rubbing my sore arm. "They're not, Charlotte."

"You're in denial." I sniffed, the tears bringing me fleeting relief. I'd known for weeks something was wrong, and it felt good to say it out loud. Even if Sy didn't—or refused to—believe me.

"You've been having nightmares for a month. I've had *one*. One. Given what we've been through, especially what you endured, this isn't that abnormal."

"But knowing what we know…" My words hung in the air.

He nodded. "We'll keep looking, okay? I promise, tomorrow I'll get together with my brothers and we'll look again. We can only look around *here*. There's no way to know what's happening on the Periphery." He used a finger to lift my chin.

I held his gaze, my heart swelling with admiration. I nodded. "I know, thank you."

He leaned down and pressed his lips to mine.

I straddled him and took his face in my hands, then covered his mouth with mine, and his lips parted immediately, his tongue diving into my mouth with electricity and fire and need.

Mere minutes later, our clothes were gone, our bodies glowing under the pale moonlight. Nightmares couldn't haunt us if we didn't sleep.

Sy grasped my hips, leaning back onto the bed and pulling me down with him.

I braced my hands on his hard chest, sinking down on him with a shudder.

He sucked in a breath, a growl escaping his lips as I leaned my head back, my long hair tickling my waist as I moved my hips. The nightmares were long forgotten while we reveled in the magic and pleasure of *here and now*. Of us.

Breathless and sated, we lay on the bed holding each other under the light of the full moon spilling through the window.

The water in the bay reflected rippling ivory moonlight.

"Did you know, lying in moonlight—moon bathing—is known to be a healing practice in some cultures?"

I smiled. "I believe it." I traced the outline of one of his tattoos.

"Yeah, it's an ancient Ayurvedic practice thought to

promote calmness and increase fertility."

"Well, then, I'd consider what we just did very high-risk behavior if you don't want kids." I breathed out a laugh.

"I wouldn't mind." He trailed a finger across my flat stomach.

The conversation wasn't scaring me the way I thought it would. We hadn't discussed kids yet. "Someday," I agreed. I was on birth control, and didn't plan on changing that anytime soon.

He nodded.

"I lost one," I whispered, somewhat hoping he wouldn't hear.

He stilled and rested his hand gently on my stomach. "What?"

"In the accident. I didn't even know I was—" I shook my head. "It was super early, but still."

He sucked in a breath. "I'm sorry. I didn't know."

"One day." I nodded again. A heavy weight lifted from my chest, a secret grief I'd carried alone for so many years, released.

"Someday, Charlotte, you'll get the chance. And whatever little soul—or *souls*—choose you, they're getting blessed with the best mother ever. You're so nurturing"—he swirled a finger over my belly—"caring"—he kissed along my shoulder—"giving"—he kissed just under my ear. "I wouldn't want anyone else carrying my child."

I closed my eyes and tried to picture my stomach rounded with Sy's baby. Between his blue eyes and my green ones, I envisioned a baby with light eyes and chubby cheeks. Boy or girl didn't matter. But not now, not yet. "She'd be beautiful," I mused.

He nudged me. "So long as she takes after you."

I jabbed him. "As if you're not aware that you are absolutely devastating yourself."

He grinned. "Me? Nah."

I grabbed a pillow and popped him with it. "Liar."

He barked out a laugh when I attacked him with the pillow again, then climbed on top of me and pinned my wrists to the bed. "Such a wild one, you are." He leaned down and kissed me.

I wrapped my legs around him, admiring the hard planes of his muscled body emphasized in the moonlight.

He dropped his head and trailed kisses along my neck. "I love you, Charlotte." He released my wrists and stared at me.

I reached up and touched the scar through his eyebrow. "I love you, too."

"Me and all my broken parts?" He quirked a brow, referencing his scars.

I ran my hand down his back and over the long, jagged scar from the terrorist attack. "Those are my favorite parts." The moonlight highlighted the irregular skin across his back, the marred scar as beautiful as the man before me.

Sy abruptly turned and rummaged through the nightstand drawer.

His body moving away from mine allowed cold air to bite at my exposed skin.

The drawer shut with a click and he rejoined me, wrapping his warmth around me once again.

"What were you looking for?"

"Well, I was going to do this differently. But, this moment *here and now* is just right." The moonlight sparkled in his eyes.

I furrowed my brow. "For?"

He trailed his hand across my jaw, tucking my hair behind my ear.

He held my face, and I nearly drowned in his deep blue eyes.

"Marry me, Charlotte."

I took in a sharp breath, my heart floating and fluttering and tumbling in my chest. Every part of me clung tighter to him, from my legs to my arms. My chest didn't feel big enough to contain the happiness swelling within it.

He pried my clinging hand away from his body, and slipped the cold ring onto my finger.

Tears bloomed and blurred my vision. I finally pulled away from him to sit upright and hold my hand up. The diamond glinted and sparkled in the moonlight. The band of white-gold held a black diamond on either side of the huge round diamond in the middle.

"For better"—he trailed a finger over the white diamond—"or worse." He trailed a finger over the black diamonds. "Even death won't keep us apart."

I held my hand directly in a stream of moonlight. I looked over at him, and he was studying my face.

Worry flickered through his eyes when my awed silence hung in the space between us.

"Yes—oh my God—yes," I whispered, falling into his arms and kissing him once again.

Chapter 8, Reality 2: On the Periphery

Charlotte

I reapplied my red lipstick and slipped into my red-soled black stilettos. I'd come home for lunch and researched Seth MacDowell, the Marine scheduled to jump at 1500 today. At just twenty years old, he lost his leg—and nearly his life—fighting for our country. There was no way I was going to allow my husband to exploit his ability to jump, especially for a client who was pulling a tantrum and looking to buy a new life since hers was now riddled with the consequences of her own actions. *Poor thing.*

Having a plan comforted me, and as I slid into my car and backed down the driveway, anticipation pooled in my stomach. Later tonight, I'd ask for a separation. I'd go stay with my parents for a month in Florida while I did some soul-searching. I wouldn't subject myself to Jared's mood swings and lies for a moment longer. After telling him *no*, I'd come home, call my parents, and book the flight.

I pulled into my reserved parking spot at the hospital and took a few steadying breaths. A huge fight awaited me, just behind the double doors that housed Quantym below the hospital before me. I sucked in a deep breath and rested my head against the seat. Deep exhaustion washed over me—fatigue that wouldn't be relieved by sleep, a tiredness that leached beyond my bones and infected my very soul. I pulled myself out of the car and headed inside, coaching myself along the way. *This will be your last time inside this godforsaken place. You can do this one last time...*

The elevator doors rolled open, and my heels clicked on the bright-white tile as I made my way to room 298. Just before entering, I caught sight of Mitch seated in the adjacent observation room, prepared to watch with some of his troops from behind the mirrored window.

Great. An audience for when Jared and I go blow-for-blow.

Bad enough I knew the whole thing was being recorded. I pretended not to see Mitch and his men and went straight into the room where Jared was already waiting.

I ignored my husband as I flitted into the room and headed straight to Seth, who was lying on the bed.

He already had his arms—and one leg—restrained. His other leg was unrestrained, amputated at mid-thigh, and his metal prosthetic leg was in place. The cloth restraints were typical protocol, preventing excessive movement during the initiated cardiac arrest and the thrashing that usually accompanied resuscitation.

I slid my hand into his, and he smiled up at me. "Have they given you something to relax you yet?"

"Gustav was in earlier, gave him the pill," Jared answered from behind me.

I ignored him, and squeezed Seth's hand.

"What he said." Seth smiled, but twitched with nerves.

"Are you scared?"

He nodded. "I've done it before. I can handle it. But

you're not gonna find a warm-blooded man alive who's telling the truth if he says he's not afraid of dying."

I nodded sympathetically.

"Why did you sign up for this?"

Jared cleared his throat behind me—a warning.

Seth's smile widened. "I want a better one of these." He glanced down at his prosthesis. "Have you seen how realistic the robotic neuroprosthetics are?"

I nodded. "The technology is amazing"—I frowned—"and expensive." My heart felt heavy in my chest. The neuroprosthetics were an incredible feat of medicine, connecting to nerves and allowing brain-controlled movement of the fake limb.

"After this mission, I'll be able to afford one," he said quietly, as if he was revealing a secret to me in that moment.

My resolve dampened. Was I going to take that away from him? By refusing to allow this jump?

"Seth, I have to remove your prosthesis."

He nodded. "That one is basic but expensive, too. Don't want you to fry it when you shock me. And I don't want anyone to steal it either," he teased, shooting a narrow-eyed glance at Jared.

I gave him a pointed look. "I'll keep an eye on it." I removed the prosthesis and wrapped linen around it. I walked over to the closet and placed it within.

"Glad you're keeping it warm, wouldn't want it to catch a chill," Seth quipped.

I threw my head back and laughed. He was a good kid. Funny, too.

Jared crossed his arms with a deep sigh.

"I know you've done this before, Seth, but I'm going to walk you through the steps, okay?" I gave him the usual spiel about what to expect during the process. While I spoke—the words so deeply ingrained in my memory I barely had to think about them as they fell from my mouth—I considered how I could get the money to this man for his neuroprosthetic leg. I could sell my car, drain my personal savings, perhaps borrow some from—

"The last doctor wasn't as nice as you."

Seth's voice brought me back to the present as I tinkered with the settings on the ventilator. I unwrapped the tubing from the sterile packaging. "Well, that's a shame."

"Are the two of you done yet? We have three more jumps happening today, so I'd like to get on with it," Jared barked.

"Anesthesia isn't here yet." I didn't bother to turn and face him.

I'd let this kid be sedated before I told Jared I wasn't going to proceed with this. I couldn't bear to watch the disappointment on Seth's face if he knew I was backing out, refusing to allow him this mission. *Was I taking from him? What is the risk-benefit? If I allow Seth this mission, I allow that celebrity the knowledge of another life she can kill herself to get to.* A war raged inside of me, increasing my anger at Jared.

The door opened, and the anesthesiologist, Dr. Carter, entered. He adjusted the wires and tubes attached to Seth's body, and turned on the screens to display his monitored vital signs. "Ready?"

"Oorah," Seth responded.

Dr. Carter placed an oxygen mask over Seth's face and looked over at me.

I nodded at the awkward doctor. He'd always given

me the creeps, with beady eyes that lingered just a few nanoseconds too long on places they had no business being.

Today, he stared at me.

"Yes. Ready," I answered, guessing he was displeased with just my nod.

I was right, and he began pushing the sedative into Seth's IV line.

Normally, a good anesthetist would tell you to count backward, or even sing to you as you went under. Not Dr. Carter. An uncomfortable silence descended, save for the low beep and thrum of the monitors.

I leaned down to Seth as his eyelids drooped, and I smiled. "You hold the key to getting anything you've ever wanted. You're a good kid, Seth. Good things come to good people."

"You showw shweet," he slurred, his voice muffled under the oxygen mask. His eyes rolled as his consciousness drifted.

I ran my fingers along the side of his face. I'd imagine it was how a mother would feel, watching her child fall peacefully asleep after a long day. I was happy he'd escape for a while, resting his mind, body, and soul, and retreating away from the harsh reality of this world.

Jared reached out and pulled my hand away from Seth. "Are you *trying* to provoke me?" he seethed.

My gaze snapped to his and my mouth dropped open.

Dr. Carter didn't hide his wide smile when he stared at my wrist entrapped in Jared's grasp. In fact, he looked excited. Like he was the type of jerk that dreamt of locking people in his basement, sedating them, and waking them to…

I pulled my hand away and stepped back. "You're mad that I'm comforti—"

"You don't have to touch him. And where's your lab coat?" Jared dragged his eyes down my body, his gaze lingering on my fitted black pants.

"Are you serious right now?"

I turned to Dr. Carter. "You can leave now."

Jared nodded. "Dismissed, Doctor Carter. Doctor *Cardoza* can intubate him." He stepped between us and glared at the doctor, staking his claim on me. He obviously noticed the creeper's stare, too.

"Yes, sir." Dr. Carter left the room and the door closed with an irritating clunk.

A quiet click indicated the auto-lock fastened.

I looked down at Seth, sleeping peacefully under the magic of medicine, then back up at Jared. "I'm not doing it."

"Yeah, you are. And what the hell was all this 'good things come to good people'?" he scorned.

"If you were a doctor, you'd understand the importance of the mental state when undergoing anesthesia. But you're not, so I don't expect you to get it."

His eyes widened and he stepped closer to me. "Who the hell do you think you are?" His jaw pulsed, the veins in his neck straining as he struggled to keep his composure.

I backed up an inch, trying to free myself from his overwhelming presence.

He stepped farther into me. "And who do you think you're talking to?" He kept his voice worryingly quiet.

I sidestepped away from him and over to the laptop. I opened the computer and began to log in. "I'm talking to my husband. Your rank means nothing to me." I lifted my chin. I wasn't one of his troops or subordinates, and it was time I reminded him of that.

He slammed the laptop closed, and I quickly pulled my hands away to avoid having them crushed within it.

He threw a file on top. "The client's file is here, as you requested."

I nearly laughed, but instead I bit back a smile. So damn obvious.

He wouldn't let me look up the case, but was going to hand me a paper file of lies. He hadn't allowed me to access the electronic chart.

Because I didn't want to give Gustav away, I refused to tell him what I knew about the spoiled celebrity client and his and Mitch's disgusting lies.

"Computers down?" I raised a brow, my voice dripping with sarcasm.

"Get over there and do this. I won't say it again."

I sighed, so tired of his empty threats. I got right in his face, something I'd never, ever done before. "Say it again, and again, and again! But I'm not doing it!"

My nails bit into my palms, nearly drawing blood from the clench of my fists. Everyone had limits, and he'd broken through every single one of mine.

In an instant, my back was flying into the wall, knocking the breath out of me. He wrapped his hand tightly around my throat as I clawed and scratched and kicked.

Screaming was impossible without air in my lungs, so I gripped onto his hand, prying his fingers desperately from my throat. Every last bit of resolve, bravery, and pride I'd carried into the room with me bled away when he tilted his head to the side, staring at me as I fought hopelessly against his grasp.

There were a lot of outcomes I'd anticipated today, but this most certainly was not one of them. He'd never put his hands on me before, and now an invisible line had been crossed. A line I didn't know existed, until this very moment. My vision smattered with black dots, and my kicking weakened as my oxygen levels dropped. *So that's what happens when I finally say no.*

I die.

The door opened, and the sound broke Jared from his trance. He abruptly released me.

I crumpled to the floor, my bones painfully connecting with the tile. I panted, sucking in breath after precious breath, while bracing myself with sweaty palms flat on the tile. I pulled myself up on shaking legs, then— in another turn of events I'd never seen coming for as long as I lived—I dashed toward Mitch. I slammed into him and grasped the sleeves of his uniform desperately as pleas spilled from my lips.

"Help me. He's not okay. Please, Mitch, *please!* He's been having these headaches, and his eyes—there's something wrong!" I panted, my words tumbling and overflowing as I shot a glance at Jared.

His hands were fisted by his side, and something raged behind his eyes—those cold eyes—that always accompanied his migraines.

Mitch pulled me against him and rubbed my back. "It's okay, Charly. You're okay," he crooned.

A sob broke free, and my shoulders shook under the force of my unrestrained sobs.

Jared took a step closer, his nostrils flaring.

I pushed into Mitch, guiding him toward the closed door. "Help me, please, get me out of here. You saw, right? Oh God, if you hadn't come in, he'd have…"

Mitch patted my back. It was a strange, fatherly gesture, coming from him. I knew he hated me, but surely he didn't want me dead.

Did he?

"Just calm down Charly, he isn't going to hurt you. I won't let him hurt you."

My gaze snapped to Jared's direction when he stepped even closer, his jaw pulsing. He stared at his father's hand on my back with disdain.

"Please, just get me out of here." I released my grip on Mitch's sleeves, a bit abashed. "Please…" My begging reduced to a whisper.

But something was wrong. Mitch held Jared's gaze and resisted when I pushed into him, attempting to guide us toward the door. A warning bell niggled at the back of my mind, seconds ticking by without movement or reaction. "Please, Mitch," I squeaked, realization dawning as my fate sealed nearly audibly.

Another two pats on my back. Not fatherly—condescending. Then, he grasped a handful of my hair, securing my strands tightly around his wrist with a quick twist.

I shrieked, and both my hands shot up to grip his wrist, trying to relieve the painful tension of his hold. Hopelessness settled, bitter and heavy in my chest.

"*He* won't hurt you, but *I* will," Mitch growled, then spun me to face Jared. He kicked the back of my knee, causing me to fall to my knees on the tile.

Pinpricks of pain flared across my scalp as he pulled my hair tighter, forcing me to look up at Jared.

"Now, say you're sorry for disrespecting your husband, and let's get on with this fucking jump."

Jared stared at me expectantly.

Apologize? No way. I pressed my mouth into a tight line, my bravery betrayed by the tears burning my eyes.

Jared ran a thumb down my cheek, catching a tear. "Well?"

When the silence stretched on for a second too long, Mitch pulled back on my hair, clawing a cry from my throat.

"S—sorry," I spat, contempt coloring my voice.

I'd sob later, but right now, I held on to any last scrap of dignity I could muster. I pressed my lips together, breathing heavily through the pain of Mitch's grip. My hands remained holding onto Mitch's wrist so my hair wouldn't be ripped from my head.

I held Jared's ruthless glare.

He smiled. "Good girl."

Mitch pulled me to my feet by my hair. He released me, pushing me directly into Jared's arms.

Jared walked me over to an unconscious Seth.

I didn't need to look when I felt the cold metal bite into my back. At gunpoint, a fleeting thought crossed my mind. What would Seth think of what was happening? He was an honorable man; he'd have helped me. The thought was vaporized by Jared's voice.

"Intubate him," he demanded.

I snapped on the blue nitrile gloves and began to work mechanically. I'd done this protocol so many times, I didn't need to think about each individual step as my trembling hands worked. I did stumble twice—my legs weak with trepidation.

Within thirty minutes, Seth wasn't just sedated—he was intubated, medically paralyzed, his body temperature reduced to therapeutic hypothermia—an uncomfortable but brain-preserving 90 degrees Fahrenheit.

"Wait. This is it, right? Get all three cameras on her." Jared spoke, likely to whoever sat behind the camera controls in another room.

If the military police were watching the cameras and didn't help me, I was truly out of hope. Jared and Mitch would get away with anything on this base—I was just a pawn in their world.

I pulled a small device out of my pocket that could count picoseconds.

Mitch held a long paper with my equation printed across it.

"Reality four," Mitch barked.

I pushed a bolus of the heart-stopping medication into Seth's IV line, anticipation building as asystole—a flat line—began to float across the monitor. My meter tracked the time that Seth's heart had been stopped in picoseconds, and I plugged the numbers into my equation. I spoke aloud, unable to stop as each number snapped into place, guiding me to the next step. I pretended Jared and Mitch weren't in the room—it was just me and Dr. Gustav—and I was training him, as I did in the early days after I'd cracked the equation.

I reached for the defibrillation paddles, adjusting the dial to deliver the correct joules. I rested my meter on Seth's bed. I stared down at the numbers, my knuckles paper-white as they gripped the paddles and pressed them into position on his chest. My voice was unrecognizable as I completed impossible mathematical figures in my head and spoke them aloud.

Finally, his flat-line converted into a fatal, but shockable rhythm—ventricular fibrillation.

I stood staring at the monitor, sweat causing my hair to stick to the back of my neck. The room fell silent, and my mind raced, waiting for the right moment when all the calculations aligned to send Seth's consciousness to reality four.

Now.

"Clear!"

Seth's body bowed off the bed under the shock of the defibrillator.

Right on target, the heart monitor showed his heart resuming a severely bradycardic—but life-sustaining—rhythm. He was being kept barely alive here, and his consciousness now resided in reality four to recon the intel he'd been trained to retrieve.

I removed the paddles from his chest, dropping my hands to my sides. My shoulders slumped, a tight coil winding deep in my stomach filled with... Dread. Regret. Sorrow. Despondence.

I looked down at the paddles in my hands, catching a glimpse of Jared at my side. His gun was tucked back into the holster at his leg. I released my grip, dropping the paddles. They clacked together as they bounced and swayed, tethered to the main device by a coiled cord.

He touched my back, and I flinched away instinctively.

I stared down at Seth, trying to swallow the sand in my throat.

Now what?

"You did so, so good." He crowded into me, bringing his lips to my ear. "When he wakes up, he's going to tell us where he was. Your protocol was streamed to the other three jumps happening just now..."

My stomach bottomed out. I wasn't sure if I was a

good person before today, but now I was most certainly going to hell. Probably already in it.

"…and they're all going to wake up in a day or two, and tell us where they've been. You better have sent him where we asked."

His threat rose the hairs on my neck, and I stiffened. I hated him. Mitch. Myself. Every fucking thing in this room, except poor Seth. I stayed silent, staring at the unconscious Marine.

"Gustav gave us the map of the Peripheries. We know how to distinguish which reality—"

"He's in reality four," I said through gritted teeth.

I spun to exit the room, and Mitch stood in front of the door. I stopped and lifted my chin to him. "Can I go home now?"

Mitch stared at his son, a smirk pulling at his lips.

A voice pealed over the radio. "We've got it, sir. Over." The transmission ended with crackly static.

"Roger that."

Mitch stepped aside, and the soft click indicated Jared unlocked the door from his phone.

Just as I went to step over the threshold, Jared grasped my elbow. "I know you're mad, but we'll talk, Charly. I'll be home in an hour."

"I have nothing to say to you." I blinked rapidly, internally threatening myself with harm if I let another tear fall in front of him.

He stepped closer. "If you're not home in an hour, you—and anyone you've ever loved—will be in grave danger."

My eyes widened. His depravity really knew no bounds.

He rubbed a thumb across my top lip with his free

hand. Then, despite my resistance, he slid his hand to the back of my neck, and pressed his lips against mine.

I winced when he sucked my bottom lip between his teeth, and slid his tongue across my lower lip.

He pulled away with a soft chuckle. "I told you I didn't like that lipstick."

I swung my free hand at his face.

Without breaking my glare, he caught my wrist.

"Fuck you," I rasped.

I pulled my elbow from his grip, and he released my wrist. I stormed out of the room.

My heels clicked down the tiled hall, my stride as fast as my legs allowed without tumbling me to the ground. I rubbed an arm across my mouth, removing the taste of him that lingered on my lips. I sucked in breath after breath after breath, and every beat of my heart ached with a devastating mix of anger and betrayal.

Just as I reached the elevator, I unclipped my badge and slammed it against the reader. The button illuminated, and just before the doors shut, I spun to see Jared watching me from down the hall, his glare filled with warning. His image was squeezed out of sight by the closing elevator doors.

I finally slumped against the back wall of the elevator, my knees unable to support my weight. Two loud sobs broke free, and I dropped my head into my hands. I composed myself and looked up at the blinking green light on the camera. Was Jared watching me right now? Just in case, I flipped the bird.

The bell chimed and elevator doors rolled open. I swiped under my eyes, straightened my back, and strode out of the facility with my head held high, ignoring the pleasantries from my former colleagues. The faster I walked, the faster I could escape Quantym, Jared, and Mitch. I was so close to my car, the first bite of freedom nipping at my neck in the form of a cold breeze. I just wanted to make it to my car without falling to the ground in front of everyone in a fit of hysterics. I was close. *So close*.

I pulled my keys from my bag, hit the fob, and went to pull the driver's door open, but a sudden presence appeared by my side. I gasped and leaned against the car for support. "Simon," I breathed, quickly running a hand over my hair and swiping at my eyes again.

"Charlotte."

"I'm sure by now Diogo told you I've resigned."

He stepped closer, his face dipping and his breath warming my ear. "Do you remember the day of the fire?"

My breath caught in my throat, and I stuttered. "I—yes. You—you saved me."

And I kissed you.

"That's not what I'm talking about." His voice was just above a whisper. "You told me something, do you remember what you said?"

I shook my head. A lie, another black tic above my head in the scheme of all the wrong things I've done in my life.

He stepped even closer, and I looked around in a panic. If Jared saw this, I didn't want to even guess the ramifications. He couldn't handle me comforting a restrained Seth, about to die, with him in the room.

"You told me I needed to help you remember. That he was going to…kill you."

And that I love you.

I froze. I should move, enter the car, go home, never look back. Comply. So the people I love don't die. *Why did I say Jared was going to kill me? Jared had never hurt me before today. My memory of the day of the fire was muddy, piecemeal—clouded by the...smoke inhalation?*

"Then," he continued, "you go and avoid me. Poof. Vanish. Cancel our meetings, refuse to take my calls, or answer my messages."

I swallowed hard and stared at my driver's seat, wanting two things simultaneously. To fall into Simon, and beg him to hide me forever. But at the same time, I wanted to push him away, escape him, and save him from the chaos—the dark cloud—that is my life.

"Do you remember, Charlotte?"

I nodded, just a slight dip of my head. I still hadn't looked at him.

"So, you need to tell me why you'd say such things—" His nose nearly grazed my temple. "—and then disappear? The only explanation is you can't escape him. Or you don't remember. So I'm here to remind you."

I closed my eyes as the warmth of his closeness gave me goose bumps along my neck. "I remember," I whispered.

A cold gust put my hair in flight, revealing my neck.

Simon sucked in a sharp breath, and his body tensed. "He's dead." He turned and stalked toward the building.

I jerked the collar of my blouse up, a feeble attempt to cover the marks I knew must be blossoming around my neck. "Shh, please! Simon, please," I begged, rushing in front of him and resting my hand on his rock-hard chest. I immediately pulled my hand back when a hot jolt lurched through my body. *How could I want to touch someone so badly after the last torturous hour of my life?*

He stilled immediately at the desperation in my voice, and his ocean-colored eyes locked on mine. A lethal glint shone in his eyes, and his jaw pulsed with thready restraint.

"I can't talk more than thirty minutes. Meet me at our spot. Where the sky—"

"—meets the trees," he finished, then nodded. He glanced at my neck again before turning and heading toward his car.

Something about the stiffness in his movements told me he was a hairbreadth away from going into the building and dragging Jared out. Dead or alive was anyone's guess.

I pulled my door open and dropped into the seat. I'd planned on sobbing the whole way home, but now, knowing I was going to have thirty minutes alone with Simon, I felt something I'd thought was lost to me forever.

Hope.

Chapter 9, Reality 1

Charlotte

"You what?" Jess squealed into the phone.

I pulled the cell away a few inches, attempting to prevent a ruptured eardrum.

"Yup." I leaned my hip against the kitchen counter and stared down at the ring on my left hand with a smile.

"Come over, please? Steve's at training, and I want to see the ring!"

"Okay, give me a half hour. Want me to bring coffee?" I pushed off the counter and pulled my car keys out of my bag.

"Girl, do you have to ask? Of course I want one."

We exchanged goodbyes and hung up, then I headed into the living room.

"I heard her scream from here. How's your ear?" Sy asked from the couch, where he was looking over paperwork.

"Throbbing. I told her I'd go over for a bit." I glanced down at the papers in his hand.

"Discharge paperwork." He held up the forms.

I nodded. His contract with Quantym—and the U.S. Government—were completed, the forms proof he satisfied his contractual obligations.

"Do you ever think about re-enlisting?"

"Funny you should ask. My commanding officer

nearly begged me when I went to pick these up— " He shook his head. "—but I'm all set."

I smiled at him, toying with the ring on my finger. I looked down, and the heavy diamond caused the ring to sag toward my knuckle. Damn gravity.

"Do you need it sized? Jeff told me how to measure your finger. I used a string, so not as accurate—"

"A string?"

He laughed. "Yeah, sounds creepy, but while you slept, I wrapped a string around your finger, and then there's this chart—"

"Oh my, that does sound creepy!" I cracked up again. The look of wide-eyed innocence on his face was killing me. "Maybe I should get it sized down just a half size or so. I can't tell if it's the heavy diamond or…"

Sy grasped my hand and gently pulled on the ring. It slipped off easily.

"No, you're right, it should get sized down."

I shrugged. "Well, not today. If I don't go show Jess, she'll kill me. I'll drop it by the jeweler's next week."

He nodded, and his phone rang—the caller ID showing Jeff's number.

"I'll be back in a few hours." I leaned down and gave him a peck.

Just as I was leaving, I heard him greet his brother on the phone.

****

I drove into Newport.

The flaming leaves on the trees were thinning, indicating winters impending freeze would blanket the area soon. The bay was void of the usual boats, and the tourist shops were darkened with signs announcing they were closed for the season.

I parked my car a block away from the lone coffee shop still open. I enjoyed the walk. Something about Newport at this time of year was magical, reserved only for those of us who lived in the area.

The crowded sidewalks and shops of summer gave way to a peaceful, almost gothic beauty in the fall and winter. The empty roads and walks were cobblestone, and the mansions that lined the water revealed their stunning age and beauty with the life of the vibrant green grass and ivy drained away. All the hustle and bustle of the tourist season masked the silent beauty—the subtleties that were more evident when appreciated in solitude.

The bell of the coffee shop tinkled when I entered, and a lone barista took my order.

I wandered over to the pastry display to ogle the decadent intricately frosted desserts within. I added a box of treats to my order and took the long way back to my car.

I pulled into Jess's driveway and gathered the tray of coffees and box of desserts and slung my bag over my shoulder. I exited the car and made my way to her front door. My cell vibrated over and over in my bag, impossible to reach given my full hands. I knocked with my foot, anticipating she'd have answered the door before I could knock like she usually does.

No answer.

My phone vibrated again with another call that went unanswered.

I balanced the tray of coffees in one hand and put the box of desserts under my arm. I rang her camera bell with my elbow. The coffees nearly launched from the tray, and I squealed, catching them before disaster could strike. I stuck my tongue out at her camera, knowing she'd tease me by sending me the video later.

Finally, the door opened, but she didn't greet me. A flash of ginger hair, and she spun and scurried back over to the TV.

"Gee, thanks," I said to the camera, before using my elbow to push my way inside. "You must be enraptured with something good. What, are they re-filming the—"

My stomach bottomed out faster than my words. There, on the TV, was General Mitchell Cardoza, giving his first formal press release.

My heart thrummed in my chest, causing heat to spread across my body as if I'd ingested molten lava.

Jess turned to me, and her brow furrowed. "Why didn't you tell me?"

My mind flooded, a gush of memories of what'd *really* happened and what the media revealed warred within me. I had to keep my story straight.

What did *he* reveal? There'd been a steady trickle of information released by the government, police, and Army since the incident in Virginia, but nothing about the assailant's relationship to the general. Or me. Yet.

"Tell you what?" My voice was hoarse. I nearly crushed the box of pastries with my grasp, and the tray of coffees trembled. My bag slumped from my shoulder and caught on my elbow.

"So, let me just make sure I have this right. You were stabbed by *Jared's brother* while you were in Virginia? Holy crap, Charlotte, there's a lot to unpack here." Her voice was quiet, confused. She turned back to the TV with her mouth hanging open. "I didn't know he had a brother," she muttered.

I stared at her radiant skin, then at her baby bump

causing her shirt to tighten around her middle. I rested the box and coffees on the side table, and dropped my bag to the floor.

Mitch's voice flooded my ears, the room around us, my very soul...

Sixteen, seventeen, eighteen...I tapped my finger on my thigh, praying to the universe the counting would ward off what felt like a heart attack coming on.

Gen. Mitchell Cardoza: *"At this point in time we're still investigating. But I have full confidence the results of the investigation will exonerate my son. His willingness to enroll in a program—offered to soldiers with PTSD—was honorable. He wanted to help others, but instead he was exploited and manipulated, and the unethical and unproven practices by the physicians and facility managers will be revealed in time."*

Reporter: *"General, did Adam Cardoza say anything to you before the incident? Were there any signs he was going to do what he did?"*

Gen. Mitchell Cardoza: *"After a particularly invasive treatment, I did mention to his team he seemed out of it. In addition, there is no evidence to tie him to any of the deaths, as the footage from inside the facility has been mishandled and subsequently lost."*

Reporter: *"There are injured victims that identified him as the assailant. Does he deny those allegations?"*

Gen. Mitchell Cardoza: *"Due to the impending trial, I am not at liberty to answer that question. What I can tell you is, instead of utilizing proven medications or therapy, the VA physicians used a protocol that hasn't been FDA cleared or approved for the treatment of PTSD, and the side effects of the experimental treatments can cause homicidal and suicidal ideation, a risk that was never disclosed to him."*

Reporter: *"If the results of the investigation reveal inappropriate treatment, will you consider suing the VA?"*

Gen. Mitchell Cardoza: *"Absolutely. Until then, I encourage anyone who had involvement in this specialized program to come forward. My contact information will be listed on-screen and on the news outlets website. There is power in numbers, and our soldiers deserve justice for the maltreatment provided by the program housed within the VA hospital."*

Reporter: *"Will Adam be allowed to serve if he is exonerated?"*

Gen. Mitchell Cardoza: *"After the appropriate medical evaluations are performed and reveal he is a victim, not a villain, I'm confident he will be able to continue to serve our country."*

"Charlotte." Jess walked over to me with her eyes still glued to the TV.

My mouth hung open, I tried to speak, but only a strangled sound came out.

Ping. My phone chimed with a text.

She rested a hand on my shoulder. "Say something," she whispered.

Ping. My cell dinged again. *Ping. Ping. Ping.* Three more texts in quick succession.

I wobbled on my feet.

"Oh no, no, no. C'mon. Over here. It's okay." Jess guided me to the sofa.

I dropped onto the couch, my mouth still open, lost for words. My hand came up to my throat.

She rushed over to the side table and stabbed a straw into my iced coffee, then scurried back over to me.

I took the drink and slurped three long swigs, the coldness a balm to my burning insides. "I didn't tell you because it's…" I shook my head.

"Unbelievable? Insane? Only something that could possibly happen to you?"

"I know." I nodded. "Unreal, right?"

"Charlotte, I mean…I'm sorry but I have to ask. Why did you go to Virginia? *Really?*" She leaned into me with her eyebrows raised.

I'd done a lot of stupid things, said even more. But this one was about to take the cake. "I was *talking* to him." The lie was bitter on my tongue.

I wanted to tell her the truth—*Jared killed his brother Adam and later assumed his identity*—but I couldn't, not without risking my life, her life, Sy's life. The government doesn't take kindly to classified intelligence breaches from a clandestine organization they funded.

She gasped and caught herself with a hand on the sofa. "Wait, what? Like, having an affair?"

I shrugged. "Not *physical.*" I rolled my eyes. "Emotional. I didn't know Jared had a brother, Jess. We connected online a while back, before I met Sy, and my curiosity got the better of me. They look so much alike…" More acrid lies bled from my mouth.

"I mean, yeah, wow, they look *so* much alike." She nodded. "Except for the scar, and his eyes are a little different, too. I think."

We both looked up at the TV, where his mug shot had been displayed intermittently throughout the segment. Other photos of him in an orange jumpsuit, being escorted in jail, displayed just before the commercial break.

I put the straw to my lips again, pulling two more cooling gulps down my throat. My eyes were wide, burning with dryness since I'd somehow forgotten how to blink. "It was his half-brother." I blurted, desperate to sprinkle *some* truth in my torrent of lies.

Ping. Ping. My cell continued to blow up with a barrage of texts.

"Guess that's why we didn't know about him. Plus, he's obviously not from around here. Wonder who his mother is." She shrugged, and her mood lightened by what she perceived as my honesty. "Sy was there, and he saved you…" Her words came out as a question.

"Sy had a hunch something was off." I shrugged. "He's got good intuition."

"I had a bad feeling when you called me that day, too. When you told me you were flying out to see your parents—your voice. You almost sounded…scared. And you were so vague." She tapped her finger on her chin.

"Yeah, Sy flew down because he felt the same. And he was right."

Her hand darted out and grasped mine as she gasped. "Oh my goodness!"

I smiled as she examined the ring.

"He saved you *and* put a ring on it. You could write a book!" Her brow pinched. "Was he mad? Jealous?"

I shook my head. "No. It wasn't like that. I told you, it wasn't physical, it was more curiosity than anything."

"What happened that day?"

I drew in my breath. "He—*Adam*—was jealous. Of Sy. There was a struggle. I tried to stop him from shooting Sy…" My voice trailed off as my mind drowned in half-truths and bloody memories.

She tilted her head. "You saved Sy, then."

"I guess we saved each other." I blew out a breath. "Listen, Jess. The media, it's like the rumor mill. Worse than the mean girls in high school. No matter what they say, come to me first, okay?"

She shifted in her seat and massaged the back of her neck. "What might they say?"

"That Adam and I were engaged, maybe?"

"Charlotte!"

"*Not* true. But he was telling his troops and his father that we were, well, *more* than what we were…"

She cackled. "Mitch must've loved that. He hated you with Jared, can you imagine…"

Coldness latched onto my spine and slithered along my arms. I managed to laugh with her, though my heart and soul felt stained from all the lies I'd just told my best friend. "Yeah, he wasn't too pleased to see me."

"So why'd you and Sy come up with the whole job-interview thing, then?"

I shrugged. "Embarrassment, on my part."

"When the media finds out you were stabbed, and you're his sister-in-law…"

"I know," I groaned. "Stop making it worse."

"Sorry! It's just so—"

"Daytime TV? Talk-show worthy?"

"Yeah." She squared her shoulders, a plan brewing in the lines of her face. "We got this, girl. You've suffered worse. We'll tackle the rumors and the reporters one-by-one if we have to." Her eyes blazed with determination.

"I just want to hide," I wailed.

"Nope. No running. We face this head-on."

"How?"

She tipped her head toward my phone, alight with

dozens of texts. "Starting now."

I sank deeper into the sofa, then groaned and draped an arm over my eyes.

"Everyone is gonna wanna know what the *hell* you were doing in Virginia with your brother-in-law." She toyed with the locket around her neck. "We have a few hours, and I'll help you. Open those texts, and we'll go through them one-by-one. And please, Charlotte, don't use the word *affair*." She rolled her eyes.

"You used it—not me!" I twisted my mouth and chewed on my inner cheek. "But when I tell people I went to meet my brother-in-law who just so happens to look like my late husband, and he stabbed me and shot my fiancé, there are going to be assumptions."

She giggled. "Let 'em talk, baby. Your *fiancé*!" She brought both fists under her chin and squealed at my use of the word.

****

After two hours of Jess helping me navigate my concise responses to the calls and texts that'd blown up my phone, our bellies sloshed with too much iced coffee and an obscene number of pastries. After what felt like millions of questions, my answers left my family and friends in want of more. I'd given the shortest, cleanest version of my lie. It'd have to do for now.

So far, the most immediate ramifications were my parents choosing to fly in this weekend for their visit. Impeccable timing, considering my mother was dissatisfied with the few details I'd revealed over the phone. I was in for it this weekend for sure.

I gathered my bag and headed for the door. "Thanks, Jess. If Steve asks, just give him the short version, okay?"

She nodded. "Trust me, I know how the gossip flies, especially in the military circles. Bare minimum." She put two fingers above her eye, giving me the scouts' honor salute.

I reached down and rested a hand on her belly. "And take care of this precious girl. No more pastries for you, little one."

Jess groaned. "I couldn't fit another in if I tried."

"One last thing—" I turned to face her from the porch. "—did the general mention a transfer earlier in the press release?"

She shook her head and her eyes bulged. "No. Why, is he getting transferred here?"

I shrugged. "Rumors, ya know?"

"Steve does duty at the prison, he'll know before anyone. I'll let you know as soon as I know."

I nodded, having hoped for that answer since Steve was an MP. "Yeah, thanks."

****

When I got home, Sy was waiting for me in the kitchen. After dropping my bag and keys on the counter, I looked up and stared at the glass of whiskey in his hand.

He rarely drank.

"Want one?" He swirled the glass.

I reached out and took his glass, downing it in one gulp, then handed it back. It wasn't going to play nice with the coffee and pastries in my belly. "No, thanks," I grumbled and shuffled to the couch.

Sy followed close behind me.

I belly-flopped onto the couch, allowing my face to smoosh into the cushions.

Sy sat beside me, and he placed a hand on my back. "I tried calling you before you got there."

"I know." My voice was muffled with my face planted into the couch cushions. "I knew this was coming at some point."

He rubbed my back. "So, you wanna talk about it?"

Sy didn't know what to make of my display.

I rolled over to face him, blowing a strand of hair from my face.

He smiled. "Hi."

"Hi." I smiled back.

We went over my version of what I'd told Jess.

It wasn't funny by any means—but the whole situation was outrageous. In a fit of—insanity? stress? disbelief?—we both cracked up laughing. The harder he laughed, the harder I did, too. I rarely saw him lose his composure, and it was exhilarating. I held on to his leg, nearly falling from the couch as we gasped in belly-aching laughter.

When we finally calmed, we stared at each other. Words were useless when our lives were beyond anything anyone would easily believe.

"God, I'm so happy I have you."

I sat up and faced him. "I was just thinking the same thing."

"So about what you told Jess…" He rubbed a hand over his hair.

"I know." I groaned. "I'll have my own reality-TV show in no time. Ugh, my co-workers, my parents. I just didn't know how else to tell her what'd happened. Once she saw the general referencing his son, and she knew I was a victim of the assailant…"

"I kept trying to call you. That's why Jeff called this morning."

I shrugged. "First, I left my phone in the car when I

got the coffee, then you must've been calling again when my hands were full. It's like the universe was *trying* to catch me off guard."

"You did good. The media attention will die down as soon as the next big story breaks."

"Well, I feel like a famous floozy now." A touch of sadness leaked into my voice.

"No. You're my wife-to-be." He rested his forehead on mine.

My eyes widened when an idea struck. "Have you thought about the wedding?"

He backed up an inch. "Well, yeah. Kind of. I mean—is this a trick question?"

"No. No wedding. This weekend. Let's do it, just you and me and…"

"And…?" A smile stretched across his face.

I wilted. "My parents. They're flying in this weekend, staying at the inn."

"That's good—right?"

I nodded. "Yeah. My mother kept texting when she heard. I know she wants more details than I'm willing to give."

"So, you want to marry me this weekend to distract them?"

"I want to marry you for so many reasons, and that is just a very small one of them." I smiled sheepishly. "Either way, crowds, remember? I'd much prefer an intimate affair."

He leaned back against the couch cushions and pulled me into him. "Well, then, it's my lucky day, because the sooner you have my last name, the better."

"Oh my gosh, I didn't even think of that!"

His brow pinched.

"Well, for the media. It's better I'm not a Cardoza for..." I trailed off.

"Ah."

I climbed on top of him and ran my fingers through his hair. "Make no mistake, Sy, above all, I can't wait to be your wife because I love you."

****

"There's my Charly girl!" My father hugged me tightly, and I squeezed him back. His glasses were crooked, and his hair in its usual organized disarray.

He released me, and I turned to my mom, embracing her and reveling in her strong perfume and signature rose-pink lipstick. The scent and sight of my parents brought me back to a safe place in my life—my childhood.

We dropped my parents at the inn. Their flight had arrived late, and I scheduled an early breakfast date with my mother in the morning. My father was going to be taking Sy to the country club to play golf, and I was almost regretful I'd be missing the chance to see his huge tattooed form playing the sport—it was certainly going to be a sight to see.

"Did you tell them yet?" Sy asked as he drove us home.

"No. I can't believe they didn't notice the ring." I held up my hand and giggled. "I mean, you weren't messing around."

He smiled.

"So, are you going to put on some white slacks for tomorrow? Should we stop and buy you one of those hats?"

He cracked up laughing. "No, I'm good."

"I feel like you may...stand out amongst the folk at

119

the country club."

He shrugged. "I'm a trained soldier, young lady. And I'll have you know, I'm a pro at blending in."

I stared at him, mouth agape. His muscled arms and body were impossible to hide behind any amount of clothes. His tattoos—an entire sleeve that stretched from his arm to his neck and to his back and chest—made him appear anything but discreet.

"Ah, yes. Discretion is your look." I nodded and bit back my smile. He was a devastatingly beautiful man. There was nowhere he could go where he'd be unnoticed.

"You look like you may want to join us."

"No way! Golfing with a bunch of pretentious dudes in a country club in Newport is my idea of hell."

He pulled into our driveway and put the car in park. "Throwing me to the wolves?"

"I never said you should go. That was all you." I gave him a pointed look.

"Well, I have to tell your father about the ring. Ask his permission."

"Kind as that may be, you're a little late asking him." I flashed the ring again and smiled.

"Easier to ask forgiveness than permission." He winked and shrugged.

****

My mother sat across from me, her light hair impeccably coiffed. Her painted nails matched her lipstick, and her aqua earrings matched her shirt. For a second, I wondered what it'd be like to be as put together as she always seemed to be.

I looked down at my sweatshirt and leggings.

Maybe I should've dressed up for the occasion.

After the waitress took our orders, I fiddled with the straw in my iced coffee. I knew what was coming.

My mother leaned closer to me across the table while fanning her napkin across her lap. "We need to talk about Virginia."

I stared at my drink and swirled the ice with the straw. "Ask away."

"Well, Charly, for starters, *what the hell*?"

I'd never liked the nickname Charly. My dad would call me Charly as a kid because he thought me a tomboy. I'd hike through the woods all day and come home with muddy legs and a backpack full of books and moss and cool rocks. The name didn't bother me until I was a teen, but luckily to all my friends I was still Charlotte. Until I met Jared and he learned of my disdain for the nickname. Then he never called me Charlotte again. Funny how I only made that connection now.

I shrugged. "I don't know, Mom. I was curious. We talked online. I never knew he had a brother, and I just was looking for a connection, I guess."

"And Simon was okay with that?"

I glared at her. "He understood my logic. I was just looking—"

"Jared's mother lives right in Cedarwood Bay Home, Charly. If you were looking for a connection, or whatever it was you needed, why not visit her?"

I was shocked by her statement for two reasons. One, Jared's mother was mentally ill and lived in an institution. And two, I'd not expected Mom to remember. I'd only met the woman a handful of times, and she was pretty far gone on those occasions. Jared and Mitch liked to pretend she didn't exist.

I shrugged again. "I don't know, Mom."

She quirked a brow. "It's because of the resemblance, right?

I took in a shuddering breath and nodded. "That made it worse."

She lifted her chin. "Look, I get why you did it. I'm not saying it's right, and you nearly got killed, but I get it." She pressed her lips together, and the parentheses between her brows deepened.

I twirled the wrapper from my straw between my fingers, unsure of what to say. A thought crossed my mind, bringing me an unfair amount of distress—Jared was implanted in my life so deeply. Too deeply. He seemed to be all I dreamt of, and now, spoke of. If there were a surgery to have him cut off me like the soul-sucking leech he was, I'd do it in a heartbeat.

"Do you have any more questions?" I twisted the wrapper on my left pointer finger, hoping she'd notice the ring and change the subject.

She clasped her hands together and rested her chin on them. She studied my face. "Did you sleep with him, Charly?"

"What? No, Mom!" I whispered harshly.

"What? You're an adult now, we can talk like—"

"No." I shook my head. "I didn't sleep with him."

"So, he shot Simon, and you hadn't even slept with him?"

"Mom, no! A lot of people got hurt that day."

"But not all by him. I bet there was something going on. Something big. Mitchell and Jared were so dedicated, and remember all those classified deployments to Virginia?" She stopped, and then sucked in a breath, her eyes lighting up with some kind of revelation.

No. No. No. Stop.

122

I nodded. "I remember, but that was a long time ago. This has nothing to do with that."

"Do you think this could be a cover-up for something else? Like a *diversion?*"

"I don't know, Mom, the knife hurt pretty bad, so yeah, that was quite *diverting.*" I twisted the wrapper around my finger until it was nothing more than a few small shreds of paper.

She reached across the table and grasped my hand. "Oh, Charly, I know. How awful." She drew in a breath and continued, like she just couldn't help herself. "But why didn't Jared or Mitchell ever tell you about Adam? There're a lot—"

"Of unanswered questions? I know, hence my little trip that almost killed me and Sy." The anger leaked around my words.

My mother leaned back. "Of course, I'm sorry. But when you're ready, it's something to think on. Talk it out in therapy. Or with me." She smiled.

"It's okay. Stop watching so many of those crime shows." I laughed, washing away the tension.

I drummed my fingers on the tabletop.

She still didn't notice the ring.

The waitress came and put our plates in front of us. My mouth watered when the smell of the eggs, pancakes, and maple syrup hit my nose.

"Can I get another, please?" I held up my glass with a smile.

"Well, look at that. That's gorgeous." The waitress took my hand in hers and examined the ring. "Someone loves you."

"The feeling is mutual." I smiled and slid my gaze to my mother.

My mother stared at my hand, her mouth hanging open.

"Well, darlin', when you find a man like that, you never let him go." Our server smiled and headed back to the kitchen to get my refill.

"Charlotte!"

I shrank back into my seat under her judgmental stare.

She stared at me for what felt like an eternity. "Well, let me see the damn thing."

I leaned forward, putting my left hand in hers.

"When?" Her voice was hesitant, cautious.

"You're here this weekend. We got the license when we found out you guys were coming to visit. We want to do it before you leave."

"So soon?"

I wish she'd expressed this kind of trepidation when Jared and I decided to get married when I was just twenty-one. Granted, we'd been together since I was eighteen, but still. I was young. Too young then.

"We're not kids. We live together. This is what we both want."

She tilted her head. "Why the rush?"

Heat rushed to my cheeks at her implication, and I pulled my hand from hers. *Geez, when would I stop feeling like a child around my parents?* "I don't know, Mom. Maybe almost dying again? Life is short."

"Well, I can't argue with that." She cut into her pancakes.

The waitress returned with my refilled iced coffee.

My mother waved the fork in her hand and shook her head. "No, no. This calls for mimosas." She raised her eyebrows at me, waiting for my refusal.

She thinks I'm pregnant.

The waitress smiled. "It sure does. I'll be right back with two mimosas."

I took a swig of my iced coffee, attempting to read the expression plastered across my mother's face.

"I like Simon. A lot. More than Jared even. Maybe," she said finally.

Her words injected cooling relief into my veins. "Really? I mean, he *is* amazing."

She shrugged. "This weekend, it is."

"I'm glad you like him. It means a lot."

She looked up and put her knife and fork down. "So, is Simon telling your father right now?"

I nodded. "Yep."

A laugh broke free from her perfectly painted lips. "Brave man." She picked up her cutlery again, then paused thoughtfully. "We both like him, Charly. We're just protective of *you*."

I looked down at my ring, spinning it on my finger with my thumb. "Well, then, I'm a lucky girl. Because that makes three of you."

She smiled, and the waitress returned with our mimosas.

My mother raised a glass, and I clinked mine with hers.

"To new beginnings."

"New beginnings," I repeated, taking a large swig to emphasize the fact that I was *not* pregnant.

A huge smile broke across my face, the happiness threatening to burst from my chest. Finally, *finally*, I was in control of my destiny. And Sy was everything I'd ever wanted.

Chapter 10, Reality 2: On the Periphery

Jared

I glared at Charly as she strode down the hall, her image disappearing behind the closing elevator doors. I spun around and headed back into the room with the unconscious one-legged Marine, then opened the laptop to document the events prior to, during, and after the procedure.

While the computer fired up, I opened my cell and accessed the cameras. I viewed Charly in the elevator, and just as her image appeared, she pegged a finger at the camera like she knew I'd be watching. A laugh broke free, and I bit on a knuckle to suppress the urge to laugh even more. She'd get over it.

At the sound of my father entering the room, I immediately homed my cell, her image disappearing behind a black screen.

"Something funny?"

I glanced at him and back down at the computer, all traces of humor wiped clean from my face. Logging into Seth MacDowell's chart, I documented the day's events, listing him as being conscious in reality four, reconning life intel for the spoiled blondie client. A shitty actress, with a shitty attitude, caught cheating on her shitty boyfriend. It was the most ridiculous mission I'd sent anyone on yet—save for the trip we sent a jumper on to reality three to assess life *there* for her, but Blondie wasn't happy with that option—she was a nobody in reality three. If she wanted to kill herself and buy a pretty new life, who were we to stop her? As long as she paid, we'd do the job.

I stopped typing when I felt the heaviness of my father's glare.

"I want you in the MTF before you return to reality one today," he demanded.

I raised my eyebrows. *The medic*? "Why?"

"Because of your little show today. It's something we've been seeing when we train someone to jump. If they jump too quickly, successively, we're noticing some…side effects."

"Side effects? I feel fine. The headaches are nothing."

He stepped closer. "Not just the headaches."

I stepped back from the computer with a sigh. "What, then?" My impatience grew, and with him in the room I couldn't check the app to ensure Charly was heading home like I'd asked. Didn't want to hear it from him.

"You almost killed her before the most important task of her otherwise useless life."

I stepped closer to him and held his scrutinizing glare.

"I didn't almost kill her," I scoffed. "And don't forget, she's also my *wife*." I wouldn't have *really* hurt her. I was just angry, and didn't want to set a precedent. She'd been testing some boundaries lately. She wouldn't be trying that again. Ensuring she and no one else in this facility stepped out of line was my *job*.

"Inhibition control," he said.

"What?"

"The side effect. Too many jumps in quick succession appears to be affecting inhibition control. Doesn't mean we stop, it means we pull back. Slow down."

"No. I'm building memories, soon I won't even need briefing. I'll be living two lives and remembering both. This was the whole *point*."

"We can still do it. Slower." My father was only slightly taller than me, and he attempted to make his presence imposing with the closeness of his stance.

I matched his gaze.

"Fine. You want me to go to the medic? I'll go. But when my tests are fine, we continue, same pace." I snapped the laptop shut.

He nodded once and turned to leave. "It's not going to break *my* heart if you kill her." He paused, and turned back to me. "But at least wait until we ensure the other doctors can do it without streaming her protocol." He raised his eyebrows at me, then left the room.

He was testing my patience, too. I steadied myself with a breath, refusing to validate his concern.

I strode out of the room, stopping in to check on the other three unconscious jumpers and documenting in their charts, too. I spoke with Doctor Carter, Doctor Gustav, and two other physicians who'd successfully completed the protocol with Charly's method streamed to them in real time.

I opened my cell and accessed the tracking app. Son of a—she wasn't home. She'd gone to…*the coffee shop*? I rolled my eyes. Of course she did, she clearly wasn't as upset as she'd pretended to be. Not if she was making a pit stop for coffee. She wouldn't leave base, my men would make sure of that.

Morgan caught up with me in the hall and clapped a hand on my shoulder. "I hear it worked." He grinned.

"We'll know in a few days." I slipped my phone back into my pocket and stared straight ahead.

I liked Morgan, and he was a good soldier. Loyal, smart, discreet.

"The MPs said she didn't want to do it," he whispered.

I stopped and turned to face him.

He shrugged and ran a hand over his shaved head. "She did it, though. It's all that matters." He corrected his tone.

Smart man.

I pulled out my phone and checked the app again. She was still at the coffee shop, and that didn't feel right.

"Morgan?" I didn't look up from my phone.

"Yeah, LT?"

"Since you and the MPs are so concerned about her, why don't you take one of them with you and see what she's up to?" I turned my phone to face him.

His eyes went to the GPS tracker showing her location.

He looked up at me. "You serious?"

"Do I look like I'm joking?" I kept my tone even and suppressed the irritation that clawed at my insides at his incredulous look.

"You're going back now? To reality one?"

I kicked the back of his knee.

He stumbled before quickly straightening.

"What's the matter, you gonna miss this side of me?" I smirked

He bumped his shoulder into mine. "I can barely

even tell when it's you from there, or you from here."

I turned and continued walking, and he fell into step beside me.

"I'm consistent, if nothing else."

He nodded. "We'll keep an eye on her. No one will let her leave base."

"Good job, Morgan. I know I can count on you."

"When's the promotion?"

I'd be ranking up from LT—lieutenant—to captain in just a few weeks, and my father hadn't made it easy. I had to work for it, just like everyone else. It was a long time coming, and I'd be glad to finally obtain the rank.

"Few weeks."

"Good, good. Hey, I'll call you in a few and let you know what she's up to. She still at the coffee house?"

I looked down at my phone and nodded.

I turned left toward the clinic, while Morgan headed right and back to the wing to grab an MP to go check up on Charly with.

A small part of me hoped she wouldn't still be there when they went looking, that she'd be home. The other part of me? A twisted part of me hoped, no, *wished* she'd try me again. I wouldn't mind seeing that fear in her eyes when I had her alone. It was intoxicating, and I had to stop myself from thinking of all the ways I could punish her that would bring us far more pleasure than pain. With a sex life like ours, it was hard to stay mad at her for too long.

I saw the way that jumper, Seth, stared at her, and I couldn't blame him. It was impossible *not* to notice her beauty, and it was a rare thing when coupled with unusual intelligence like hers. Especially when she did stupid things like wearing lipstick or not wearing that oversized lab coat over her fitted clothes. Even dumber still was her choice to flirt with him in front of me, intentionally provoking my anger today. I'd burn those tight black pants when I got home, I decided. My patience had already been tried enough for one day.

I strode into the clinic and was brought into an exam room immediately. The small white-walled room was just as bland as the rest of the facility. A few glass jars of cotton swabs and tongue depressors were lined up across the counter, and a sign about PTSD was posted on the back of the door.

A see-through plastic replica of a head was on another counter, and I picked it up to examine it. The fake sinuses, eyeballs, and brain were visible through the clear plastic. I popped the top of the plastic skull off and poked the fake brain. It was realistically squishy.

That's why bullets always tear through the head like butter.

The door opened and I quickly put the replica head back on the counter. The eyeballs popped out and bounced across the floor.

I went to get them, but the medic stopped me. "I got it. Everyone seems to love these model heads." He chased the eyeballs across the room. "You're the third guy to do that this week." He chuckled and popped the eye back in place. After he got the second eye in, half the brain fell out onto the counter. It wobbled like Jello.

I handed him back the clear plastic skullcap in my hand.

He flushed, laughed, and put it on the counter, alongside the half-brained head.

"The general had some concerns about symptoms you've been experiencing. Thinks it may be related to successive jumps."

"I'm fine."

"Well, we just have to document we performed a quick neuropsych exam. Shouldn't take more than thirty minutes."

I nodded, cringing at the psych part of the word. Always made me think of my mother.

The exam was fairly quick, and I aced it. The only time I may have had a few points taken off was when the medic spoke of Charly. Mentioning her was of no significance in the scheme of things, it was personal, and quite frankly, had no business being part of the exam that was assessing my ability to continue jumping.

The medic, Rogers, handed me a printed form.

"I'll talk to the general. Your physical exam is completely normal, and most of the neuropsych, too."

"Most?"

"Some of your vitals gave you away at the mention of your wife. But nothing to indicate a contraindication to jumping. If you're having marital problems, we can certainly refer you to a counselor."

"There are no problems," I bit out.

He looked at me, then sighed. "Okay. I'm going to need to reassess weekly."

"Weekly?" My blood pressure rose, and I could feel the arteries in my neck pulsing.

"Yes. It's protocol now. Rapidly successive jumps can be detrimental to inhibition control, so we'll keep a close eye on it. I'm sure you'll be fine."

I nodded and slid off the exam table.

"Good to see you, sir." He held out his hand.

I stared at his hand, then met his gaze. I turned and left the room.

I'd be discussing weekly exams with my father. I didn't have time for this nonsense. I stuffed the forms into my back pocket and opened my phone as I strode out of the clinic.

Charly wasn't showing up on the GPS at all. I closed the app and saw two missed calls from Morgan.

I hit the button and he answered on the first ring.

"LT," he answered, breathless. "Don't worry, we found her."

"Found her?"

"I have Jackson reconning now, do you want us to bring her in?"

"What the hell is going on? Where is she?"

"She's on base, behind the coffee shop. The woods there has a dead zone. That's why she disappeared from the app. I ran back to call you; she doesn't know we found her." He was still breathless. "You want us to bring her in?"

I opened my car door and slid inside, then slammed the door and rolled my neck, relief surging as the bones cracked.

"What is she doing in the woods?" I knew the exact place he spoke of. Charly had mentioned going there before. The woods behind the coffee shop was an old training ground, but with its odd ability to inhibit radio and cell transmissions, it'd been allowed to grow over, no longer used. The perimeter was secured with fencing and barb wires. She wouldn't escape.

"She's talking with—"

I could hear Jackson say something in the background.

"Recon! Now!" Morgan yelled at him.

"With?" I grasped the steering wheel until my fist

burned, the slight discomfort bringing some relief from the fire licking at my insides.

"Simon Donovan."

I closed my eyes. I'd be returning to reality one any minute now, and I'd be left to make this decision with my alternate consciousness if I waited much longer.

"Recon only, find out what they're talking about. I'll be back in the morning. Do not let her off base."

I could only hope I was making the right choice. *She's convincing him to sign on at Quantym, just as I'd ordered*, I reassured myself. Just as Morgan responded, my mind drifted, like I was almost ready to pass out.

"You got it, LT. Recon."

"And he doesn't touch her," I growled.

"Yes, sir, no touching…"

His voice was muddled, as if I was listening underwater.

****

"Rise and shine," my father crooned, louder than necessary.

The room was crowded, between him and the two doctors standing beside my bed. Medical equipment filled every available space left in the room. I squinted when the overhead light infiltrated my eyes. I was back in jail, in the seg room, and nearly puked when the doctor pulled the vent tube from my throat, extubating me.

My chest was sore and tight as I huffed and heaved. The ICD had to be burning me from the inside out.

"Remember anything?" my father asked, boredom lacing his tone.

"Almost everything." I gasped, trying to adjust to my body's rapid rewarming.

He nodded. "Good." He turned and left the room,

squeezing through the maze of equipment in the confined space. He left me with the doctors while I fought to regain control over my own shivering body. Every inch of me ached, especially my chest.

The doctors didn't speak as they monitored my vitals, and for once, I felt starkly alone. Like I was still dancing on the knife's edge between life and death. I decided not to tell the doctors, since I didn't want to delay or slow down the succession of my jumps.

Instead, I pulled in a sharp breath and closed my eyes. *Pain is weakness. Feel nothing*, I commanded myself.

I recalled the events from reality two, and the bleed-through was about to beckon her to me the way a predator lures its prey.

And I'd be waiting, with sharp teeth hidden behind a tight smile.

I'd be waiting.

Chapter 11, Reality 2: On the Periphery

Charlotte

The car skidded to a halt as I parked at the Ground House and stuffed my cell into my back pocket. I slid off my heels, then grabbed my running shoes from the back seat and pulled them on.

I slammed the door shut and looked over each shoulder before jogging straight into the woods. A tiny makeshift path had been created from all the times our shoes pressed upon the earth here, deterring growing plants and brush away from where our feet trudged through. It was an old training ground, and a long while ago, we'd pulled a leftover footlocker beside the pond within to use as a bench. Gone were the days where we'd only meet at the hospital or in Quantym's conference rooms, though we continued to meet there, too.

Simon and I would sit and talk on that bench, sometimes for hours, one time until night fell and the stars twinkled above as we sat under the line of trees— where the sky met the trees—hence the nickname we'd coined for the spot. The meetings had always been with one motive—get him to sign on at Quantym for Jared, and for me, as his former surgeon, to assess his recovery. But he'd never signed and was now completely healed.

Over time, he'd become my true friend, my only friend. Our conversations veered away from his surgery and Quantym, and on to our hopes, dreams, and sometimes discussing theories of the universe or Simon teaching me about the constellations in the winter, spring, and summer sky. The changing backdrop of stars with the changing seasons were the only indicator we had of the amount of time we'd spent in that woods, and the stars above were the only witnesses to how much we'd talk under the cover of trees in an area so enchanting, it even drowned out any means of radio transmission or tracking.

It wasn't a secret Jared and his men tracked my movements even when we weren't fighting, or when I wasn't needed at Quantym. I never told him I knew, and I'd hoped all the tracking would reassure him of my loyalty, but over the years it seemed to do the opposite. The more trustworthy I'd proven to be, the tighter he squeezed, until it felt like he was choking the air from me. Today, that analogy became a literal reality.

Jared *demanded* I meet with Simon after learning he was a jumper, and I'd always regretted telling him Simon's words when he woke from surgery.

When Simon saw me for the first time here, in recovery, he told me he already knew me, he'd seen me "on the other side." He'd connected with me in reality three through his brief death, but he'd always refused to reveal the nature of our relationship *there*.

Jared didn't seem concerned, either. His only concern was getting Simon signed on as a jumper, and he insisted I help with that.

And while I should feel guilty about all the meetings with Simon, I justified it as complying with Jared's demands.

Get him to sign; don't give up, whatever it takes.

I pushed through the last of the ferns and my foot sank into the mud as I neared the pond. "Crap," I muttered.

Simon was already seated at the bench, wearing a brown military-issued tee and his camo trousers. He turned to face me when he heard my voice, then looked down at my shoe and suppressed a chuckle.

He came over to me and offered his hand.

I took it, and goosebumps rose along my arms.

His gaze dragged across my arm, and the corner of his lip curled as he tried not to smile.

"It's cold," I said quickly, shivering to emphasize the point. I grasped his hand tightly as I pulled my foot from the mud with a loud *thwap*. I tried stepping forward again, but my other foot sank.

"Ugh, these were my newest pair." I looked down at the other sneaker, now completely swallowed by the thick mud.

Without warning, Simon reached down and lifted me into his arms, effortlessly slinging my legs over his strong, tattooed forearms.

I gasped, then looped an arm around his neck to make the muddy trek easier. I toyed with the dog tags around his neck, ignoring the feel of my skin against his while I was in his arms.

He carried me through the rest of the mud, and gently placed me on the bench.

"Thank you." I looked around, avoiding his gaze until the blush that heated my cheeks could cool.

The pond was hugged by trees alight with fall colors. The setting sun cast a golden glow across us through the canopy of flaming leaves. Under different circumstances, I'd be basking in the beauty of it all, but the citrine glow was tainted by the darkness leaking from my soul. I wondered if Simon could sense it, that I was a pariah—a stain—on a place as beautiful as this, and in the presence of someone as genuinely *good* as him.

"Anytime."

He smiled, and it nearly undid me. I blinked away the tears that pricked at my eyes, and glanced down, noticing his boots were a muddy mess. "Hope you have another pair before duty tomorrow."

"I do." He kicked the footlocker, dislodging a few clumps of mud from his combat boots.

I glanced nervously at his watch. "I don't have much time."

He brushed my hair from my shoulder, and gently ran his fingers along a tender spot on my neck. "Tell me what happened."

I drew in a breath. *Right down to business. Okay.* "Long story short, I discovered something at Quantym. Something evil, unethical. I decided they shouldn't use it, but Jared doesn't tolerate the word *no*."

"I'm going to kill him, Charlotte," he said calmly.

"No, you'll get *yourself* killed. You do understand that he and his father own this base, and almost all of these troops?"

"Not everyone is as loyal as you think. There's a group of us who are tired of the corruption. Our group is getting bigger every day, and we're working on eliminating it."

I dropped my head. "I'm one of the bad guys, too."

He ran his fingers down my cheek. "No, you're not one of them. I see you."

I swallowed and blinked, trying to hide the shame. "You're wrong. I'm worse. If you knew what I did today—" A strangled sound escaped before I could slap a hand over my mouth.

"You were forced."

I shook my head. "I won't let you paint me as a victim. I worked on that equation, I studied it, trained Gustav, *wanted* to crack it." My shoulders slumped. "But when the exhilaration of cracking it settled, and I realized what they were using it for, I couldn't—" My throat constricted, cutting off my voice.

"The day of the fire, you said you remembered?" He dipped his head to meet my eyes.

I nodded. "Not everything, but enough."

"I think I know why your memory is so spotty." His deep voice was low, soothing.

"Why?" I looked up at him, hoping he'd have all the answers for me. Answers for questions beyond this very conversation.

"You jumped from the main reality. Had a near-death experience and went back." He slid a little closer and rested his hand next to mine on the bench.

I gasped.

"We're connected there, here, and on reality three, I saw it myself. That's what you were trying to tell me. You were warning me about the main reality."

I gaped at him. "How did you figure this out?"

"In the main reality, I signed on at Quantym. I'm a jumper. The last time I jumped, I started to retain, recall more of my other life and for longer periods. But I haven't jumped since the day I set the fire—"

"*You* set the fire?" I stared at him wide-eyed.

"I guess in every life, I'm hell-bent on taking out the corruption that is Quantym." He let out a humorless laugh.

The sound of a snapping twig made both our heads shoot up. I glanced around, and Simon stood to survey the area.

"Probably another bunny," I said quietly. They'd often hop through the woods, their speedy rush causing me to startle a few times before.

He sat beside me again.

"I can't believe it. A jumper, me?"

He nodded. "Yes, you. And me."

"I guess, now that you say it…" God, did it ever make sense. The idea that he and I were connected in three lives was astounding. But other than the main reality, where no one could travel to—not without melting their mind—and Gustav had successfully put a ban on that, Jared wouldn't know, couldn't know. Could he? If he was sending jumpers here, maybe. Or…

"Is Jared?" Panic colored my question.

"A jumper? No."

I wanted to ask *how* we were connected in the other realities, but the pieces all started to snap in place. "So, if I warned you that he was going to kill me, and I jumped, that means—"

"He already tried." His jaw pulsed, and he pulled his hand away, draping it over his knee. He leaned forward and hung his head.

I sucked in a breath. Before I went into Quantym today, I knew I had to escape him, but now, it wasn't something I could delay. "I have to leave." I glanced at his watch again.

"You can't go back there." He turned to face me.

"I don't plan on staying. I'll pack my stuff and take a flight out tonight. This morning, I'd already decided I was going to leave and stay with my parents in Florida."

I'd be able to think clearer once I was out of state, maybe even get a restraining order, before filing for divorce. I was powerless on this base.

He dipped his head. "He tracks you."

"I know," I said quietly. "I'll leave my phone at home."

"He recently started tracking me, too."

"I'm sorry." Heat rushed to my face. "Probably because he wants you to sign."

"Not your fault. Found it, and kept the tracker on. Then, got this." He held up a new phone.

"Huh. That was smart." My shoulders were still slumped, but now I had a plan. "Simon, thank you for listening and not judging. I hate to do this, but can I ask one last thing of you before I leave?"

He nodded, his ocean eyes hardening with determination.

"I swear I'll pay you back. Can you book the flight for me? If I use the cards, or my phone—"

"On it." He typed furiously into his phone, and within minutes, he got me a seat on the red-eye to Florida.

I didn't even want to know how much I owed him. Either way, I wasn't taking a dime from our accounts— Jared would know. I'd borrow it from my parents, pay him back, and get a job in a neurology clinic in Florida. Then, I'd be able to pay my parents back.

"I'm going to pay you back," I repeated.

"I'll see you in Florida in a few weeks. To check on you. And get my money." He winked. "I have plenty of leave time stocked up."

"Yeah, why don't you ever take your leaves?"

He shrugged. "Everything I wanted was here."

My heart pulled itself back together. Maybe this wasn't goodbye after all.

A cold breeze flew by, bringing up a slew of leaves. When it settled, more snapping branches and twigs. Definitely footsteps.

We looked around, and there was nothing—no one.

Unease prickled the back of my neck, and I shivered. I sat beside him on the bench one last time.

His hand slid closer, and he wrapped his pinky around mine. A small gesture, one that someone probably wouldn't even notice if they were watching us.

"I'll pick you up tonight, and take you to the airport. Have everything ready, and meet me at the corner of Rosewood and Holly Lane at 0200, sharp."

"Got it." Rosewood and Holly were only a few minutes from my house, and if I ran…

"You're going to be okay, Charlotte. Just don't be late. If I think he's stopped you, I'm going inside your house, and I'm shooting him."

My eyes slid shut. I could hear the truth in his voice. He was a sniper; two seconds was all it would take. I couldn't bear to be the reason for more evil, for more death, and I didn't want Jared *dead*. I just wanted to get away from him.

"I won't be late," I whispered.

Chapter 12, Reality 1

Charlotte

"You ready?" Sy smiled as he parked the car.

He looked amazing wearing a button-down shirt and black slacks.

"I'm excited," I said, smiling back.

I smoothed my long-sleeved ivory sweater dress. My mother would judge my choice of clothing, an outfit too casual for a wedding, but I was too excited to care about something so trivial. I'd worn my long espresso hair down, and even curled the ends. The only jewelry I wore was my engagement ring.

We'd ordered our wedding bands the day before, but they wouldn't be ready to pick up until next week. We'd both settled on bands with a deep-cut black infinity twist that wrapped around the ring, contrasting against the white gold, complementing the black diamonds in my engagement ring beautifully.

The excitement of marrying Sy today helped me shake off last night's nightmare easily, and given the nature of the dream, Sy didn't even know I'd had one, thankfully. I didn't thrash because I dreamt I was restrained to a bed in Quantym. I didn't cry out—frozen from fear—seeing Jared standing over me with defibrillation paddles in his hands. It'd been the oddest, most unsettling dream yet. I pushed the dream from my mind and focused on the day ahead.

The day ahead was a real-life dream come true. Nightmares be damned.

My parents' rental car was already parked. They waited for us at the front doors. My mother had a professional long-lensed camera slung around her neck. Both my parents were dressed to the nines. My mother must've gone shopping after breakfast the day I'd told her.

"Ah, I see you've arranged photography for the occasion," Sy teased, squeezing my hand as we walked toward the doors of the courthouse.

"I had no idea. But I'm glad she'll capture the moment." I looked up at him, my heart nearly bursting when he smirked and his blue eyes sparkled with excitement.

We'd decided to have a reception after the winter to celebrate with all our friends and family, when the warmth of spring returned. Today was the day we'd commit to each other in the eyes of the law, but we'd already committed to each other in our hearts and souls. I'd love him in more than just this life. I'd always love him no matter where we were in space and time.

I'd never been sold on the idea of a soulmate until I met him. Years ago, I'd have scoffed at the notion we were born as just a half a piece, and needed to find our other half to become whole. Now, no one could convince me otherwise. He was my destined other half, and I didn't have to question that I, too, completed him.

We entered the courthouse, signed some paperwork, and provided our ID's.

My mother grumbled something about how unromantic the affair was.

I looked up at Sy as he handed back the papers to the clerk.

He smiled at me, and grasped my hand.

We stood before the judge.

My mother's camera clicked furiously as Sy and I stared at each other, smiling like fools.

The judge nodded, adjusted his glasses, and began. "Do you, Simon, take Charlotte to be your lawfully wedded wife, to have and to hold, from this day forward?"

"I do." He gave a huge smile and pulled me closer.

"And do you, Charlotte, take Simon to be your lawful wedded husband, to have and to hold, from this day forward?"

"I do." My smile widened as I stared into Sy's deep-blue eyes.

The judge smiled at us. "By the power vested in me by the state of Rhode Island, I now pronounce you husband and wife. Simon, kiss your bride."

Simon pulled me close and pressed his lips to mine.

We kissed until my father cleared his throat, and I pulled back, breathless and high on the moment.

"I love you, Charlotte." Sy turned to my parents. "I'll always take care of her."

"We know you will." My father responded.

My mother dabbed at her eyes with a tissue.

"Now, let's go get something to eat." My father smiled and grasped my mother's hand.

****

My parents had made reservations for a fancy lunch at the country club, and Sy and I met them there immediately following the ceremony.

My father embarrassed me by telling Sy about days

I'd spent in the woods growing up, freaking my parents out when I'd go missing for hours on end while I explored the fairy-tale-like forest that surrounded my childhood home.

Sy was engrossed in the stories of my childhood, and I laughed along with them.

I'd already told him I was an odd kid—an outcast who preferred the forest and books over people.

Sy told my parents about his childhood, and about his aunt who raised him and his brother, Jay, alongside his cousins Jeff and Max, who'd become more brothers than cousins. Right up until the brothers had each enlisted in the military one by one. He told them of the treehouse they'd built, and how it'd become the boys' meeting place from childhood right through the teen years, creating the parallel that Sy and I were both odd forest dwellers.

I laughed, fondly remembering the treehouse he'd taken me to—our official first date, so many months ago. Long before I knew about the Periphery or our connection beyond this life.

"I hope to meet her soon," my mother said to Sy.

He leaned toward her. "I'm sure you'll both get on great. She wanted to come today, but Jay is getting deployed, and she wanted to see him off. I told her she'd get the chance to meet you at the reception."

Today was an informal affair, and we'd discouraged more than just the two needed witnesses from attending. After the winter, we'd have the celebration that allowed both families to celebrate and feel included equally. I hadn't even told my friends about today. Yet.

"You've seen *my* spot in the woods, so you'll have to take me to yours one day," Sy said, smirking at me from across the table.

I chewed on my lip. "We'll have to trespass to get there."

He shrugged. "Scared?"

I scoffed. "Absolutely not. I know those woods better than anyone. I'll take you someday. There's a creek, and back in the day, there was a huge moss-covered tree that'd fallen across it, making a bridge to the other side." My eyes glazed as I remembered my favorite childhood spot.

"Is that the tree you fell asleep on and we almost called the police to report you missing? Geesh, you were only thirteen. You could've drowned." My mother shook her head.

"I was fifteen. And, no, the tree I fell asleep in was *near* the creek. I climbed it and fell asleep in a divot where the branches cleaved, that looked like a papasan chair. It's where I'd read."

She tilted her head. "So you could've fallen and broken your neck instead of drowned?" She pointed her fork at me. "Oh, Charly, you were an unusual child." She shook her head and laughed.

I rolled my eyes. "I made it." I waved my hands across my body to remind her of my presence in the here and now.

We all laughed.

****

My parents left to return to Florida that night. We'd dropped them off at the airport and returned home.

In traditional fashion, Sy carried me over the threshold into the house.

When he put me down, I attacked him. I tore his shirt off his body—buttons flying and fabric tearing—and while it was mostly a joke, because he'd done it to me so many times before in the heat of the moment, the humor of the situation only heightened our desire. Between laughter and breathlessness, we devoured one another. Again and again.

Sy and I lay in bed, holding each other. After two rounds of worshipping each other's bodies thoroughly, and after the day's events, we were exhausted.

"My wife," he whispered into my ear as he caressed my back.

The small sliver of moonlight from the waning crescent left most of his face shrouded in darkness.

I found his lips anyway and kissed him.

The night was so dark the water on the bay was nearly invisible, making it feel like we were staring into outer space when we looked out the window. Just blackness and dim stars and a sliver of a moon sat beyond the bed we lay together in.

"My husband." I trailed my fingers along his chest.

Charlotte Donovan. I smiled at the thought. My co-workers were going to lose it when they found out. I'd go tomorrow to sign the forms to apply for a badge with my new name on it. Then I'd return to work on Monday as scheduled. I was glad at the thought of settling into a routine.

With Jay deployed, Sy was going back to work to cover for him at the construction business, too.

He kissed my forehead, and I drifted away, my mind lingering on the edge of wakefulness and slumber. His strong arms held me, keeping me safe.

****

He's coming, a vaguely familiar voice crooned.

I pulled myself from Sy's arms, and sat up in bed.

The clock showed two in the morning.

Sy snored quietly beside me.

He's coming.

The woman's sing-song voice sounded again, softer, just barely audible over the sound of the wind whistling outside. In the distance, the sound of waves crashing on the rocky shore sang a hushed lullaby. I sat in silence, listening for the creepy voice again.

When I heard it again, I scrambled for the light. I snapped on the small lamp beside the bed, hoping to bring my mind completely back to reality and away from the dream.

With the light on, the window before us became more like a mirror, the black night disappearing behind the reflection of us in bed. I stared at my reflection, my dark hair in disarray.

Feeling exposed, I wrapped myself in the throw blanket from the foot of the bed, and grabbed a tank and shorts from the dresser.

He's coming. The voice was even fainter this time, singsong and eerie. A separate entity from the lullaby of the waves, maybe even coming from inside my head.

My back stiffened, and I pulled the clothes on quickly. My gaze darted around the room. I ran to the lamp and shut off the light, the window revealing the night sky again.

Was I still dreaming? I stilled, listening for the voice.

I turned toward the bed, my gaze roving over a sleeping Sy, and to the nightstand—both our cells had black screens. Both off.

I went downstairs and confirmed the TV was off.

Maybe exhaustion from the long day had taken a

toll.

I went back upstairs and used the bathroom. I splashed water on my face, drying it roughly with a towel, then dropped the towel into the sink.

I looked up at my reflection.

Jared was reflected in the mirror standing just behind me. I gasped and knocked over the soap dish, the ceramic shattering on the tile below.

I whirled around, and no one was there. I stabbed at the shower curtain, pulling it back. Nothing.

I huffed and gasped, turning back around to grip the sink. I stared at the drain below, too afraid to look at my reflection again. Too afraid of what I might see.

Avoiding the mirror, I kneeled on the tile and carefully scooped the broken dish into a pile.

An image burst through my vision of me in the same position, hands planted flat on the tile, gasping for air, my throat burning from the grip that'd been around my neck—

The image disappeared, and I resumed cleaning up the fragments, tossing the largest pieces into the small trash can. I huffed and gasped, trying to focus on cleaning the ceramic, counting to calm the panic searing through every vessel and nerve ending as if I'd been electrocuted.

He won't hurt you, but I will.

I stopped counting and stilled when I heard Mitch's voice. My heart pounded in my chest, and the blood rushing in my ears deafened me.

I went to stand, and knocked my head on the edge of the sink with so much force, it caused me to fall back to my knees.

I groaned, and my hands flew up to cradle the

explosion of pain where I'd hit my head.

Another flash took my vision, this time, my hands were flying up to release the tension of the grip on my hair, my face being forced to look up at Jared, as he smiled down at me.

Now, apologize for disrespecting your husband...

Mitch's voice faded, and I lowered my face onto the tile. My arms and thighs leaked pinpoints of blood from the shards of ceramic that pierced my skin. I slid on my own blood, bringing my knees to my chest and hugging myself into a tight ball.

Well? Jared's faraway voice prompted.

I counted each gasping breath I dragged into my lungs, the panic hijacking what was left of my sanity. *It wasn't a dream. I was awake. I was bleeding, if I needed any further proof.* This was my reality—I was either going crazy, or being tortured...

Tortured. The thought caused me to pause. Maybe I was being tortured *there?* Was Jared that evil in both lives? Or was he controlling the narrative in both? Something told me it was the latter. It'd taken me a long time to trust my intuition, but right now it begged—screamed for my attention.

He was doing something intentional, haunting me somehow, in both lives.

Two could play this game. I wasn't going to run, or shrink away from him this time. No.

If he wanted to play, I'd come out and play.

It was time to show him I wasn't the meek eighteen-year-old he'd manipulated, controlled, then eventually married.

I was all grown up now. And my sharp adult teeth had finally come in.

I pulled myself back into bed, and wiggled up against Sy.

He unconsciously wrapped an arm around me, pulling me close.

Tomorrow, I'd investigate. These weren't dreams anymore, these were flashes—visions.

The bleed-through effect.

Tonight, I'd rest. And tomorrow, I'd fight back.

****

He's coming. I heard the soft voice one last time before waking to hear Sy swearing in the bathroom.

I sat up and squinted at the bright light of morning.

The sky was gray, and spots of rain were collecting on the windows.

I suddenly recalled where I'd heard the voice before—it was Jared's mother's voice.

I walked into the bathroom.

Sy was sweeping remnants of the shattered ceramic from the floor.

"Sorry about that." I leaned on the doorframe.

"What happened? There's glass, blood, and…" He stopped and gasped when he looked up at me.

I looked down at the dried blood that still clung to my arms and thighs from when the ceramic pierced my skin after I'd lain on the tile. "Oh crap. It was quite a night." I rubbed my arms and thighs, as if I could dust the blood off like glitter.

"Oh man…" He stared at a spot of blood on the underside of the sink.

I patted the top of my head. I didn't even realize the blow had broken skin. "Aw, shit."

He dumped the remainder of the ceramic into the trash and walked over to me. "Let me see."

153

I rested my forehead on his chest.

He gently parted my hair, searching for the injury.

I winced when he found it.

"Sorry," he said. "There's just a small cut, and a bump."

I laughed. "The nighttime is a dangerous time for me, apparently. I tried cleaning up the ceramic, then I hit my head, then I got a few cuts from the leftover shards when I went to—"

"It's okay." He smoothed my hair with one hand and wrapped his other arm around me, holding me close.

"Sorry I did a crappy job cleaning it up. It was late, dark, and I didn't want to wake you."

"I would've helped."

I pulled away and looked down at myself. I was a bloody mess. "I need a shower."

"Well, since you didn't let me help clean last night, the least I can do is help you clean up now." His eyes gleamed.

"I wouldn't mind that one bit." I smiled and turned to start the shower.

****

After getting ready, I noticed two texts were waiting for me on my cell. I ignored them and sat to have coffee with Sy before he met his brothers at the construction site.

Jeff planned on bringing him up to speed on the project before they resumed work tomorrow.

"It's raining. I'm surprised Jeff didn't cancel," I said.

"They finished the foundation and bones of the house before Jay left. We'll be working inside."

"Oh, that's good."

Sy put his mug in the sink, then came over to kiss my forehead. "You going to get your new badge?"

I smiled and nodded. "Yep. I need to drop off my ring for sizing and go to the registry, too. Update my license." I stared at my engagement ring, hating the idea of parting with it until it was sized. I'd pick it up when our bands were ready, too.

"Be careful. It's supposed to pour all day."

"I will."

He knocked twice on the counter, his brow furrowed in thought before he grabbed his keys and headed out the door.

I slid my phone over and checked the messages. Jess.

—Steve said today before two. The transport van left overnight.—

I wanted to be shocked by the timing, but Jared's mother's voice already gave me fair warning last night.

He's coming.

I parked outside work and went inside.

Nelson was the first to greet me when I came through the double doors, his loud baritone voice alerting the others of my arrival.

"Charlotte!" Angela darted out from behind the triage desk and nearly plowed Nelson over to hug me.

"Stop acting like you haven't seen me." I wrapped my arms around her tightly.

"Not *here*, though!" She released me and jumped up and down.

Brian emerged from the back and came over to me. He shook my hand, and I pulled him in for a hug.

"I've worked for you for far too long to be that informal."

He patted my back. "Glad to see you, kid. How you feeling?"

"Great."

"It's gonna be good to have you back. Keep her in line." He tipped his head at Angela.

She rolled her eyes. "The mama bear of the clinic is back!" She squealed. "I even have a few new office supplies waiting for you at your desk."

I strolled over to the triage desk and leaned over the counter to peek. "You've got to be kidding." I held up the banana pen and the penis eraser.

Nelson and Brian laughed.

"So, what brings you in, Charly?" Nelson asked.

"Um, well. To see you, actually."

"Me?" He pulled his chin back, then leaned on the triage counter.

"I need a new badge—" I rummaged through my bag and pulled out the marriage certificate. "—because I have a new last name."

"Well, well, congratula—"

"You *whore*!" Angela screeched, cutting off Nelson.

"Thanks, I was expecting congrats, but—"

She pulled my left hand up and examined the ring. "Thor's got good taste." She referred to Sy as the Greek god of thunder—a nickname she'd given him on her own.

Nelson and Brian leaned in for a look.

"Told you, she needs to be kept in line." Brian shrugged. "Congratulations, Charlotte. James is gonna freak out when I tell him. Maybe we can set up a gathering to celebrate?"

I nodded. "We were thinking of a spring reception."

"Sounds great, gives plenty of planning time. Hey, I

got to get back, see you tomorrow?"

"I'll be here."

Angela stood in front of me with her hands on her hips. "And you didn't call me? To be a witness?"

"My parents were here this weekend."

"Ah. Guess you're forgiven. Maybe." She narrowed her eyes at me.

"C'mon, Charl, let's go get your forms filled out for that badge."

I followed Nelson and turned to shoot Angela a joking glare over my shoulder.

She mouthed *call me*, before perching back on her seat at triage.

It was pouring when I left the clinic.

I started my car and blasted the heat. The windshield cleared with a swipe of the wipers, and a van drove by on the road parallel to the lot. I pulled out of my spot, and keeping a safe distance, followed the van through the winding main road on base.

It stopped outside the prison, as I knew it would. If I had any question of who was in it before, the Virginia plates on the van answered my silent question. I pulled over on a side road, my car concealed behind a line of bushes. I watched the MP open the sliding van door and escort the cuffed prisoner out.

Jared looked over both shoulders before he disappeared through the side door of the building.

I pulled away and left base. I wanted to scrub the vision of Jared from my eyes. He was cuffed, contained. He didn't appear smug or happy. And if he hadn't been haunting the hell out of me, I'd almost feel pity for him.

Almost.

Chapter 13, Reality 2: On the Periphery

Charlotte

I pulled into the driveway so fast the car screeched to a halt, just an inch from the garage door. My heart raced, relief surging through me when the garage opened and Jared's jeep wasn't there. *I'd made it home on time.*

I balanced the tray with two coffees in my left arm, and gathered my bag and heels in the other hand. I stomped my feet in the driveway, dislodging some of the mud from my sneakers before heading inside through the garage.

I placed the tray of coffee on the kitchen island, then pulled off my muddy sneakers, dropping them on the back deck to dry. I darted upstairs to pack a small bag.

I took only enough clothes to sustain me for a few days. My parents had a washing machine, so I'd make do. I threw a toothbrush, comb, and my makeup bag inside—things Jared would never notice missing. By the time he did, I'd be long gone.

I stashed the bag in the coat closet near the front door, shoving it all the way to the back, and slammed the door shut when I heard his jeep pull in and the garage opening.

I ran back to the kitchen and slid the coffees out of the tray, stabbed a straw into both drinks, and discarded the tray in the trash. I spun to the fridge, and pulled out the roast I'd prepared the night before. I quickly turned on the oven, and popped the dish inside just as the side door shut, then grasped the island counter for support just as he clomped into the kitchen.

I looked up and his eyes were set on me, gleaming with...curiosity, maybe?

He dropped a briefcase of folders onto an island chair, and removed his uniform jacket. His brown tee was soaked in sweat. "Hey," he muttered.

He always trained before and after his shift, and today was apparently no different.

"I got you one," I said quietly, sliding the coffee across the island toward him. It killed me to do it, but I didn't want to arouse suspicion. It was safer if he thought me docile.

He turned back to me, then stared down at the coffee.

An emotion flickered in his eyes so briefly, I couldn't identify it. *Guilt? Shame? Remorse?*

He took the coffee and headed upstairs.

A few minutes later, I heard the shower running. I slumped my head, glad we didn't have to talk about today. There was nothing left to say. And before the sun could rise tomorrow, I'd be gone. Relief surged through me at the thought.

Jared came back downstairs in a white tee and gray sweatpants, and the heady smell of his eucalyptus-and-cedar soap wafted past me as he went to the stove to peek in the oven. For an instant, sadness washed over me, but anger quickly stomped it out when the harsh memory of his hand on my throat infiltrated my mind.

"Smells good." He closed the oven door.

He stepped close behind me and brushed my hair

away from my neck. He touched a sore spot on my neck with gentle fingers. "I could've hurt you. But I didn't."

My heart jackhammered in my chest. I didn't want his lack of apology to hurt, but it did. An apology wouldn't have kept me from leaving, but maybe it'd make it hurt a little less. "I think the words you're looking for are *I'm sorry.*" I sank my teeth into my lower lip to stop myself from saying more

A puff of breath hit my neck.

Was that a laugh? Don't cry. Do. Not. Cry.

"What did you expect? I had my father, military police, and three doctors watching. No one talks to me like that without repercussions."

"But I'm not one of your soldiers."

"In that facility, you are. In fact—" He pulled me around to face him. "—our vows do mention *honor and obey.*"

I swallowed and held his gaze. "Love."

He raised his eyebrows. "What?"

"The vows. They're to *love*, honor, and obey. What you did today isn't something you do to someone you love."

His shoulders shook with a scornful laugh. He pushed his tongue into his cheek, shook his head, and left the kitchen.

I darted up the stairs and turned on the shower.

I took the longest shower of my life, allowing the hottest water I could tolerate to assault my back. I opened the shower door and clumsily felt around for the towel on the rack.

Jared stepped forward.

I yelped in surprise as he wrapped me in a bath towel and locked his arms around me.

"I do love you, Charly." He spoke into my ear. "And if you love *me*, you'll obey me."

I stilled as his words settled. "Get off me." I broke out of his arms. "*Obey* you? Ugh." I stormed into the bedroom, gripping the towel at my chest.

He followed me into the bedroom and crossed his arms over his chest. "Those are the vows."

I pulled clothes from the dresser and dropped my towel, purposely choosing clothes I could sleep in *and* wear to the airport.

His eyes locked on my body, and he froze.

Good. Get an eyeful for the last time, jerk. I put the leggings on and pulled a camisole over my head.

Jared moved toward me, his intent clear in his eyes.

"Don't even *think* about it."

He stopped short, then looked up at the ceiling as he dragged a breath into his lungs. He dropped his head to look at me again. "I'm not going to apologize. You can't talk to me like that."

I barked out a laugh. "Then don't." I shrugged and turned to leave the room, balling up the towel and tossing it into the hamper before heading for the stairs.

He was close on my heels, and I stopped short.

He looked down at me with a furrowed brow, a question dancing in his eyes.

I stomped past him and back into the master bathroom, pulling open the medicine cabinet and tearing open the foil pack that held nighttime cough medicine. It's not like I could set an alarm for 0200, but if the meds knocked me out right after dinner, I'd definitely be awake by midnight. I tossed back a capsule, and drank water straight from the faucet to wash it down.

"What was that?" Jared asked from the doorway.

I turned to face him, wiping my mouth with my arm. "Do you ever stop watching me?" My heart picked up pace when his eyes hardened at my words. "It was my birth control," I quickly lied.

His brow smoothed and he smirked.

I wanted to punch him for that look. *Dream on, asshole.* I went downstairs and pulled the roast from the oven.

Jared came up behind me again, and his breath whispered across my neck. "If you're thinking about leaving, I want to warn you. Just because I didn't hurt you, doesn't mean I wouldn't. Under the right circumstances."

My knees went weak, and I grasped the counter for support. Was my whole life a lie? I never, ever imagined this side of him existed. My breathing picked up, and the more I tried to stay calm, the more my body tried to revolt. *Run. Get away. Now.*

He put his hand on my ribcage, and pressed his front to my back. "I can feel your heart racing. Do I scare you, Charly?"

I straightened my back and turned to face him. "No."

He leaned so close our noses almost touched, and his minty breath fanned across my face. He tilted his head, and for a moment, I thought he was going to try to kiss me. Instead, he uttered one word that sent a chill through me. It dropped from his mouth as a statement, yet rang with warning.

"Liar."

He turned away from me, opened the cabinet, and pulled out a plate.

I left dinner on the stovetop and stomped back upstairs. I wasn't hungry, and even if I was, I couldn't bear to sit with him.

I flopped onto the bed, and the sounds of him fixing himself dinner downstairs enraged me even more. His indifference was beyond imaginable.

I slammed my phone onto the nightstand and curled into a ball, hugging my knees tight in an attempt to ease the thorny heartbreak. It hadn't always been like this.

I stared at our wedding photo atop the dresser. I'd worn a fitted white gown, and he wore his Class A uniform. We faced each other with huge smiles, our hands joined in front of us, his dark skin juxtaposed against my strangely fair skin. We were opposites in many ways, but I'd always thought us the perfect fit. From the moment we met, until only recently, we'd laughed so much together—the type of belly-aching laughter that causes sore bellies and gasping breaths. Mitch never seemed happy about that—but we didn't care. We'd shared a thirst for happiness and knowledge and meaning and purpose.

But things changed when Quantym grew, and their ranks and positions took precedence. Jared's time became scarce, his laughter and smiles dimming under the stress of the new organization.

His recruiting me was supposed to bring us closer, allow us more time together, at least that's what he'd told me. We were supposed to grow old together, keep laughing together, have children.

But now, it was bad, worse than I could've ever imagined, and his demeanor over the last year nullified the positive memories, making me wonder if I ever really knew him at all. Before I could stop them, the tears overflowed. I sniffled and quietly shook with sobs until the meds kicked in, and I fell asleep.

I jerked awake, and Jared was asleep beside me. He had an arm draped over my waist, and I gently removed his arm and got out of bed. It was one in the morning. In one hour, I'd be on my way to the airport, and within five hours, I'd be out of state, in Florida. I was nauseous with anxiety.

Jared stirred, and I stilled. When his breathing resumed its deep regular pace, I left the bed and used the bathroom, then pulled on a sweatshirt before lying back in bed. I watched the clock for forty-five minutes.

I stared at Jared's sleeping face, saying a silent goodbye to my marriage. Too bad he'd been hiding a monster behind that beautiful mask. I left my phone on the nightstand so he couldn't track me, then I quietly left the bed and headed downstairs.

I pulled my bag from the coat closet, slid on my old sneakers, and slipped out the front door. I ran the whole way. My breath created small clouds in front of me, and my fingers ached from the bite of the cold night air as I neared Rosewood and Holly in less than ten minutes. Running soothed the adrenaline pulsing through my veins, but when I reached the intersecting streets, Simon's car wasn't there. I glanced at my watch, and it was just past two. A surge of panic flowed, and I looked up and down both dark streets. No signs of life.

What now?

If Simon didn't show, I didn't even have my phone to call anyone else. I walked to the top of the street, looking down the main road for any signs of life, and was greeted with dark silence. My shoulders slumped, hopelessness settling.

I'd walk down Rosewood one last time. If he didn't show, I'd walk to a gas station and call someone for a ride. Becca Diogo and I worked together at Quantym, and I wondered if I could trust her to help me. Another bitter realization dawned—without my cell, I didn't know her number.

My fears were vaporized when headlights illuminated the street ahead. Simon's black car pulled toward me, and I jogged to the passenger side. When the car stopped, I pulled the door open.

"You're late," I teased, dropping my bag inside before sliding in. I pulled the door shut and drew my sweatshirt sleeves over my freezing hands to warm them.

"Going somewhere, Charly?"

His voice ripped through me violently, and I whipped my head to the left to confirm what I already knew but my brain refused to accept.

Mitch sat behind the wheel with a sinister smile painted across his face.

I sucked in a loud breath while scrambling and clawing for the door handle, shrieking when my vision was taken out by a hood thrown over my head. The car jolted forward, and we were speeding away.

I screamed and kicked as I was dragged into the back seat with a strong arm around my neck. I continued to kick and scream and claw as forcefully as I could until I was put into a tight chokehold that could break my neck in seconds with one move.

Gasping, I dragged in breath after breath after breath, while my heart stuttered and stomped in my chest.

"I warned you not to try me," Jared murmured in my ear through the hood.

As I squirmed and kicked, his hold tightened. I grasped his forearm around my throat. "Please don't do this. Don't," I begged on a sob.

"I have a show for you. I came back just so I could be *here* for this." Excitement dripped from his words.

"What are you talking about?" I kicked my legs and tried squirming again as I gasped and huffed, the black cloth over my head triggering a severe bout of claustrophobia.

"Not long ago, in another place in time, I made you a promise." He tightened his hold on me when my panic caused me to expend more energy trying to uselessly fight him.

"Jared, please! What the hell? I'm your *wife!*" Desperation laced my words.

He clicked his tongue, and I stilled.

"You've been very, very bad. *Here and there.*"

I struggled and twisted, gaining no purchase. "What are you talking about?" I started screaming again, panic overriding every other thought and instinct.

I distinctly heard Mitch let out a dry laugh and say, "Put her to sleep."

"You'll find out soon enough." Jared laughed, and the sound was full of scorn. "Goodnight, Charly."

A pinprick stabbed my thigh, followed by burning pressure. "No! No, Jared!" I screamed, my body weakening almost immediately.

"Shhh." He pulled the cloth from my head and ran his fingers through my hair.

His face before me blurred, and I fought against heavy eyes.

"Please, don't do this." I whispered.

Simon. Oh my God, where was Simon?

Chapter 14, Reality 1

Charlotte

I was up and ready for work two hours earlier than necessary. I ran on the treadmill, showered, and drank two coffees.

Sy had already left the house—his first day back to work at the construction site with his brothers.

The longer I waited, the more my anxiety increased, so I decided to go to work early.

The commute to work was different now, traveling from Portsmouth, as opposed to my old house that was minutes from Newport Base. I enjoyed the quiet cold morning, and took in the sights as traffic pulsed with the typical heavy morning stop-and-go.

Most of the leaves were gone, the fall melting into an early, dark winter. The days were noticeably shorter now, too.

I pulled right up to the gates of the base. It was early, so a line hadn't formed yet.

PFC Goodman scanned my badge and waved me in.

I glanced at the clock, confirming it was still laughably early. I made my way inside the building and dropped my things at my desk. I glanced down at the gag office supplies Angela had left for me and laughed.

"You're early."

I whirled around. "Hi, Brian. You scared me." I put

a hand to my chest.

"Didn't mean to. How you doing, Charlotte?" He smiled, his brown eyes twinkling under his wire-rimmed glasses.

"Good, good."

He wheeled a seat toward me and sat. He crossed an ankle over a knee, and his lab coat fell open, revealing a plaid button-down. "Really?"

I plopped down in my chair and nodded.

He studied my face, allowing silence to hang in the air between us.

"Okay. Yeah, I'm nervous. I'm glad to be back to a routine, but—"

"But?"

I shook my head. "I don't know. It's weird, ya know? Something unimaginable happens to me again, and life just goes on. I can't explain it, but sometimes, I feel like it's not real. Like nothing that happened is real." I immediately regretted my rambling, and my face heated.

Brian gave an empathetic smile. "It sounds like you're still processing everything. That's totally normal. Still in therapy?"

"No. I went, but I just need…time."

He nodded. "Understandable. Hey, this is going to sound weird, but…" He ran a hand through his tousled chestnut hair.

"But?" I crossed my arms, a smirk pulling at my lips. It wasn't often Brian was at a loss for words.

"The injury?"

"Say no more." I smiled and stood, lifting my shirt to reveal the scar on my torso. It was only about two inches long, but it was still angry in color. Being a medical provider, I wasn't surprised by his curiosity. I'd have wanted to see it, if the boot were on the other foot.

He pushed his glasses up his nose and leaned closer. "Oof. Still tender?"

"Not really. Itchy sometimes." I dropped the hem of my shirt back down.

"Put the sticky silicone pads on it. That scar won't even be noticeable in a year."

I shrugged. "Doesn't bother me. It's tiny."

Loud singing announced Nelson's arrival, followed by Angela's chipper voice.

"Time for work."

Brian headed back into his office, and I logged in to the computer.

The day was steady, and just before lunch, I stepped into an exam room to take vitals on a pleasant elderly Vietnam veteran.

"Hello, Mr. Jones! Tell me what brings you in today." I smiled at the old man, one of my favorite categories of patients—not just war heroes, but gentlemanly and usually wisecrackers, too.

"I'm here because of this damn ear again." He pulled out his hearing aid and jabbed a finger toward his ear.

"Ah, looks like the last time you were here, you needed some antibiotic drops. We'll have you fixed up in no time."

I took his vitals and grabbed the otoscope.

"You married?" he asked loudly.

"Actually, yes. As of this weekend." I smiled.

"Ah! You pretty ones are always taken."

"Too bad you didn't come in Friday, you'd have had a chance," I teased.

He snapped his fingers. "Damn."

I threw my head back and laughed. "Mind if I take a look?"

He nodded and turned his head, allowing me to examine his ear with the otoscope.

"Yep, looks like otitis externa again. Brian will be in in a few to double-check and get you a prescription."

"Thanks, dear."

You did so, so good.

When I heard Jared's voice, I grabbed onto the wall and gasped. I slammed the otoscope back into the wall holder.

"You okay, dear?" Mr. Jones reached his hand out toward me.

I nodded. "Fine," I whispered, grasping the wall and stumbling my way toward the door of the room.

You—and anyone you've ever loved—will be in grave danger.

A whimper escaped my lips when I heard his voice again.

"Dear?" Mr. Jones stood.

The exam room door opened and Brian speed-walked in. Typical. He stopped short when he noticed my condition.

He grasped my shoulders. "Charlotte?"

I looked over his shoulder, too embarrassed to meet his eyes. "I'm okay. Just need some air."

"Geeze, you're sweating. Panic attack?"

"I'm okay," I squeaked.

"Take an early lunch. Seriously."

Nodding, I dashed out of the room, then pressed my back against the cool wall outside the door and counted each breath I drew into my lungs.

Twelve, thirteen, fourteen…

"Charl?" Angela sped over to me. "What's going on?"

"Brian's sending me to an early lunch. You'll cover for me?" I swiped a hand over my damp forehead.

"Yeah, sure. Of course." She nodded heartily. "You sure you're all right? Need company?"

I shook my head. "No, just need to be alone for a bit. Grab a bite. I'm fine. Promise." My tone was clipped, cutting off the conversation. I strode out of the clinic and straight to my car.

Then, I dropped into the driver's seat and pulled out of my spot.

"Here I come, jerk," I muttered.

Driving down the main road toward the prison, I pulled into a spot and without further thought, strolled straight into the facility.

"Ma'am?" A fully-uniformed MP stopped me at the door.

"I'm here to visit Adam Cardoza."

"Badge."

He scanned my badge and escorted me inside.

I handed over my ID and filled out visitation paperwork.

The MP handed back my ID with wide eyes. "Charlotte Cardoza?" He glanced back down at the paperwork and up at me.

I nodded, heat rushing to my cheeks. I didn't bother correcting him. My new ID, with my new last name, would be mailed to me in a couple weeks anyway.

"All right. Have a seat. It'll be a few."

"Ms. Cardoza!" A short, stocky guard called out from behind the glass reception area.

I stood.

"Follow me."

A loud buzzer sounded, a door opened, and I was escorted deeper into the facility. I was brought into a small room, and a guard stayed inside with me, standing beside the door we'd entered through. I took a seat at the long metal industrial-looking table in the center of the room.

The windows were covered with bars, and other than the table, two chairs, a wall clock, and another door, there was nothing else in the room.

I shifted in my seat, and my arms prickled with goosebumps.

A buzzer sounded, and the door at the back of the room opened.

I sucked in a breath, my heart raced in my chest, and sweat began to form along the back of my neck.

A guard entered, and just behind him, Jared followed, with his hands cuffed behind his back. A second guard stayed at his heels.

"Hello, doll." Jared smiled widely at me. The top button of his orange jumpsuit was undone. He'd grown a thin bit of dark facial hair, and his black hair was freshly buzzed.

One guard grasped his elbow, and he sat.

I crossed my arms over my chest and leaned back into my seat, sinking farther inside my fleece coat.

He looked up at the guard. "The cuffs?" He raised an eyebrow.

The guard turned to me. "Ma'am, your call. There will be a guard in with you at all times."

"Keep him cuffed."

Jared let out a short laugh.

The two guards exited the room, leaving just me, Jared, and the guard by the door who'd escorted me in.

Jared tilted his head. "Missed me?"

"Yeah, right."

"I knew you'd come." He leaned back into his seat, squirming with the discomfort of having his hands cuffed behind him.

"Comfy?" I nodded at his restrained arms.

He leaned forward. "With you here, yes. Yes, I am." His smile pulled slightly askew from the scar trailing down the left side of his face from the car accident.

But now, somehow, the scar was like a crack, allowing me to see through the beautiful face to the monster beneath.

Silence descended.

I started counting the tick of the wall clock.

His eyes widened with anticipation. "You must need something if you're here."

"I don't know why I came. This is stupid." I stood and backed away from the table.

"Wait, Charly. Sit." He tipped his head at the chair.

I stopped and held his gaze.

His dark eyes gleamed. "I know why you're here."

I turned toward the door and took a few steps, ready to leave. "Bullshit."

"The dreams. They're unsettling, aren't they?" he called out.

His words were like a kick to the gut, halting me in place. I finally turned to face him.

"Ah. The bleed-through can be so...*unforgiving*."

I stomped back over to the table. "What the hell are you doing?"

He shrugged. "Sit. Let's talk."

I lowered myself back into my seat.

"It's not going to stop. You've made a poor choice, Charly. Simon can't save you from this."

"From what?"

He pulled in a deep breath. "Your destiny."

I rolled my eyes. "And let me guess, you're my destiny, Jared? Ugh, how romantic."

"The name is *Adam*," he warned, shooting a glance at the guard. "You know what your problem is, Charly? You think you're better than everyone else. You're not. You hide behind people like me, to put your own selfish flaws in the shadows."

"You don't even know what you're talking about."

"But I do. See, Charly, you think you're too good for me, or my—" He cleared his throat. "—organization. Truth is, it's right up your alley. In fact, on the Periphery, you're quite an important part of it. By choice, might I add."

"You know nothing about who I am."

He sighed and rolled his neck.

I winced when I heard the bones crack.

"After almost seven years of marriage, I certainly do. That's why people like you go into health care, and marry people like me. You hide who you really are behind service jobs, become a noble military spouse, but it's all a farce, and I see you." He leaned forward. "I see right through you."

"I don't have to sit here and listen to this." I slid to the edge of my seat, a part of me ready to leave, another part of me begging to stay, to find out if Quantym was still actually up and running.

"If you don't, there will be repercussions."

I crossed my arms and rested them on the table. "Do

you remember the night we met?" I looked down and traced invisible lines on the metal table with my finger.

His eyes lit up at my question, and a wide smile broke across his face. "How could I forget?"

I looked at him through my lashes. "I thought you were a hero back then."

"So, what you're saying is, it's not your fault. I tricked you? My uniform dampened your panties, and then I ended up being the big bad wolf?"

I curled my lip. "You're not the person I thought you were."

He shifted in his seat. "That's where you're wrong. I'm consistent, if nothing else." He inhaled sharply. "That was the night all your friends died. Except you."

I closed my eyes at the memory. He was at the bowling alley—on leave with another soldier when he struck up conversation with me. I was just eighteen and with my date, Tyler, and a couple friends. We were celebrating graduation, the guys in the group probably more so than the rest of us, and I was uncomfortable. Jared insisted my date was drunk, and asserted he'd bring me home safely. I'd tried to tell Tyler that I was leaving, but he was already making out with another girl, and I was humiliated, angry, and hurt. I went with Jared—he was a few years older, and being in the military, he radiated responsibility and honor.

Tyler lost control of the car that night, killing himself and three others.

"I didn't think they'd... I told them not to drink and drive."

He nodded. "But they died, and you didn't. Kind of like *our* accident. Amazing how you always end up the poor little surviving victim."

"Really? You think either accident was my fault?"

"I'm not saying that. I'm saying you have a skewed perspective of things. You always come out on top, but feel jaded."

"You're a narcissist," I spat. "You think tearing me down will make you bigger? It won't, so save it."

He threw his head back and laughed. "A narcissist? No, you're mistaken. My father—now, *my father* is a narcissist. I'm just a man who knows what he wants and knows how to get it."

I rubbed a hand over my face, then glanced at the wall clock; my break was nearly over.

"A narcissist would belittle you, hurt you, chip away at you to get you to stay, or to do what I want. I've never done that. What kills you is that it was always *your* choice, I never had to force a thing. And, despite what you may think, I've never, ever cheated on you. From the moment we met, it was only you. Always only you."

I chuckled. "You've always been a liar."

"Is this what you came here to do? Accuse me of being a cheater or a liar? I'm neither. I'll tell you what I am. Unstoppable."

I glared at him. "Narcissist."

He leaned forward. "That night we met? I slashed the brake lines on that asshole's piece-of-shit car and brought you home. Even your parents liked me after that, for saving your life. Know what else I did? I snuck in through your window, night after night, talking to you, making you laugh, refusing to touch you—until *you begged me* to defile you." He laughed and shook his head. "God, I wanted you, but when I ended up being your first, there was no hope for you after that. I bent the *world* around us to make you mine. So, if Simon sold you some shit about dying for you, just remember I sold my *soul* for you."

"You're lying." I clenched my jaw.

There was no way. No.

"You don't want to believe me, because that validates my initial point. You knew, deep down, doll, you knew. And you loved me—*married me*—anyway." He smiled. "Hiding who you are behind me doesn't make you better. The absence of bad deeds doesn't make you good."

"Shut up." My heart raced in my chest, too fast to count the fluttering beats.

A memory of sliding into his passenger seat flashed through my mind, and how I'd noted the flashlight and wire-cutters on the console. How was I to know what he'd used them for?

He leaned forward over the table and held my gaze. "I never hid who I was. You just pretended not to see."

I shook my head. "No. That's not true."

"Yes, it is." He lifted his chin and smirked. "Don't be ashamed. Morally gray suits you well."

I sat staring at him in frozen silence, ignoring the chill that danced along my spine.

"Simon's a good man, yeah?" He leaned back into his seat.

I stared into his dark eyes. "Yes, he is."

"Did he ever tell you he got a purple heart? For what happened with the terrorist attack?"

"No—yes. Yes."

"Ha! Calling *me* a liar? It's okay, now you know."

My shoulders slumped, and my heart continued its marathon in my chest. *Why didn't I know that? I should've known that.*

177

"Speaking of, does Simon know you're here?"

"Of course," I lied again, and I swear I could feel my soul dim, feeding his assertations about me.

His eyebrows shot up. "You'll never be a good liar, Charly." He smiled widely. "Your secret is safe with me." His tongue darted out and ran across his lower lip, and his eyes remained locked on mine.

I glanced at the clock. "I have to go."

"You must have more questions for me."

I leaned forward, horrified that the conversation veered as far off as it did. "What do you want from me?" I whispered.

"I'll be out of here soon, Charly. And I want you to help me with something. Something for me and my father's organization."

Now it was my turn to laugh. "No. You're nuts. You stabbed me—"

"Charly." He let out a deep sigh and closed his eyes for a few seconds. "You're hiding again. You stabbed me *first*, remember?" He opened his eyes and pinned me with a glare.

A wave of nausea hit me. I stood. "I have to go."

"Back to work, huh?" His gaze went to my scrubs.

I nodded.

"Come back, we have more to discuss."

I turned around, and the guard opened the door for me. I glanced over my shoulder one last time.

"Oh, and Charly...sweet dreams."

As soon as my feet hit the asphalt outside the building I ran to my car. Now, I was having a real panic attack. I huffed and gasped, bringing in ragged breaths that did nothing to feed my hungry lungs. My heart hammered in my chest so fast, numbness tingled my lips.

Why did I come here? What did I expect?

I dry heaved twice. Thankfully, my stomach was empty.

Pull it together, Charlotte. Pull it together.

I finished the rest of my shift in near-silence, and drove to the jewelers to pick up our rings afterward. Then, I went straight home.

****

Sy could tell I was off. He'd asked me repeatedly over dinner if I was okay, and each time I deflected and said I was just tired. The more I lied, the more guilty I felt—for lying and visiting Jared—and an evil voice in my mind cackled with Jared's words.

You're no better than me. Stop hiding.

Later that night, as I lay on Sy's chest in bed, I slid his wedding band onto his finger.

He smiled. "You picked them up today."

"Yup." I held my hand up, with both the band and the diamond now on my left ring finger.

"Now everyone knows you're mine."

"It didn't take a ring to solidify that." I rested my hand on his chest again.

He toyed with my rings. "Feels good just the same. They suit you."

"You really did pick the perfect ring," I mused, lifting my head to stare at the set again.

"No, I picked the perfect woman."

I put my head back down, a cold hollowness settling in my stomach. He thought me good. I'd once thought that of someone, too. And I'd been wrong.

But Sy was good, through and through.

After a heartbeat of silence, I asked him about the helicopter crash. "Tell me about the terrorist attack again."

He rubbed my back and drew in a deep breath. "We were only a month away from coming home from that deployment. I woke up with a bad feeling that day. We'd almost made it back to base, when gunfire came at us. The copter went down, and I knew I was hurt bad. I pulled Jeff out. I couldn't walk, but somehow helped pull him out from the metal pinning him down. I wanted to get him out before the whole thing blew."

I held my breath, waiting for him to continue.

"There was no hope for the other two. They were dead on impact. A terrorist ran up behind Jeff as he was pulling me out, and I shot him and one other. They went down like bags of lead. Clean shots, right through the head." He whistled, the sound like a bullet. "Jeff then pulled me away from the burning helicopter as I started to lose consciousness."

I blew out a breath. "I'm sorry I never asked before."

"Sorry? It's not a pretty story. I'm kind of surprised you're asking now."

"I want to know everything, Sy. You know all my demons. I want to get to know yours."

I felt his head nod, and his silence indicated he was reliving the horrible experience.

He let out a gruff laugh. "Me and Jeff both got purple hearts, but it didn't change anything. Our men still died, and I still signed on at Quantym so I could afford the surgery."

"I'm sorry."

"Don't be, Charlotte. I told you, dying was the best thing that ever happened to me. It's what brought me to you."

I drifted off to sleep with a heavy heart, wondering

which version of myself I believed to be true. Jared's version, who thought me willfully ignorant and no less evil than him, or Sy's—who thought me good, and worth dying for. Perhaps I was a bit of both.

****

He's coming.

"No! Stop!" I cried out.

I have a show for you. I came back just so I could be here for this.

"I'm here, Charlotte." Sy's voice drove away Jared's.

I grasped Sy's arms, and the dream melted away.

"It's five." He smoothed my hair.

I kept my tight hold on him, my nails biting into his skin. My damp shirt clung to me, the coldness causing me to shiver. "I have to get ready anyway. I want to run before work."

"Another dream?" he asked.

I sat up and nodded, slowly releasing my grip on him. "Have you had any more?"

He sighed. "Last night. But we did have a charged conversation before bed, so…"

"Sorry about that."

"Stop apologizing. I have to get ready. I'll go make us coffee." He left the room, and I sat on the bed trying to calm my breathing.

This had to stop. I wouldn't allow this to go on.

As soon as Sy left for work, I dialed Brian and called out of work. I apologized profusely, telling him I was going to see my therapist to get an anti-anxiety prescription.

Another freaking lie.

I got ready and left the house, driving straight into

Newport and pulling up at Cedarwood Bay Home by seven-thirty.

"Good morning." A nurse's assistant in a colorful scrub top greeted me at the front reception desk.

"Hi, I'm here to visit Caroline Cardoza."

The woman's eyes lit up. "Oh my! Caroline hasn't had a visitor in years!"

A pang of guilt hit me. "I'm Charlotte."

"Cardoza." The woman's smile widened. "She's been talking about you lately."

I dipped my head. "Really?"

She nodded energetically. "Yup. Well, in her lucid moments. Have a seat, and I'll go make sure she's freshened up and ready for a visitor. It's early, so you can have the rec room to yourselves."

The woman obviously had a good relationship with Caroline. The few times I'd met the woman, I hadn't noticed even a second of lucidity.

Though, living in these quarters the staff got a better chance at being around for those fleeting moments.

"All set, Ms. Cardoza. Follow me."

I was brought into a large room, where a green sofa was placed in front of a wall-mounted TV, and two round tables sat off to the side. Boxes of games and books were lined along the deep windowsills.

Caroline sat at a round table, staring down at an unfinished puzzle before her. Her long blonde hair was straggly and obstructed most of her face. She wore a pink housecoat and rocked slightly in her seat.

I was escorted to her table, and took a seat across from her. "Is she…does she get…agitated?"

"Oh, heaven's no!" The aid smiled. "She gets confused, but never aggressive. I can keep the door open."

I shook my head. "No, it's fine, then. Thank you."

She left the room.

I stared at Jared's mother across from me, searching for Jared in her features. Jared's skin was a blend of Mitch's dark tone and his mother's fairness. He had her eyes, but almost everything else was Mitch's. Even his personality.

Caroline didn't look up as she held a puzzle piece in her hand, her gaze roving along the puzzle, looking for the right spot.

"Hello, Caroline."

She didn't respond.

I eyed the piece in her hand, then slid a bit closer, examining the puzzle. "May I help?"

She grunted, then slid the puzzle piece into place with a soft click. She finally looked up at me, and her mouth went slack with a small intake of breath. "He's coming." She leaned toward me. "He's coming."

"Jared?"

She shook her head. "The monster." She looked down and grabbed another puzzle piece, pinching it between her fingers as she searched the puzzle with her gaze again.

I picked up a piece. "I always liked puzzles, too."

I looked over the puzzle, and Caroline's breathing picked up pace.

She rocked back and forth in her seat, her eyes glazing. "He's coming. He's coming."

"Who, Caroline, who?" I whispered.

Great, agitate the mentally ill, Charlotte. Great plan.

"The monster. Save my son." Her eyes filled with

183

tears.

"Shh, Caroline. It's okay. Your son is fine. In fact, I just saw him yesterday."

Finally, someone I could speak the truth to.

She shook her head. "No. No. *No*. It's going to destroy him...and you." She sobbed and slammed her fist on the table.

Puzzle pieces jumped, and some sprinkled to the floor like confetti.

I spoke to her as I picked up the fallen pieces. "Caroline, I promise you, it's going to be okay."

She shook her head aggressively, and her long hair whipped back and forth. "There is only one way, *Charly*." Her voice deepened noticeably when she uttered my name.

I rubbed the shiver that slithered up my arms.

"Save him! *Save him*!" she growled.

"The monster?" I stared at her with compassion. How tragic to be imprisoned by her own mind.

She nodded, tears streaming from her eyes. "He's coming."

The nurse's aide bustled in. "Oh, dear. She can get cranky when she's hungry. Join us for breakfast? I can bring you both to the cafeteria."

"No, thank you. I have to get to work," I lied.

"It was good seeing you, Caroline. Next time, we'll do the puzzle together, okay?" I reached across the table, and brushed her hand with my fingers.

"Save him." Her whisper was strangled. "Seven saves him." Another glistening tear rolled down her cheek.

I looked at the aide. "Does she always say that?"

"For as long as I've known her. No matter how far

the mind goes, there is one thing my patients have in common. The love for their children isn't robbed by their mental illness. Sometimes, they feel guilty they cannot be there for them. And, when they're not visited by their children, sometimes the mind copes by making up scenarios. Like the child isn't coming because they're hurt, or in danger."

I nodded. "Caroline, I'm going to see Jared today. Do you want me to tell him anything for you?"

She stood abruptly and grunted. "I want to see his face." She reached into her housecoat pocket and fished something out. She held her hand out to me.

I reached out, and Caroline dropped a wrapped butterscotch candy into my hand.

"For him." Without another word, she turned and stiffly walked out of the room.

I left the facility, and it was sunny but cold as I sat in my car, allowing it to warm up. Caroline was undoubtedly severely mentally ill, and what the aide had told me made sense. Her utterances weren't new. Ridiculous that I'd thought I was actually getting a message from her in my dreams.

But why was I hearing her voice in my dreams?

He's coming.

What was she *doing on the Periphery?*

****

I drove the short distance to Newport Base. PFC Goodman scanned my badge, and I drove right past my work and to the prison.

This would be my last time. I'd try to get intel about whether Quantym was still running, and if he gave me nothing, I'd let it go. I had no other choice. Jared was talkative yesterday, and I could only hope he would be

185

today, too. Especially when he learned it was my last visit.

It's now or never.

The MP standing guard remembered me from the day before. He took my ID and bag, and made a quiet call to someone.

Within a few minutes, I was escorted to the visitation room by the same stocky guard as the day before.

Jared was already seated at the metal table in the center of the room. He looked up at me with a huge smile.

The guard stood by the door, and I took a seat across from Jared.

"You just can't get enough of me," he gushed.

I scowled, unimpressed with his arrogance.

He folded his hands on the table and leaned toward me. "I knew you'd be back."

I stared at his hands and hugged myself a bit tighter.

"You want me cuffed?" He lowered his voice. "Scared, Charly?"

I narrowed my eyes at him. "No. I want to know if your father is still running his...business." I tried to appease him with my discretion in front of the guard.

"Quantym? Of course. You managed to slow us, but not stop us."

I wiggled in my seat, and heat prickled along my hairline. Something felt...off. "What do you need my help with?" I was referring to his request from the prior day.

"It's simple, really. Mathematics. Help us access all seven peripheries."

My eyebrows raised. "Seven?"

"Yes. After that, the great beyond." He stretched his arms out dramatically. "Seven chances to live your best life. And we already know you picked me in two of them." He brought his hands back together, clasping them on top of the table. "I'm told you picked me in all of them. You and I are more alike than you'll admit." He chuckled.

"I don't believe you. Besides, I've made some new decisions here."

He shook his head dismissively. "You and your boyfriend won't make it a few more weeks, if that."

I leaned forward. "You mean my husband?"

His back straightened instantly. "Liar."

I shook my head slowly, then shrugged out of my coat. "I'm widowed. I'm free to marry the man I love." I folded my hands on the table.

He glanced down at my hands, his gaze zoning in on my rings, and his eyes widened infinitesimally.

Something resembling hurt distorted his face for half a heartbeat, before his mask slipped back into place, hiding everything but the anger. His eyes darkened, and he cocked his head to the side. "Annul it."

I laughed. "Are you serious? I'm not here to discuss my marriage. I'm here to ask what you want from me so I can move on. You want help with Quantym, fine. Just tell me what to do, then leave me the hell alone."

He flew from his seat, and I nearly fell out of my chair.

I scrambled toward the guard. "Okay, I'm done here. We're done."

The guard stared straight ahead as if I was invisible and he was deaf.

Jared sauntered over to me slowly, drawing out the

anticipation, feeding on my fear.

I am the dumbest person alive with a death wish.

I circled around the metal table, desperate to put distance between us.

"What do you want from me?"

He smiled, splaying his hands in front of him. "Don't be scared. I just want to talk." He kept his gaze pinned on me, and I eventually stopped my waltz around the room.

I tilted my head. "Jared, when was the last time you visited your mother?"

He walked right up to me. "Trying to insinuate I'm crazy like her?"

"I saw her today."

He reached up to touch my face. "Such a liar."

I backed away. "Don't touch me." I pulled the candy from my pocket and held it in his face between two trembling fingers.

He stopped and stared at the candy. He ripped it from my hand, unwrapped it, and popped it into his mouth, pushing it into his cheek. "And what did she say?" He brought his face down to mine, the tip of his nose grazing my cheek.

"She wants to see your face."

He breathed a laugh. "Maybe I'll go pay her a visit. My time here, in jail, is nearing its end."

"What do you want from me, Jared?"

He took another step forward, and his body pressed against mine. "I don't just want your help. I want you to admit it. Admit you'll never escape me. And admit that you don't want to."

"No. You're getting out? I'll help you with whatever stupid math you need, but you have to leave me alone after."

"Ah, see? Not so noble, are you? There go those morals you always tout. What do you think Simon would think of that deal?"

"Leave him out of this." I closed my eyes to avoid his gaze.

"Look at me, Charly. It's so hard to admit it, isn't it? To have a mirror held up and face who you truly are. You think I didn't know you were up to something in Virginia? I did. But the night we danced at the gala, I felt you yield to me, like you always do. Your mind. Your body. Your very soul."

"No." I blinked as tears pricked my eyes. "Stop it. I said I'd help."

"You kissed me back that night. Even my father saw it. But you're so obsessed with proving yourself honorable. If you'd just stayed, let Simon finish his mission... You think about that, don't you, what life would be like right now had you made that choice?"

"No, I don't. Do we have a deal or not?" My voice cracked, and tears finally spilled down my cheeks.

"No deal," he whispered. "Annul your marriage, and we'll have a deal."

"No."

He dragged his lips along the trail of tears on my cheek.

I turned away and whimpered. "Stop." Bleakness settled heavy in my chest.

I hate him, but I'll never escape him.

"You always choose the hard way." He sighed, wrapping one arm around my back, while his other hand grasped the back of my head, pulling me into his chest. "I guess if you won't agree, I'll just bend the world around us. Again."

My shoulders wilted, and with my forehead on his chest, I said, "Why won't you just let me go? I'll help you, then you can disappear again, and I won't tell a soul."

"Is that it? You're still mad about the four years you thought I was dead?" He sighed loudly. "My mistake, I should've come back sooner. But you know how stubborn my father is. Always about *sticking to the plan.*"

"I've moved on, Jared. I suggest you do the same."

"No." He dropped his head back, staring at the ceiling for a few heartbeats. Then, he charged into me. The wall connecting with my back took my breath away as he clamped his mouth onto my neck, causing me to cry out.

I clawed and pushed at him. "Get off me, asshole! Stop it!"

The wetness from his mouth slid across my neck, but never broke connection. When I felt the burning, horror set in.

He's giving me a fucking hickey!

I kicked and squirmed, screaming every profanity I could think of at him.

The guard turned his head, pretending he was in another dimension.

Jared removed his mouth from my neck with a loud smack. He rubbed an arm across his face and chuckled. "I'd like to see how you're going to lie your way out of *that.*"

I lost all control and began attacking with a torrent of kicks, fists, and drawing blood as my nails scraped across his skin in my seething tirade. I kicked his groin hard enough that he stumbled, and I was able to push him to the ground as I continued my attack, but the smile never left his face, even as he writhed in pain.

"I hate you!" I panted while kicking him again and again while he was down, then dropped to my knees, straddling him and punching him, over and over.

He blocked most of my swings, then grasped my hips, holding me in place on top of him. "I quite miss this." He dug his fingers into my hips, his strong grip sure to leave bruised handprints behind. "Oh, gonna have to explain those now, too." He threw his head back and laughed again.

I swung and landed a hit right across his face—a perfect shot.

His grip on my hips disappeared as he brought his arms up to block his face.

I landed a second punch, then wailed when pain exploded through my hand. I crumpled to the ground beside him, breathless and heaving, my energy running out.

"Feel better?" he asked.

"No. I hate you. I hate you so much." I moaned, wringing my injured hand.

He slid to a sitting position, draping his arms over his bent knees. "Done now?"

"I hate you," I whispered through coarse breaths, bracing myself with my palms flat on the filthy tile while my heart thundered in my ears.

"No, you don't."

I looked up at him and gasped. "You bastard!"

My attack had torn open the first several buttons of his orange jumpsuit, exposing his chest. I stared at the scar, my experience as a nurse telling me exactly what it was—an ICD device. He was controlling both lives, being put in arrest and resuscitation whenever he wanted to. He wasn't a jumper, but somehow, he and his father had figured something out.

He smirked. "You've always been stubborn. Why can't you just admit it? You and I are drawn to each other for more than just the explosive chemistry." He winked. "We're drawn to each other for a *purpose*."

"No." I shook my head. "I'm not drawn to who you've proven yourself to really be, or Quantym, for that matter."

"I'd love to stay and chat—" He lifted himself from the ground. "—but I have a mistrial to attend with my father. You still want to do this the hard way?"

"I told you! I'll help if you agree to leave me alone afterward!"

He shrugged and walked over to the guard. He mumbled something that sounded like "*Call them*," and the guard nodded once.

The door opened, and he glanced down at me on the floor one last time. "Shame. The hard way is so *painful*."

The door was left open, and he and the guard both left the room.

I waited at the reception desk for over fifteen minutes to get my things returned. I tugged on the collar of my shirt, attempting to hide the mark Jared'd left.

What was I going to tell Sy? My heart broke at the thought. *I'll never deserve him.*

The guard finally appeared and handed over my belongings.

I rifled through my bag before leaving the facility, my energy and hope completely expended as I dug for my keys. I just wanted to go home, shower, and call Sy.

I was going to tell him the truth. He'd understand. That's what he's always said. *Come to me first, I want to be there for you.* He knew I hated Jared, and he knew how stubborn I was. He'd know I only visited Jared to see if he was still involved with Quantym. And given the scar across his chest, the organization was as alive as it'd ever been. Intel that I'm sure Sy and his brothers would want—need—to know.

I finally got my keys in hand and pushed on the double doors, a cold gust greeting me as I freed myself from the grip of the nasty facility. A microphone was thrown in my face, and I gasped, lurching backward against the door that'd closed behind me as chaos ensued.

A crowd formed around me, closing in faster than I could make my way to an escape.

"Mrs. Cardoza! Mrs. Cardoza! Will you give a statement?" A journalist leaned into my space, elbowing the other reporters to maintain his position.

I turned my face, and jerked the collar of my shirt over my neck.

I was bounced into another reporter. "Mrs. Cardoza, do you support the allegations that Adam was a victim of an unauthorized mental-health program?"

"Stop, please, let me by." My voice was drowned out by the flurry of news reporters. Cameras and microphones and voices were everywhere I turned. The steady click of cameras and subsequent flashes disoriented me.

You always choose the hard way. Guess I'll just bend the world around us. Again.

"Is it true you're engaged to your late husband's brother?" A female reporter asked.

An older man, his hat indicating the local news, stumbled forward, "Tell us, what did he say? Did you visit today to show your support?"

"Charlotte, are you going to marry him while he's still in jail?" A light on the woman's camera blinked, recording the scene.

Another young woman ambled into my path. "Did he really stab you, or was it a cover-up for something else?"

A middle-aged woman scurried alongside me, throwing the microphone into my face. "Just what is your involvement with the general and his two sons?"

I folded in on myself, jerking my coat up to cover my face. The crowd grew more impatient, bouncing me around like a ping-pong ball, salivating for answers to their questions.

"Move! Give her space!" A loud voice bellowed, and the crowd parted.

I didn't remove my jacket from my head. An arm looped around me and ushered me away from the chaos. Questions were continuously thrown toward me, cameras flashed and clicked, and as I was navigated away, I stumbled on feet that kicked into mine.

"You have a *lot* of explaining to do, Charly." Mitch laughed as he opened my car door for me. He whispered into my ear, "Appearances are *everything*. Thanks for your help in making him an innocent man."

The crowd of reporters closed in again, and I dropped into my driver's seat.

Mitch shut the door, drowning out the shouts of the reporters. He turned to talk with the unrelenting journalists, gaining a moment for me to drive away and escape.

I was beyond screwed. *Please help me,* I begged the universe. *I'll never lie again. I'll make better choices. I'll do anything. Please, help me.*

Ding. My phone chimed. *Ding. Ding. Ding.* Then, it blew up. It rang with a flood of calls and texts. Half the reporters must've been live, and between the news and socials, my secret was out with a capital *O.* I silenced the ringer.

Adrenaline dumped into my system. My life was over. The life I'd built with Sy, my friends, my parents, my co-workers. I was done for. An embarrassment, a shame. And I'd humiliated Sy, undoubtedly hurt the one person I loved the most. He couldn't forgive me, even if he claimed otherwise. There was no coming back from this. Jared was leaving me nowhere to turn but to him and Mitch.

Why wasn't my agreement to help enough? What did he really *want?*

I was undeserving of love or forgiveness. My stupidity brought me to a place of no return, it was all darkness now, like a black hole, sucking in and crushing any ounce of light that dared enter.

I wanted to will myself to disappear, so I brought myself to a place where no one would find me. Not Jared or Mitch or even Sy.

The woods. *My woods.*

Chapter 15, Reality 2: On the Periphery

Jared

Mitch pulled into the back lot of the hospital. It was late, and the place was a ghost town. I lifted Charly from the back seat and carried her inside. Her arms and legs swung loosely as I made my way down the hall with my father striding beside me.

Morgan caught up with me. "All set. Room 298, sir."

I grumbled a laugh. "That won't do. Tie him to a chair in the shooting range."

"Sir?"

"Are you questioning me, Morgan?"

"No, sir. It's just he's—"

"A jumper? I know," I bit out. "Keep him sedated, too. Don't let him wake up."

That stupid Marine was more trouble than he was worth. I didn't feel like wrestling the two-hundred-pound brute if he tried to be a hero. I'd just put a bullet in his skull and really piss off my father for wasting assets.

"Yes, sir." Morgan turned on his heel to set up Simon for the show.

"Two more jumps happening tomorrow. Once we confirm they can do the protocol without her, we can get rid of her, too," my father said.

I nodded and glanced down at an unconscious Charly in my arms.

Nope.

"She's a jumper. Why waste assets?"

My father gave a scornful laugh. "Time to cut overhead. Bad enough I'm keeping the other one until we can make enough of our own."

"It's going to take time to build our own. I have a few clients, small missions I can send her on." I strode into room 300 and placed her on the hospital-like bed.

"Wake her, and let's get this done." Mitch turned and headed in the direction of the shooting range.

I sat on the edge of the bed and pushed her hair from her face.

"Charly," I crooned. "Time to wake up."

She stirred, then rolled to her side.

I sighed and rubbed my eyes. Damn, it was late, and I was beat. We should be home and in bed, tired from a warm meal and a good fuck. I tapped the side of her face, and her eyes fluttered open for just a second, then shut again. I stared at her for a moment, drinking in the soft angles of her face. She was striking, and no amount of time married to her ever dimmed that. Too bad she was a traitor, a liar, insubordinate, and possibly even a cheat. She couldn't hide behind that angelic face, any more than I could hide behind my father's monstrosities.

It's what made us a flawless match.

We were both selfish creatures. Her, hung up on pretending to fight for morality, while being immoral herself. I owned the fact that morality was just another human-made weakness that stopped us from obtaining power and wealth and chose to do as I pleased to get both.

"Charly…" I hummed again, watching her long black lashes flutter.

Her eyes opened wide and she gasped. Her panicked gaze flew around the room, then settled on me. "Jared."

I bit my lip when my name fell from her mouth, like it was as natural to her as breathing. I lowered my face to hers, pinning her arms in place. "Ready for the show?" I smiled.

Her face twisted in horror as she tried to wriggle away, but I tightened my grip. The meds were still doing their job. She was weak, slow to digest my words, and her panicked breaths and blank stare revealed her struggle to comprehend the gravity of the situation.

"Jared, please."

I dropped my face into the crook of her neck, inhaling deeply. "I love it when you beg."

She tried fighting beneath me, and all it did was drag a laugh from my throat.

"It's not what you think," she choked out.

"Oh, but it is. You did this on the other side, too."

Her brow pinched. "What? No, I was—"

"Every lie that drips from those delicious lips, will only guarantee you more pain."

"He was bringing me to the airport, and I was going to stay with my parents! Jared, you *attacked* me! Let me go!"

I paused at her words. I hadn't considered that. Perhaps she wasn't fucking the Marine I'd assigned her to recruit *here*. But assumptions weren't going to get me anywhere. The meds were wearing off, and her strength was coming back. All five feet nothing of her thrashed beneath me.

"Prove it, Charly," I growled.

"You—you were in his car. The ticket, there should only be one. Mine. Look it up!"

"Were your parents expecting you?" Not sure why I was even entertaining the liar.

"No, I was going to show up, and—"

"Sir?" Morgan stepped into the room.

Charly stilled beneath me, her chest rising and falling with heavy breaths.

"The general said it's time."

I nodded. "Morgan, do me a favor. Check—" I glanced down at Charly. "Airline?"

"Southern Lights. The red-eye to Lauderdale." She panted.

"For?"

"Her name, moron. And keep this between us."

"Yes, sir."

I flipped her onto her stomach and pulled a zip tie from my back pocket, securing her hands behind her back. "Time for the show," I purred, pulling her off the bed.

"Wait, let him check, prove that I'm not—"

"Oh, no matter." I waved my hand through the air. "I'm killing him no matter what. *Your* fate lies in what Morgan finds."

I threw the hood back over her head when she started screaming; I was so, so tired of hearing it. It was too late, and I had to be up far too early to have a migraine. She resisted when I started dragging her down the hall, so Morgan joined me, each of us grasping an elbow and dragging her—screaming and flailing— toward the range.

****

My father was a sick man, no question. The setup

couldn't have been better. I entered the range, and an unconscious, bloody, and beaten Simon was tied to a metal chair. Too bad I hadn't been the one to do it. No matter, Charly wouldn't know the difference. And after the show, I was quite sure she'd never be the same again. Pity. Sacrifices were never easy.

I'd been dreaming of getting this revenge ever since the incident in the main reality. The incident where I shot Simon, Charly stabbed me, and I stabbed her. Then, I ended up in jail so Quantym could be covered up. Not just by us, but the government, too. Wouldn't want the populace finding out what they were funding. Typical corruption bullshit I'd been taught about for as long as I could remember.

I wasn't mad that I had to take the fall and end up in jail in the main reality. But what really frosted my ass was that Simon got to take my wife and my father got to maintain his rank and appearances. I'd had to give up my rank when my father had me fake my death and reenlist as Adam. Sacrifices were made, over and over, and only by me. Until now. Now, my wife could share that burden.

Morgan helped me drag Charly into the room. Her flailing had weakened, and her body stiffened. It was a funny thing, what terror could do. One minute you're begging for your life, the next, your cells won't even communicate, and you're forced to watch a crisis through eyes in a frozen body.

Her legs gave out, and she fell to her knees. Her head was slumped, and when Morgan pulled the black hood off her head, her hair was in disarray. She looked up, saw Simon, and shrieked, as I knew she would.

I bent to speak into her ear. "Not long ago—in the main reality—I promised you I was going to kill him and make you watch. Today is that day, Charly."

"Please, don't. He's innocent! He did nothing!" She struggled against her restrained wrists, her gaze darting between me and Simon.

I paused, allowing time for her to take in his appearance. He was unconscious—drugged, but she didn't know that. His chin rested on his chest, and most of his exposed skin was bruised and bloody.

"In the main reality, you love him. Do you love him here too, Charly?"

I pulled the gun from the holster at my leg.

"No! Please don't…Jared, no!" Her voice echoed through the concrete range.

"How good of a shot do you think I am?" I asked my father, drawing out the situation and heightening her fear.

"I'd say first try you get him straight through the skull."

Charly's screaming intensified. She pleaded and begged, leaning into my leg and sobbing the whole time.

Morgan looked down, and I stared at him, waiting to see if his loyalty was as deep as he'd made it out to be. He felt my stare and met my gaze. "I'd say first shot hits the chest, second through the head." He smirked, then stole a glance at my wife.

He had pity for her, and I considered that an infraction. One I'd deal with later.

I looked down at Charly. She was going to pass out, no question. She screamed until it sounded like her throat was going to bleed, her voice hoarse and raw.

I nodded once at my father.

Morgan put the hood back over her head, taking away her vision.

I pulled the trigger, and the gunshot thundered through the concrete range. I shot to the left of Simon's head, and my father kicked his large, unconscious body off the chair. He landed with a thump just inches from Charly's knees.

She screamed and cried, falling forward onto the cement floor when she heard his body drop. "No! No! Oh God, no!" She was going into shock, her body twitching and her voice lowering as she chanted *no, no, no* beside her fallen...*lover? Confidante? Friend*? Whatever he was to her, in her mind he now ceased to exist. And nothing would make me feel bad about that.

She'd never know my father hadn't allowed me to kill him.

He was an asset, after all. A jumper, and those were expensive.

She'd never know the difference.

And what difference was there, really? He'd be tied to a bed, going on missions for Quantym until we didn't need him anymore. He was as good as dead no matter how you sliced it.

I put the gun back into the holster at my leg and pulled Charly to her feet. Her body gave out, so I dragged her all the way back to room 300. She huffed and gasped and panted, and even *my* excitement about the situation was waning. Once the high of getting revenge wore off, I was tired as hell. I wanted to feel bad for her, but my anger wouldn't allow it.

I tossed her onto the bed and removed the hood from her head.

She was pale, clammy, and seconds away from heaving all over the place.

"Do not puke on me, Charly," I warned.

"You're a monster. Evil. Like your father." She said between breaths.

I chuckled. "And *you* are now property of the U.S. Government, under the organization known as Quantym, headed up by none other than yours truly."

I pulled her hair aside, exposing her neck. "Move your head to the side."

"Don't."

She knew the protocol. I pulled out the microchip gun and held it in place at her neck. She cried out when I pulled the trigger, and the GPS microchip was deposited under her skin with a loud snap.

"Wouldn't want to lose assets acquired by the company," I mused.

"What the hell is wrong with you?"

I laughed again. "I quite like you. Being married to you didn't work out, but I'll keep you anyway. Did you know that you're a jumper?"

Her body slackened, hope draining from her faster than water in a paper bucket. "I figured it out."

I leaned down, my lips grazing her cheek. "Liar. Simon told you."

She didn't bother denying it.

By now, I'm sure she figured out I'd had Morgan and Jackson track her and heard her conversation in the woods behind the coffee shop with Simon. It was what landed us in this very situation, after all. I'd have to thank the guys for that intel but hadn't gotten around to it yet.

I stood abruptly when the reader buzzed, and within seconds my father opened the door and came into the room.

I walked over to him.

Mitch didn't spare more than a one-second glance at

Charly.

"It's done. Tomorrow, you have PT at 0600, and we're working on two jumps at eight. If Gustav and Carter can pull it off, we can—" He glanced at the bed and back to me. "—eliminate her, too."

I nodded, but planned on discussing that idea further. It'd be a waste to eliminate her. I didn't want to yet, either. For more than one reason, most of which my father didn't need to know. But if I could sell him on her value, I could keep her long enough to figure out how to get everything I wanted.

"We'll talk," I told him. "I'm tired as hell, and I don't want anyone in here except Morgan or Jackson."

Mitch raised his eyebrows. "Oh?"

"I don't trust anyone but those two. I'll keep the cameras on. She's restrained and chipped. I have a few missions for her, anyway."

"Speaking of Morgan, he told me to give you a message. He said her name wasn't on any of the flights out to Florida."

My heart rate kicked up, heat flaring from my head to my feet.

"Charly?" I whipped my head to look at her.

"He's lying. Mitch, tell him! Jared, look it up right now!"

I sauntered back over to her. "You're a little fucking liar. You were going to run off on me with him, weren't you?"

She struggled uselessly with her arms still restrained behind her back. "No! He's lying! Mitch, you bastard!"

Her voice was so hoarse, I knew every word must hurt. Good.

"I'll tell you what, Charly. I'm not going to kill you.

But I'm not going to let you have what you want. Not here. Not there. I'll keep you tethered to this damn bed until the day you die, old and gray. No chance for your consciousness to live a better life, in another place on any periphery."

She whimpered. "Look it up, Jared! Two seconds is all it takes. Get your phone."

"You're calling my father a liar? Morgan, too? Who the hell do you think you are?" I stood glaring down at her.

She turned her head to the side and squeezed her eyes shut. Dead giveaway for a liar, she wasn't even trying to convince me anymore.

"Get on with it, Jared. You're going to be woken soon, and you have a big week ahead." My father rubbed his temples impatiently.

She whipped her head over and looked up at me. "Woken? You're…from the main reality? Is this why…" Her voice trailed off, her eyes clouding as she put the pieces in place.

"I'm both. Turns out while you were doing your research to navigate the peripheries, we were learning that jumpers could be built. I'm remembering, Charly. Everything from there, to here. It's like I'm two people in one."

"The side effects. Inhibition control, anger…" She spoke to herself.

I wasn't surprised she knew it was possible, and I wasn't surprised she hadn't told me. Building jumpers, because of the side effects, was probably another one of her moral hard-stops. She'd never want the tech used. Too bad it wasn't her choice to make.

She looked up at me. "I don't know what's

happening in the main reality, but do you really think it's fair to punish me for something I have no control over?"

I cocked my head to the side. "Oh, there was a lot of …intent in your behaviors. You even *stabbed* me over there." I snickered. "The bleed-through caused you to be a traitor here, too, didn't it?"

"Instead of telling her about it, why not show her instead?" my father said from behind me. "Traitors should be shown the error of their ways. She was cheating on you, Jared." He walked up beside me. "Show her. In both lives, she betrayed you."

My father's words stoked the flames of anger in me, turning the embers into a raging inferno. "Brilliant," I whispered. "Instead of relying on the bleed-through to confirm or deny what you've done, why don't I just show you?"

She sucked in a loud breath. "No," she growled. "I've never cheated. If you send me backward, I'll die there."

"Not right away, you won't. First—" I dragged a finger down her cheek. "—you'll go crazy. Then, you'll die. It's the perfect plan—now, he can't have you, and you can learn everything I know, too."

I turned to my father. "Get the device."

He nodded, and left the room.

"If you're wrong, Jared?" she asked.

I looked down at her. "I'm not."

If I was wrong, I'd put a bullet in my own skull. I was torturing her, but it was for a good reason. My training rendered me capable of pushing emotion aside for moments like this. I trusted Morgan and my father. They had no reason to see her tortured. They wouldn't lie about her betrayal. I leaned down and pressed my lips to hers. I could taste the delicious fear on her, and it sent a thrill through my body. She'd probably do absolutely anything to stop me from doing what I planned to do.

As I pulled away, she spit in my face.

I wiped it with a sleeve. "Brave. Let's see how long you can hold onto that nerve."

"You're making a mistake. Don't do this." Her chest rose and fell, faster and faster with her waning courage.

The lie about staying with her parents was the final straw. She wanted to leave me for that sonofabitch *there and here*? I'd make sure they weren't together no matter what life they were in.

My father returned with the cart holding Gustav's banned device—the AED that would shock her backward, to the main reality. Once she was there, she'd have a mental breakdown, robbing her of her life there completely. Once I brought her back here, she'd be fine, except, because she was a jumper, she'd have all the memories from *there and here*. The perfect torture. To know what was taken from you in both lives.

Her eyes lit with terror, and she thrashed uselessly.

I cut the zip ties from her hands, then fastened the four-point cloth restraints, tethering her to the bed. I ripped her shirt open, and placed the wired AED stickers into position on her chest. Her begging fell on deaf ears.

Today, she was going to be like me in more ways than one. First, I let her know the pain of sacrifice when I pretended to shoot Simon, and now, I'd let her see what it was like to live in one life with the knowledge of two. *Just. Like. Me.*

It didn't break my heart that she'd be incapacitated over there. She'd visited me in jail there, told me she married Simon, flaunted her ring. That was a painful memory I had to live with whether I was there or here, now that my memories were becoming stronger, more permanent. Her marriage announcement was a kick in the gut, just as she'd intended it to be. Now, here, in reality two, I could make her atone for all her sins in both lives.

"Don't," she begged.

I leaned down to whisper one word while holding her desperate gaze. "Clear."

The AED fired twice, programmed to deliver the shocks at specific intervals that would send her into a fatal arrythmia and back to the main reality. I looked at my watch. She wasn't intubated, so I had to be mindful of time so I didn't render her brain-dead.

I covered her mouth with mine and puffed a breath into her lungs, then started compressions.

My breath was keeping her alive, and I reveled in the heady feel of that.

I glanced at my watch again, leaving enough time for her consciousness to go back and collect nearly *all* her memories from that life, before I brought her back.

I puffed another breath into her lungs, her chest rising and falling with my breath, then started compressions again.

Finally, I stood and hit the button on the AED.

Her body bowed off the bed with the shock.

I brought my fingers to her neck, feeling a thready pulse. "She's back," I crooned.

She moved her head side to side, and her lashes fluttered. Her eyes opened, barely focusing on me standing over her.

I leaned down, dragging my lips across her cheek. "What did you see, Charly?"

She blinked rapidly, and tears escaped from the outside corner of her eyes, disappearing into her dark hair. Her green eyes were dull, lackluster, and her voice was no different when she finally answered me. "Everything," she whispered.

Without another word, I ripped the AED patches off her, and to my surprise, she didn't react.

She stared unseeing at the ceiling, her eyes glazed, her spirit broken.

Something in my chest constricted. A foreign, strange feeling. Maybe all the jumps were taking a toll on *me*.

My father wheeled the AED device out of the room without a word.

I turned to leave, allowing her the night to sift through the memories burned into her from the main reality and here. I badged the door open, and ensured it locked behind me. I slipped my cell from my pocket, to double-check the cameras were on.

Before I could access the cameras, I noticed a text. I clicked it open and stopped my stride, pulling in a deep breath. It was a text from Morgan. A screenshot. I stared at the itinerary showing Charlotte Cardoza booked on the red-eye to Lauderdale—alone—just as she'd said.

I tried dragging in another breath, but my chest was too tight, the pain too severe. I stumbled over to the edge of the hall, resting my sweaty palm flat on the wall for support.

The pain and pressure increased to an intolerable point, and my attempts at breathing became useless. It finally became clear what was happening.

A heart attack. I was having a fucking heart attack.

Chapter 16, Reality 1

Charlotte

I parked my car on the small, dirt road next to my childhood home in Massachusetts. It'd only been a thirty-minute ride, and my phone was alight with dozens of calls and texts. I'd silenced the ringer but could see the notifications piling up.

By now, I was sure my friends, family, co-workers, and Sy and his family had seen me on the news leaving the jail with a three-inch hickey on my neck, escorted through the crowd by a deceitfully tender Mitch. *Holy crap, that looked bad.*

I was dizzy with shame, and Jared was behind it all. I thought I could visit him, determine if Quantym was still running and escape with that intel. But I never walked away from Jared unscathed, and this time was no different. He would ruin me, and no matter how much I resisted, how much I ran, it was just an inevitability.

I exited my car, stuffed my phone into my pocket, and headed straight into the woods. Maybe I'd be attacked by a bear or eaten by a coyote. All better options and a more dignified death than what awaited me if I faced the consequences of today. I couldn't bear the loss of Sy, or the look of pity on my friends' faces. I was disappointed in myself, and I was determined to hide. Even if just to pull myself together for a few hours.

It wasn't easy trudging through the woods that used to be my second home as a kid. The briars and prickers had grown over, and they pulled at my scrubs and scraped my skin as I clomped deeper into the darkening forest.

Soon, I arrived at the creek, and the moss-covered tree-bridge was still there, just as I remembered. Several meters away, I found my tree, the one with the papasan-chair-like divot in the middle. I climbed the tree and settled into the hollow, allowing the tree to embrace me. It was more than what'd happened at the jail, and with the media. My soul was aware something was coming—something big. Something insurmountable, a tragedy so big, it warranted tears before it even arrived. It was like the earth was pulsing with the energy of this event, injecting awareness into my veins, allowing me to grieve before the loss.

I hugged myself into a ball, and I wasn't surprised when I heard Jared's faraway voice.

Not long ago—in the main reality—I promised you I was going to kill him and make you watch. Today is that day, Charly.

I couldn't hear my own voice answer, but I answered in my head. *No. Please, don't.* I knew that was some variation of what I'd say, and now I was out of time. This was happening, somewhere on the Periphery.

Somewhere, Jared was the thing of nightmares. Everywhere, Jared was the thing of nightmares.

In the main reality, you love him. Do you love him here, too Charly?

"Yes, I do," I whispered out loud, allowing the universe to hear the truth. It's not how I'd answer on the Periphery. No, I'd deny it there, escape him eventually, find Sy and live happily ever after if I allowed myself to dream that life was fair.

The sun dipped lower in the sky, the air colder, and I hugged myself tighter. I pulled my sleeves over my hands, and jerked the fleece coat collar up to cover my cold ears. I closed my eyes and prayed for strength, a miracle, or some variation of both. Somewhere between the tears, the cold, and my prayers, I passed out.

"Charlotte!"

Voices called my name, over and over again. When I opened my eyes, the forest was dark, the air so cold each breath created a cloud in front of my face. I shivered, then heard Sy call my name again.

"Charlotte!"

A man's voice called out to him. "Sy, over here!"

Was that…Jeff's voice?

"Her cell is within meters, she's close."

Definitely Jeff's voice. They'd tracked my cell.

I sat up, and slid from my spot in the tree. The truth. I would tell them all the truth. *The truth would set me free.*

"Sy!" I called out. "Sy, I'm here." My legs were numb from the position I'd been in, and I stumbled through the trees and over the roots, branches, and briars.

"Charlotte!"

His voice was getting closer. Their footsteps sounded just a few feet away.

"I'm here." I pushed through evergreens and empty branches, my feet crunching through the fallen leaves.

Sy emerged from behind a large pine, and I stared at his striking blue eyes as he closed in.

Suddenly, the crown of my head went numb, and my legs wobbled beneath me. "Sy," I croaked.

My vision blurred, and a fuzzy image of Jared standing over me appeared, causing me to inhale a loud gasp of breath.

"Charlotte, are you okay?" Sy ran the rest of the way toward me.

I grasped his shirt, fisting the fabric in my hands as my knees gave out, and I saw the forest through new eyes.

A rush of memories hit me so hard, my breath was stolen from my lungs. I imagined it was what one sees before the true, final end, when they die at an old age. A total life review, but this review was foreign to me. It was me, but different choices, different minutiae; it was me, but not *me here*. It was my life—on the Periphery.

A strangled sob released from my parted lips, a puff of mist forming from my warm breath released into the cold air. My grip released on Sy's shirt, and I collapsed into his arms.

The last thing I heard was Simon calling my name.

Such a beautiful man, with a beautiful voice, calling me. But he was too far away.

Because now, there was nothing.

Nothing but numbers.

Chapter 17, Reality 1

Simon

"Charlotte!" I called out, my voice echoing in the rapidly darkening forest.

The panic made my voice unrecognizable. Something was wrong. First, she'd gone missing after appearing on the news, outside the prison with Mitch. Then she didn't answer calls from anyone, including me. Hours passed, and by nightfall, there was nothing that would calm me until I found her. *I just had to find her*. The rest I'd deal with later. As long as I found her, everything would be okay.

I was lucky Jeff was able to get in touch with Jay, who walked him through using his tech to ping her phone. It's not something I'd have normally condoned, but given the circumstances, and the fact that I was beyond certain something was gravely wrong, I insisted we do whatever it took to find her.

Now, as I mazed my way through the woods near her childhood home, I prepared myself. Whatever the outcome, Jared and Mitch were going to die, and by my hand. I could only hope and pray she was alive, unlike the recurring dreams that'd been haunting me. The dream always ended the same—her cold, lifeless body, left for me to find, lying beside a creek. Then, I'd hold her and scream and beg the universe for her back. But this wasn't a dream, it was a nightmare, and I wouldn't let it end the way the dreams did. If I had to rip the fabric of the sky in half, I wouldn't let it end that way. Not while I was alive.

No one could call me a weak man. I'd faced death more times than I cared to count; I'd faced injuries that'd bring a grown man to his knees with a stoic face and determined heart. But here, in this cold dark forest, each time I shouted her name and silence followed, I was certain it was the one thing that could break me. I'd once told her she'd be my undoing, but what I didn't tell her was it wasn't finding her that would do it. It was losing her that would.

"Sy!"

Her voice was a lullaby, soothing my panic as I picked up pace toward her. I called her name again, nearly falling to my knees with relief when she responded.

"Sy! I'm here!" She was ducking under a low-hanging branch. Her speed picked up when our gazes met, and her feet shifted like she was ready to full-on sprint into my arms.

I stalked forward, relief running through me so powerful I was nearly high off the feeling. I kept my eyes locked on hers. My arms were ready to catch her; she was so close I could smell her vanilla shampoo.

A heartbeat later, her body jerked, as if she'd hit an invisible glass wall. "Sy," her voice was weaker, my name almost a plea as it fell from her lips.

She stumbled into my chest as I called her name over and over, but her jade eyes were glazed, her vision unseeing, her face indicating she could no longer hear my voice. Her delicate hands fisted my shirt, and I crushed her into me as her knees gave out.

A strangled gasp left her lips.

Jeff ran up behind me. "Sy! What happened?"

I continued calling her name, over and over and over.

It won't end like this. If I had to strike a deal with the heavens, or experience the pain and death of every enemy I'd ever sniped, I wouldn't let it end like this. I'd drink all the blood I'd spilled. I'd willingly step into the depths of hell and stay there so she could live, but *I wouldn't let it end like this.*

Shit, what was even happening?

I turned to look at Jeff. "Something's wrong. I found her, then she…"

She what?

I swung her up and into my arms, but then she began to thrash and wail.

"Charlotte, it's okay, I'm here. Charl—"

She kicked and thrashed, screaming and grunting in a voice that wasn't hers.

"Put her down, Sy. Maybe she's hurt." Jeff stepped beside us, his hand reaching out to console her.

I slowly lowered her to the forest floor.

She swiftly rolled to her side, then sat up on her knees, and began digging furiously through the leaves without looking up. Her dark hair hung around her face, swinging loosely as she dug and dug, searching for something.

Jeff and I squatted beside her.

She didn't acknowledge our presence or our voices when we spoke.

"Charlotte! Stop, look at me!" I tried grasping her arms, and she immediately shrugged away with a loud grumble.

She continued to dig through the leaves, crawling until she grasped a small branch. A small sigh escaped her lips, then she used both hands to clear a spot on the forest floor. With the stick, she began to write in the dirt.

Jeff stood and slanted his head. "It looks like...numbers?" He glanced at me then back to Charlotte.

"Charlotte, what is it?" I spoke softly.

She didn't answer, but continued using the branch to write in the dirt.

Jeff turned on his cellphone flashlight, illuminating what looked to be an equation she was drawing into the forest floor.

"Okay, Sy. We're gonna have to get her out of here. She needs help." He snapped a photo of the numbers she continued to write into the ground.

I nodded once. "I'm sorry love, but I have to get you home. I'm going to carry you."

She didn't respond.

I swooped her into my arms, and she began to thrash and squirm, her agitation heightening as we made our way back toward the car. By the time we reached the edge of the woods, she was full-on screaming.

"Aw hell, man. What happened to her?" Jeff looked at Charlotte with a furrowed brow.

"I don't know, but I can tell you, I'm going to kill them. Whatever this is, happened after she saw *him*."

"You think he drugged her?"

Good point, I hadn't thought of that. My brain wasn't firing adeptly, not with her in such a state. I'd been able to function with a broken back and under the duress of a terrorist attack, but with Charlotte screaming,

I could barely formulate a sentence. I just wanted to make her better, bring her back.

I shrugged. "Let's get her to the hospital. If you plan on driving any slower than ninety, let me drive."

"I got it, man. Just try to keep her calm." Jeff pulled out the keys and slid into the driver's seat.

I got into the back seat with her, then pointed to the console.

"Get a pen and paper from in there," I directed Jeff.

I tried speaking to her, but it was no use.

She was too far gone, her eyes were clouded, her body agitated to a point of no return.

Jeff rifled around and finally handed me a pen and paper.

As soon as I handed them to Charlotte, she quieted, quickly scribbling numbers over the paper.

We pulled up to the emergency room, and before Jeff even stopped the car, I was swinging the back door open and hauling her inside in my arms.

She rested the paper against my chest, continuing to write numbers—nonsense—all over the page.

Three hours later, I found myself sitting in the vinyl visitor chair in a private room in the ER, staring at my wife scribbling numbers all over the crinkly white table paper the nurse had provided her with to calm her.

She'd already filled half the roll with the jargon.

The used, written-on half was crumpled in a heap and almost spanned the length of the room.

She was on her hands and knees, and until the results of her tox screen came back, I wasn't willing to allow them to sedate her.

She didn't respond to me, the doctors, or the nurses. I hadn't let Jeff come in, instead I told him to get rest and

I'd keep in touch. When I'd been asked to change her into a hospital johnny, I was glad for that, and nearly lost all control when I saw the mark on her neck and handprints on her hips.

What the hell happened? Didn't matter, really. Jared and his father were going to die.

Whatever happened, Jared was behind it, and Charlotte fell into whatever trap had been laid. I didn't need to question her motives or intent, I was two-hundred percent certain those marks were left against her will. But I didn't have confidence that she'd know in advance my trust in her. She could be her own worst enemy at times, and nothing I said or did was ever enough to save her from herself.

"Mr. Donovan." A young doctor entered and shook my hand. "How long has she been like this?"

"No more than four hours," I replied, sliding to the edge of my seat to touch her shoulder.

She immediately shrugged away from my touch.

"The good news, is her toxicology reports are negative. So, I'd like to sedate her now, allow her some rest. Then you and I can talk."

I nodded. "I'll get her on the bed."

I squatted beside her. "Charlotte, come here, love." I pulled her against me, and damn if my heart didn't break when she struggled to get free. I held her tighter, swinging her legs over my arms to carry her to the hospital bed.

"I'm going to give her an injection to calm her, then we can have the nurse come in to start the IV."

I placed her on the bed as she wriggled and groaned, trying to get back to the paper on the floor.

The doctor walked up to the other side of the bed,

and I pinned her arms down, bringing my face to hers. I looked into her unseeing eyes, murmuring that I was there, that she was going to be okay, that it'd all be figured out soon. I could only hope I wasn't lying to her.

Her body loosened after the doctor finished pushing the plunger of the syringe and depositing the sedative into her.

Her eyes rolled, glazing over before they fluttered shut. Her breathing slowed, coming in soft, regular breaths, like when she was sleeping peacefully at home and in my arms.

I stepped away from the bed and slumped into the seat beside it. It took all my strength to continue to feed my lungs deep breaths of the thick air that refused to calm my need to kill Jared. I wanted him dead, *now*. I grasped the edges of the chair, veins protruding from my arms under the strain.

Two nurses came in, and began bustling around my wife, hanging bags from IV poles and attaching wires and electrodes and monitors to various parts of her.

"Sir, I'd like to first discuss her test results and history." The doctor's voice broke me out of my thoughts, and I turned away from Charlotte to face him.

I nodded.

He stared at my hands grasping the chair, before speaking again.

Try as I might, I couldn't release my grip. If I did, someone was going to die.

"The good news, is that all her results are normal. Her head CT is stable, her lumbar puncture doesn't indicate any kind of infectious or inflammatory brain condition. Her labs and tox screen are all normal, too."

I waited for the bad news while holding my breath.

"The unfortunate news, is that I don't know what is causing her altered mental status. We'll keep her for a few days for observation, and—"

I pinched my thumb and forefinger on the bridge of my nose. "But you have an idea."

"Well, we'll know better—"

My hands flew back to the armrests of the chair, gripping it until the wood cracked audibly.

The doctor sighed. "She has an extensive medical history, Mr. Donovan. The accident left her with a brain injury years ago, and—"

"A brain injury." I shook my head. "She's fucking brilliant."

"Just because it resulted in the rarest manifestation—savant syndrome—doesn't make it any less of a traumatic brain injury. And the unfortunate thing about head injuries is how unpredictable they can be. Some resolve spontaneously, even years later. Others *worsen* inexplicably, years later."

I shook my head. "Fix her. I don't care what it costs, or what it takes, fix her," I growled.

"I'm going to do my best. Be patient, and we'll figure this out. You're a Marine, yeah? Me, too. We got into this because we're not afraid of a challenge. I don't give up easily."

I nodded, the doctor gaining some of my respect. His words rang true. We didn't give up easily, as long as our hearts were beating, we didn't give up. And, even then…

"Her case is complex. I'll consult with some of my colleagues tomorrow. Tonight, you and she need to rest. Maybe we'll have more answers tomorrow."

After the doctor left the room, I lowered the bed rail and slid onto the bed beside Charlotte. I pulled her small frame into my arms. Before drifting away, I sent a plea out to the universe.

Help me fix this. Show me how to fix this. I cannot lose her. I'll do anything. Anything.

****

Two weeks passed, and her condition hadn't improved. Over the course of two weeks, I'd fielded visits from her co-workers, parents, friends—all who had questions that I had no answers to. By now, everyone—including her medical team—had seen her on the news and come to their own conclusions about what led up to her mental breakdown.

I didn't care. The trial was underway, and I already knew a mistrial was looming. Another systemic manipulation by the Cardozas. I wasn't fazed. Both were dead men, as far as I was concerned. Jared would be out of jail soon, and that didn't bother me—it'd be easier to kill him on the outside, anyway. Their deaths were a simple certainty, so I focused all my efforts and attention on Charlotte.

After her parents returned to Florida and the visits died down, I was asked to make arrangements to have her transferred to a long-term care facility.

Cedarwood Bay Home wasn't a bad place—I'd been there before to visit Jared's mother when we were gathering intel about Adam and Jared Cardoza, long before I'd placed myself into Charlotte's life. I wasn't thrilled they'd be at the same facility, but I was able to ensure they were kept in completely separate wings. Here in the smallest state in the country, our options for long-term care were limited, and it was going to be a temporary stay, anyway. At least until we could figure out what was wrong and how to fix it.

After getting her settled in and hauling a case of butcher paper into her room, I opened a box of black markers for her. She kneeled beside me, unaware of my presence as she grabbed a marker from the box and unrolled the paper, beginning a long day of writing her numbers.

I stood and stared at her. She was a shell, locked inside of herself and unaware of the outside world as she wrote. I took note that her writing wasn't going from left to right, rather, the equation was being written from *right to left*. Backward. Odd. I took out my phone and snapped a photo of the paper containing her numbers.

I squatted beside her and scooped her hair into a ponytail, clearing it from her face so she could work. "I'll be back soon, Charlotte. I'm going home to take a shower and get a few more of your things, okay?" I foolishly waited for a response.

She continued her torrent of... *numbers, math, nonsense?*

"Do you want me to get you anything?" Another pause followed, punctuated only by the sound of her marker squeaking along the paper as she continued to write.

"I love you." I leaned in and kissed her forehead, my eyes closing when my lips connected with her soft skin. She smelled of vanilla and honey.

I tore myself away from her, and left the facility. As I headed home, my cell rang. It was Becca Diogo.

"Hey, Donovan. I heard about Charlotte from Joel. How is she?"

I drew in a breath, my fist tightening around the steering wheel. "Same."

"I'm sorry, man. Listen, I'm up at Fort Dix. They've

transferred a lot of us out of Virginia. Mind if I come see her?"

"When were you thinking?

"This weekend, I'm off. Maybe I can try talking to her or something?"

"She's been transferred to Cedarwood Bay Home."

"Listen, I know this is tough, but I've seen her in action. Don't underestimate her. She's gonna be okay."

Her words were a balm. Not many knew the tenacity of my wife. She hid it well under her slight exterior. "Thanks, Diogo. Any new intel?"

"Maybe. You know he's going for a mistrial, right?"

"Good. Easier to kill him when he's out, anyway."

"Figured you'd say that. But there's more. We didn't shut them down, we just slowed them. They're still up to their shit. Got my hands on some financial records. Investors, especially those in the government, are still funneling money to an offshore account. I got a hit the other day, so Joel, Jay, and I cracked in to see where money was being withdrawn from."

I raised my eyebrows. "Where?"

"Right there in Rhode Island."

I blew out my breath. "Dammit!"

"Donovan, I don't think the main operation was just in Virginia. I think they've got facilities on bases all over the states. Anyway, there's still the team from when we infiltrated in Virginia. It's bigger now, more organized, more set on clearing the corruption."

"Clearing?"

"Well, yeah. The team is more set on...commandeering the tech rather than trying to eliminate it now. They want to regulate it. Eliminating it has proven to be an upstream battle. One we aren't going to win."

I wasn't surprised. "Thanks, Diogo. I guess now I know what I have to do."

"What's that?"

"Pay my commanding officer a visit. I want in on the team. If it's going to be regulated, re-formed under new command, they're going to need soldiers who know what the hell this is all about."

"Hell yeah, they are." She couldn't hide the excitement in her voice. "I'll see you this weekend, Donovan. Don't go killing anyone without me."

I hung up just as I was pulling into the driveway, my eyes hardening as I stared at Charlotte's car that I'd had towed and parked in front of the garage.

Whatever it took, even if it meant re-enlisting, killing, or becoming the leader of Quantym myself—I was going to bring her home, intact both physically and mentally.

And with that thought, I stomped on the gas, floored it out of the driveway, and headed back toward Newport Base, ready to sign my life over.

Again.

Chapter 18, Reality 2: On the Periphery

Jared

"LT? You alright? I got your text." Morgan ran the rest of the way toward me with Rogers following close behind.

I'd texted him to meet me outside room 300 discreetly and with a medic. They'd undoubtedly thought it was for my wife, so I wasn't surprised when they both approached my sweating, slumped form on the floor beside the closed door with wide eyes.

"I think it's—" I put a fist over my chest, and both men pulled me off the ground.

"Save your energy, we got you, man." Morgan stared straight ahead as they hauled me to the MTF wing.

After several hours and reassuring test results, I was given a diagnosis of a panic attack. Morgan reassured me of their discretion, and I took it as an opportunity to lay into his ass for the text.

I fisted the collar of his uniform and dragged his face close to mine as I lay on the stretcher. "Why did you lie to my father about Charly's flight?"

He resisted, pulling his chin back. "I didn't say anything! That's why I texted you!"

I released my grip on him and he stumbled back.

"The cameras." I groaned. I was two hours away from having to show up for PT, and I hadn't slept at all yet.

"What happened with your wife?" Rogers approached the bed.

Bad move.

"None of your damn business, Rogers," I bit out, flying into a sitting position.

He backed up, his fat ass stumbling into the medical tray behind him.

I sucked in a breath when the pressure returned to my chest. "Give me more." I nodded at the sedative tablets he'd given me to snap me out of what'd felt like a heart attack.

He handed me the bottle of pills and I tossed one under my tongue. I swung my legs over the side of the stretcher and stood, stuffing the bottle into my pocket.

"Did you kill her?" Morgan asked, holding my gaze. His throat bobbed.

I stared at him, sauntering over to him slowly. "Why does it matter to you?"

He shrugged. "Did you?"

"Not yet. Your assignment is to ensure no one, and I mean absolutely *no one* other than me, goes into room 300. Got it?"

"Yes, sir."

Rogers watched the exchange with a ramrod-straight back, and nodded his acknowledgement of my statement.

I left the MTF, and headed back into room 300.

Charly looked over when I entered, and when she saw me, she quickly turned her head away toward the wall. Her arms and legs were still strapped into the cloth restraints, and her torn shirt was hanging open, revealing her full breasts in a lacy black bra. The AED had left angry red patterns where they'd been attached to her chest.

Now that my rage had subsided, I chided myself for leaving her like that. There were more than a few men who had access to the cameras, and I'd left my most prized possession exposed for any one of them to fantasize to.

I'd be sure to limit who had access as soon as I got some sleep.

I unfastened the restraints and pulled her ripped shirt back together to cover her.

She didn't speak or look at me.

"You'll feel better after sleeping." I wasn't sure why I said that, but I wanted her to look at me. "The memories won't ever go away, but they'll fade. This is your life now. No use dwelling on what was."

She stared at the wall, unblinking.

I pulled the pills from my pocket. She needed rest. I took a small tablet and pushed my finger into her mouth, pressing the pill under her tongue. "It'll help you sleep."

Her throat worked, taking what little solace I could offer in the form of drugs.

"I won't restrain you, in case you need the bathroom." I nodded in the direction of the bathroom attached to the room. "But if you try anything stupid, you'll lose that privilege."

She didn't respond, so I left the room, ensuring it locked behind me. I wasn't sure what my plan was just yet, but after a few hours of sleep, and a meeting with my father, I was certain I'd figure it all out. Mitch wanted her eliminated.

And I had no idea what I wanted.

****

A few weeks passed, and Doctors Gustav and Carter still couldn't pull off the protocol on their own.

When Mitch would get Charly from the room, she'd help, wordlessly and mechanically, before being shut back into the room that'd become her cell.

I tried to keep a distance from her during those missions. Something burned behind her aurora-colored eyes that scorched my soul, but after the facility cleared out at night, I'd go see her.

She'd rarely respond to me, and tonight was no different.

I stared down at her, untethered but lying still on the bed as if she was anyway. Her ribs were visible beneath her shirt now.

"Starving yourself?" I raised an eyebrow and perched on the edge of her bed.

The staff had been documenting the food and drinks they'd been bringing in, and now I had them documenting what they were taking out, too.

She'd barely touch a thing most days.

"That last jump you helped with, the client is a former president, you know. He's hired us so a jumper can find a life where he hasn't run for election yet." I laughed. "He knows how to build a following, I'll give him that. He lost re-election, so he wants to try again…elsewhere. Start over."

She stared at the ceiling, and silence descended upon us when I stopped speaking.

"I, for one, believe in second chances. That's what most of our clients are buying from us. A second chance. Can't fault anyone for wanting that."

She didn't move, didn't even blink. She remained still, emotionless.

"I know what you're thinking—that our alternate consciousnesses live there, and I should care more. But let me tell you a secret." I leaned down to whisper in her ear. "Those of us who help put people in power are the most powerful of all. Everyone knows who they owe their life to, and they don't forget that."

She finally blinked.

I sighed. "You're more trouble than you're worth, you know." I tipped my head back and stared at the ceiling, unsure of what I was even expecting. After Gustav and Carter were able to send jumpers to all the peripheries, I'd be ordered to eliminate her. My chest tightened at the thought.

A slight movement, and I looked down to see her head loll toward me.

"What day is it?"

I stilled at the sound of her voice. "It's November twenty-seventh. Yesterday was Thanksgiving. Why?"

She shrugged, then turned away again.

I stared at her while absently rubbing my chest, an ill attempt to ease the pain there. "Why did you want to know the day?" I asked through gritted teeth.

She swallowed, her throat working with the effort. "My parents…"

I sighed. "Don't worry about them. We've got your voice down pat with an AI program. You've spoken with them, wished them a happy holiday. You told them you couldn't attend their gathering since you were hosting at our house this year." A rare pang of regret stabbed me in the gut.

She nodded as a look of relief combined with hopelessness settled over her face.

"Do you want to die?" I held my breath while the

silence stretched on.

She shrugged again. "Doesn't matter. It's the same everywhere. You told me—"

"Ah, yes." I nodded. She was referring to what I'd told her in the main reality, when she visited me in jail. *You'll never escape me.* "You should be more grateful."

The bed shook when she released a scornful laugh.

I continued to stare at her, surprised she'd finally given up on the silent treatment.

"For?"

Wow. Really talking today.

"All the things I'm capable of, and I've yet to *really* hurt you." The words felt like acid in my mouth.

Her head turned toward me slowly. "You've got to be kidding me, right?"

I waved my hand. "Oh, I'm not saying I've gone easy on you. But physically…"

"I'd rather you have tortured me physically." She pressed her lips into a tight line, steeling herself.

I smirked. "I still can, if that's what you're into."

She didn't laugh.

"You found out he lied. I can see it in your face." She still stared at the ceiling.

Dull pain gnawed inside my chest as I reached out and trapped a lock of her hair between my fingers, twirling it as I spoke. "Doesn't change anything. You're only useful to us until Gustav and Carter can pull off the protocol, and that day is closing in soon."

So maybe she didn't lie about going to her parents, but the intent was the same. She thought she could leave me in the night, with Donovan giving her a ride to escape to the airport. No matter how you cut it, she was a pretentious defector. What happened to vows? Loyalty?

Respect? She thought herself better, yet her actions proved her no better than any other traitor.

"Yes, it is. I barely even helped them today."

I shifted my leg under my knee and scooted farther onto her bed. "Tell me, Charly, why so talkative today?"

"You've got the psychology degree, why don't you tell me?"

I clicked my tongue and sighed, suppressing the urge to chide her for her disrespect. I was projecting all my anger toward her, though she was only responsible for some of it. "So many possibilities. Humans aren't meant to be isolated as much as, well, as much as you are right now. So maybe you just need connection. Then, there's Stockholm Syndrome, or even the possibility that you're trying to decide whether or not you want to kill yourself. If so, you're trying to determine the benefits, if any." I twirled her hair around my finger, the softness of it sliding through and around my rough fingers as I spoke my thoughts out loud.

She blinked rapidly, but didn't speak.

I leaned down, bringing my face to hers. "So, which is it?"

She stared at the ceiling, refusing to meet my gaze.

I grasped her face into my hand tightly, forcing a whimper from her lips.

"Answer me," I growled.

She refocused her eyes away from the ceiling, and onto mine. "Do it for me."

I released her and inhaled sharply at her words. *She was asking me to kill her.*

"Afraid of tainting that pure little soul of yours? You think if you do it, you'll go to hell after the seventh periphery?" I laughed mockingly.

Her eyes hardened, and she pressed her lips together, ending the conversation.

"Tell you what, Charly. You continue to not eat, and I'll have Carter stuff an NG tube down your throat to feed you. I hear it's *very* painful."

Her chest rose and fell harshly with her quickened breath, whether from fear or anger, I couldn't tell.

"Coward."

In a second, my gun was pressed under her jaw, the metal biting into her soft skin.

"Is this what you want? Is it?" I was shouting now, standing over her breathing heavily while my chest constricted and the pain mounted.

Say no. Say fucking NO.

She closed her eyes. "Such a damn coward."

I pulled the gun away and stuffed it back into the holster at my leg, then turned and left the room before I could do something stupid. I popped a pill under my tongue, desperate to stop the crushing pain in my chest. That woman was going to be the death of me, so I'd have to eliminate her first. As soon as the protocol was cracked and the others could do it without her, she'd get her wish.

****

Two days later, once they'd been woken from their mission, we confirmed Carter and Gustav were able to get three jumpers to the fifth periphery without Charly's assistance.

One jumper, a young man, was awake and being interviewed by Doctor Gustav about intel he'd garnered from the fifth reality. His story aligned with that of the other two who'd awakened, confirming where he'd been by providing details we'd mapped out—who the president was in that reality, which certain social, civil, and financial events had taken place, and where a particular client was residing, and with whom.

My father met my gaze over the jumper's bed. Deep creases trailed from the corner of his eyes. He was a force, and his cold, black eyes told me he was about to say something I wasn't going to like.

"We need to confirm they can get jumpers to the seventh periphery."

I narrowed my eyes at him. "No one, not even Charly, has been able to get anyone there yet. If it goes bad, we lose them."

He shrugged, sauntering over to me. "Have them try it on her."

I steeled myself and stared at him. "Why her?"

"She'll be able to confirm if they get her there or not, by process of elimination. She knows the maps of the other peripheries. This one will be new, unknown. She'll know if they did it correctly or not."

"She could lie."

"She won't. It's not something she does often, and I'm surprised you don't know that."

I balked at the dig, his reference to his lie about the flight. We hadn't spoken of it, but his words just now told me he knew that I knew.

"And," he continued, "if they screw it up, it's only one loss. A loss we were planning on, anyway." He lifted his chin, challenging me.

"I'll talk to her tonight. Ensure she knows what's at stake if she lies, or makes this more difficult than it has to be."

He slid his hands into his pockets, and looked down as he sidled closer. "You've been talking to her a lot, yeah? Keep your emotions out of this, Jared. Final warning."

"I've been trying to get her to eat. If she doesn't, there's no one to train the others." I clenched my jaw, staring at my father. "You lied about the flight. You raised me to trust and honor your word. Fucking laughable."

His eyes darkened. "I didn't raise you, Jared. I *trained* you."

I inhaled a deep breath, considering how much my father continued to steal from me in this life, and in the others. I puffed out my chest, lifting my chin and standing inches from him. It was my turn to challenge him.

"You hate her so much." I smirked. "Why? Does she remind you of my mother?"

He laughed, nodding. "She does. But I never treated your mother the way you do Charly. But, alas, that's not why I hate her. No." He shook his head, biting a smile. His gaze flitted to the ceiling, then back to me.

"Why?" I asked through my teeth.

"Because I don't like weakness."

I raised an eyebrow and sneered. The last few weeks proved to me just how tough she was. I'd seen soldiers go through less emotional and physical isolation and torture, and weep to be freed.

He brought his chest to mine, meeting my challenge. "She's *your* weakness. I didn't train you all those years to have a chink in your armor."

I stepped back, his words hitting me like a bucket of ice water. "I have no weaknesses. We send her when I get back." I turned and left the room.

Tomorrow morning, I was leaving for a week to take

the APFT—army physical fitness testing—before being promoted to captain. I was taking the test at a different base, two hours away, in Arlington. The travel time would allow me time to think, and I looked forward to the opportunity to be away from my father *and* Charly.

I headed straight for Charly's room, my heart hammering in my chest the whole time. I wanted to say it was because I was mad at her, but I had no reason to be. My father's words repeated again and again in my head.

I never treated your mother the way you do Charly.

He was a liar. I bet he'd done worse. I did what the situation required, what my training prepared me for. It wasn't my fault she had a sharp tongue and defiant nature. No, that was all her doing.

I pushed the metal door open as soon as my badge caused the electronic lock to release, and it hit the wall with so much force the crash thundered through the room.

Charly was sitting on the edge of the bed, and her head snapped up at the sound. Her eyes widened when she saw me enter the room with ferocity.

"Get up," I commanded.

Surprisingly, she stood. Confusion danced in her eyes as she held my glare.

I stood before her, my chest heaving with each breath as I looked down, towering over her.

"You're going to be sent to the seventh periphery. You have a death wish, let's see if the universe decides you're worth sparing."

"You're sending me?"

"If you think you can lie, just know—I can track you there, too."

She tilted her head slightly, her mouth twisting as she considered my words. "When?"

I calmed at the sound of her voice, surprised she wasn't more afraid. "When I get back. I'm going to APFT for the week."

She nodded acknowledgement, her gaze locking across the room in thought.

She was getting exactly what she'd asked for if things didn't go right. Death. She was as good as dead in the main reality, tethered to me here in reality two, and about to possibly die in reality seven. Her options for life were diminishing, and quickly, at that.

I pushed forward against her, prodding her silence. "What's the matter, you going to miss me?" I slid a hand behind her neck.

She tried to pull back, but I tightened my grasp, dragging a small sound from her throat.

I let out a low hum, taking in her face as she studied me. Her body heat bled through my uniform where our bodies connected, and I knew she felt it, too. The scorching chemistry between us, despite the fucked-up situation, was palpable.

"Morgan will keep an eye on you. You'd better eat, Charly."

Her lips tipped up at the corners, and she glanced at my mouth before meeting my eyes again. "What's the matter, Jared? Can't win this one, can you?"

I closed my fist around her hair. "Win what?"

Her jaw pulsed, and she pressed her lips together, breathing through the pain. "My reaction. Whether I eat or not. Whether I care about being sent to periphery seven or not."

"You only pretend not to care."

"No, Jared. You're the one pretending. I can't believe you let Mitch take it this far. This isn't you. You're a monster, but I never thought you capable of being worse than him."

I released her. "Well, you thought wrong." I stood over her, unable to stop staring into her eyes. I automatically reached up to touch her face.

When she turned away from my touch, I spun and left the room, slamming the door behind me.

Chapter 19, Reality 1

Simon

It'd been a month. A whole damn month since my wife had become incapacitated after visiting Jared in prison. In that time, I'd gotten her treated at the hospital, admitted to a mental-health care facility, and signed myself into a new military contract, similar to the black-op contract I'd signed on when I did missions for Quantym. I'd completed the PT testing, and went to drill with the guys every morning at 0600. This time, I was part of a team intent on taking over the program, and ousting Mitch and Jared's corruption within the facility.

In the last month, the general was well on his way to having Jared exonerated. The trial had veered off to vilifying the facilities managers at the VA where Quantym was housed in Virginia. The public no longer saw Jared as the enemy. Instead, the corporation that led medical care given to soldiers on that base became public enemy number one. Amazing, yet unsurprising, how easily the media had been bought, selling people on a falsehood that redirected the blame.

The details of the trial took a back seat while I focused on Charlotte. If finding a way to heal her meant signing over my life, I was happy to do it. Today, Joel, Jeff, and Diogo were coming with me to visit her.

She'd been talking more, but nothing that made

much sense to any of us.

We'd sent photos of her equations to some doctors on our team, and they were busy investigating if the math was part of an equation that would be used to help them navigate all seven peripheries—something our internal jumpers learned she discovered in reality two.

I squatted beside her.

She was more agitated than usual. She chanted the numbers out loud, rocking on her heels as she wrote.

"Charlotte." My voice soothed her panicked musings.

She continued to write furiously across the paper, her handwriting nearly illegible from the speed at which she wrote.

"You have some visitors. Diogo, Jeff, Joel…" I smoothed her hair.

She didn't look up, bringing her face down closer to the paper. Her breathing picked up pace, and she began making a deep sound, anticipation building as her hand worked, filling in more numbers in the equation.

Silence descended as we all watched.

Diogo jumped when Charlotte began screaming, her fists slamming into the hard floor, her bare feet kicking at the paper.

She threw the marker across the room as she huffed and wailed. It was a shocking scene to the others, but to me, I'd seen it play out dozens of times over the last few weeks.

"It's okay," I soothed, rubbing her back while she wept.

The others looked down at her with compassion.

"I don't know, Sy. Listen, man, maybe she's really…"

"Shut up," I snapped.

Joel's teeth clicked when his jaw shut. Smart move.

Diogo got onto her hands and knees, pushing the hair from Charlotte's face. "Hey, baby girl. Remember me?" She swiped a tear away with a thumb.

Charlotte grunted, pulling away from Diogo, and began sifting under the wrinkled paper for another marker. She grabbed one, uncapped it with her teeth, and began her torrent of numbers across the paper again.

Diogo cocked her head, then dragged a finger across some written numbers and abbreviations. "Picoseconds?"

Charlotte nodded, never looking up.

My heart swelled in my chest. Was it a coincidence, or did she really just respond to Diogo? Maybe she wasn't completely lost inside her mind after all.

I looked over the paper. I picked out another barely legible acronym—VF—*V Fib*, it was tattooed on the EKG rhythm on my damn hand. I spoke the words aloud, and she grunted an acknowledgement.

I looked over to my brothers. "Let's bring her in. Maybe if she sees the equipment for jumping, it'll help her..."

Jeff shook his head. "Sy, it's a long shot. She'll scream if we try moving her."

"It doesn't hurt to try."

"We can't just smuggle her onto the base. Whatever she's working on, if it's the equation to get to all seven peripheries, she's getting close. She freaked out at the end of this strip." Joel walked along the length of the unrolled paper where her jargon began fresh this morning. "She's trying to finish it."

"So, what then, you think she'll be magically cured

when she does?" I seethed.

"No, let's give her some space. Go talk to Xavier, show him and the docs the updated pictures. See if they agree."

"I'll meet you outside in ten."

The room cleared, and I spoke with Charlotte. I didn't care if she didn't—or couldn't—respond. I'd talk to her every day for the rest of my life if this was all she had left to give, and I'd take it gratefully. I told her what I was leaving to do, before lifting myself off the floor and meeting the others outside.

****

Diogo, Jeff, Joel, and I reported to the briefing at Newport Base. We sat at a long conference table, and our commander, Lt. Xavier, remained standing as he dropped a heavy folder onto the table in front of him.

"I just came from a meeting, and a few jumpers returned from reality two last night with some...concerning intel." His gaze found mine.

I stiffened, holding his stare.

"None of the jumpers have been able to locate you, Donovan. Or Charlotte."

I sucked in a deep breath. *Were we killed in reality two? If so, why was Charlotte incapacitated here?*

"We've had the jumpers case your barracks. You haven't been seen for a couple weeks, but you haven't been reported AWOL yet, either. As for Charlotte, Jared has been coming and going from the house, but she's been missing for weeks as well."

We ran off together. My chest swelled, and shoulders relaxed, I couldn't help the smile that pulled at my lips. *But what was wrong with her here? Was it really just her head injury worsening?* The cold realization mutilated my smile, and I furrowed my brow at the thought.

I sighed. "On her last jump, she may have altered things there. She...told me she loved me, and that Jared was going to kill her. Over there, I probably helped her escape."

Jeff shook his head. "They'd have reported you AWOL by now, Sy."

I clenched my fists.

Lt. Xavier spoke. "They're building jumpers now. By undergoing the protocol multiple times, they've learned they can cause troops to begin building retainable memories and become jumpers."

"Shit," Joel muttered. "Guess you're not too special now, Sy."

I narrowed my eyes at him.

"But, not without repercussions," Lt. Xavier continued. "Inhibition control, physical and mental ramifications..." He raised his eyebrows and found my gaze again.

What was he implying?

"So, while the easiest way to find out where you are, Donovan, is by sending you, it's too risky. You've been on too many missions, and you'll start to suffer those same ill effects the more you jump and return."

"Send me," I growled. I didn't care about ramifications. I didn't care if my inhibitions slipped more than they already had. It was a side effect I'd been dealing with in silence for years now, anyway. Funny they were just finding this out. I'd known after my first jump, the subtle changes. I'd heal faster, my intuition would improve, but I'd also be more short-tempered, more likely to chase what I wanted. Charlotte included.

Diogo leaned forward. "You're risking *more* than just your life, Sy. Look at what happened to Charlotte. Do you think, between the brain injury and two jumps, it's possible it caused her—"

"No!" I snapped.

"We've been considering that." Lt. Xavier sighed and rubbed a hand over his shaved head. "The equation she cracked in reality two is beyond complex, and it's the key to navigating all seven Peripheries. Another theory is that somehow, they sent her consciousness backward, intentionally incapacitating her. They likely knew her wires would get crossed, and she'd become fixated with cracking it here, too. But that theory is challenged by the fact that no one survives being sent backward."

Lt. Xavier opened the folder and slid a photo over to each of us. On one side was a photo of Charlotte's scrawled numbers on the butcher paper in the care home. The photo caught the back of her, her dark hair spilling down her back in waves as she sat on her heels, marker in hand. On the other side, a sketch—presumably from a jumper—included a snippet of an equation. The numbers on both sides looked like useless jargon.

"From a jumper?" I looked at Lt. Xavier. They'd been bringing back bits and pieces of the equation for days now, and we'd had no matches tying her musings to the equation from reality two.

He nodded. "As soon as he woke up, it was his sole mission. Bring back a *confluent* piece of it, instead of multiple pieces, no matter how small." Xavier turned and snapped on the overhead projector. "And, voilà." He slid two zoomed-in portions of the photos together, and in one area, they matched seamlessly. "The proof we needed, so we're leaning more toward this now. But there are no guarantees, Donovan."

Finally!

I nodded, swallowing harshly. "Send me." I nearly crushed my molars, clenching my jaw.

Lt. Xavier sat, his eyes hooding with unsurprise by my response. "You'll need to sign a release, and be briefed on all the side effects. I want you to reread the map of reality two, as well. Ensure you're aware of where you—"

"I'll know if I'm in reality two by the memories." I drew in a sharp breath, willing myself to maintain control. If they knew just how much my inhibitions had slipped since my last jump, they'd never let me go. "And if I'm dead in reality two, and I end up in reality three, I'll be sure to let you know when I get back." The sarcasm dripped from my words. *Oops.*

"Watch it, Donovan." The lieutenant's eyes hardened.

Joel said, "You can't go now. We need to—"

"No, he can. The staff are here. No one will be surprised by his—" Xavier pinned me with a glare. "—insistence on going right away. Inhibition control, remember?" He raised an eyebrow.

I stood at the same time as Xavier.

I shot a glance at Joel. "No time like the present, sweetheart."

Joel grimaced and stood, Jeff and Diogo following suit.

I laughed and turned to follow Xavier out the door, and all of us headed toward the small new wing that held the equipment to jump.

****

I nodded at the two doctors and Xavier, who all

crowded around the bed after handing back the signed release forms.

One doctor fastened the cloth restraints, while the other adjusted the IV pumps.

Xavier scanned the intubation equipment that was prepped on a cart to the side.

I was wearing only military-issued scrub bottoms, and I was shirtless for the inevitable defibrillation that'd follow cardiac arrest. There wasn't an ounce of fear in my body, only electric anticipation.

Jeff, Joel, and Diogo were behind the two-way mirror, watching, and that didn't bother me. I was a pro at this. Years of this malevolent protocol were what led me to Charlotte and led me here, and I wouldn't change a damn thing.

"Donovan, listen to me, and I mean it. Don't think you can't get kicked off the team if you go rogue on us. You're going over for no more than thirty minutes."

I nodded, adding a wink for good measure.

Xavier wasn't impressed, and his mouth tightened into a hard line. He leaned down, his lip curling. "If you really give a shit, you'll follow orders, understood? We don't want the Cardozas getting their hands on that equation here as much as you want to save her. We've all got interests in this," he warned.

"You got it, LT." I smirked. I'd try not to go off mission, but if I could get to Charlotte, there'd be no stopping me. *Inhibition control issues, remember?* I closed my eyes and smiled, the idea of being able to see her, actually talk to her, caused my heart to pick up the pace and my muscles to tighten.

Xavier backed away to the corner of the room while the doctors worked.

Soon, the room was filled with the beep of my heart rate on the monitor, and a bolus of sedative was being pushed into my line. As my consciousness drifted, impatience flared within me, and I nearly fought against the drugs to tell them to just *stop my heart already.*

Minutes passed, and my eyes snapped open. Something was wrong. Did the jump fail? I looked at both arms tethered to the bed, but the room was empty.

How much time had passed? Where was everyone?

I closed my eyes and focused. A rush of memories tumbled into my brain so fast, I gasped as the headache grew to an explosive point.

A flash of memory caused me to groan, the sound reverberating loudly in the room.

I was supposed to pick her up, help her escape.

I was heading to get her; I'd brought my .45, because I'd be putting lead into her husband if he tried to stop us.

I slid into my car, leaving plenty of time to arrive at Rosewood and Holly early. A pinprick stabbed my neck, followed by a flaring burn where I'd been stuck. I spun around and swung, my fist connecting with someone. There were two of them, in all black, waiting in my back seat. Damned rookie mistake I'd made, to think he hadn't tracked her and heard our conversation.

"Hit him with another. The dose wasn't enough for his size!"

I knew that voice. Morgan. I'd served with this guy; he was better than this. Another man sat behind me, and a metal bar was pulled over my throat. I grasped the bar, swinging wildly, trying to connect with either man who threatened to stop me from getting to Charlotte.

If they were here because they knew, where was

she? The thought dumped adrenaline into my system. I hit the push start on the car, dropping the shifter into reverse. I stomped the pedal to the ground, tires squealing, while another pinprick stabbed my neck. My vision blurred, the car bumped into a stone wall, and both men in the back scrambled out of the car when it came to a halt.

My door swung open, and I was dragged from the driver's seat, drugged and stumbling. Pain exploded through my body from a relentless attack of the metal bar across my arms, back, and legs. I fell to the ground, my eyes losing focus as booted footsteps made their way toward my car.

"Time to pick up your girlfriend." General Cardoza sneered. "Shame. You're a soldier. You know what we do to traitors, and she's about to find out, too." He laughed, and the sound was cut off by the slamming car door.

He took off in my car as I lost consciousness.

I woke up tethered to the bed in Quantym. Days passed, then weeks. I'd been shocked and resuscitated too many times to count, being forced to gather intel from one of seven peripheral lives, or sometimes with no mission at all—just being sent to see what'd happen after so many jumps in quick succession, like a lab rat.

I looked around the empty room, struggling against the restraints. I stared at one wrist, then glanced at the other. Deep scars marred both. I'd gotten out of these tethers more than once, healing faster with each successive jump. I tried blocking the memories, so I could focus on the mission from the main reality. *Charlotte*. It'd be too easy to get swept up in the thoughts and memories of reality two and lose focus.

But I was still locked in this hellhole room, and I needed a plan.

Think.

There was no telling where Charlotte could be, or if she was even still alive. But either way, people were going to die, starting with both Cardozas. I bowed my back, a yell coming deep from my chest as I pulled against the restraints, blood spurting from both wrists when the restraints finally snapped, releasing all my limbs. Blood dripped down my ankles, soaking into the white bed linen.

I shot up in bed, heavy breaths sawing in and out of me. I stood on the bed, bringing my face close to the camera, the flashing green light mocking me.

"You're going to die. You're both going to *die*," I growled.

I hopped off the bed, sauntering over to the mirrored window. I leaned close, my breath creating a patch of fog. A slight movement indicated someone was just behind the glass, watching. A feral smile stretched across my face, my muscles winding tighter with the knowledge that just inches away was someone I could kill. Who, didn't matter. I was like a starved vampire, ready to drink a century's worth of blood. I was going to enjoy every fucking minute of it, too.

I licked my lips, the hunger increasing to a devastating point, then pulled my arm back, and delivered a shocking blow to the mirrored tempered glass. It bowed, cracked, and was only one more hit away from buckling out of its frame, allowing me to kill. The need to spill blood was overwhelming, intoxicating, all-consuming.

I didn't give a shit that the amount of jumps they'd

sent me on in an incredibly short time irrevocably changed my mind and body. I'd still be the same man with Charlotte. I'd never hurt her. I pulled my arm back again—

****

I gasped at the burning pain searing my throat, which caused me to gag and cough.

"What the hell is going on? Wake him up! Why isn't he waking up?"

Was that…my brother?

"Donovan!" Lt. Xavier's voice was muddy, far away. "Did you extubate him too soon?"

"He's adjusting, be patient," another voice spoke, adding confusion to my agitated and confused state.

"Sy!" Jeff's voice sounded from above me.

One quick zap of energy pouring out of my soul allowed me to pull on both tethers, snapping them simultaneously. In another fluid movement, I was airborne, tackling the first body that got in my way.

"Stand down! Dammit, Donovan, stand the hell down!" Xavier's voice came from beside me, but it still sounded too far away.

I needed to kill.

I pulled my arm back, ready to finish whoever was beneath me with one blow.

Three bodies surrounded me, all pulling back, preventing me from delivering the blow.

"Get the hell off me!"

Joel bucked.

I stumbled back, and Diogo, Jeff, Xavier, and I all fell on our asses.

"What the hell was that?" Joel stood quickly, then glared down at me.

Good question.

"I-I don't know. She wasn't there, but someone was. I wanted to kill—" I heaved, breaths coming faster and faster. "They've got me tied to a fucking bed in Quantym, forcing me on mission after mission." I braced my palms on the floor, sweat dripping from my temples as I scrambled to dig up the memories before they could fade.

The room remained silent, allowing my memories to be spoken aloud, uninterrupted.

"My strength and healing have increased to an impossible point. I have scars, deep scars on both wrists from trying to escape, and healing from each failed attempt." I wheezed, my chest tightening. "They drugged me, stopped me from picking her up, helping her escape. Cardoza said—"

I leaned forward, vomiting violently before I could finish.

Both doctors rushed over, each grabbing an elbow to help lift me off the floor, and guiding me back to the bed.

I leaned forward, heaving again.

"Damn, man." Jeff rushed to the other side of the bed. "Your body can't keep going through this. I don't give a shit if you think you heal faster, your heart—"

"Continue," Xavier barked.

"The Cardozas have her. I think."

You know what we do to traitors, and she's about to find out, too.

My back bowed off the bed, a yell clawing its way out of my raw throat as my body rejected the memory of Mitch's words.

"Send me back," I demanded.

Lt. Xavier and Jeff both shook their heads.

"No can do, Donovan. Pull yourself together!" Xavier looked over at Joel.

Joel shrugged. "Send him. He says he can handle it. You send him, and he comes back a monster, we can deal with that. But if you keep him, he's a demon, and I don't trust demons."

I stared at Joel, considering his words.

Xavier looked at the doctors, and both shook their heads.

"Twenty-four hours of observation, minimum," one doctor said. Dr. Cabral, his uniform indicated.

"No," I snarled. "Tonight."

"Men, dismissed. I need a word." Xavier cleared the room with a sweep of his hand.

I closed my eyes, the memories from reality two rapidly fading. I wish I'd seen her, even if just a glimpse, to know she was still okay, still there, somewhere. Something told me if I could just lay my eyes on her, she'd tell me how to fix her in the main reality.

Xavier hovered near my bed and slid his hands into his pockets. "We'll send more jumpers tonight, Donovan. Let the doctors do their jobs, observe you after that jump, ensure you're not compromising your health."

I grit my teeth. "You don't understand."

"I do understand, Donovan! I get it, really, I do. But you're no good to her if you incapacitate yourself!"

His words settled, and I hated to admit he was right. If I didn't proceed with caution, Charlotte and I would both be put in Cedarwood Bay Home, and live out our lives there—her scribbling nonsense, and me in a straightjacket for my bloodlust.

"Classified intel, Donovan. Can you handle that?"

I nodded.

"She's worth a lot of money. There's bound to be more than one or two people who are well aware of her worth. There, they've already got her locked away, but here—"

I sucked in a breath. "What are you saying?"

"Tonight, we've got a team, we're going to take her. Keep her safe here. Let her work on the math, maybe let her see you jump. Might help her remember who she is, and it'll get the Cardozas' attention. I can't imagine Jared will jump to reality two once he learns she's missing here. He and his father will be preoccupied with a manhunt. Here."

"Doesn't matter. He's building memories. Doesn't even matter if he jumps or not. They know what the mission is, and what they need her for."

"But they send jumpers all the time. You don't think word won't get back to them in reality two that she's missing here? I mean, wasn't that the whole mission? To get her to crack the code here, since no one can travel backward without dying?"

I blanched. "Maybe they don't die right away if they get sent backward."

He shrugged. "What are you getting at, Donovan?"

"Maybe that's what happened to her."

He nodded. "I didn't want to say anything, but based on recon a few jumpers brought back...that's exactly what we think happened to her. We have to get her here to keep her safe, first. Then, we'll infiltrate reality two. There's got to be an antidote."

I nodded stiffly. There better fucking be. I didn't like the idea of her being abducted, manhandled, or picturing how she'd scream when taken from her numbers.

"Let me do it. Or at least help get her."

Xavier nodded. "I planned on that."

Jared and Mitch were about to be lured into the lion's den, and I was looking forward to ripping both their throats out with my teeth.

Chapter 20, Reality 2: On the Periphery

Jared

I strode away from room 300 with my teeth locked, my jaw aching from the pressure. She knew how to get under my skin, and while I wanted to say that pissed me off, it also pulled me in.

A part of me wanted to turn around, go back into her room, and get her going again. At least when she showed anger, I knew she wasn't dead. But I needed rest, and I'd been getting an insufferably little amount of sleep lately. Sleep deprivation was used as a torture device for good reason—it weakened the mind, the senses, judgement, and insight.

Did I want her dead? No. Was I really going to let Mitch send her to the seventh Periphery?

Maybe.

I pulled my cell from my pocket and accessed the cameras. She was sitting on the edge of the bed with her head hanging and her dark hair obstructing her face.

Was she crying?

I almost hoped so. Her lack of...*everything* lately was unsettling. At least if she cried, it showed she still felt *something*.

Why did I care so much? She was trying to run off on me.

Her image was overlayed by an alert across my

phone. The stupid, insignificant Marine was acting up again. Pity, must be hard being turned into an unhinged animal, drugged, zapped, resuscitated, and kept in a state not quite alive, but not quite dead, either.

I sighed and headed to the adjacent observation room to see what the issue was this time.

With a soft click, I closed the door behind me and stepped up to the two-way mirror. He was standing on the bed, his wrists and ankles bleeding from the tethers he'd snapped yet again. He looked into the camera and said something. I didn't bother logging in. I could watch the video later if I truly wanted to.

I crossed my arms in front of me when he strode over to the mirrored window. He stared through the glass, and for a moment, it appeared as if he could see me. I tilted my head, noting the absolutely unhinged look in his eyes. Shame, now that we were learning excessive jumps helped increase healing and strength, it was quickly learned it wasn't worth it, and looking into his eyes it was evident why. Sure, you'd be strong as a bear, vicious as a beast—but lacking the self-control that defined you as human, too. And even lions could be caged.

Maybe I'd show Charly what'd become of him one day. Maybe she'd be a little less broken if she learned he wasn't dead, but incapacitated beyond repair. Which would she find worse? I'd have to think on that.

I was broken from my thoughts when the senseless animal punched the glass, the two-inch thick shatterproof glass bowing in toward me. He really was a monster, and by the looks of it, and dumb as one, too. Another blow hit the glass, and the large piece loosened from the frame.

I backed away, calling over to Morgan on the radio. "Code blue. Drug him and use extra restraints this time."

An alarm went off, signaling my men to subdue Simon. It was becoming a biweekly affair, but we knew how to handle him. He was nothing more than a gnat on my radar when I had more important things to tend to.

I looked down at my phone and swiped the alert away, staring at Charly on cam again as I left the observation room. I stopped mid-stride when I saw her talking to my father, and turned the audio all the way up to hear over the alarms and troops stomping by. I popped an earbud in, just in time to hear her soft voice answering his.

"No. You're wrong." She shook her head and let out a scornful laugh.

I kept my eyes on my phone, watching and listening, curious as to why my father was with Charly and what he was questioning her about. I didn't have time for this. I was going to be woken soon, and I needed rest for my travel and testing this upcoming week. I didn't plan on jumping for the week. My mind and body needed rest from jumping from the main reality. Plus, I didn't need my main reality consciousness present for the APFT.

Intent on watching from my house whatever interaction they were having, I made my way down the hall. It couldn't be too important if he hadn't come to me first. I hit my badge against the reader and entered the elevator. The doors rolled shut, then the car ascended with a jolt.

The doors rolled open, and I strode down the hall, ready to go home, take a shower, and ensure everything was packed for my week-long trip.

Mitch laughed. "Wanna bet? he challenged.

I'd missed something—service was always spotty in the elevator. I exited the facility and headed toward my car, still listening and watching.

"I don't make deals with the devil," she said.

Pulling open the door to my jeep, I froze, watching the scene from room 300 play across my phone.

Charly's small frame was slammed against the wall, my father's hand around her throat, as she struggled and thrashed.

He was going to kill her.

I'd done the same thing to her not long ago, but I knew I wouldn't hurt or kill her, I was simply sending a message. This, no, this was different. I knew my father's tells. The stiff spine, the cold set of his face. He was all in, and she was going to die.

No.

I threw my door shut and ran back into the building, sprinting toward the elevator. I slammed my badge against the reader, tapping my foot and swearing as the floor buttons slowly illuminated one by one until they lit up the first floor. The doors opened impossibly slowly, and I used both hands to force my way inside, punching at the Close Door button furiously.

The elevator descended, and I glanced down at the phone. Her kicking had slowed, and a trail of blood was dripping down the wall behind her.

No, no, no, what had he done?

If I didn't stop him in the next few minutes, she'd be dead. The image of a cold, dead Charly lying in room 300 flashed across my mind, and the image caused me to pull my gun from the holster as I sprinted to her room.

I smashed my badge against the reader and forced the door open as soon as the lock unhitched.

"Let her go!" I pointed the gun at my father.

He turned to me, a smile flashing across his face as he released his grip.

A weak scream escaped her lips as she crumpled to the ground gasping. Blood was soaking the back of her shirt.

"What the hell is going on?" I demanded, glaring at my father as heavy breaths caused my chest to heave.

He waved his hand dismissively, looking down at her on the floor. "Just proving a point. Right, Charly?"

Her shoulders rose with each gasping breath she took, her eyes cast downward. She was trying not to pass out.

"Did you—?" I stared at the blood on the wall and on her shirt. There was a small, metal hook jutting out from the wall he'd slammed her into.

"Oops. That wasn't planned." He slid his hands into his pockets. "Stand down, Jared. If I report this, there will be no promotion."

I lowered my gun. I knew the point he was trying to prove—that she was my weakness. The realization hit me heavy in the chest. *Shit.*

He stepped closer. "So, what are you going to do about that weakness?"

I shrugged. "I don't have time for this. I have to report—"

He nodded. "Ah. You have to report for a whole week. So many things could happen to her while you're gone. Just think about it. A facility full of men, some tasked with manning the room while she showers…"

I narrowed my eyes at him. "I have Morgan. I'd say you, but you've proven yourself untrustworthy. Dishonorable."

"Watch your mouth, soldier. I am your superior, above all else." He lifted his chin, meeting my glare with his own. "If you take care of it now, you'll free your mind for your testing. You won't have to worry—"

I threw my hands up in frustration. "I thought you wanted her sent to Periphery seven?"

He smirked. "We have plenty of disposable jumpers, and the Silencer has been costing us money, what with the outbursts and all. I'd rather send him."

Charly snapped her head up at his words, her eyes rounding. Hope colored her face, and it made me pull the gun from the holster at my leg.

I pointed it at her.

Her lips parted as she stared at me with wide eyes.

A stretch of silence passed, broken only when my father sighed loudly.

Charly lifted herself from the ground, wincing and reaching a hand around to the wound on her back. She took two small steps toward me. "Just do it already." Her gaze held mine, challenging. "Do it, Jared. Do it!"

My father pulled his gun out and pointed it at her. "She gave explicit permission. If you can't do it, I will. You'll thank me later." He cocked the gun.

I plowed into him, grasping his collar and slamming him into the wall. "Leave," I ground out. The veins in my neck throbbed with my desire to kill him, but if I did in this facility, I'd be good as dead, too. She'd be bait on a hook in this room when the guards stormed in, and I wouldn't allow it.

He pressed the barrel of his gun under my chin. "Touch me again and kiss that promotion goodbye. Final warning."

I released my grip on him and stumbled away as I

stuffed my gun back into the holster. My thoughts raced, and my heart thundered in my chest.

He leered at Charly. "I think we've all learned a lot here today." Then he turned to me and raised his eyebrows. "I won't tolerate weakness." He turned and left the room, and the door slammed shut behind him.

Charly began trembling, her bottom lip quivering, and it nearly sent me out into the hall to put a bullet into my father's skull.

"What the hell was that?" I asked her.

She shook her head, and when she tried to answer, just a pained squeak came out. Her green eyes filled with tears, and a sob broke free. She slapped both hands over her face to hide the emotion.

She'd been hiding it all along. She wasn't broken, after all. Just tough as steel.

I strode over to her and stiffened when she fell into me, both her hands fisting the front of my uniform as she sobbed. I slowly wrapped my arms around her, bringing my face down to her dark silken hair.

She didn't forgive me; that much I knew. But humans could only withstand so much, and she'd been through a lot—emotionally and physically. My father was wrong; she wasn't my weakness, but dammit, I was human, capable of some small semblance of compassion for the petite woman. *I'd been married to her for years, what did he expect?*

I swallowed hard at the feel of her soft body against mine, and forced the longing that bloomed in my chest down, down, down. Allowing weakness now would be like signing my own death certificate, and I'd be damned if I proved my father right. She always yielded to me, so I'd expected this at some point, but I wasn't happy about the circumstances leading up to it. And the small snippet she heard about Simon might even be compelling her to try to gain my trust, to learn if he really was alive. I was on my guard, and traitors couldn't be trusted.

I pulled away.

She stood before me, trembling, bloody, and cold.

"Turn around," I ordered.

She complied.

I lifted her shirt. Ouch. The hook had torn into her skin deeply, just under her bra line, maybe even catching a rib. I called Morgan on the radio to come take a look and bring Rogers with him to room 300. She was going to need stitches.

I pulled the bloody shirt off her, and walked her over to the bed. "Sit."

She lowered herself onto the bed, and I tried not to look at her in her black bra and facility-issued drawstring pants. I wrapped a blanket around her shoulders, and she hugged it tightly.

I went into the bathroom and wet a washcloth with warm water.

When I returned to the room, she hadn't moved. Her eyes were closed, her head slumped. I sat on the bed behind her and pulled the blanket off her shoulders. It wasn't my fault my body responded to her the way it did, but I hid it flawlessly with a quick adjustment.

She jumped when the soft cloth connected with her bloody waist.

"I won't hurt you. The medic is coming, I'm just going to get you cleaned up."

She nodded and sniffled with her back to me.

I gathered her hair into my hands, then pushed it over the side of her shoulder. Goosebumps rose on her skin as I dragged my fingers down her arm, then continued cleaning the blood with the cloth, keeping my free hand wrapped around her arm.

I cleaned her waist, and then up to the area around the wound. I unhooked the back of her bra, and brought the cloth close to the wound, accidentally grazing the torn skin.

She flinched and whimpered.

"I'm sorry." The words fell from my mouth before I could stop them, causing a fissure in the wall I'd built around the empty cavity where my heart should be.

She huffed, her back straightening at my words.

I pressed the cloth over the wound gently, and her body shuddered.

Leaning closer, I brought my lips to her ear. "I'm so sorry, Charly. So, so sorry for everything. I never wanted to hurt you, I never wanted to take it this far." My words were sincere, pouring from a small place within me where I held the only light that'd ever leaked in. Without her, it'd only be darkness. All darkness.

A sob broke free, and her shoulders shook with the emotion. "I trusted you."

"You want to ask if he's alive?" A plan brewed, and I prodded her into my bait. I wouldn't tolerate the pain, the hollowness in my chest that ached like a heart-attack.

She nodded.

"Are you sure you want to know the answer? It's going to be hard to hate me when you know the truth."

She turned her head, glancing at me over her shoulder.

I studied her profile—a porcelain doll.

"What's the truth, Jared?"

Her answer was further proof that while she wanted

to hate me, she didn't.

"I'm not the monster you think I am." The tip of my nose grazed her shoulder as I leaned closer.

"He's here?"

I nodded, and she turned her body to face me.

"He signed. But his body didn't handle the protocol well. We're trying to treat him, but it's proving fruitless."

"Don't lie to me." Her eyes hardened.

I widened my eyes innocently. "I'm not. I'll show you, if you want." I looked at her through my lashes. "Now, since we're spilling truths, do you love him?"

"I was trying to get him to sign, dammit! Just like you asked, no—*commanded, assigned, ordered* me to do!"

"If he got better, would you leave with him if I made arrangements, so Mitch doesn't kill you?"

She paused, her eyes darting back and forth to search mine. She didn't trust me. Smart woman.

I brought my hand up to her face. "I don't want to kill you."

She held my gaze. "What's wrong with him?"

I drew in a deep breath, dragging my gaze to the ceiling. "Inhibition control. Temper. Complete mental break after a few jumps. You've seen it happen to some of the...weaker jumpers."

She nodded. "How bad?"

"Tell you what. I'll show you when I get back next week, then you decide. Okay?" I kept my voice gentle, placating. "But I'm going to have some strict rules, to keep you safe, of course." I leaned closer to her, and her breath whispered across my lips. "But Charly, if you don't love him, why do you care so much?"

"Because I've ruined his life. He was doing me a

favor, giving me a ride to the airport. And now—" Her shoulders slumped and another tear fell.

I nodded, then leaned in. "Just a ride? That's it?"

"Yes, Jared. That's it."

She looked down.

She wasn't asking *me* to take her from Mitch, but I hadn't offered, either. Once she saw the state Simon was in, she'd be left with only one choice, anyway. It was the first of many steps I'd have to take patiently to get her back home. Luckily, I was a patient man, about to get everything I wanted.

Mitch couldn't stop me from keeping her as my wife if she proved loyal. He'd had no choice the first time, and this time would be no different. Charly wasn't just my weakness. I'd always been hers, too. Even now, hovering just inches from her face, my lips nearly grazing hers, she didn't dare back away.

I struck like a viper when I heard a badge hit the reader, bringing my hand to the back of her neck and pressing my lips to hers.

When the door opened, I released her and we exploded apart. From Morgan's and Roger's perspectives, it appeared we did so because they'd entered.

Both men froze, staring at us while Charly gaped at me.

Excellent.

I pulled the blanket over Charly's shoulders, covering her body from them.

Charly turned around, and I moved the blanket to expose the wound.

"That looks like it hurt," Morgan said.

"A pinch," she retorted sarcastically.

Rogers stepped closer. "She's gonna need stitches. What happened?"

I nodded at the wall where a splotch of her blood stained around the metal hook where Mitch had slammed her.

"The general is no longer allowed in room 300, understood?"

Morgan cleared his throat.

"I don't give a shit if he outranks me, Morgan! You code all these electronic controls, remove his access. Unless you wish to see my wife dead?" I glared at him.

Morgan pulled the laptop over and began clacking away. "Got it. Removing his privileges now. Hey, don't you have to be up in a few hours to head up to Arlington for APFT?

"I'll sleep when she's fixed."

Morgan stared at me, questions hanging from the tip of his tongue. His gaze darted to Charly, then me again. "Back together?" he asked quietly.

I nodded. If the men thought us together, I saw it as insurance they wouldn't dare try anything stupid while I was gone, like allowing Mitch access to her room or offering to help her escape.

"We're going to need an X-ray, too. It might've gotten a rib." Rogers touched gently around the wound on her back.

Charly recoiled when he touched a particular spot.

I grasped her hand for comfort.

Her gaze shot to me, questions floating in her eyes at my behavior. She played along, uncertain what my end game was.

Her. The end game was her.

Chapter 21, Reality 1

Jared

Opening my eyes, I nearly vomited as the tube was pulled from my throat. My father wasn't in the room, which didn't surprise me. I was shivering and shaking and cold, waiting to acclimate while two emotionless doctors monitored my vitals wordlessly.

Taking controlled breaths, I forced myself to maintain control, trying to ease the trembling and the pain. I thought about Charly in reality two, and the fierce desire to protect her from Mitch. I was disappointed I hadn't been able to keep my consciousness on that side long enough to see her stitched up and safely in bed. But no matter, I'm sure my alternate self was doing a fine job of it, and I'd attain those memories next time I jumped. I'd be at APFT for the week in reality two, and Morgan would keep an eye out for her, but I couldn't help but wonder how she'd feel in my absence. Probably isolated and lonely—but that could benefit me upon my return in a week.

****

The next morning my father and I were in court, and we'd been able to buy my freedom in the form of a shoddy mistrial verdict. Such a shame the courts and attorneys mishandled sensitive information, and the insane international coverage made a fair trial impossible. Once we'd involved Charly—tipping off the media so she'd be caught by reporters on cam deliciously marked up outside the prison that day—the news sank their teeth into our supposed backstory, and the American people got enraptured with the dramatics. The tabloids and magazines were already salivating for an interview.

My presence and the proceedings had all been done to keep up appearances, anyway. Mitch had the judge in his pocket, along with several members of the prosecution team. By day's end, I was a free man. Alongside my father, I gave a couple of statements to the media, and the people at large were quite sympathetic to my situation. And who could blame them? The system was known for treating soldiers and vets poorly. My widely publicized case brought out the justice-seekers, and every other commercial on TV now seemed to be for one organization or another that was collecting funds to help soldiers who'd been wronged like me—legally or medically.

My legal proceedings were far from over, but I wasn't concerned with that. Patience was just another one of my virtues.

I pulled into a spot outside Cedarwood Bay Home and parked.

I went to see Charly first, and when I entered her room, she didn't look up.

She was on her hands and knees, scribbling numbers on a long roll of paper laid out on the dingy tile floor. She was in a sweatshirt and leggings, with thick fuzzy socks on her feet.

The jumpers from this side had already briefed us about her condition. It was a pleasant surprise she'd begun working on the equation here in her insanity, but it made perfect sense. The overwhelming influx of memories from reality two wouldn't be complete until she cracked it here like she had there.

I squatted beside her. "Hello, doll." I tucked a stray lock of hair behind her ear.

She kept her gaze on the equation she continued to write, unaware of my presence.

"Broken, but still beautiful," I murmured. Something dark and cruel in me was delighted to see just how bad a state she was in. It was the ideal revenge on Simon, especially when just hours ago I had my lips on hers in reality two.

She let out a small sound from her throat, her eyes glazing as she stared at an empty spot on the paper where the equation stopped abruptly.

She'd crack the equation soon enough, and Mitch and I would be able to offer designer deaths in the main reality, too. She wasn't just training the docs over there, I was retaining the protocol and would be able to help train the doctors once I had the equation. Afterward, she'd end up dead. Like most who'd been sent backward when the mind had nothing else to sink its full strength into, it'd collapse and she'd end up dead here and conscious in reality two. With me.

I took the marker from her hand.

She fought me, squirming and screeching.

I slid behind her, sat on the floor, and pulled her into my lap as I wrapped one arm around her body, and clasped a hand tightly over her mouth.

She struggled with all her might, attempting to thrash and wiggle out of my grip, but gained no purchase. A person of sound mind would've given up after a few minutes, but she continued trying to fight me, breathing heavily from her nose with my hand over her face. If I let her, she'd break her own neck trying to get back to her numbers.

"Doll, you won't escape, so just listen. Shhh. Listen. I know you're in there, somewhere. How does it feel having your life commanded by someone else? I warned you, and you didn't listen."

She let out muffled groans under my hand and continued to wriggle.

"I'd never normally tell you this, but since you're shattered, I might as well. It *hurt* when you betrayed me in Virginia and stabbed me. How does it feel, Charly? To be incapacitated and hurt by someone you love?"

She tried twisting out of my grasp, so I closed my legs around her, completely subduing her.

Her body finally weakened, but she continued moaning and groaning beneath my hand.

I kissed her temple. "I know why my father hates you, and I don't blame him. I thought marrying you, being with you long enough would dull my obsession with you. But it only made it worse, and then you ended up a *necessity*, with your equation and all. Do you know what that's like? To *love and need* someone so much you nearly hate them for it? I wasn't raised to have any weaknesses, yet here you are—weakness incarnate."

She moaned, her body limp in my arms.

"You have a chance to make it right, though," I said thoughtfully. "I'm going to make you the same offer I did a while back, when I had you come to Virginia with me. This time, you'll be with me in reality two. If you betray me again, you'll end up just like this again. And I'll chase you across all seven lives if I have to, destroying you until you yield to me fully. Or cease to exist. Your call."

She whimpered, her gaze scanning the floor in search of her numbers or her marker, who knew?

"You and I have work to do. We have clients who are going to pay very well for designer deaths, so I'll let you get back to it. You always were a hard worker." I snickered.

I released her, and she scrambled from my lap back to her paper. She grasped her marker and started writing furiously again, as if nothing had happened at all.

I lifted myself from the floor and glanced at her one last time with pity. I almost regretted her condition for selfish reasons, but quickly recalled the self-satisfaction in winning against Simon. In this reality, I'd broken even.

I left the room and headed toward the opposite end of the building to see my mother. I entered her room, and she was sitting in a recliner, a tray of untouched food in front of her.

She stared blankly at the flickering TV.

"Hi, Mom." I perched on the armrest of her chair, and rested a hand on her shoulder.

She slowly looked up at me and reached for my face with a quivering hand.

She looked so much older now. Devastatingly so.

"He's coming," she whispered, and her eyes filled with tears. "He's coming." She nodded through the tears, patting my cheek. "My son, he's coming."

"I'm *here*, Mom. Have any candy for me?" I smiled.

She fished into her housecoat pocket, then handed me a butterscotch with a smile.

I popped the candy into my mouth and stared at her.

Her eyes were glazed, slightly unfocused. "He's coming," she whispered again. "The monster will destroy you."

I tilted my head. "Hmm. The monster, you say?"

Her back straightened. "Yes." She nodded enthusiastically. "Yes. Yes. Yes. Yes."

I smirked. "That would be me."

"No," she growled and shook her head vehemently.

I let out a deep sigh. "You remember my wife, Charly? She's here, too, you know. But she's okay. We're just working through some stuff." I shrugged. "She lost a pregnancy a few years back. Do you remember the car accident?"

My mother stared at me with her glazed eyes glistening with tears. She nodded.

"I wouldn't mind a kid or two," I confessed. The thought of her body being irrevocably changed by my seed sent a thrill through me. An image of a preciously rounded Charly flashed into my mind, and I smiled at the thought of tethering her to me in such an irreversible way.

My mother nodded continuously, a small smile pulling at her lips.

"Imagine that." I raised my eyebrows. "You'd be a grandma."

She reached for my face again, trailing a gentle finger over the scar on the left side.

"I'm working on base with Mitch, um, Dad, and—"

She began screaming, clawing at me in desperation.

"Mom, stop. Mom! I wrapped a tight hug around her to subdue her.

Realization hit me in the chest so hard, I nearly passed out.

She whimpered, tears streaming from her eyes.

"You were a psychiatrist. I remember. Smart and kind and caring." A few distant memories attempted to claw their way out. I fought against them. What were the odds they were accurate, anyway? I couldn't have been older than four, and I wasn't even in school when my mother would take me to the park and push me on the swings or buy me a cone of soft-serve chocolate-and-vanilla swirl on a hot day or read bedtime stories. She was under pressure, being both a mother and a father to me during Mitch's deployments in his younger years. Then, before I could truly appreciate her, she'd broken.

And then Mitch had to raise—or as he said—*train* me.

I never forgave her.

She nodded. "The monster, Jared. The *monster.*"

"Mitch? Mitch is the monster?"

She wailed, grasping my shirt and burying her face into my chest. She continued nodding. "Seven, seven, seven! There's *seven!*"

Seven lives. And he sent her backward from one of them. *Son of a bitch.*

I whispered into her ear. "I'll kill him."

"Seven," she whispered. "Seven. *Seven!*"

"I'll do it for you, Mom. I didn't know, all these years, I never—" I swallowed against a constricting throat. I hadn't cried—hadn't been allowed to—since I was a young kid, and I imagine this was what it would feel like if I did. I didn't allow the tears to fall, instead, I pulled my mother into me, steeling myself.

"She helps you," she wailed.

Charly probably *would've* helped me realize it sooner, if I hadn't incapacitated her first.

"Yes, she does." I rubbed my hand over her hair, willing my sadness to morph into rage, a feeling I was more familiar—comfortable—with.

"Caroline, aren't you a vision?" My father entered the room.

I released my mother and kept my gaze on him.

My mother looked at him with wide innocent eyes.

He walked over to her, trailed a finger down her cheek, then leaned down and gave her a peck.

I froze. I'd never seen him affectionate with anyone. Ever.

He turned to me. "And I presume you've already visited your wife?"

I nodded. "She's getting close."

"Any day now, and we'll have designer deaths on the menu. I was hoping she'd have it cracked before you got out." He scratched his temple.

He might as well have said *I wish she'd died before you got out.*

Fury welled in my chest, and I considered killing him right here, with my invalid mother as a witness. Her testimony would never be allowed in court, anyway. But I had to remove emotion, be calculated, ensure my innocence when he met his untimely demise. Charly and I could run things at Quantym no matter what life we were in. The only thing Mitch added was his rank, connections, and experience. Nothing I couldn't obtain in time, especially being his surviving son.

"What treatments have they tried on her?" I tipped my head toward my mother. If they'd gotten my mother to survive, maybe Charly...

"Well, the late nineties were a wild time for mental illness. They used shock treatment a bit too...liberally."

"Ah."

"I'd visit her after her treatments, and each time she became more and more subdued. But never cured." Mitch dragged her tray of food closer to her.

"Do you think she'd have gotten better without the treatments? Maybe that's what made her end up like…this."

He shrugged. "No telling. But she's safe here. She's got her puzzles and a dedicated caretaker."

I stared at my mother, and she held my gaze with deep knowing eyes. Fried as her brain was, even she could detect his bullshit. But she wasn't dead. Maybe the shock treatments were good for that. But wouldn't she be better off dead, and living out a life on the Periphery where she wasn't trapped in a body by a mind unwilling to let go? I thought about her in reality two, and even there, she was in a mental institution. *What life had he sent her back from?*

"Before we go, I have to head to the bathroom. Keep an eye on her. She's been agitated."

Mitch nodded and laughed. "Charly, too. Have you seen what she does when you take her marker?"

I clenched both fists until my hands ached, trying to slow the painful thundering of my heart. He wasn't a narcissist. He was a sadist. And I failed to protect two of the most important people in my life from him. *I'd even helped him.*

What did that make me?

I never believed in an afterlife, but now, I was certain there was a hell. That's the only place people like Mitch or me could have come from, and we brought pieces of it wherever we went, leaving a black mark on anything pure we touched.

I ducked into the private bathroom in my mother's quarters. Moments later I was sending an anonymous text to a person I never thought I'd dare ask a courtesy from—Simon the Silencer.

—I can offer you a clear shot to his head. Latitude: 41.5033, longitude: -70.2840. Ten minutes.—

—Who?—

—My father.—

****

After washing my hands and saying goodbye to my mother, I strode down the halls of Cedarwood Bay Home with my father. We exited the facility nine minutes after I'd sent my text.

I kept my eyes straight ahead, not that Simon's movements on one of these rooftops would be seen, but I made sure to walk along the far side of the brick path where trees grew high along the edge. He'd never have a clear shot at me.

I kept my stride a half-pace behind Mitch, and when the whistle of the bullet sounded, I hauled ass for cover.

My father dropped like a brick, with a clean shot through the head.

Shame, he didn't even suffer.

Guess there was a new head of Quantym in the main reality now. I was glad I wasn't going to be in reality two for a week.

Mitch was going to be pissed.

Chapter 22, Reality 2: On the Periphery

Charlotte

I paced in the small room, trying to get my blood flowing. I'd been locked in for what had to be more than a month now, and my strength—and will—were diminishing rapidly. Jared was gone for the week, and for some reason, that unsettled me. I was able to read my husband, and after our last interaction, the war that raged within him was obvious. Mitch had trained him to be a monster, but beneath it all, there was a still spark of humanity in his eyes. I could only hope that spark wouldn't be snuffed out by another inhibition-stealing jump from the main reality next week when he returned.

It had to be close to evening now, and this is when Jared would normally come to talk, or instigate, me. I guess I didn't have to worry about that for the next few days. But I was completely sick with loneliness and isolation, with far too much time to think—the worst torture of all.

I wanted to say I feared dying, but I didn't. With the memories from reality one, and the terrors from here in reality two stalking my mind and stealing my ability to sleep, nothing could be worse than this isolated purgatory. A pit hollowed out in my stomach, its depths allowing a chill to echo through my chest when I thought about Simon, locked somewhere in this contemptible place because of me.

I knew better than to get him involved, and that I ruined anything good that I touched. But it didn't stop me from accidentally stealing his pure life out from under him. In the main reality, he loved me, and now, over there, I was incapacitated and could give him nothing in return. Here, I got him imprisoned.

A beep and click sounded.

Someone was about to enter the room.

I backed away from the door.

"Good evening, ma'am." Morgan smiled at me. He brought a tray of food in, and kicked the door shut behind him.

I tipped my head in greeting, fidgeting with my hands.

"I have to document what you eat. Make it easy on me, okay?" He placed the tray on the bedside table.

I nodded.

"Do you need anything else?" He put his hands on his hips and stared at me.

"No. Thank you."

Morgan stepped closer. "He's still gone. Don't worry."

"I'm not."

He slid his hands into his pockets. "Gustav just found out you were staying here."

I raised my eyebrows. "He didn't know?"

Morgan shook his head. "He just figured you were coming in to work with Jared every day to train them and going back home at night. He had no idea."

I tilted my head. "Why are you telling me this, Morgan?"

He shrugged. "He likes you and would never

condone what's...happening."

I stepped closer to him. "And you do?" I challenged.

He balked. "I never said that."

I glowered at him. "How did it feel that day, capturing Simon and watching me scream 'til I almost puked when Jared pretended to shoot him? Did it make you feel loyal? Powerful?"

He held my glare. "No. But I have to uphold my duties, and that means following orders."

"In this facility you're not in a combat zone, where challenging authority puts your unit at risk."

"Wanna bet?" He toyed with a button on his army fatigues. "What's happened to you when you've challenged him? Or his father?"

I blanched. Fair enough. "I'm not hungry."

He sighed. "If you forgo more than three meals, Carter's been ordered to put an NG tube in."

My eyes widened and my heart thrummed so quickly I thought I might pass out, or climb the wall. Instead, I stalked over to the tray and swung my arm, causing the tray and its contents to fly across the room. A metal cup spun on the tile loudly before slowing to a stop.

"I ate, but dropped the tray." I fisted my hands. "Looks like I touched a bit of everything."

He stalked over to me, and I lifted my chin, holding his stare.

"I almost don't want to tell you why I'm still here." He bared his teeth, then glanced at the camera.

I followed his gaze to the camera. The light was red, indicating he'd turned it off. Fear pooled in my empty stomach as I put my hands on my hips and steeled myself. "Why?"

"Gustav and me—we talked, and we'll help you escape. But it has to be at night and while he's gone, which is only for a few more days. I'm only making this offer once. When I come back tomorrow morning, have an answer for me. And have this cleaned up." He looked down at the mess I'd made.

A surge of relief washed over me. At least cleaning it would give me something to do.

He turned to leave.

"Morgan, wait. I'm sorry."

He looked at me, zoning in on my shaking hands.

"I'm just going crazy in here, alone with my thoughts. And memories." I pressed my lips together, refusing to show him the emotion, but my trembling gave me away. "I wasn't unfaithful, I followed his orders, just like you, and yet still—" I had to stop speaking to swallow back the burn that threatened to close my throat.

"Charlotte, even if you didn't, you still wouldn't deserve this."

I covered my face with my hands. I hadn't heard someone use my full name in so long.

"Hey, listen, we'll get you out. But he'll probably find you."

Ah, how decent. He and Gustav were willing to help me to alleviate their guilt, and whatever happened to me after Jared caught me wouldn't be their problem.

I removed my hands from my face without letting a tear escape. I appreciated his honesty. Jared *would* find me. Rubbing the back of my neck, I trailed my fingers along the tiny scar where he'd put the GPS chip in.

Morgan's gaze went to my neck. "He chipped you?"

"Yes," I whispered, and my face reddened. Microchipped like an animal.

He stepped a little closer and inspected the scar.

I turned my head to give him a better look.

"I can remove it. A little lidocaine and tiny incision."

"Let me sleep on it. Think."

"I'll be back in the morning." Morgan looked down at the mess again, then proceeded toward the door, stepping over the strewn tray contents.

"Thank you." My brow pinched as my thoughts raced.

Morgan pulled the door open, then turned around and stared at the floor. He bent and picked up a package of crackers, then tossed them to me.

I caught them.

"You're not hurting *him* when you don't eat." He left and the door slammed shut behind him.

I tore open the package and popped a cracker into my mouth. My stomach rumbled at the promise of sustenance. I glanced up at the camera where the flashing green light resumed, then I looked over at my reflection in the two-way mirrored window.

Now what?

****

Morning came, and I hadn't slept much, really. But that wasn't anything new. I'd usually just zone in and out, pace back and forth, and eventually rise when my body rejected lying supine any longer. This morning, my back ached more than usual, and a shiver wracked through me. I had no windows, no clock, no way to tell what time it was. I only knew morning came when I'd hear boots stomping past the room from the hall. There was a night shift, but I presumed they mostly sat in front of the cameras.

I glanced at the camera facing my bed and thought about Jared. He was a couple hours away, and would return with his promotion. Before this mess, I'd have planned a special dinner for his return, and even as much as I always disliked Mitch, I'd usually invite him to things like that, too. The man hated me but liked my cooking. Go figure.

Thoughts rushed and tumbled over me when I heard the soldiers in the hall starting their shift. I was supposed to have an answer for Morgan, and despite thinking on it all night, dread roiled my stomach at the thought of telling him what I'd come up with. He'd think me crazy, but I had a plan. A plan based on a gut feeling, and as a doctor, that went against my need for evidence, for research. But I needed an answer for him and finally settled on one.

I went into the bathroom and undressed for a shower, then turned to glance into the mirror to examine the wound on my back from Mitch's attack a couple days ago. The wound was stitched, but red and angry looking. I'd pulled the bandage off after accidentally getting it wet the other day, and never got another. After Jared left, the medic, Rogers, never returned.

After showering, I hugged a towel over my shoulders and opened the linen cabinet, pulling out a pair of facility-issued drawstring pants and a T-shirt. Another shiver shook through me as I donned a pair of thick socks. I went to the bed and wrapped a blanket over my shoulders to stave off the cold.

Finally, Morgan returned to the room.

"Morning. Breakfast awaits." He placed a new tray on the bedside table, and removed the old one.

I'd cleaned up the tray I'd tossed last night, and had

the items neatly stacked on it for him, and had even rinsed out the dishes.

He smirked. "I bet doing that felt good."

"It was dramatic, but satisfying." I waved my hand across the table in slow-motion, mocking my tray-swatting the night before. I glanced up at the camera. The light was red.

"Well?"

"I don't want to escape."

He dipped his head. "Really?"

I nodded. "He'll find me. You know it. I know it. What I want, and I need you to tell Gustav this, is to be sent to the seventh Periphery. I need to see something."

"You've got to be kidding." He placed the empty tray down and stepped closer. "Why?"

"I have a hunch about something. And if I'm right, it'll change everything, everywhere."

"You gonna tell me?"

I shook my head. "No. But I have another ask."

He lifted his chin.

"I want you to help Simon."

He rubbed his forehead. "You're kidding, right?"

"You and Gustav made me this offer to alleviate your guilt. What's wrong with wanting to alleviate mine? He got into this mess trying to help me, by giving me a ride to the airport. He doesn't deserve this."

"Um, Charlotte. Simon's not...the same anymore. You..." He sighed loudly. "You can't save him now."

I fought against the fire in my chest to answer. "If his heart is still beating, there's a chance."

"No, really. He can't be released. I'm sorry." He shook his head.

"I'm a doctor, dammit! I can fix him."

"Just how many chances and how much time do you think we have? I'm willing to help, but I won't make it a suicide mission."

I blanched at his tone; I wasn't going to win this one. "What if you happened to leave something in the room, or loosened a tether, just before Mitch…"

Morgan laughed without humor. "He's snapped all the tethers. We've had to sedate him, and Mitch would never go in his room, anyway."

I blinked rapidly. "I'll come up with something, after I get back from the seventh—"

"About that. I'll have to see what Gustav says. I can't make you any promises."

"I know the protocol for reality seven. I hid it, because I didn't want to risk it on anyone else. But I have it, and I know the numbers. I trust Gustav can do it. He's succeeded accessing the other peripheries without my assistance recently, and this protocol isn't much different."

"So you're not suicidal?"

I shook my head. "Absolutely not."

He rubbed a hand over his shaved head. "I'll tell Gustav. I have to leave. The cam has been off too long now."

He grabbed the empty tray, and before heading out the door, he turned to me. He stared at my face for a moment before shaking his head, opening the door, and allowing it to shut behind him.

The light on the cam went from red to green, and I slumped down onto the bed.

Morgan's words replayed in my head.

Simon's not…the same anymore. You can't save him now.

I clenched my fists and stared up at the camera while biting my lip. Perhaps Jared was watching me right now. The thought caused me to turn and swipe the tray off the side table again, temporary satisfaction warming my stomach when the dishes clanged to the ground. Another cold shiver wracked my body, so I grabbed the blanket from the bed and hugged it tight around me as I hauled myself into bed.

I fought against the memories from reality one, memories when Simon and I lay in bed, with the views of the bay before us. Then, a memory from *here* flashed before me—when I'd coached him as he attempted to walk again during his rehab, and a moment when he'd stumbled into me during that process. I'd caught his arms, and our faces nearly touched. He'd flashed me a smile that day, and after that moment, I knew his determination would heal him. I was right, he walked flawlessly by the end of the week. I squeezed my eyes shut, the memories taunting a feeling of loss that was too painful to bear. At some point, surprisingly, I fell asleep.

****

"What the—" Morgan's voice woke me. He looked around at the tray and its contents strewn about.

Morgan, Gustav, and Mitch were in my room. I hugged the blanket tighter around me and shivered violently.

"Leave," I grumbled. My eyes slid shut.

"Hello, Charly. I hear you want to go on a little trip?" Mitch's voice sounded from above me.

I nodded with my eyes still closed.

"What's wrong, Charlotte?" Gustav touched my forehead. "She's burning up."

"Aw, man. She's sick, maybe that's why she's not

285

eating. I'll call Rogers," Morgan said.

Mitch spoke, "Not necessary. She wants to go on a trip, let's send her. She'll be treated when she returns." He tapped my cheek. "Look at me," he demanded.

My eyes fluttered open, and I stared at him before my heavy lids shut again. I was so, so tired.

Morgan muttered a few profanities—it sounded like he'd stumbled over something. Probably something from the tray I'd tossed. A boot full of eggs. The thought amused me, but I didn't have the strength to smile. Oh well.

"Get her ready and clean this shit up. We send her today. I want to do it before Jared gets back."

"Sir?"

"What is it, Gustav?" Mitch barked.

"We have some jumpers returning today. We have an important briefing at noon. Let's send her tomorrow."

I opened my eyes and stared at the men; Morgan had begun cleaning up the mess I'd made.

Mitch nodded at Gustav. "Tomorrow by noon, I want her sent to Periphery seven. No more delays." He exited the room and the door shut behind him.

Morgan chuckled. "Gustav, how do you think he's gonna take the news?"

Gustav sighed loudly, perched at the edge of my bed, and patted my hair. "Not well."

I stared at Gustav, waiting to hear more.

He looked down at me. "Charlotte, a few jumpers came here to deliver an important message."

He looked like he was trying to suppress the smile that pulled at his lips.

"Mitch was sniped in the main reality."

I fought against the fatigue, allowing a huge smile

to break across my face. Another violent tremor shook through me. Every inch of my skin hurt, so I tried not to move.

"You think it was the Silencer?" Morgan asked.

"Maybe," Gustav answered.

"Absolutely," I whispered.

"Rest, Charlotte. I'm going to call Rogers and get you some medicine. Here. Drink."

I pushed up onto my elbows and took two big swigs from the water bottle, then handed it back to Gustav. "Gustav? I need a favor."

"What is it, dear?" He leaned down toward me.

"The banned device, to get sent back to the main reality. What they used on me—" My voice cracked.

"They used it on you?" His eyes widened.

I nodded.

"Ah, shit." Morgan rubbed a hand over his face and puffed out a breath.

"Charlotte, I'm so sorry. Really, I never thought, I never *knew*—"

"It's okay, Gustav. But please, just this one thing. I need you to store that device in Simon's room. In a closet, a cabinet, somewhere, okay?"

He raised his eyebrows and nodded. "But, what—"

I closed my eyes. "I'm so cold," I whined, then shivered.

A heaviness was placed on me, and I opened my eyes to see Morgan laying two more blankets over me. I wanted to thank him, but my eyes slid shut, the fatigue winning.

****

A day or two had to have passed. When I woke up, my body was heavy and sore, and my room was full of equipment. Something felt tight on my face, and I reached up to touch it.

The small NG tube was taped to my cheek, and snaked up my nose and down into my stomach. I had IV's running into both arms. My gaze landed on Gustav.

"What happened?"

"Glad you're doing better. You were going septic from the wound on your back, but the antibiotics are kicking in. I don't think you're stable enough to go—"

"She goes today. Jared returns tomorrow." Mitch spoke as he entered the room, staring at a file. "This yours, Charly?" He turned the folder toward me.

It was the protocol to get to Periphery seven. I nodded.

He spoke while he looked at the protocol again. "You trust it enough to risk your life?"

I nodded again, the movement bringing pain. "Everything hurts."

"He had us stop the pain medications because of the protocol. We don't want anything interfering. As soon as you get back, we'll treat the pain." Gustav tried to console me.

Morgan stepped forward and began fastening the tethers to my wrists and ankles.

I didn't move. I'd wanted this, but didn't expect to be so sick when it happened. I feared my compromised state may threaten my memories, then all hope would be lost. Perhaps it was good they'd stopped the pain meds temporarily, despite the discomfort.

Doctor Carter joined Gustav and the others in the room, and they began prepping the drugs and equipment needed for my jump.

A flash of panic arose. *What if my heart wouldn't re-*

start here because I was so sick? Would Simon be left to rot tethered to a bed in Quantym forever?

I inhaled deeply, bringing every ounce of physical and spiritual strength I had left in me to the surface. I turned my head to the side as Carter began pushing the bolus of heart-stopping meds into my line.

He flashed a sinister smile when he caught my stare.

Mitch's voice was the last thing I heard before going to the last available life on the Periphery. "Sweet dreams, Charly."

****

I never spoke upon my return to reality two. They resuscitated me, and I retained the memories from the seventh Periphery. It fed what little strength I had left.

Mitch threatened me, and even put a gun to my head, but I wouldn't tell him what I saw, and I hadn't uttered a word since coming back. I was still processing it and was certain the team considered I may have brain damage from the jump while septic.

I assume it was evening when my room cleared out.

Morgan came to visit me, probably before leaving the facility for the night. "Say something, Charlotte. You don't have to tell me what you saw, but—"

I stared at the ceiling, unblinking.

"My girl's pregnant, have I ever told you that? A good man takes care of his family, and I thought by working here, the pay increase would help me be a better—" He swallowed loudly. "—a better, I don't know, partner, father, maybe. I'm not making excuses, I just...I don't want you to die, and watching what's happening to you is really messing me up. Damn, if someone did this to my girl, I'd be so—"

"Don't worry, Morgan. You didn't kill me."

He puffed out a loud breath. "You scared us. Glad you're okay."

"I'm not okay. Everything hurts. It all hurts so bad." The dam finally broke, and I cried in front of him.

"You gotta be strong, it's all gonna be okay…" His hands hovered over me, never making contact, as he tried to figure out how to console me. "Shit. Hang on. I'll get Rogers to give you some of the good stuff, and it'll take your pain away. All your pain." He smirked. "And if you eat something, I'll even make him take that out." He pointed at the NG tube.

Within thirty minutes, Morgan made good on his promise.

I ate, Rogers removed the NG tube, then injected me with something that took away all my mental and physical pain. I was high as a kite.

"Give her a shot every six hours until she's better," Rogers told Morgan as my mind drifted.

And finally, with memories from three realities flowing through my overwhelmed and grieving brain, I slept.

Chapter 23, Reality 1

Simon

When I got the anonymous text with exact coordinates and a promise of a clear shot, I slipped off base mostly undetected and headed straight for Cedarwood Bay with my heart in my throat.

Initially, I'd hoped it was a defector offering me Jared's head. But when I asked who the target was, and he answered, *"My father,"* that put a fire under my ass. *Had Jared visited Charlotte, or abducted her? Was offering Mitch's head a setup?*

I'd slung my rifle case over my shoulder, and took the fire escape up to the roof of a building that faced Cedarwood Bay's lot. If I could get a clear shot, I'd be putting a bullet through both their skulls.

Jared was the devil, but he wasn't dumb. He kept himself shrouded in the shadow and cover of heavy trees and stayed a half step behind his father. Two seconds, and Mitch dropped when the lead kissed his temple. Jared disappeared, but he was living on borrowed time, too.

I couldn't enter Cedarwood; within minutes police and media swarmed the lot where the general's lifeless body lay. But I was able to call to ensure Charlotte was safe, and I was confident she'd remain so since the facility was on lockdown with a shooter on the loose.

Me.

I'd be seeing her tonight, anyway, when I helped the team break her out of the home and set her up on base. Normally, I'd do things the right way, sign her out, leave a paper trail, but I couldn't take chances now that Jared would be running Quantym. He'd need the equation and her—especially with his father now eliminated.

****

I slipped back onto base and set myself up in an empty barrack to disassemble and clean my rifle. Just as I was snapping the case shut, Xavier stormed in.

He stopped two paces away and glared at me. "I told you, Donovan, no going rogue on us!"

I looked up at him with feigned innocence. "Duly noted, LT."

"It's all over the news already!" He paced restlessly, then rubbed a hand over his face. "Last warning."

I smiled. "It was more painful for me to offer him a painless death. Besides, with all the coverage of Jared's case, there were probably a lot of people who wanted his head."

He nodded. "Well, you fucked us for tonight. The facility is going to be on lockdown, and we're going to have to postpone getting Charlotte."

"No can do, LT. I'll sign her out if I have to. Jared offering up his father means he's up to something, and I have a feeling he needs her now more than ever."

"Jared offered up his father?"

I held up my phone with the anonymous text.

Xavier scanned the message then looked at me with raised brows. He blew out a breath and sat on the bunk across from me. "Shit." He dropped his head into his hands.

"What are you thinking?"

"I don't know what to think, but it's making me uneasy as hell. I didn't see it coming."

I puffed out a short laugh and nodded. "Yeah."

My cell rang and I answered it on the first ring.

"Mr. Donovan? Hi, it's Corrine from Cedarwood Bay. You asked that I call with any changes…"

"What happened?" I barked into the phone.

"Nothing, just a status change. She stopped writing. And she said your name."

My heart thrummed violently in my chest, and I tried to stifle the hope that rose like the tides during a full moon. I strode out the door and Xavier followed close behind.

"Is she still talking? What is she doing? I'm on my way right now."

"Well, she's not doing anything, really. She appears to be in a state of catatonia, but before that, she was writing as usual, and then she screamed. That's why I went in to check on her. She stopped her writing, uttered your name, and hasn't said a word since."

I pulled my door shut and took off before Xavier could even pull his closed. He muttered something as I stomped on the gas and headed for the home.

"I'll be there in five. Thank you for calling me."

"Sir, I wasn't trying to get your hopes up, just following the instructions you left."

"You did good, Corrine. Tell her I'm coming."

I stormed into the facility, and while I knew Xavier was on my heels, I wanted to be alone with Charlotte. No matter what happened here and now, she was coming with me. She was still inside herself somewhere and she *said my name*.

I strode into her room and fell to my knees in front of her "Charlotte," I whispered. I cupped her face.

Her gaze found mine, and my heart nearly stopped.

I couldn't help myself, I leaned down and kissed her.

She grasped my wrists, holding my hands in place. Her eyes locked on mine, then she gazed at the paper laid out on the floor.

She'd finished the equation.

"Charlotte, you finished? I know what this is. It's to navigate all seven peripheries, right?"

She shook her head. "Six," she whispered.

She slid from my grasp and sat on her heels. Her eyes glazed and locked on the paper in front of her.

She solved the equation, but she wasn't fully better.

I tried talking to her, touching her, holding her, but she remained catatonic, with unseeing eyes and a stiffened body.

"I'm taking you out of here, love. I'm going to get you better."

Xavier and I argued a bit about signing her out. He was hung up on sticking to the plan, but I wanted Jared to see she was with me. Let him come straight to me, but he'd never, ever get to her. I'd be glad to put a bullet in his head and end him when he tried.

Charlotte came with us, silent in her catatonic state.

I'd rolled up the paper with the equation and brought that with us so we could show the doctors and keep it under lock and key.

****

Later that night, Xavier had set Charlotte and me up in a barrack that was under high security. I didn't want to take her back to the house and risk anything. Not that I planned on sleeping, but at least on base I had the team looking out for us.

Jared had access to base but had no idea I'd signed on with the team as far as anyone knew. Besides, he should be plenty busy tending to the media and arranging a funeral, what with his father's untimely demise and all.

Charlotte fell asleep, and I climbed in beside her, my chest constricting at the thought that with the equation now completed, she was likely to die soon.

Every jumper who got sent backward eventually did, presumably when their mind collapsed under the duress of all the memories of two lifetimes attempting to occupy one brain.

There had to be a way to change her fate. I'd stop at nothing to ensure she didn't die. I ran my fingers along her soft ivory cheek.

Her black lashes fluttered, but she didn't wake.

"I love you, Charlotte," I whispered.

After two hours, I got out of bed. Attempting to sleep was useless when I felt like I should be *doing* something. I couldn't spend a moment resting when I could be putting a bullet into Jared's head or jumping to another life to take him and his father out there, too.

I paced, then did fifty push-ups, followed by fifty sit-ups, but nothing burned off the uneasy energy that flowed around me.

A soft moan caused my gaze to fly to Charlotte.

She lay still on the bed, her dark hair a halo around her. Then she whispered something.

I slowly walked over to where she lay, ready to wake her if she was dreaming. Maybe she still had her nightmares.

Her soft voice sounded again. "The multiverse may be real, but the possibilities are not infinite. If you don't have it in you to kill, in no reality are you a killer."

My back stiffened. She was repeating Jared's words to her many months ago before he'd stabbed her.

I sat on the edge of her bed and smoothed her hair. "It's okay, Charlotte. I'm here." I sucked in a breath when I saw her green eyes were open but unseeing. She wasn't dreaming.

"The multiverse may be real, but the possibilities are not infinite. If you don't have it in you to kill, in no reality are you a killer," she repeated. Her brow pinched, and her lower lip quivered.

My heart beat painfully in my chest.

"Charlotte, look at me. Please. Look at me," I damn near begged.

Her gaze locked on mine.

My heart rate kicked up, and I grasped her face in both my hands. "Yes, great job, love. It's me, Sy. I won't let anything happen to you."

Her eyes filled with tears, and one escaped from the corner, disappearing into her hair. "The multiverse may be real, but the possibilities are not infinite. If you don't have it in you to kill, in *no reality are you a killer*." Her tone had changed. Now it sounded like she was pleading.

I pulled her into my arms, and she locked her arms and legs around my body.

"Help me, Sy," she whispered.

I wasn't a man who prayed often, but in that moment, I begged. *God, please help me help her.* "Anything, love, anything. Tell me what you need." I held her so tight, I was afraid I'd never be able to let her go. I buried my face into the crook of her neck, rocking slightly as she held onto me as if it may be the last time.

"Please help," she croaked.

"Tell me how, dammit!"

She sniffled and sobbed into my shoulder, and my heart shattered in my chest. I'd survived death more than a dozen times, but this was it. This was what was going to take me out.

"The multiverse may be real, but the possibilities are not infinite. If you don't have it in you to kill, in *no reality are you a killer*."

"I'll fucking kill them for you. All of them. I put a bullet straight through Mitch's skull today. Did I tell you that yet? It's all over the news, and his son is next. I'll make him suffer for what they've done."

She kept her arms and legs wrapped around me, and I was certain that if I didn't come up with something, I was going to have to witness her lose it and die right here in my arms. Would it be like Alzheimer's patients who would get so lost in their mind that they'd forget to breathe? Would her rushing thoughts bring her heart into a fatal arrythmia or give her a stroke? Fuck, no. *No, no, no.*

"I'm taking you to the wing here on base where we've started our own facility to allow jumps. I know the tech is immoral, but we're looking to regulate it since we didn't stop it. Think of it as the end of a prohibition era."

I stood, and she stayed clinging to me.

I carried her down the dark empty halls and to the small wing where I'd been sent to reality two the other day.

She kept her head buried into my shoulder, chanting about not being able to kill and asking me to help her.

I set her down and she stood frozen, staring at the equipment.

After several moments, I followed her gaze as it

went from the hospital bed to the four-point restraints to the ventilator, the defibrillator, and the glass-door fridge that held all the meds and IV bags.

She began slowly walking the room, running her hands along the equipment. Her movements became more rushed, panicked.

"What is it?" I stared at her, then turned and badged the closet in the room open. I took out the paper with her equation and unrolled it on the bed.

She walked over and ran her delicate hands over the paper. She pointed at a portion of the equation, and I recognized it from Diogo pointing it out the other day.

Picoseconds.

The meter, she needed the damn meter. I turned back to the closet, opened a drawer, and pulled out the meter that counted picoseconds.

She took it from me, stared at it, then looked up at me and smiled.

She fucking smiled.

Two strides, and my body was nearly against hers as I brought my face down to meet her eyes. "I'll figure something out, Charlotte. Don't give up on me. You're going to fight, and we're going to get through this. I know you're in there, and I'm going to get you better."

She nodded, then closed the small space between us, pressing her body fully against mine as she walked into me with both her hands on my chest, guiding me toward the bed.

When the bed hit the back of my thighs, I sat and pulled her into me, and she slammed her lips against mine.

She pulled away, breathless, then put her hands on my chest and pushed me down onto the bed.

"Charlotte, wait. Hold on." I glanced up at the cameras in the room, and as much as every part of me wanted to jump her right here and now, she wasn't wholly there.

She pulled away, then guided one arm toward the tether on the bed.

I cocked an eyebrow.

She pointed at the other tether, then turned to glance at the ventilator. She wanted to send me on a mission.

I shrugged. "If you send me, I'll kill them in every life you send me to."

She looked down, then slumped onto the bed beside me. "The multiverse may be real, but the possibilities are not infinite. If you don't have it in you to kill, in *no reality are you a killer*."

"You can't know I'm going to kill them," I spoke to myself aloud. I turned to her, and took her face into my hands. "Send me, Charlotte. I won't hurt anyone; I just want to see. Show me. Show me what you can't say."

She nodded eagerly.

It couldn't have been more than thirty minutes, and she moved as if this protocol was second nature to her. She obtained the meds from the fridge, set up the vent and defibrillator, started my IV and fastened the tethers.

Not gonna lie. It was the first time I was ever afraid to jump. I was literally putting my life in her hands, and her mind was most definitely not at full capacity. But something shone behind her sage eyes, a spark of fire, of intellect, that I trusted with my soul. I was going to allow her this, and if I could die to cure her, great. If I died trying, I was okay with that, too.

Charlotte unrolled the paper on the floor beneath her, her gaze dragging along the length of the equation scrawled on it. She positioned the meter that could count picoseconds onto the bed, then prepared to put a bolus of heart-stopping medication into my IV line.

Before attaching the syringe, she leaned close to me, her gaze locking on mine. Her eyes closed, and the tip of her nose grazed my cheek. Her lips found mine, and she kissed me gently. A tear escaped when she pulled away, then attached the syringe and depressed the plunger.

A flash of panic hit my nervous system, and I nearly tore out the IV before the meds could hit. But I stared into her knowing eyes, and held her gaze until the pressure in my chest increased, then darkness descended.

****

I returned from the jump with a shock to the chest and fire in my veins. Or maybe it was bloodlust. Adrenaline. Satisfaction from cold-blooded murder of the two people I hated most in this world. This was her plan, and it was a damn good one. Strike in the middle of the night, when no one was suspecting it, before anyone even knew she'd cracked the equation in a reality where she wasn't locked away. And sending me to the furthest Periphery first ensured jumpers couldn't go backward to warn them I was coming. Brilliant.

I bellowed out a yell of...*agony? Pain? Frustration?* She'd already extubated me, but whatever the hell I was feeling was addictive, and I wanted more. *More.* I pulled at the tethers until Charlotte was over me, running her hands over my chest, attempting to chase away the fire.

Hard breaths sawed in and out of me. *How much do I tell her?*

She didn't speak, and I stared at her as bitter realization dawned. She still wasn't cured.

My focus returned, my body relaxed, and my breathing slowed. "It's OK, Charlotte. I saw what you wanted me to see. I saw. Send me to another." I gritted my teeth.

She shook her head, then rested her forehead on my freezing-cold chest.

I lifted my head, unable to hold or touch her with my hands still tethered. "I can do it, Charlotte. I can handle it. My body always reacts this way to waking up. I want to see. Please send me," I coaxed. And… time was of the essence.

She was taking an educated guess on how quickly she could wake me, estimating how long it'd take me to find them and end them.

It felt faster the second time, and even quicker the third time, even though hours and hours had passed. In what felt like mere minutes, and she was pushing another bolus into my IV line, and darkness spread from my heart to my brain as my consciousness drifted away to another life on the Periphery.

It wasn't Charlotte over me when I started on my bullshit after being shocked back to this life.

It was Xavier, screaming my name over and over and over as I attempted to get out of the restraints and kill.

Charlotte stood behind him, wide-eyed and gaping, her hands trembling.

I finally calmed, but my heart slammed relentlessly inside my chest. Memories of three lives, and what I saw, haunted me. *How could I have not known?*

"Do you have a damn death wish, Donovan?!" Xavier was beet-red as he hollered at me. "I told you, no going rogue! And you—" He spun to face Charlotte.

She shrank away, her gaze darting from him to me.

He sauntered closer to her. "You're barely coherent one minute, and the next you have the capacity to send him on not *one* but *two* trips to the Periphery?" His tone was laced with accusation.

"Three," I clarified.

He glanced at me, then glared at her. "If she can do this protocol—" His gaze drifted to the paper on the floor. "—she can speak for herself. Unless she's—"

"Stop, Xavier," I warned.

Charlotte scurried over to me and unfastened a tether. She turned to face Xavier when he stepped closer to her.

I sat up and unfastened the other restraints.

"Well, Charlotte?" He put his hands on his hips. "Unless it's not really you. I've heard of the things they've tried, experimented with. Imagine that, turning you into a mindless dummy they control and using that against him."

She backed away, shaking her head.

In a heartbeat I was on him, my arm wrapped around his neck from behind. "She can't speak, but she showed me why. Now, stop hurling accusations at my wife and wake the team. You're all going to want to know what I just saw. And did."

I released my hold on him, and he stumbled.

"Wake the team? It's almost noon! I went looking for you last night. Jared showed up at Cedarwood Bay, just after midnight, likely to abduct her—" He tipped his head at Charly. "—and Joel took him out. He's dead."

I ran a hand over my short hair, electricity thrumming up and down my spine. "Good."

"Then you missed morning PT, and I went nuts

looking for you two, thinking maybe he'd gotten to her here!" He paced again restlessly. "You've gone too far, Donovan. Too far! You're out!" He straightened and got in my face. "You will not come in here, think you're going to command my team, and take matters into your own hands! I don't give a—"

"She can't speak because she's being held in all six lives. If Jared'd succeeded last night, he'd have her here, too."

Xavier stiffened, his chin rising, his gaze locked on mine.

"She sent me to reality six, and it turns out, in that reality, he kidnapped her. I shot him and his father, and got her back. In reality five, they were acquaintances, and I found her chained by the ankle in his house. In reality four, she'd just been reported missing this week, but guess where I found her? And we already know he has her locked away in reality two. I sniped both of them—Mitch and Jared—in every life she sent me to."

Xavier blew out his breath. "You think saving her in the other lives will snap her out of it?"

I nodded. "Without a doubt." I rubbed a hand over my face. "He knows her value, and she's the key to him running Quantym in all the lives. Her plan is brilliant. She sent me from reality six, all the way down to four, in the middle of the night, so no one saw it coming, and no one can jump backward to warn them. There's only one problem." I glanced down at the paper on the floor.

"What?"

"The equation can only navigate six peripheries."

Xavier turned to her. "There's no access to the seventh?"

I shrugged. "If you can't travel backward, I guess

303

there's no need for Quantym to exist in the seventh Periphery..." I spoke my thoughts aloud. "But we should still be able to travel to there from here..."

Charlotte glanced at the paper and back to him. She opened her mouth to speak, but a heartbeat too long passed, and no sound came out. Color drained from her face as her eyes rolled.

I stalked over to her, my own body wooden and stiff and shivering, and caught her before she could crack her skull on the tile.

She trembled and shook, completely out of control.

Xavier called for backup over his radio.

A seizure. She was having a seizure.

Chapter 24, Reality 2: On the Periphery

Jared

I returned to base from Arlington in the early morning and went straight to room 300. I stood over a sleeping Charly, drinking in her soft features, her hair a dark cloud scattered across the pillow behind her.

She was in a deep sleep, her breaths slow and even, her body completely unmoving. When she wasn't running her mouth, or challenging me, she was quite pleasing to be around—she was smart, funny, affectionate.

I almost didn't want to wake her and ruin the peaceful moment, but I'd missed her. "Charly," I whispered, running my fingers along her cheek.

She stirred, turning on her side toward me, then reached up and rested her hand on my stomach. "Jared," she murmured.

I raised my eyebrows and grasped her hand, holding it in place on me. "Missed me, doll?" I sat on the edge of her bed.

She nodded.

I nearly choked before a smile spread across my face. I leaned down until my nose almost touched hers. "Open your eyes."

She opened her eyes, then reached up and touched my face. "Hi, baby."

I straightened my back and recoiled away from her touch, then stared down at her.

Her eyes were glassy, her skin warm, and her cheeks were flushed deep pink.

"Hi," I responded cautiously, the word coming out sounding like a question.

Her eyes slid shut. "Did you water my flowers for me? I forgot to."

"Your flowers? It's December, Charly."

"Mmm…" She shivered.

"What the hell do they have you on?" I muttered to myself, rising and pulling the laptop over. I logged in. They'd documented no medications, but she was high as hell.

I turned back to her and rubbed her back.

She moaned softly—it sounded like appreciation.

"I want a hot shower. I'm so cold." She hugged the blankets tighter with her eyes still closed, and a shiver wracked her.

"I can do that." I went to the bathroom and turned on the shower, then went to the closet and pulled out some towels. I stared at the empty shelf that should've held her clothes. Shit. I'd forgotten to bring more of her things before I left. A surge of panic hit my chest, and I stalked back to her bed.

I pulled on the blanket, and she resisted.

"I'm cold," she whined.

I yanked it off her, and she was in just a hospital gown. Morgan was going to get ripped for this. No wonder she was so fucking cold. And Rogers, too, for not documenting her meds.

"Come here, it's warmer in there. I have the shower on." I grasped her arm.

She sat up, and the movement was unusually slow.

The johnny fell off one shoulder, and I stared at her exposed skin as she reached up and ran a finger over my new captain rank insignia on my uniform.

I pulled her into me, and she didn't resist. She wrapped her arms around me, and I lifted her, carrying her into the bathroom.

She looked up at me as I sat her on the sink in the room full of hot steam.

I brushed the hair from her face, then brought my face down to hers and kissed her.

And she kissed me back.

I peeled the gown off her shoulders, exposing her naked body. Inhaling sharply, I looked down, taking her in.

She shivered again, pulling me back to her.

I started unbuttoning the top of my uniform, and my lips were on hers again as I pushed my tongue between her lips and she let me in effortlessly, her tongue twining with mine. And there it was, revealed—the nuclear chemistry between us that could light up an entire city. In an instant, parts of my uniform were strewn on the floor, my dog tags clinking as I stepped out of my boots, and my pants fell to the tile.

She wrapped her legs around me and I carried her into the shower—my chest ready to explode with need. Wherever her anger and memories and hatred had gone, or whatever drugs they were hiding behind, could be dealt with later. For now, I was going to re-claim my wife.

I gently placed her down, and she stood under the stream of hot water.

"Shit," I muttered. "Be right back." Stumbling out

of the shower, I scrabbled for my phone and turned off the cameras in the room. Charly wasn't a traitor, or a weakness, as Mitch alleged. She was loyal to a fault, and she obviously didn't hate me, regardless of some of the fucked-up shit I'd done.

I stepped back into the shower, and she was still standing under the hot stream of water with her eyes closed. Stepping closer to her, I began running the bar of soap over her hot skin. Her head lolled back, and a sigh escaped her lips as I took my time, using the opportunity to run my hands over every beautiful part of her. I slid my hands over her full breasts, her small waist, the swell of her hips and ass. Her head fell forward, onto my chest, and I continued rubbing soapy circles along her lower back.

Mine. The thought infiltrated my mind so loudly I couldn't be sure I didn't mutter it aloud.

I brought my hands up to her hair, and massaged shampoo onto her scalp.

She moaned and kept her eyes closed.

"Tip your head back."

She complied, and the hot water rinsed her hair free of the lather.

"Turn around," I ordered.

I ran my hands over her body again, washing away the soap. Her dark hair was slick to her back. I turned her again and stared at her.

"Look at me."

She opened her eyes and looked up at me, then her gaze darted around a bit disoriented. "Jared?" Her arms flew up to cover her body.

"You asked me to shower you." I gently pulled her arms away from her chest. "What did they give you?"

"Give me?" Confusion colored her face.

Before she could think too hard on it, my mouth was on hers again, and her lips answered, as I knew they would. Her body responded to me whether her mind wanted it to or not. I never had to force a damn thing.

She ran her hands up my chest, pressing herself closer to me.

My patience came undone like nuclear fission in that moment, lighting my body on fire. I locked my arms around her as my tongue dipped into her mouth again, violent and wanting and searching.

She moaned into my mouth, and I spun her around. She braced her forearms and splayed her hands on the tile wall, then rested her forehead onto her biceps.

Mine. Mine. Mine.

I grasped her hips, ready to take her, when the hot water ricocheting off my shoulder hit her, parting her long dark hair and revealing her back.

The wound from Mitch's little experiment last week was massively infected. The stitches were in place, but the edge of the wound was red and angry, with dark pink streaks snaking from the wound and down toward her waist.

"Son of a bitch!" I punched the tile on the side of her head, and she recoiled. "Stand up, Charly."

She obeyed.

"How long has it been like this?"

"What? I-I don't know." She shivered.

I pulled her under the hot stream of water. "It's okay, I'll get you fixed up." I ran my hands over her hair, then kissed her forehead. "Then we'll go home. Does that sound good?" I drew her into me.

She nodded, then shivered again as her eyes slid

shut.

****

After I'd reamed out Rogers, Morgan, and Gustav, they met me in room 300 to assess her infection. I'd had Morgan return with clothes for her, and I took her into the bathroom to get her dressed.

Rogers hung a bag of IV antibiotics, asserting that the oral antibiotics had already kicked in, and she was better than she was a couple days ago.

I looked her over. "You call this better? Why didn't anyone call me?" I gritted my teeth.

Morgan cleared his throat. "The general said no distractions for you. Rogers initially gave her IV antibiotics, but had to stop them for—"

Gustav interjected. "After her jump, we gave injections of pain meds and oral antibiotics—"

"Her *what*?" I stomped over to him, ready to knock the old man out.

Rogers cleared his throat. "She couldn't have any meds outside the protocol during the jump, and afterward, we felt she was improving enough to spare her the IV. Carter had already put the NG tube—"

"NG tube?!" I pulled my gun out and paced back and forth.

Breathe. Just breathe.

"Those were your orders," Morgan blurted.

I spun to face him, and stuffed my gun back into the holster.

Inhibition control, I had to get a grip. Those *were* my orders. I just didn't think she'd call my bluff and continue on her bullshit. "Give her something to reverse…this." I waved my hand over her splayed out on the bed drugged out of her mind.

Rogers scrambled over to her, and sprayed something up her nose to reverse the effects of the narcotics.

Almost immediately, the haze in her eyes began to clear.

"And let me guess. It was my father who orchestrated her jump? To the seventh Periphery?"

"Actually, it was *her.*" Gustav slid between me and Morgan.

Morgan pinned Gustav's back with a glare, as if he was betraying some unspoken truce.

I turned to Charly, laid out on the bed, still high as a bird but coming down. "Charly?" I stomped over to her.

She nodded. "I wanted to see."

"And?"

She lifted her head, and her gaze shifted toward the other men.

I turned to them. "Out. Now."

The room cleared, and I lowered myself to the edge of her bed. "Tell me, Charly. What's on the seventh Periphery?"

She sucked in a deep, shuddering breath. "You." She wilted, and her glassy gaze found mine. "You were right. It's always me and you."

A huge smile broke across my face, and I climbed on top of her, bracing my forearms on either side of her head. I smoothed her hair. "I told you, doll. And you know for a fact I can't alter things in that life. You're the first to jump there." I snickered. "You have no idea how happy this makes me, for you to finally see—accept—the truth."

"It doesn't make sense," she whispered.

"Yes, it does. You've always loved me, and I you.

311

Just because you don't like some of my actions, doesn't mean I'm not your weakness. I told you, in every life, you choose me."

"The human variable." Her brow creased. "Love."

"Ah, yes. The complexity of our choices." I tilted my head. "Did you think Simon was your soulmate? That you'd have to fight that hard to be with someone? No, doll, no." I laughed. "He was just some cuck hung up on stealing you from me. To covet another man's wife is a sin, you know."

She closed her eyes when I uttered his name, and that was unacceptable.

"Look at me," I demanded.

Her aurora eyes locked on mine.

"Now, tell me why you're not happy about it."

"You don't deserve it."

I sucked in a breath. "Your love? Yes, I do." I could feel my features rearranging as the anger hijacked my composure. "I've lived a life filled with darkness. No mother, Mitch for a father. I was a trained soldier before I was even old enough to enlist. Why shouldn't I be allowed a small glimmer of light?" I gritted my teeth. "I don't give a shit if I had to steal you in the other lives. In these three—"

"Wait, what?"

"Nothing. It doesn't matter. Where it matters, you *chose* me. And, maybe it's not me that's undeserving, maybe it's *you* that deserves *me*."

Her eyes rounded and lips parted as she took in my words.

The IV clicked softly in the background, pushing meds into her system.

I still wanted to kill the men for not caring for her

properly. "You and I—" I rubbed my thumb along her jaw. "—are going to run Quantym together, everywhere. My father is approaching his *permanent* retirement." I let the implication of my plan to kill him in all lives hang between us.

Her eyes darted back and forth, searching my face. "Steal me?"

I smirked. "Just think about it. Limitless money, power, us…" I brought my face closer to hers. "We're not just destined because of *love*." I kissed her frowning lips softly. "We've got a job to do, and we're the only two qualified. You want the rest? I can give you the rest—kids, a home, whatever stupid idea of love is ingrained in you, I can fulfill."

"The bleed-through effect," she whispered and her eyes widened. "Not just for the bad—"

"It's not all bad. Nothing ever is." I dragged my lips along her cheek, then kissed her neck, ready to finish where we'd left off in the shower. "We're all just at the mercy of our very human condition, after all."

Her head snapped toward the door when my father entered.

I pulled myself off of her, and stood to meet him.

He stepped around me and stared down at Charly.

She sat up and faced him.

"So, that's what you saw, huh?" He barked out a laugh. "I almost shot you for not telling me, and that's all that it was? Your disappointment silenced you?" His shoulders shook with another scornful laugh.

A tear escaped and rolled down her cheek, the diamond wetness glistening as it hung from her chin. She broke his gaze and found mine.

My eyes softened when they met hers, and I

captured the tear on her chin with my thumb.

He'd either been standing behind the two-way mirror, or watching the cameras. I was glad he knew. It was the last parting gift I'd offer him.

He turned to me. "My permanent retirement?" His eyebrow raised.

"Your old ass won't be able to run this place forever."

He nodded. "You won't succeed like you did in the main reality."

"That wasn't me. You have a mark on your back. Your permanent retirement is imminent, but not by *my* hand."

He turned to Charly. "Well, *she's* not a killer. And the Silencer is locked up. Who should I be looking out for, Jared?" He sauntered closer to me.

"When you find out, do let me know. Clearly, you haven't heard yet. They took me out over there, too. I don't need to wait for a jumper to tell me." I tapped my temple, anger rising at the memory. I'd been minutes from snatching Charly from the Cedarwood Bay facility, then woke up in reality two with a blaring headache and memories of both lives. I'd been sniped. No matter, she'd be dead there soon, too. Quantym was more advanced on this side, anyway, and I was tiring of running things in both lives. I had the upper hand in reality two regardless.

I lifted my chin at him. "Now, I have one last promise to make good on before I take *my wife* home."

"You really think she'll remain loyal? With everything you've done? She's breaking down your walls, just to stab you through the heart again."

"There is only one person in this room who has continually lied and betrayed me, and it's not her."

He sneered. "Blinded by love?" He clicked his tongue. "You don't deserve that promotion. You're *weak*."

I ignored him and turned back to the bed. "Charly, get up."

She stood and stumbled over to me.

I grasped her hand. "I told you I'd let you see what's become of Simon, and after you see, we're going home."

She took in a deep breath, the fading drugs still causing her to sway on her feet. She shivered, then grasped her IV pole.

I cocked a brow at my father. "Care to join us?"

I pulled Charly out of the room with me, and headed to Simon's room, a mere two doors down the hall. Poetic how close they'd been all along. The sound of my father's footsteps followed us.

I slipped into the adjacent observation room, and Charly followed me in.

When she saw Simon, she immediately stepped up to the two-way mirrored glass and gasped. She rested her palm on the window.

"Simon," she breathed. The glassiness in her eyes finally cleared.

I ran a finger around my collar. The sound of his name on her lips temporarily constricted my airway. This was the last piece of the puzzle, and I couldn't back out now. Once she knew I was her only option, life could move forward. Quantym could move forward. *We* could move forward.

It was never about forcing her. It was about showing her, letting her see the truth and *choose*. She wouldn't hate me then. There was no way around it—for her, I was just an inevitability, as was her role at Quantym.

I turned to her. "He's dangerous, Charly. He can snap the tethers and kill you in seconds. But, if you want to go in, I won't stop you. You need closure, so I'm offering it."

Mitch stepped up to the glass beside us, intrigue written all over the lines on his face.

Charly looked up at me. "I want to go in."

I was disappointed, but not surprised. Sitting on the bench in the small room, I slid a folding knife from my boot. "Don't underestimate him. Protect yourself." I placed the knife in her hand, then slid the clamp onto the IV tubing, and disconnected her from the pole. "I don't want this holding you back from running if you have to. We'll hook you back up when you're done in there."

She nodded and glanced down at the knife in her hand. She closed her fist around it.

I pressed my badge against the black reader pad, and the door buzzed before unlocking. I gently pushed her into the room.

She spun to face me as I slammed the door shut.

Good, I wanted Simon to see her turn to me in her panic.

She turned to face him, and he lifted his head off the bed.

"Charlotte?"

She stepped closer to him, unspeaking. Her gaze darted to the mirror and back to him, fear written all over her face as she searched for me in her reflection.

I sat on the bench, and Mitch joined me to watch the show.

He chuckled. "You're not boring, I'll give you that."

I interlaced my fingers behind my head, and crossed an ankle over my knee. "There's a few ways this can end.

Care for a wager?"

He shrugged. "A hundred thousand says she stabs him."

I raised my brows. "She's not a killer." I laughed. "But sure, I can spare the change."

He shook his head. "To free him. Put him out of his misery."

I tipped my head side to side and twisted my lips, considering his guess. "Maybe. But I think he's going to try to kill her, or pretend to try, to get one of us in there."

Mitch stared at Charly in the room, stepping cautiously closer to Simon's bed.

I leaned forward.

"Simon—oh, Simon, what've they done to you?" She brought a trembling hand down toward him.

He mumbled something unintelligible, and she nodded.

I reached forward to turn up the volume that fed the speakers into our room.

In one fluid movement he snapped the bedrails that held his tethers—now handcuffs—and bolted upright to face her. "What have they done to *you*?" His statement dripped with accusation as he looked her over, his gaze lingering on her clamped IV.

She backed up a step. "Simon. I'm so sorry. I never meant for any of this—"

He flew from the bed and stood over her, his shoulders rising with each breath, the cuffs hanging from each bloody wrist on either side. "I should've gotten you away sooner. I knew he was going to hurt you, and by the time I tried to help, it was too late. And now look at you, glancing at that mirror like he'll save you from *me*."

She tipped her head back to look up at him, her

knuckles turning white as she gripped the knife in her trembling hand.

His gaze went to the knife in her hand, then to his own reflection in the mirror. "Trying to re-write history here, are we?"

The statement was meant for me. I smiled and rose from the bench, stepping closer to the window.

Charly stared up at him. "Tell me how to help you, so you can go free. Then you'll never have to deal with me—or them—again." Her voice quivered.

How noble. Offering hope disguised as freedom that she had no authority to give.

He looked back down at her. His body was wracked with a tremor, and he rolled his shoulders. "You think that's what I want? I'm going to kill them, Charlotte," he said calmly.

She took a step back. "Stop. No more killing. I can't—I can't stand any more death."

He stalked over to the mirror, pulled his arm back, and landed a blow to the tempered glass.

I crossed my arms over my chest.

"Is this what you want her to see?!" He yelled into the mirror. "You want her to see, come in here yourself, so I can show her what you've made me!" His voice reverberated and echoed in the room.

Charly shrank away from him, stepping backward toward the door.

"You're afraid of *me*?" Pulling his arm back, he landed another hard blow, cracking the glass. "Come on, Jared. Even your wife isn't too scared to come in!" Two more ferocious blows to the damaged glass busted open his knuckles. His chest heaved with rough breaths, and his hands were bloody and raw.

Charly jumped, fear blazing in her eyes as he revealed the depths of his hatred, fury, and lack of control as his entire body vibrated with savagery.

"Alright. She's seen enough. I'm taking her out." I unfolded my arms and backed away from the glass.

Mitch held up his hand and stood from the bench, joining me in front of the window. "Wait. He's just toying with you."

I slid my hands into my pockets. "A hundred grand, you said? I guess we can see where this goes for a few more minutes."

My father side-eyed me, then returned to watching Simon, who now sauntered closer to Charly.

I flicked a glance down at the gun in my father's holster, then returned my gaze to the room.

Simon stalked toward Charly, and she backed away from him, until she bumped into the closed door. She winced when her back connected with the cold metal.

Simon touched her face and she whispered something to him.

His back stiffened, and he froze.

"That's enough." I stomped over to the door and hit my badge against the reader. The light turned green and the buzzer sounded, but the door didn't open. I pulled and pulled, allowing a deep growl of frustration out from my chest.

I pulled out my radio, hit the button, and spoke. "Morgan, room 298, fix the auto locks, *now*."

Morgan's voice came back almost immediately. "On it."

I hit my badge against the reader again. The green light lit, the buzzer sounded, and I finagled with the door handle.

Mitch looked over at me, stepping closer.

"What are they doing? What's—" My panicked gaze flew to the window, then to my father, and back to the door handle. I kicked the door and turned to him.

My father laughed. "You're gonna take the loss so soon?"

"You can have your hundred grand! Get her out—"

Mitch stepped up to the reader, and he put his badge against it. The green light flashed, buzzer sounded, and with an easy pull, he opened the door.

I caught his eye and smiled before simultaneously pulling his gun from the holster and kicking the back of his knee.

He stumbled into the room, and I immediately shut the door.

The lock hitched with a click.

Morgan's voice sounded over the radio again. "Captain, try it again. I'm not seeing any issues on my end. All the coding is fine. Over."

"My bad, Morgan. There was nothing wrong, after all. Over."

Then I stepped up to the window to watch the show.

Chapter 25, Reality 1

Simon

Charlotte's body trembled and shook, and soon the room swarmed with medics and doctors.

She was lifted onto the bed, an IV started, and an anti-seizure med was pushed into her line.

Within minutes, the seizure stopped, and she looked over at me, her heavy eyes revealing just how hard she was fighting her failing body.

"Donovan, you ready to go?" Xavier stared at me. "The team's here. We'll look out for her. If your theory is right, you're running out of time."

I nodded. "Let's do it."

Charly was moved to a small stretcher, and I was hooked back up on the bed.

Doctors and medics worked furiously around me, before my brothers stormed into the room.

Charlotte fought against the medics treating her, struggling to sit up. She cried out, "Three!"

The doctors and medics stopped and stared at her.

Xavier stepped forward, and spoke to the doctors surrounding my bed. "She'll help you get him to reality three. Move!"

The medics resumed setting up for the jump.

"Sy, what the hell?" Jeff bellowed. "You're going to put your life in her hands? She's post-ictal, and not...all there."

Xavier stepped in between the men and me. "Let him go. I'll bring you up to speed while he's under. Charlotte is going to die."

The men looked over at her, and back to me. "And? What's he going to do to stop that?" Jeff asked.

"Kill them in just two more lives. If he's right, she lives. If he's wrong, justice is served either way."

Charlotte stumbled off the stretcher, reached for my hand, and shook her head. "Just three." Her weak knees buckled, and my brothers caught her elbows to hold her upright.

I stared up at her. "What about reality seven? Or reality two?"

She shook her head slowly.

Xavier stepped beside her. "You'll take care of them in seven and two?"

She nodded.

I stared at Charlotte. "But, *in no reality are you a killer…*"

She pulled out of my brothers' grips and stepped back, then her gaze went to the doctors and medics.

I raised my eyebrows at Xavier, the questions hanging in the air between us.

He shook his head. "I don't know, but if you want to trust her, I'd suggest we get you to where she says."

Joel stepped forward. "Godspeed, brother." He grasped my arm tightly and nodded.

I nodded at him as my consciousness drifted, and Jeff's loud voice was heard bitching about something in the background. He never shut up, and when I got back, I'd tell him to do just that.

Chapter 26, Reality 2: On the Periphery

Charlotte

Three almost inaudible buzzes sounded as someone tried to access the room where Simon and I stood staring at each other. I walked over to him, glancing at the door, then bringing my gaze back to his. "Please trust me," I whispered, referring to my earlier statement.

He nodded with one dip of his head.

We both abruptly turned to the door when it opened, and Mitch stumbled in. A half-second glance allowed me to see Jared's sinister smile before the door slammed shut.

Mitch steadied himself upright and reached for his gun. His holster was empty.

I stared at my reflection in the mirror, knowing Jared was watching.

"Simon." I kept my tone stern, in control. I couldn't let him lose focus now.

He strolled toward Mitch, unhearing, his eyes locked in like a predator that just had prey dropped into its cage.

"Simon." I said his name louder, and he didn't acknowledge me.

Mitch wasn't a small man. He was over two-hundred pounds of smart, well-trained, experienced muscle. But it wasn't more than a minute before he found himself on the floor, being killed by Simon's bare hands.

My screams did nothing to stop him, and there was no breaking him from his trance. The predator they'd created to kill, was doing exactly that. His sheer rage was foiling any plans I had to save him, and soon, I'd be left to choose—my life, or his.

The sickening *thud, thud, thud* of his fists connecting with Mitch's face, and the resulting skull cracking and blood spurting caused me to fold in on myself, refusing to look, but still able to hear the horrific scene.

A regretful glance revealed that Mitch was unrecognizable, and a blood-covered Simon still couldn't gain control, completely zoned out and hung up on violence and vengeance and punishment. That half-second glance would live forever rent-free in my head, worse than any horror movie scene on earth.

My resolve shattered, and I ran to the window, slamming my hands upon the glass. "Please, please, get me out! I can't take it anymore, please!" Tears streamed down my face, and despite my begging Jared for help, Simon continued his tirade, his viciousness and fury bringing him to a place of no return.

The buzzer sounded, and I was at the door before it even opened.

Jared held a gun by his side.

"Don't." I put both my hands on his chest and pushed him into the observation room, allowing the door to slam shut behind us. I sucked in breath after breath, my body violently trembling and shaking. Sinking down onto the bench, I dropped my head into my hands while trying not to puke.

Jared took a knee in front of me and cocked his head.

"Hmm, quite the show," he mused.

I held my breath, trying to regain control and push the violent, bloody images of Simon killing Mitch out of my mind.

"He'll never be the same, Charly."

"Stop talking. Please stop talking." I huffed and gasped, then slapped a hand over my mouth.

Jared stood. "If you're going to puke, leave the room. That's disgusting."

I regained control, swallowing the bile in my throat, and followed his gaze to the glass.

Simon finally stood from Mitch's decimated body and approached the window. His pupils were dilated, and the blue of his eyes had darkened to a raging stormy sea. He cocked his head and a feral smile broke across his face. "Next."

Jared's back stiffened, and he tapped the gun against his thigh, then radioed Morgan. "Code blue. It's that damn Marine again. No sedatives or restraints, shoot to kill. He's killed the general." He looked around, his gaze going to the lights that remained off. The alarms hadn't sounded—Morgan hadn't responded or called the code.

An ounce of hope blossomed in my chest. Maybe he and Gustav could atone for their wrongdoings after all.

Simon backed away from the mirror and strolled toward Mitch's body.

I squeezed my eyes shut, not daring to look at what he was going to do.

"Morgan!" Jared barked into his radio again.

Silence followed.

The cold bite of metal hit my cheek as Jared tapped his gun on my face. "Open your damn eyes! See the truth. Simon's a monster, Mitch is dead, and you're here, with me. *By choice*."

I glanced into the room and spotted Simon heading toward the door with Mitch's badge in his hand.

I brought my gaze back to Jared. "You're the monster."

The buzzer sounded, and before Jared could turn around, the door exploded open.

Jared grabbed and spun me around, using me as a human shield, and pressed the barrel of the gun to my temple. "Well, that's what you're into, apparently."

I grasped his forearm while staring at Simon, whose eyes were locked on the gun at my head. He didn't deserve any of what'd been done to him, and yet, here he stood, still trying to stop me from dying as a result of my very own poor choices. Choices I'd repeated again and again, lifetime after lifetime.

Jared.

"Tell me, Simon, is your thirst for revenge worth her life?"

Simon studied Jared for a moment, narrowing his eyes. "Maybe."

Jared laughed. "I'm going to give you a gift and call it even. I offered my father's head to you in two lives, and you got your revenge on me in reality one. Take that badge, get your ass out of here, and we're square."

Simon rolled his shoulders, then stretched his neck side-to-side. He was covered in Mitch's blood. "I don't like that deal."

"You are positively obsessed with my wife." Jared clicked his tongue and sauntered closer to the door. "Move, or I'll shoot her."

I whimpered when he held me tighter, and a stitch on my back let go with a painful prick, followed by the warmth of blood. Crap, the meds had most definitely worn off.

Simon took one step back.

"Good, now toss my father's badge over to me."

The badge clattered onto the hard bench.

"Charly, get that."

I swiped the badge off the bench.

"Good girl." Jared backed us up to the door, and badged us into the room. He tossed me in, and I landed near the unrecognizable bloody corpse formerly known as Mitch.

Another stitch felt like it popped, and more warm blood began soaking the back of my shirt. I screamed, the sound bouncing off the cold gray walls of the room.

The gun went off, then the door slammed shut.

Jared and I were locked in the room that'd been Simon's prison.

The mirrored glass shook and bowed in. Simon's bellowing roars could be heard from outside the room.

Jared charged toward the control panel on the wall and pulled the emergency alarm. The lights in the hall lit up red, throbbing as an alarm wailed. In minutes, the area would be secured.

And Simon would be dead.

I ran to the mirror.

It shook again with another blow and a crack splintered across the length of it.

I pressed both my hands upon the glass. There were speakers in the observation room, so I didn't have to raise my voice. I knew Simon was there, I could feel his presence even though I couldn't see him. "Please, take the deal. Go. They'll kill you, and I can't live with that."

A slight movement and shadow appeared behind my

hand on the other side of the mirror—his hand, pressed upon the glass, just under mine.

"I'm *choosing* him. This is what I want, there's nothing to save me from. He's my husband, Simon. Please, go."

The shadow remained under my hand, but the blows to the mirror and his loud roars of frustration silenced.

"Please, go. If you try to save me, I'll just run right back. It's always what I choose," I whispered. "I'm sorry for everything."

Loud voices sounded in the hall, followed by stomping boots and the continuous alarm.

The shadow beneath my hand disappeared.

I turned, and Jared was right behind me. He smiled. "There, the truth doesn't sting so bad once you see it for what it is. There's no shame in admitting I'm your weakness."

Nodding, I swallowed and stared at the blood-streaked tiles beneath our feet.

"I'm a patient man, but I'm still mad about this, Charly." He put a knuckle under my chin to lift my face toward him. "I told you the night we met we'd never be apart. I knew you were it, and I meant it. Not because you're my prisoner, but because you can't let go, either. You're mine, but I'm yours, too." He reached down and snapped off the speakers. The sounds of the alarms in the halls and boots stomping silenced. "I would've bought you tickets. Hell, I'd have gone with you to visit your parents. There wasn't any need for all of this." He waved his hand around us.

I took a step forward and closed the gap between us, twining my arms around him and resting my head on his chest. I stole a glance at the mirror, and Jared was staring at his reflection, triumph written in the smirk on his face. He wanted Simon to see what I was. A traitor. A liar. Addicted to poison.

He sighed deeply and wrapped his arms tightly around me.

I winced. "My back. I think a few stitches broke."

"Mmm. We need to get that IV hooked back up, too."

Stepping around Mitch's corpse, I walked over to Simon's bed and slumped down. Then, I pulled up the back of my shirt.

"Oof. Yeah, two or three, I can't tell." He grazed his fingers near the wound, then badged into the supply closet in the room. He took out supplies to clean and cover the injury. Before sitting behind me, he handed me two painkillers and a bottle of water.

"The guys can't fix your stitches just yet, they're…busy right now." His voice held a smile. "They'll let us know when the threat is…neutralized, and the area is secure. Then we'll go home."

I threw back the pills and took a big swig of water. "You made Simon a deal. Will you let him go?"

Jared laughed softly, and looped a finger around the loose fallen strap of my tank top, gently bringing it back up to my shoulder. "Charly, the orders were shoot to kill. He didn't accept my deal. And he killed my father." He sat behind me and began cleaning up my wound.

A gasp escaped my lips at the memory of Mitch's demise.

Jared sighed. "Death is inevitable. At least you know Simon's going to get another chance out there, somewhere. Most people don't live with that knowledge."

I nodded again, swallowing back the burn of emotion. "It's my fault, though."

He shrugged while taping gauze over my broken stitches. "Not really. Remember, if you don't have it in you to kill—"

"—in no reality are you a killer." I finished for him. Those were his words from long ago, in the main reality.

He pulled the back of my tank down, covering the dressed wound, then turned me to face him. "You really do have all your memories from reality one, don't you?"

"Yes." I nodded.

"Me, too. You'll be dead over there soon, and we're going to run the most powerful agency on earth. You'll never want for anything. The main reality doesn't matter." He didn't look up as he packed away the gauze and tape into the first-aid kit.

"I don't want those memories."

He shrugged again. "Then don't think about them." He rose from the bed and put the kit back in the closet.

I stood and opened and closed a few cabinets in the room.

He cocked a brow. "What are you looking for?"

"This." I pulled out the case that held Gustav's banned device pre-programmed to send jumpers backward. "I knew Gustav had it in one of these rooms, and there's something I want to show you."

He slid his hands into his pockets and strolled over to where I stood, then leaned against the wall right next to me.

"I never told you, but I made this device. I didn't want it used, of course." I pressed my thumb onto the print reader, and the case unlocked with a bleep.

Jared huffed out a laugh. "Of course." He rolled his

eyes.

"So, we called it Gustav's device, because he helped me with the mechanics of it. But I did all the coding, believe it or not. And there's an Easter egg hidden inside." I pulled the device from the case and ran my hands over the shiny red exterior. "Even Gustav doesn't know."

Jared rubbed a hand along his chin as he stared at the device. The same device he'd used to shock me to the main reality and torture me with the memories of two lives.

"Do you have a screwdriver?"

He reached into his back pocket and pulled out the folding knife.

I pointed to the two screws, and he used the knife to loosen the screws.

I pulled the cover off the device, then turned to face him. "Before I show you, you have to promise you will never, ever use this tech." I stood on my toes and brought my hands up to cup his face.

He looked up, sighed, then nodded.

All the tells that told me he'd use it if he damn well wanted to.

Then, he dropped his gaze to my mouth and leaned down to kiss me.

My lips answered his, not bothering to fight against the truth for another second. It was like napalm and nuclear warfare, and either way, I was going to perish from the blast or the fallout.

Jared pulled away with a smile, running his fingers along my cheek.

I turned back to the device.

"If we're going to run Quantym, I want you to know

what I'm capable of. And it's more than I've ever let on."

"Okay, let's see it." His voice dripped with impatience.

I used my nail to lift away a thin metal sheet, and he peered at the two handheld paddles within.

He shrugged, appearing disappointed. "I like the sticker pads better."

I lifted the paddles from the casing. "These aren't ordinary paddles. They're pre-programmed with a protocol, perfectly timed to deliver the shocks."

"No way! Reality seven?" A wide smile broke across his face, revealing my favorite dimple of his, just one, on his right cheek. "You really are the uranium, Charly."

"That's not all." I discreetly snapped on the device. "See these?" I lifted the paddles so they were near his face, revealing the buttons on the underside of each handle.

He dipped his head to look at the buttons where my index fingers rested when grasping the paddles.

"Watch this." I pressed the paddles to his chest, and before he could step away, I had both my fingers squeezing the buttons. "Oh, they're wireless too. Cool, huh?"

He froze, his features twisting with shock as he quivered with his back against the wall.

"It's a small current, eliminates the need for tethers—I always found them barbaric. But paralyzes you nonetheless, doesn't it? I'll spare you the details, but it's how the nerve pathways work."

"S-s-top. S-stop!" His eyes widened, and his body was completely incapacitated by the current I'd programmed into the paddles.

"Don't be such a pussy, Jared. Sometimes, love hurts."

"S-stop." He trembled, frozen in place, his wide eyes locked on mine.

"Keep watching, Jared. This isn't the end. This is an opportunity," I said sternly, mimicking his voice.

"Y-you're n-n-not a kill-kil-" He tried speaking, but the small voltage made him sound like a broken doll.

How fitting.

"I'm not a killer. Correct. But I'm not killing you, I'm saving you. The bleed-through isn't just for the bad. It's for the good, too. In reality seven, you're good. So, so good. That's what I've always been attracted to—drawn to—*loved,* and held onto in these other lives. That glimmer of—" My voice shook with emotion. Dammit, I'd never be able to deliver a punishment as well as him. "—the bleed-through effect."

"Ch-Charly." His wide eyes pleaded.

"I hate that nickname. Goodbye, Jared." I used my thumbs to simultaneously press both buttons on the upper side of the handles.

His body shook with the blow, the joules delivered directly to his heart in two pulses. He crumpled to the ground when the current stopped.

I fell down with him, burying my head into his chest and chanting his name over and over and over again. I never wanted him dead. I wanted him good.

After several long moments of grieving over his lifeless body, I released my grip on his shirt, unclipped his badge, and stood. I packed away the paddles and re-covered the casing, hiding my secret.

I walked over to the mirror and snapped on the speaker. There was only silence on the other side. No boots stomping, no alarms, no movement at all.

I pressed Jared's badge to the reader, and slowly opened the door. The hall was filled with heavy silence, the tangy scent of blood, and multiple dead bodies—Jared's corrupt troops.

My lungs were too tight. I sucked in a breath, and it did nothing to feed me the oxygen my body so desperately needed.

The heavy metal door slammed shut behind me, and the sound boomed through the hall.

"You really are a brilliant woman." Simon sat on the bench in the observation room, covered in blood. "Morgan and Gustav are safe. They called in my commanding officer and his team. They helped us."

I stared at him with wide eyes, trembling as my mind and body began to succumb to the shock. I took two steps forward, and he stood, catching me as I fell into him, sobbing.

I wasn't worried about the monster they'd made him into. I knew the cure. In fact, I knew a lot more than I'd ever let on. I masked my abilities well, knowing they made me different. Alien. I'd barely shown my husband and his crew a fraction of what I was capable of, and they'd already coined me a tool to be possessed, or mocked my intelligence as an illness to be treated.

Simon's case was simple, really. Jumps increased adrenaline, and by injecting beta-blockers into him for several weeks, in conjunction with negative biofeedback, his body would eventually stop producing so much. Then, the meds could be tapered, and he'd be cured.

I only wished healing my heart was so easy.

"It's okay, Charlotte. I've got you, you're okay."

Simon murmured into my ear, as he lifted me into his arms.

"I saw us in reality one," I whispered.

"I jumped to here from there more than a few times, but my memories are spotty. Maybe you can help me fill in the blanks."

"We're happy...blindingly happy." I held onto him, allowing the emotion I'd tried so hard to suppress over the last few months spill out, and the tears soaked his shirt. I finally felt safe enough to show just how much everything had hurt.

"I knew that." He smiled.

"Distract me from all the other...the *bad* memories. Tell me about the stars, Simon."

"I'm going to replace the bad memories, one by one, with good ones." A laugh rumbled from his chest, and as he carried me toward the elevators he began speaking. "Cassiopeia was a vain queen, and she's represented by five stars in the northern sky. As the legend goes, her boasting angered Poseidon, and he sent a monster to destroy her kingdom. Cassiopeia bound her daughter, Andromeda, to a rock as prey for the monster, but she was rescued by Perseus, who she later married."

I sniffled, and smiled against his chest. "I've never heard that one before."

"When you're ready, I'll show her to you in the night sky."

I nodded and clung to him the way I imagine Andromeda clung to Perseus when he rescued her from the monster.

Chapter 27, Reality 1

Charlotte

I pushed away from the bed and held my head in both hands. "My head." I groaned. "It hurts!" Stumbling back, I fell on my ass onto the hard tile while cradling my head.

"Charlotte! Medeiros, get her!" Xavier hollered.

The medic rushed over, and the pain swelled to an overwhelming point.

"Look at me, Charlotte." The medic flashed his light into my eyes. "Breathe, okay? I know it hurts, just breathe through the pain."

Groaning, I waved my hand to get his light out of my face. "Stop. I'm okay, I think. Where's Sy?"

"Xavier, tell them to wake him. It's done, she's back!" Jeff's voice sounded from close to where I sat.

Back? Where the hell did I go?

I glanced around the room. My equation was laid across the floor, written on a piece of...*was that butcher paper*? The memories of the last month began flooding my brain. Simon took care of me...I was incoherent...Jared sent me backward, melting my mind here and leaving me trapped within myself and memories...

No one survives being sent back. How am I alive?

My gaze landed on Simon.

He was strapped to the bed, extubated, and the medics were unwrapping the cooling packs.

I groaned again, and held tighter onto my head, allowing my eyes to close. "Give me something for the pain!" I wailed. How could I help wake him if I couldn't stand due to the incredible pain?

Medeiros stood to help the other doctors as they swarmed a slowly waking Sy.

"Look at me, Charlotte." Joel grasped my shoulders.

Opening my eyes, I blinked rapidly at the brightness of the room. "Oh, help, there's too much...it's too much...I can't—"

"Slow breaths. It's all the memories. Take slow breaths. Focus on something," Joel coaxed.

"Count." His voice sounded over all the commotion.

My gaze snapped to Sy, who was shivering on the bed, his eyes locked on the lights above him as his monitor beeped with a slowly increasing heart rate.

He shivered and moaned around gritted teeth. "Tell her to count."

"Count, Charlotte. Look at me, count." Joel's dark eyes held mine.

"One...two...three...four..." My breaths slowed, my heart rate calmed, and the vise-like pain around my head loosened. "Five...six...seven..."

"There. That's it." Joel's grip on my arms loosened, but our eyes remained locked.

"Where are we? This isn't Quantym." I broke Joel's gaze and glanced around the room.

"Focus, Charlotte."

My lips moved as I continued counting, whispering the increasing numbers.

I glanced up at Sy, and he was staring at me.

Joel helped me off the floor.

A medic threw warming blankets over Sy's shivering body, and I sat on the edge of the bed, putting both my hands on his chest. "Sy…I'm so sorry. I—"

He brought his arms out from under the blanket, pulling me into him. "I told you, Charlotte, nothing will stop me from finding you, or loving you."

I grasped onto him with everything I had, with every ounce of spirit and strength and physical fabric from which I'd been formed. "I have so many memories."

"I saw so many beautiful lifetimes with you…" he murmured, running a hand over my hair.

I pulled back and stared at him. "Before they fade, tell me, Sy. Tell me what you saw."

"In reality six, we're engaged. In reality five, we're married. In reality four, we're dating—" he laughed. "In reality three, we're engaged."

I laughed with him, then added, "In reality two, we're about to start dating. You like to tell me stories about the stars."

He grinned. "The stars?"

"The constellations." I smiled.

"I do something like that here, too. Moon bathing, remember?"

I laughed and brought my head down to his chest, nodding against him. "How did you fix me?"

"He tried to take you from me in all the lives, called you his 'uranium.' You were the key to Quantym, and once he knew that, he and his jumpers took you. But I killed him and Mitch and stole you back."

"In five realities?"

"Yes." He smoothed my hair. "What about reality two?"

"You killed Mitch. As for Jared—" I swallowed hard. "—I took care of it. The bleed-through isn't just for the bad." The memory was still raw, and while I didn't want to lie, I didn't want to tell him what I'd done, either.

"The good bleeds through, too, and while there will always be bad, the good is so much more potent. Without all that negative bleeding through, fracturing you, and with the swift treatment of the seizure, you can handle the memories. The good outweighs the bad now, and your mind is exceptionally strong."

"The seizure?" My eyes widened.

"You were treated immediately. I assume the others who'd succumbed after being sent back weren't."

"We're soulmates." I kissed him, and his cold lips were a cooling balm to the overflowing memories igniting a fire in my mind.

He sat up and pulled me into him. "You're just realizing that now?"

I sank into him, not ready to let go. "And here, in reality one—the main reality—we're married." I closed my eyes, ignoring the crew bustling around us. None of it mattered, just that he was back, and I was back, and we were together.

****

Simon never asked me about reality seven, and I never offered up what I knew, either. It was an unspoken secret, a mystery in its meaning and execution and existence.

I'd once thought about how I wished I could cut Jared off me like the leech he was. The thing with that is, in medicine, it's a well-known fact that you cannot make a clean cut—a cure—without clearing margins. That means you must take a healthy piece from around the area, to ensure the bad piece is cut out completely.

That's how I cut him off me, I suppose. By agreeing to give him one-seventh of myself, allowing the universe that small piece that'd caused me to make certain choices over the course of multiple lives.

In reality seven, I was Jared's, and he was mine. But there, he was good and we were happy. I'm not sure what that means, or how that affects the universe or what the deeper meaning to that is. And I'm not sure I'll ever know, because that's part of being human and being alive. The great mystery of the universe and life and love and all that.

And I'm glad, that despite all I know, there's still a little mystery to keep me seeking the very meaning of it all.

Epilogue, Reality 1:Six Months Later

Charlotte

I draped my legs over Sy's, and the waning sun shone across the beaded bodice of my dress, casting dancing rainbows across his face. The May weather was delightful, balmy and warm, but under the shade of the trees, it smelled of pine, and the breeze brought with it a cooling salve to our heated skin. We'd eaten and danced and celebrated for hours with our closest friends and family, finally celebrating our marriage.

"How does it feel, Mrs. Donovan?" Sy wrapped his arm around my waist, and I looked around at the crowd of people who'd joined us to celebrate.

"It feels…long overdue." I turned to him and smiled.

"The honey is always sweeter when you've had to fight for it."

I elbowed him. "Honey? Really? You'll never stop teasing me about bees, will you?"

He barked out a laugh. "Nope. It's gonna be forever with me."

My smile faded and I met his gaze. "It'll never be long enough." I rested my forehead on his.

Frantic clicking caused us both to look up.

My mother smiled from behind the long-lensed camera, snapping pics faster than the paparazzi. "Look at you two! If that isn't love, then I don't know what is!"

We turned to each other and smiled again, allowing her the photo op as the clicking continued.

"She's right, you know," Sy murmured.

"I know." I swiped a curl away that'd escaped my hairpin and danced in the spring breeze. "I have a wedding gift for you. Wait here." Without another word, I stood and flitted away from the crowd, gathering my gown up so I could make my way through the mossy bed that led to our favorite weeping willow.

James and Brian had set up tents, tables, streamers woven with flowers and lights, and tulle and chiffon to decorate our oasis in the forest. Just steps away from the setup was the treehouse built by Sy and his brothers as kids. I ascended the wooden makeshift ladder and ducked into the old house.

I slid out of the gown and pulled my backpack from the corner where I'd stashed it. I pulled on my white tank, running shorts, and sneakers. I descended and headed down the hill, deeper into the forest.

"It's time?" Jeff called out. Max sat beside him with a wolfish grin and paint gun in hand.

I nodded and laughed, hopping into one of the two-seater four-wheelers—Sy's gift—and pulled safety glasses over my eyes.

Sy never even noticed his brothers had slipped away.

Jay, Jeff, and Becca revved their engines, each with their own quad ready to go.

Joel sat beside Jay in the four-wheeler, also armed with a loaded paint gun.

"At least give him a minute to process. Sixty seconds, okay?" I called out.

The brothers all looked at each other and smirked. They weren't going to give him a second.

"Sy!" I called out his name and drove the quad over the roots and uneven earth of the forest. I pulled up beside the weeping willow, and called out to him again.

Sy emerged from the crowd with his hands in his pockets, and a mischievous smile pulled at his lips.

"Quick! Get in!" I motioned frantically with my hand.

His eyes widened. "What...?" He quickly removed his black jacket and tossed it aside, then started unbuttoning the top buttons of his shirt.

A whistle, then a splatter of paint hit him in the chest.

"Son of a—"

I floored it and cut the wheel, bringing the vehicle close enough for him to hop in.

Sy hopped into the quad, immediately picking up the loaded paint gun and aiming. "Bad move, Jeff!" He fired.

Jeff swore loudly when he took the shot to the side of the head.

Before we could cheer, Sy was pelted with another shot to the arm, and the paint spattered, lacing my hair with the bright-orange paint.

I squealed with glee, flooring it and taking off out of the line of fire.

We chased each other, quads revving, brothers shooting at one another, laughter echoing throughout the forest.

Becca pulled up beside me. Her girlfriend, Jill, sat passenger, and aimed right for me.

I cut the wheel, bringing up a wave of mud that covered them both, before disappearing between two trees and into a darker part of the forest. Several more shots rang out, and I knew Sy'd connected with at least two of his brothers by the sounds of their cussing.

They might've had a head start, but I had the sniper.

An hour later, when our ammo ran out, we were mud-covered and laughing and breathless. We parked the new vehicles under the old treehouse, and rejoined our wedding guests.

"I figured it was better than the classic throwing of rice." I smirked at Sy when some guests gasped at our paint-splattered and muddy appearances.

"I haven't had that much fun in a long time."

I pulled him down to me and kissed him, the paint and mud on my hands marring his face under my grasp. "I've thought about it, and I want to help at Quantym. I can be a contract employee. Like you."

He pulled back. "Are you sure that's what you want?" He'd signed on to help me and was contracted to the organization for another five years. At least this time, Xavier and the team were trustworthy, and knew the importance of keeping the intel classified and out of hands that'd use it to make a profit.

I nodded. "I can't outrun destiny. Can't beat them, join them." I shrugged. "And, I'm more than qualified, I have firsthand experience." I raised a brow.

Sy's lips twisted as he pondered something. "Xavier mentioned needing a head for the ethics committee. We'll talk to him when we get back."

My skin tingled with anticipation at the thought of our two-week honeymoon in the Bahamas ahead of us.

Clicking sounded again, and we looked over at my mother, who captured the moment once again, this time with us covered head to toe in paint and mud.

"Charly, you really are an odd one." She bit her lip and shook her head disapprovingly.

"She's met her match." Sy lifted me into his arms, slinging my muddy legs over his strong forearms.

I looped my arms around his neck, and matched his sky-blue gaze as he rubbed a thumb across my cheek, covering it in sticky orange paint. "I most certainly have," I agreed, kissing my husband once again.

Our loved ones cheered.

Indeed, the honey was sweeter after the fight.

Acknowledgements

First and foremost, I want to thank God: Thank you, Heavenly Father, for your guidance and presence at all times in my life, in both the light and the dark. Thank you for listening to my prayers, for giving me only what I need, when I need it, and at your discretion, not mine. I trust you.

To my brilliant editor, ELF: thank you for your advice, guidance, kindness, and patience, and for polishing the Periphery duet to shine. Working with you has been amazing, and I'm looking forward to doing it again!

To my husband, Tony: I adore you. You're my pedra, my love, my life. Thank you believing in me, and in Periphery, even when I just wanted to delete it and forget I'd ever penned a novel. Thank you for being my weapons-and-military resource, and thank you for your service to our country and our family, and for championing my books to anyone who'd listen. There's no one I'd rather be on this crazy journey with than you!

To my Alexander and Ethan: I love you bigger than the universe. You'll both always be my reason for being. Nothing is impossible, never stop dreaming, and always choose to be the light this world needs. Thanks for being my inspiration to be the very best version of me.

A huge thank you to my sister, Jill, for being the voice I never had—my PR rep, my cheerleader, my bestie, my confidant, and my shoulder. Words cannot express my gratitude for having you embark on this journey with me. Thank you for believing, even when I didn't.

Thank you to my parents, who always told me to

reach for the stars, and that nothing was impossible. You both fed the dreamer in me, no matter how prone to darkness she may be. I'm still not sure if my strange brain is a blessing or a curse, but it motivates me to bring light to those who need it most in whatever capacity I can.

To my brother: thanks for all the "character development" growing up. You're humorous, but still the voice of reason when times get tough, and I look up to you.

A special thanks to Jessica August: my friend and fellow reader of all things deliciously dark and twisted. A heartfelt thanks for believing in me and my story. Thanks for all the "work therapy," beta reading, and for listening to my crazy rantings and ravings and anxiety over getting exactly what I wanted. Shine on, you magnificent black diamond—thanks for being uniquely, wonderfully you.

To my laboratory work crew at CMH—you're not co-workers, you're family! The support I've received from co-workers and friends has blown me away. Every like, share, conversation, attendance at events, and words of encouragement you've given mean the world to me.

To my street team, including, but not limited to: Jill, Jess, Hannah, Andrea, Louise, Sarah, Joanna, Adam, Wendy, Irene, Linda, Steph, Christina, Emily, Angie and all my precious ARC readers: THANK YOU.

Dear Readers:

In love with the *Periphery* series? Sign up for updates at aadasilva.com where you can learn how to gain free access to two bonus epilogues that reveal a glimpse of Jared's fate on the Periphery, and Simon's final thoughts about all that transpired.

Thank you for choosing to live in my universe for a while. I hope you enjoyed your stay. Being an author is a dream come true, but it's not without its challenges. Motivation can run low, imposter syndrome can creep in, and doubts can get loud in a mind filled with ideas yet to be explored. Reviews help authors grow, can be great motivators, and help authors like me gain visibility and reach. Please consider leaving a review at retailer and reader sites.

Thank you again for exploring the Periphery with me. In every life, I choose to explore the unknown with all you amazing dreamers.

AA DaSilva

A word about the author...

Born and raised in New England, AA DaSilva has a degree in clinical laboratory science and brings her love of science and writing together via science fiction. When she's not writing or working in the lab, she can be found with a book in one hand, and a cup of iced coffee in the other. She resides in Massachusetts with her husband, two sons, and pup Didi.

For the latest updates on new releases and events, sign up for email updates at aadasilva.com and follow her on socials.

Thank you for purchasing
this publication of The Wild Rose Press, Inc.

For questions or more information
contact us at
info@thewildrosepress.com.

The Wild Rose Press, Inc.
www.thewildrosepress.com